Winter Park
PUBLIC LIBRARY

THE RUSSIAN AFFAIR

Also by Michael Wallner

April in Paris

NAN A. TALESE

Doubleday

New York London Toronto Sydney Auckland

THE RUSSIAN AFFAIR

A NOVEL

MICHAEL WALLNER

Translated from the German

by John Cullen

This book is a work of fiction. Names, characters, businesses, organizations, places, events, and incidents either are the product of the author's imagination or are used fictitiously. Any resemblance to actual persons, living or dead, events, or locales is entirely coincidental.

www.nanatalese.com

Book design by Michael Collica
Jacket design by Michael J. Windsor
Jacket photograph © Dennis Hallinan/Getty Images

Library of Congress Cataloging-in-Publication Data
Wallner, Michael
[Russische Affäre. English]
The Russian affair / Michael Wallner ; translated from the German by John Cullen.—1st American ed.
p. cm.
Originally published: Munich : Luchterhand Literaturverlag, 2009 under title Die Russische Affäre.
(alk. paper)
1. Self-actualization (Psychology) in women—Fiction. 2. Moscow (Russia)—Fiction.
I. Cullen, John. II. Title.
PT2685.A4742R8713 2011
833'.92—dc22
2010023149

ISBN 978-0-385-53239-6

PRINTED IN THE UNITED STATES OF AMERICA

2 4 6 8 10 9 7 5 3 1

First American Edition

For my cousin Susan

THE RUSSIAN AFFAIR

ONE

Anna laughed and pivoted to the left, turning her back to the harsh wind. The man in front of her folded his handkerchief, laid it across his empty shoes, and stepped to the brink. Instead of using water to wet himself down, he scooped up some snow and rubbed his chest with it. Then, accompanied by the bystanders' expressions of compassion and encouragement, he arched his back, sprang forward, and disappeared into the black water. Small chunks of ice bobbed against one another. Anna watched as the man swam underwater to the far end of his improvised swimming pool and surfaced there. His beard, white and unkempt a moment ago, was now gray and plastered to his cheeks.

"He ought to get a life guard's badge," the woman next to Anna cried out, pulling the fur trim of her cap down over her ears. "That way he could charge admission."

"The Moskva River belongs to everybody," a man wearing eyeglasses replied. The snowy wind bent his umbrella to one side. Anna dodged the pointy wire ribs and watched the bearded swimmer as he propelled himself through the water with increasingly powerful strokes. She pushed her way out of the group of spectators and hurried along the riverbank. Under the Krasnopresnenskaya Quay, she climbed up the icy steps and soon reached the bus stop. On the ride home, people on the bus discussed the weather. It was getting warmer, they said; tomorrow the temperature was supposed to rise above twenty below zero. That meant that the cold holidays would be ending soon, and the schools would open again. The thought elicited a satisfied nod from Anna. When Petya didn't have to go to school, everything was thrown into disorder.

With a jerk, the bus moved out of the middle lane. Anna noticed the policeman who was waving the heavy vehicle to one side; at the end of the avenue, a large, dark automobile appeared and rapidly came closer. The bus rolled into the right lane. The Chaika was already right behind it. When the big car pulled alongside, Anna could see a lady in the backseat, her hair waved, a magazine on her lap, and then the Chaika shot past. Although the policeman, too, must have noticed that the car carried only a female passenger, he saluted it as it sped away.

Anna got off the bus at the Filyovsky Park stop. The queue of people waiting on the corner indicated that the canned peaches must have finally arrived. Should she get in line? It would be her fourth queue of the day. Anna banished all thoughts of peach compote, turned into her street, and entered Residential Building Number Seven. On the fourth floor, she unlocked the door to her apartment.

"Did you get toilet paper?" her father asked.

"No, Comrade, I have procured no toilet paper," Anna answered, in her best Communist-youth-organization voice.

"If you think we can keep on using newspaper, you're wrong," Viktor Ipalyevich said, stretching out both arms and pointing from one end of the apartment to the other. "The paper in the windows was letting in drafts, so I had to replace it."

"In the living room, too?" Anna asked, putting her purse on the table.

"In the living room, in the kitchen, wherever it was." Since his daughter was paying his gesticulations no heed, he let his arms drop, took the dark brown chessboard from its shelf, and began setting up the pieces. His peaked cap, which he wore even inside the apartment, made him look younger; only his goatee betrayed the fact that the poet Viktor Ipalyevich Tsazukhin had gone gray.

Anna raised her nose. "Have you been distilling again?" Her eyes narrowed, and the blue irises grew dark.

"That's no reason to glare at your own father as though he's some sort of reprobate."

He tried to bar her way to the kitchen, but Anna was faster. On the stove, she found the telltale system of metal pipes: a many-dented teapot served as a condenser; above, in another pot, the first distillation was cooling. In the next stage of the process, the once-distilled liquor would be sent through the labyrinth again.

"Even when you close the window, the neighbors can still smell it," Anna said, looking at the elbow joint where the last pipe emptied into a converted paint can.

"And will the neighbors run to the police on account of a little glass of Four-Star Tsazukhin and denounce Viktor Ipalyevich as an unproductive Soviet citizen? Or will they hope to be invited into the courtyard on the next sunny day and served by Viktor Ipalyevich in person?"

Refusing to engage in a rhetorical battle with her father, Anna turned off the gas flame that kept the mechanism in operation. He said, "That's the way to turn Four-Star Tsazukhin into rotgut," and went into the living room, shaking his head. The velvet curtain that hid the sleeping alcove moved and a small hand appeared, followed by a child's face—the image of Anna when she was a young girl. The child's hair covered his ears and was cut straight across his forehead, just above his eyebrows. Long lashes screened his light eyes; he had a strong nose, and his mouth was a little too big.

"Are you finished now, Grandfather?" the boy asked.

Anna stepped into the living room. While the poet was announcing that the game could begin, he answered her anxious look with a nod. She formed the word *temperature* with her lips; her father pointed a finger upward and answered inaudibly, "Ninety-nine point seven."

"You can play only until dinner," Anna told her son by way of greeting.

Petya clambered out of the bed where they both slept and embraced his mother. In his dark blue pajamas, he resembled a miniature sailor. He jumped up onto the chair, squatted down, and moved a white pawn two squares forward. Anna carried her shopping bag into the kitchen, took out two cans, placed one between the windows, and opened the other. In order to prepare the soup, she had to move Viktor Ipalyevich's private distillery to one side.

"I have to go out later," she called into the living room. "Will you put Petya to bed?"

"You're going to the combine again?" Anna's father asked absently. "I wish I knew why you have to attend every meeting."

"To get a Category One." She dumped the red beets into the pot.

"And what's the difference between a Category One painter and the rest of them?"

Anna looked at her hands, at her gray, chapped skin, at the cracks around her wrists. "A Category One painter doesn't have to put her hands in lime anymore."

The soup began to boil. She stirred it, remembering that the meeting of the building combine wasn't scheduled to take place until the following week. The thought of her real purpose made her feel languid. She could heard her boy wheezing in the next room; the game excited him.

Shortly before seven o'clock, Anna left the apartment. The collar of her overcoat was turned up, and her fur hat was pulled down on her forehead. No one could have maintained that the cold wasn't the reason for these precautions. On the ground floor, old Avdotya, a fellow resident, was fiddling with the mailbox. "Anna Tsazukhina, I'm at my wits' end!" she cried out. Avdotya was nearly deaf. Since everyone spoke loudly to her, she took that for normal procedure and bawled at everyone in her turn.

"Have you misplaced your key again, Avdotya?"

"Indeed not! There it is!" The old woman looked up imploringly.

Anna considered the little metal drawers. Rust had made some of their numbers unrecognizable. "Isn't yours seven-oh-six?"

"Seven hundred and six, exactly!" Avdotya pointed to her key ring, which was hanging awry from one of the little doors.

"But you're trying to get into seven-eight-six." Anna stuck the key into the right hole and turned the lock. The mail drawer was empty.

"I'm waiting for a letter from Metsentsev!" Avdotya explained, without looking into the mailbox. "He's going to write me about . . ."

But Anna had stepped out of the building, and the closing door swallowed Avdotya's last words. Anna left her street behind, turned into Mozhaisk Chaussée, and crossed to the side where the streetlights were no longer functioning. In such cold weather, fewer people than usual were out and about, but Anna kept her eyes open for someone standing still where there was nothing to see, someone who slowed his pace in the icy wind. Only when she was certain that everything on the avenue looked normal did she slip into an alleyway on her left, a narrow passage that was closed to traffic. And yet Anna knew that at the end of the alley, for the past several minutes, a black automobile had been waiting with its engine running; the driver didn't want to get cold while he waited. She hadn't taken more than a few steps on the hard-trodden snow before the car's headlights flared and a rear door opened.

"Good evening, Anton," she said, settling into the backseat.

The driver tilted his rearview mirror so that he could see her. "You're early. That's good." His full, deep voice always caused Anna to wonder if he'd once been a singer.

"Why is that good?" She took off her cap.

Anton didn't answer as he made a skillful turn in a small space and drove out onto the avenue. He paid no heed to the onrushing traffic; as he expected, all vehicles braked when their drivers realized that a ZIL government car was jumping into the inside lane. Anton accelerated, the limousine hurtled forward, and Anna was thrust back in her seat. She was so warm that perspiration ran down her spine. A bright light made her look up; Anton was overtaking the bus for Nagatino. Passengers sat in pale light. Some of them stared after the long automobile; ZIL limousines had "Special Right-of-Way." Except for weddings, driving a black automobile was forbidden. Anna smiled: If you got married, for a few hours you enjoyed the privileges of a prominent road user. She watched the bus getting smaller, certain that the weary shapes it carried figured her for a woman who was being driven, at state expense, to visit her hairdresser or pick up packages in Granovsky Street.

Anna put a hand over her eyes. Once upon a time, she would have set out on this drive full of happy expectation; she would have gazed at her reflection in the passenger's window and fixed her lipstick and adjusted her hair. Two years ago, when she was twenty-five, and after three years of marriage, her husband Leonid had finally been transferred to Moscow. To avoid having to live in a shared flat on the outskirts of the city, they had accepted Viktor Ipalyevich's offer and, together with Petya, moved in with him. Anna had obtained a good position with the building combine, earning more than her husband, who drew a lieutenant's pay; it was she who took on the chief financial burden of her four-person household.

Then, in April of that same year, her building combine had been ordered to paint the facades of several buildings along Kalinin Prospekt for the May Day celebrations. Yarov, her foreman, had opined that a new coat of paint made no sense if the rust on all metal surfaces were not removed first. There wasn't enough time for that, he was informed, and he should use colors that guaranteed anti-rust protection. Anna had kept Yarov from gainsaying this instruction, and work had begun. The plaster was loose and dry rot had invaded many walls; nevertheless, the building combine's skilled workers covered the facades in friendly shades of yellow and light gray. In order to meet the deadline, they had worked in four shifts. On the afternoon of April 30, a committee that included the government's Deputy Minister for Research Planning inspected the results. Anna didn't know who the powerful man with the greasy hair was, but the fine fabric of his overcoat gave him away as a member of the nomenklatura. While scaffolding was being dismantled and hauled away on all sides, Anna gave the arch she was working on a final stroke of her brush. Alexey Maximovich Bulyagkov stepped under her ladder and praised her flawless brushwork as the other members of the committee formed a group behind him. The Deputy Minister wanted to know how long it took for a person to learn to make such a perfectly straight stroke.

"At twelve, I joined the Pioneer Girls," Anna answered properly. "When I was sixteen, the combine offered me a trainee position. I received training to become a skilled worker, and two years ago, I passed my qualifying examination." She straightened her headscarf; her work clothes were tight on her, because under them she was wearing her heavy sweater and a pair of pajama pants. While she was trying to remember some of her building combine's outstanding accomplishments, Bulyagkov asked her name.

Anna came down the ladder. "My name is Anna Tsazukhina, and I'm twenty-seven years old."

"Are you related to Tsazukhin, the poet?"

Anna could not have said why she'd introduced herself by her maiden name. "He's my father."

Two members of the committee put their heads together.

"I'm an admirer of his work," Alexey Maximovich said, setting his foot on the ladder's lowest rung. "Of some of his work." He held out his hand; although her own was covered with flecks of paint, Anna laid her brush aside and clasped hands with the Deputy Minister.

"All the best, Anna Tsazukhina," he said, gazing at her with merry eyes. Then he turned, and he and his colleagues moved on from the archway.

Six weeks later, Anna had accompanied her father to a poetry reading; after some brief resistance, Leonid had agreed to go along as well. They had taken the subway to the Pushkinskaya station and climbed up into the light of a bright June evening. Viktor Ipalyevich bit his lower lip and nervously chewed his beard, which he'd trimmed the previous day.

Viktor Tsazukhin was a veteran of Soviet literature; his early poems had evoked the Red Army's battle for Berlin. He was known as a forerunner of the artistic generation produced by the Revolution, and his analytic, future-oriented style had served as a model for many later poets. In recent years, his publications had become rarer and their print runs smaller. The state publishing house no longer printed his volumes, which now appeared through the auspices of a small house dedicated to "special Soviet literature." Since Viktor Ipalyevich lived a secluded life with his family, he had no idea whether or not he still had a following as a poet and, if he did, no idea how his descriptions of the present found their way into his readers' hands.

When Viktor, Anna, and Leonid reached the area in front of the Conservatory building, the poet was overwhelmed. Countless young people were causing such a tumult that ushers and police were having great difficulty in keeping the entrance open to ticket holders only. Groups of female students, hoping they might still be able to secure tickets, gathered around latecomers. Automobiles were thickly parked up and down Gorky Street; drivers just arriving were waved on.

Someone recognized Tsazukhin, and within seconds, the crowd began to close in on him and Anna and Leonid in such numbers that the three were unable to take another step forward. People greeted the poet; those standing nearby asked him to take them with him into the auditorium. Helpless with happiness, Viktor groped for his daughter's hand, while Leonid directed his efforts toward opening a passage for them. But they needed help from some of the policemen, who steered them away from the colonnaded doorway to a smaller entrance nearby, where a door opened for a moment to admit them. The poet, his two companions, and a nimble student—a girl in a plastic raincoat—slipped inside; the door closed at once, separating them from the throng of people trying to press in behind them. Doctor Glem, the chairman of the artistic board, was waiting for Viktor Ipalyevich and his family on the stairs. The chairman exchanged hasty greetings with the poet and his family, in which, without many words, the student was included. While an assistant showed Tsazukhin's companions to the box assigned to them, Doctor Glem escorted Viktor Ipalyevich backstage.

Leonid helped Anna out of her jacket. Enjoying her elevated vantage point, she let her eyes wander over the auditorium. Usually, the large hall was used for concerts, with room for seven or perhaps eight hundred people; tonight, there were surely a thousand, and more were still shoving their way inside. In the parquet section, she recognized Plissetskaya, the ballerina from the Bolshoi Ballet, and not far from her, the comedian Rodion; Brezhnev's personal interpreter took a seat in the middle. Older gentlemen were standing in the aisles and ascertaining who had come besides themselves; above all, however, Anna saw sons and daughters. The moment touched her, and when she sat down next to her husband, her face was burning. There below her sat Moscow, not some small collection of admirers still loyal to a forgotten poet, but the citizenry, come to hear her father. When the lights dimmed and the applause began, Anna realized that her father had made his entrance onto the stage. Doctor Glem offered Viktor Ipalyevich the seat reserved for the guest of honor and stepped to the lectern. The audience, however, would not allow the chairman of the artistic board to speak; the clapping grew so unanimous that Tsazukhin had to get to his feet again and make another bow. Even now, his peaked cap remained on his head. Minutes passed before Doctor Glem could deliver his speech of greeting. It consisted of a patriotic profession of faith in the new Soviet lyric poetry, properly declared and congenially applauded. Glem thanked the audience, introduced Viktor

Ipalyevich, and left the stage. Anna's father slowly walked forward. The folder he placed on the lectern remained closed. He pushed back his cap, which left a red stripe across his forehead. Wide-eyed, he peered into the darkness of the parquet and at the packed rows of seats beyond it.

"The weathercock rotates. That's his line of work . . ." he began. The microphone sent his words all the way to the last row.

Anna leaned on the balustrade. Viktor Ipalyevich wasn't like the young Moscow literati who looked upon the cat-and-mouse game with the Soviet state censors as good sport and were content to publish clandestinely. He wasn't one of those writers whose works appeared as closely printed typescripts and got passed from hand to hand and whom neither jail sentences nor publication bans could intimidate. Viktor Ipalyevich Tsazukhin figured in official Soviet literature; the state had seen itself represented and embellished by his work. Anna knew the program for the reading. In accordance with the wishes of the literary committee, her father was to begin with the conformist verses of *Sling* and continue with some longer passages from *The Red Light*. Now, however, he was declaiming a poem, "The Weathercock," that he'd only recently written. No one had ever heard these verses.

Tsazukhin's voice rose as he spoke the last lines:

I do not hold
with the cock on the roof,
yet I know which way the wind blows.

The silence in the auditorium was palpable. He marked a pause, and then, when he opened the folder to begin the scheduled reading, spontaneous applause interrupted him. This time, he didn't accept it, waving the plaudits away and reading the first lines while some in the audience were still clapping. The people understood: first a bit of provocation, followed by adherence to conventions. The official program was under way.

During the intermission, Anna and Leonid strolled around the upper foyer. Leonid wanted to get them something to drink, so he joined the line for the bar. Anna took a few steps with him and then stood still, listening to what the people around her were saying. "Viktor Ipalyevich challenges our feelings," she heard someone say. "He elicits our humor." A man quoted a passage in which the poet brought his irony to bear on the tactic employed by people who, while waiting in a line, jot down their place number on their wrist so as to keep pushy interlopers from getting ahead of them. Amused, Anna turned her head and saw a large, powerful man with a blue tie bearing down upon her.

"Are you enjoying the evening?" he asked.

She needed a few seconds to recognize him as the man who had stood under her ladder a few weeks earlier.

"Your father is an exceptional poet," said Alexey Maximovich Bulyagkov.

"Do you like his poems?"

"I don't think I do." He examined the people around him. "But they touch me. Judge for yourself which is more important."

At that moment, Anna felt as though a ray of light had gone through her. It came from the magnificent chandeliers, from the excited chatter of the large crowd, and, above all, from the marvelous experience she was sharing with her father. At the same time, she wondered how the Deputy Minister had recognized her without her work overalls on and with no scarf on her head; she was wearing the lime green dress she'd bought with a month's salary.

"Are you here alone?"

"My husband's over there." She pointed to the commotion in front of the drinks bar.

"What does your husband do?"

"He's an officer in the armored infantry, stationed in north Moscow."

Bulyagkov bowed and walked over to a lady in a floor-length gown, who greeted him volubly.

Two weeks later, Anna received a small parcel in the mail, a copy of a volume called *My Beloved Does the Wash*, which was a collection of all her father's love poems. When she deciphered the sender's name, she hurried to the apartment and withdrew into the sleeping alcove. Leonid was sitting at the table with Petya, cutting his bread into bite-sized pieces; two arm's lengths away, Anna read the Deputy Minister's letter. He requested that her father write a personal dedication and sign the book, and he suggested that Anna look at the poem on page 106. Strangely excited, she turned to the page and read these verses:

Come see us tomorrow, uplift and gladden us!
Today's rain refreshed us, and the forecast is glorious.
And should we want stormy weather,
We'll make some together!

There was a handwritten note on the margin of the page: "Would you return this volume to me personally tomorrow evening at seven o'clock?"

Anna and Leonid had been married for three years; Petya had come into the world a few weeks after the wedding. Neither of them had ever made the other feel that their little boy was the only reason they were still together. Leonid behaved himself, drank little, and treated her father with respect. Anna didn't dream about anything out of reach; she wanted a good education for her son, her own apartment, and perhaps, eventually, a car. And she had never, at least until that day, knowingly done anything wrong. She was forced to think about some of her colleagues, who reported on casual flings that apparently enlivened their marriages. Such accounts were accompanied by declarations that an affair didn't mean that much these days; there was a real thirst for life in the city of Moscow. Anna resolved to take the Deputy Minister's note as a joke and his offer not very seriously. However, when she climbed out of the alcove, she avoided Leonid's eyes and hid the book in her bag.

The following day, she worked the early shift and was home by three. At dinner with her family, she pushed the volume of poetry across the table to Viktor Ipalyevich and said, "A girlfriend from the site asked me to get your autograph."

Still chewing, her father took his fountain pen out of his breast pocket. "For whom shall I sign it?"

"Just your name's good enough. It's going to be a gift." Anna held the book open to the first page to avoid the possibility that he'd flip through it to the telltale note.

"Even on worksites, people are reading my poems," he said. Smiling, he wrote, "With Best Wishes, Viktor Ipalyevich Tsazukhin." Anna blew on the ink, closed the volume, and laid it on the bookshelf.

Leonid helped her do the dishes. "Maneuvers start tomorrow," he said. "I'll probably sleep in the barracks tonight."

"I've got another combine meeting," Anna replied, running water into the sink.

While Leonid lit up his evening cigarette, while her father got the chessboard out and shoved a pair of cushions under Petya, Anna changed into her summer dress with the brown dots, put on a jacket over the dress, and took leave of her family. As she went down the stairs, she felt incomprehensible relief at the thought that she wouldn't have to see her husband again later that night.

The return address on the parcel indicated a street on the opposite side of the city center. Anna took the wrong bus and missed the appointed time. She hurried along the avenue and turned into a side street. The dimly lit sign read DREZHNEVSKAYA ST. The secluded place, the unprepossessing buildings threw her into confusion: It wasn't conceivable that the Deputy Minister lived here. There was no café, there weren't even any shops; where had he invited her to go? Anna reached the address she was looking for and stepped back. On this bright July evening, not a single window showed a light. She hoped that there had been some misunderstanding, considered once again the possibility that she was the victim of a practical joke—the big shot from the Ministry, she thought, had allowed himself a laugh at her expense.

"You're too late, Anna Tsazukhina." Bulyagkov, wearing a light summer suit, was coming toward her from the other end of the narrow street. "Of all bad habits, tardiness is the worst," he said, looking at her so merrily that her confusion only grew.

Without further explanation, he unlocked the door and went in ahead of her. Anna followed him to a nondescript staircase, which he went up three steps at a time. At the door of an apartment with no nameplate, he used his key again. The opening door revealed an elegantly furnished flat; stray beams of sunlight greeted Anna as she entered. Bulyagkov tried to help her out of her jacket, but she kept it on.

As her host made no effort to begin the conversation, Anna said, "Here's the book."

"How is our poet?" Bulyagkov said, glancing at the dedication before laying the volume aside.

"Since his reading, my father has been interrogated several times in the headquarters of the Writers' Association."

"Were there accusations?" The Deputy Minister stepped over to the sideboard in the living room.

"He was asked to review the political usefulness of his poems."

"What did you expect?" Bulyagkov uncorked a bottle of wine. "Your father behaved like a bull in a china shop. Now he's got to bare his bottom and sit on the shards."

The crude image startled her. "Do you think his poems are 'unidealistic' and 'morally inadequate,' too?"

"I don't understand a thing about poetry," he said, pouring himself some wine. "Nobody gets upset about a little sideswipe." His light eyes measured her. "But what Viktor Tsazukhin did was deliberate provocation. And so now he has to take a couple of raps on the knuckles." He took a sip and held the glass high. "I should have opened the bottle earlier. And you, Anna, how are you?" He gestured, offering her a corner seat on the sofa.

"Why does that interest you?"

"I like your dress. Did you make it yourself?"

"I can't sew."

Bulyagkov skirted the coffee table, sat on the sofa, and leaned back. "This light makes your hair look red."

She didn't like the way he was looking at her as she slipped into her seat. He placed a full glass in front of her and, without waiting for her to pick it up, clinked it with his own. "Tell me about yourself."

"You know most of what there is to tell."

"Far from it. For example, I wonder why your father didn't see to it that you received some other kind of education."

"I'm satisfied."

"That's not an answer."

After a pause, she said, "Viktor Ipalyevich is a poet."

"A man of intellect," said the Deputy Minister, nodding in agreement. "So why would his daughter become a house painter?"

"He's a poet—and nothing else." Anna gripped the stem of her wineglass with two fingers. "Until my mother got sick, she worked for us all. Then she died. Man cannot live on poetry alone."

He looked toward the window. "It's hard when you can't do what you have the talent to do."

"I'm not talented," she replied, "and I like my work. It's well paid." She drank, tasting the heavy wine all the way down. "Why not tell me about yourself, Comrade?"

"Oh, how boring," he sighed. "I'm originally Ukrainian. I came to Moscow when I was fifteen, and I've gotten about as far as a non-Russian can."

"Your Ministry is responsible for research planning. That can't be boring."

He shook his head and said, "Administrative work. Our office makes money available. In the laboratories, in the big science cities—that's where the meaningful work takes place. We're just puffed-up bureaucrats." He looked at her. "What about your husband? What's he doing this evening?"

"He's taking care of Petya." She straightened her upper body. "No, I'm wrong. He has to go on maneuvers."

"Does he like his unit?" Bulyagkov drained his glass.

"He's stationed in Moscow, and that counts for a lot."

"It's hard to obtain a right of abode for Moscow."

Throughout the following hours, Anna found the Deputy Minister attentive and calm, and possessed of a charm the likes of which she'd never known. Usually, when men became confiding, they made jokes and accompanied a bit of flattery with some harmless touching. Anna had never before encountered such seriousness in a man, an almost intimidating interest that seemed to require her to show her best side. It was an effort for her to be this *interesting* Anna, the exertion weakened her, and she was afraid that she didn't deserve such an elevated level of attention. She would have liked their get-together to be more relaxed, but at the same time, Bulyagkov's steady pressure made the encounter unique. She envied his travels—not only did he know Kiev, Vladivostok, and Prague, but he'd also seen Havana and Helsinki; he liked reminiscing, and he answered her questions at length. During the conversation, he went into the kitchen and returned with an already-prepared platter—little liver pâté sandwiches, bread, and ham. Between them, they emptied the bottle of wine. Only once, in the midst of an animated description, did he lay his hand on hers; otherwise, he didn't make the slightest attempt to touch her.

Physically, he wasn't Anna's type; the men she found attractive were wiry, with long limbs and thick hair. The Deputy Minister was a brawny man with a pronounced paunch; his face might have been angular once, but now it looked puffy. She liked his eyes, which had something of the

Arctic wolf about them. Was it shyness that prevented her from asking him what he expected from her? As for Bulyagkov, he acted as though he thought it a natural thing for a high state official and a house painter to spend an evening together. They conversed some more, followed the zakuski with a few glasses of vodka, and darkness fell, which at that time of year meant that the midnight hour was approaching. Without explanation, Bulyagkov stood up and disappeared into an adjoining room, which Anna presumed was the bedroom. She figured that the next item on the program was at hand, but before she could work out what her own behavior was going to be, he came back. His damp temples indicated that he'd merely gone to comb his hair. He hated to say it, he said, but the time had come for her to go. He answered her surprised look with an invitation to name a wish—the first wish that came into her mind.

"Faucet washers," she said, and then she had to laugh at herself. "The faucets in our apartment drip. They take standard washers, but I can't find them anywhere."

"Washers." Bulyagkov escorted her to the door. "I'll see if my influence extends that far." He took her by the shoulders and gave her a brotherly kiss. Anna started down the stairs. On the way home, she realized that the granting of her wish would mean that this wouldn't be their last meeting. The thought of the Deputy Minister's clever move made her smile.

Two weeks had passed, and Anna assumed the matter had been forgotten. But one afternoon, a black ZIL parked in front of her building. An inconspicuous man got out, presented himself as a messenger, and, when Anna came down, handed her a small package no larger than a bar of soap. The man was Anton, whom she saw from the front for the first time.

"That's from Alexey Maximovich," he said, stony-faced. "If you have time this evening, he would be delighted to receive a visit from you."

Anna wondered whether Bulyagkov had chosen the date at random or knew that she was working the early shift that week. "How long do I have to think it over?"

"Come to Gospitya Street at eight," Anton replied. "I'll wait for you there."

"If I can't make it, how can I reach you?"

"Don't worry, Comrade. Gospitya Street, right off the little square." He got back in the car and drove away. Anna opened the package while she was still on the street. Upstairs in the apartment, she announced that she'd finally been able to scare up some of those confounded washers. Viktor Ipalyevich congratulated her and got out the pliers.

That had been the evening when Anna was Anton's passenger for the first time. He took a surprisingly short route to Drezhnevskaya Street. She admired how smoothly he weaved in and out of traffic without making use of the privileged status accorded to government vehicles. In front of the now-familiar building, she got out of the car and told him goodbye, but Anton indicated that they'd see each other when she was ready to go home.

Bulyagkov opened the door with two potholders in his hands, and soon he was serving her Tartar-style chicken ragout. When Anna asked who had done the preparation, he confessed that the delicatessen on the Kutuzovsky Prospekt had delivered the food right on time. She thanked him for the washers, the most sensible gift she'd received in a long time. He opened a bottle of wine and showed her the label. She couldn't decipher it.

"It's a pinot blanc. I picked it up at my house."

"What does your wife say when you leave with a bottle of wine under your arm?" Anna didn't wish to be impertinent, but his casual attitude, which was again on display in this, their second meeting, made her nervous.

"Medea is home even more seldom than I am," he said. He raised Anna's hand, the one holding the glass, to her mouth. "Taste it."

Although she found the wine so acidic that she grimaced, she praised it dutifully. Then she asked, "What does your wife do?"

"She's on the Soviet Council for Inter-Republic Cultural Cooperation. Since so many touring theater companies are constantly arriving in Moscow, she goes to the theater very often—so often, in fact, that she ought to have a bad conscience." He took a drink.

"Do you have a bad conscience, Comrade?"

"Why?"

"Because so far you haven't given me a single reason why we're together." She felt her forehead beginning to burn. "Or are you going to tell me that we have these meetings because you like my father's poems?"

"What sort of future do you dream about, Anna?"

For a moment, the right answer went through her head: *I dream about the realization of world communism, equality for all people, and the end of imperialism for the benefit of every individual.* She said, "When Leonid and I applied for an apartment, we were told that something would be available in Nostikhyeva soon. That was three years ago." Anna pushed her plate away. "I'd like Petya to go to the Polytechnic. He's got a talent for logic—he's already beaten Viktor Ipalyevich twice at chess. But they take only so many students."

"How about you, Anna? What would you wish for yourself?"

"I'd like to see Stockholm."

His face took on a look of affectionate surprise. "Why Sweden?"

"Viktor Ipalyevich has a book at home, a thick volume with pictures. Stockholm's a city on the sea, and it doesn't get hot in summer." She smiled. "I don't like hot weather." Her host refilled their glasses. "When are you going to try to kiss me, Comrade?" Anna asked. Maybe it was the wine, maybe it was the intimate setting, but in any case, Anna thought the question was justified.

"Does that mean you want me to?"

"You're doing everything possible to soften me up." She pointed at the remains of the exquisite snack.

"Do you suppose that I'm trying to seduce you with chicken ragout and white wine?"

"Aren't you? What do you want from me, Alexey?"

He turned serious. "I watched you that day we first met. You were standing on the ladder, and I was under you. It's something I'll never forget."

She moved away. "I don't believe you."

"You don't think it's a pleasure to look at you?"

"But we can't just . . . sit here and eat, and I tell you about Leonid, and you talk about Medea . . ." Anna forcefully laid her hand on his. "And then I go back home?"

"There are things I can imagine doing with you." He stroked her thumb.

She raised his hand and pressed it against the base of her throat, expecting his fingers to set out on their own.

"I'd like to see you naked," he said. "We could keep sitting here and talking—I won't touch you."

"No," she said curtly.

He drew back his hand. "I understand."

"Not because I'm too modest," she went on more softly. "Not because of that."

"But because . . . ?"

"I can't undress in front of you."

"A scar? Perhaps a third nipple?"

"I can't let you see my underwear."

He leaned back, smiling. "You think I can't imagine what kind of underclothing a female house painter from combine four-one-six wears?"

"With these things on, doing a 'striptease' in front of you is out of the question." She pronounced the unusual word slowly.

"You could go to the bathroom and fold your clothes in a nice neat pile. I'll wait here."

"Will you get undressed, too?" Anna could feel sweat forming on her upper lip.

"Good gracious, no." Bulyagkov folded his arms as though trying to cover himself.

He pressed her with neither gestures nor looks. Anna cast her eyes around the apartment, taking in the chandelier, the pattern of the wallpaper, the brass curtain rods. From outside came the light of an interminable dusk.

"Please close the curtains."

As if they were at the beginning of an experiment, Bulyagkov got to his feet and they moved past each other without exchanging a glance, Anna heading for the bathroom and her host for the window. Anna walked down the hall, turned into the bedroom, and stopped in surprise: The bed wasn't made. She gazed at the blue-and-white-striped mattress with the folded duvet on top of it. Whatever the Deputy Minister had in mind for her, it wasn't the obvious thing. When she entered the bathroom, the turquoise-colored tiles gave her the feeling of stepping into a dream. She ran her fingers over them. Where could you get such beautiful materials? The pale gray grout between the tiles wasn't the crumbly stuff Anna had to work with on the job. She continued to discover further details as she undressed. Since Anna and her family had moved in with her father, casual living had come to an end. Viktor Ipalyevich, who had sung of many a body in his poetry, detested displays of real nakedness and wouldn't allow Petya to sit at the table without a shirt, not even on hot summer days. Anna took off her shoes, her blouse, and her skirt; a glance in the mirror confirmed her belief that her gray brassiere was not made for a stranger's eyes. She removed it, quickly slid her panties down to the floor, and beheld the naked house painter. Her bosom was glistening with perspiration, and her muscular arms bore witness to the countless buckets of paint she'd hauled up and down scaffolding. Anna pinned her hair back and washed herself, but she still didn't like what she saw in the mirror. She put one foot forward, raised her chest, threw her head back; then, at last, she opened the door into the bedroom. A sudden feeling of shyness overcame her, followed by a bad conscience: While she was undressing herself for another man, Leonid was putting Petya to bed. Anna covered her breasts and started to return to her clothes, but then she heard Alexey's voice. He was calling her from the hall; she answered that she was coming. While she walked to the bedroom door, she could feel the vein in her neck throbbing. Alexey was waiting for her in the dimly lit anteroom. Gravely and lovingly, he kept his eyes fastened to hers. Then he led the way back into the living room.

Anna jerked around in her seat. Outside, an icy wind was beating against the window through which she'd watched the bus for Nagatino disappear.

"You passed it up!" she cried out to Anton.

He raised his eyes to the rearview mirror. "A small change in the routine, Comrade."

The ZIL shot onto Vernadsky Prospekt, heading southwest. "Where are we going?" Anna asked. When she got no reply, she leaned forward over the seat. "I have to be back before midnight."

"By midnight, we'll all be in bed," Anton said in his soothing bass.

With a jolt, they drove onto the icy bridge; the limousine was taking the expressway out of the city, already leaving behind the big housing developments to their right. Soon Anton turned off onto a road snuggled amid white hills. Anna saw the silhouettes of bare trees against the dark gray sky. The headlights repeatedly tore a patch of frozen forest out of the darkness. She asked no more questions. A DEAD END sign appeared, and under it a notice banning all vehicles. But a freezing policeman waved the automobile through without looking into the backseat. On two sides, Anna saw walls, in front of which young birch trees had been planted. A second man in uniform opened a barrier for them, and the ZIL drove into a pine plantation. Only the road had been cleared; otherwise, the snow lay knee high on all sides. Anna could see no building of any kind until Anton rounded a bend to the left and stopped on a steeply sloping concrete slab. When she got out of the limousine, ice crystals stung her face. Here on the slope, the trees stopped. In spite of the darkness, she was sure that the river lay before her, compelled to a standstill, as it were, by the cold.

There were lights in three windows at ground level, and then lights came on outside, too. Around the door, Anna could see wood carvings of some pale color; the house itself might have been blue. Anton, without a coat, walked ahead of her. Alexey Maximovich appeared in the doorway, wearing a white shirt under a woolen jacket. "We have visitors in the city," he sighed. "My wife needs the apartment." Without making sure that his visitor was following him, he went back into the house. The door closed behind them.

The most impressive thing, Anna thought, was the stove, a massive construction covered with blue tiles that radiated an immense amount of heat. She let her coat slip from her shoulders. "I thought your wife . . ."

"Medea knows about it. I've had the Drezhnevskaya apartment since long before you came along." There was a dull sheen on his cheeks and chin; Anna was sure that he'd just finished shaving.

Finding it hard to look at him, she let her eyes wander. There were carpets on the wall of Kyrgyz workmanship, and a gigantic Persian rug formed the centerpiece; she followed the patterns with her eyes, the meanderings in blue and ochre, as if writing were concealed in them. Upholstered furniture faced the fireplace. Above the dining room table was a hanging lamp; its weak light conjured up days of old, because this house was still lit by petroleum lamps.

"Are you hungry?" Alexey sat on the bench sofa and arranged a cushion for Anna. "Anton picked up a few things." He nodded toward a passageway, which she supposed led to the kitchen.

"Is Anton going to stay in the car?"

"Are you worried about him?" he asked with a grin.

"It's cold."

"He can go into the summer house."

Anna walked through the passage to the next room and found the light switch; the kitchen still looked rustic, but it was equipped with every urban convenience. "Shall I fix us something?" she asked.

"Yes, make something for us, Annushka," he called out.

After checking the pantry and glancing at the clock, Anna took out onions, eggs, and sour cream and heated some oil in a small iron skillet. If it takes us an hour to eat, she reckoned, there will still be an hour before Anton has to take me back. If Alexey comes with us, he'll have Anton drop him off first. She turned on the oven, cut the onion into thin slices, and dressed them with cream and paprika. After beating some eggs, she poured them into the skillet and put it in the oven. She heard Alexey moving around in the living room, and soon afterward came the sound of music, a sleepy hit tune featuring lots of violins. He walked into the kitchen. Anna said nothing. Every time, she found the preliminaries more difficult. She hoped he'd start the conversation on his own. With his fingers, he combed her hair aside and kissed her ear, but it wasn't a caress; it was rather a kiss of welcome, as though he were just now greeting her. Without interrupting her work with the two-handled chopper, she leaned her head against his cheek.

"A hard day?"

"The comrades monopolized me for four long hours. The office was overheated, my secretary's coffee undrinkable, and the representative from Tambov had such foul breath that I stood up and pretended I had to walk around in order to think." Bulyagkov leaned on the sink. "I'd love to see you cook naked."

"Not tonight." She looked into the oven to see whether the eggs had set yet. "Was the Minister there?"

"He knows what sessions he should stay away from." With the reserve that she had liked in him from the start, Alexey put his hand on her waist. "It's always about money. Every oblast wants to distinguish itself through particular achievements in research. The farther they are from Moscow, the more money they want." He clasped the back of her head, and she enjoyed the pressure of his fingers. She wrapped a cloth around her hand and took the little pan out of the oven.

"Take a seat." She strewed chopped onion onto the cooked eggs.

"Do you know that this is a Ukrainian recipe?" Alexey asked. "I was often served this dish as a child."

"What were you like when you were a boy, Alexey?"

"Happy." He went back into the front room.

Anna heard the sound of a bottle being uncorked, followed by the tinkle of glasses. When she carried in the food on a tray, Bulyagkov, who was standing in front of the liquor cabinet, turned around. She served; he took a seat and started eating.

"Seventy-four percent," he said after a few bites. "With the help of the technological revolution, they want to boost petrochemical production by seventy-four percent."

"Isn't that . . . extraordinarily good?"

"There is no 'technological revolution.' Seventy-four percent is beyond all reason. It's not even an incentive, it's a fantasy." He drained his glass and refilled it at once. "But Kosygin wants to *announce* it. And therefore I have to put on the necessary performance for the Minister." With a sudden blow, he jammed the cork back into the bottle. "They want units of greater capacity, gigantic power station units to improve primary processing." He broke off a piece of bread and used it to wipe the traces of egg yolk off his plate. "But things aren't so advanced as that, not anywhere in the country. In Murmansk, they thought they had the problem solved. Twelve million rubles, and during the trial run, everything blew up in their faces."

He took Anna's wrist. "You're not taking care of yourself," he said, waving her hand back and forth.

"I've used your cream." She wanted to pull her hand away.

"Rough and blotchy," he said, spreading her fingers.

"It's the lime."

"Why don't you wear gloves?"

"They don't help."

"You're beautiful, Annushka." He let himself sink back against the cushion. "Are you cold? Shall I put more wood on?"

"It's fine." She shifted to the side and took off her boots. While she let her blouse drop and slipped out of her underskirt, she had the feeling that, for her, deceit and reality were getting more and more mixed up. Every day a new piece of her integrity went missing, and her feelings slipped away from her. Obviously, her life was a lie.

Without touching her, he stood up, took a step back, and pointed at her body with an outstretched hand. Calling her affectionate names, he watched as she unzipped her skirt and slid off her pantyhose. Finally naked, Anna set the plate in the skillet and put the remains of the bread on the plate. With a glance at the wall clock, she made sure that there was as yet no reason to hurry. In semidarkness, she sank down onto a rug, and her mood grew darker and calmer. She couldn't help thinking about Anton. Had he made himself comfortable in the summer house? He was probably sitting in the car with the engine running.

TWO

At three in the afternoon the next day, when she boarded the special bus on Durova Street, it was already getting dark. At the end of a thirty-minute trip, twenty workers, seventeen of them women, were dropped off in Karacharovo. The worksite was an elongated, twelve-story apartment house that was supposed (according to the plan) to be ready by May. Trouble began because the painters were unable to do their work, and that was because the plasterers were two weeks in arrears on theirs. The walls and ceilings on five entire floors had yet to receive their final coat of plaster. The person in charge defended the delay by blaming it on the unrelenting cold: Not even the propane heaters that burned day and night on every floor could make the surfaces dry. Anna and the other women complained that the plasterers' dillydallying would cause them, the painters, to fail to fulfill their responsibilities in the plan as well. What happened in the end was what usually happened: The women laid aside their paintbrushes and picked up trowels. This was dirty work, and so a settlement for the cost of cleaning the painters' work uniforms had to be reached. When that was done, Anna and some of her colleagues climbed up on the scaffolding, while others mixed the lime plaster. In order to counteract the cold, they used quick-drying cement; the women on the scaffolding had to work very fast. A tub of fresh plaster was hoisted up to Anna; using a hawk with one hand, she scooped up some of the mixture and spread it on the ceiling with the trowel in her other hand. The plaster was too runny, and some of it dripped onto her face. She cursed and called out to the mixers to use less water. Then, with circular movements, she distributed the remaining plaster over the smooth surface.

An hour later, her head and shoulders were sprinkled with gray. Even though she was wearing a headscarf, she could feel wet plaster in her hair and her eyelids were gummy with it, but her dirty gloves prevented her from wiping off her face. Nevertheless, she'd managed to plaster half of the ceiling. Anna jumped down from the scaffolding, crouched next to the propane heater, and drank a glass of tea. One of the plasterers, a nice-looking, broad-shouldered man, squatted down beside her; after taking a few sips of his own tea in silence, he thanked the comrade for her help.

Is Petya asleep already? she wondered. Will the inhalation treatment give him a more restful night, or will he utter that strangled groan again and sit up in the bed, because he can't get enough air when he's lying down? As long as he was running a fever, she had to let him stay home from school, but spending the whole day together with his capricious grandfather wasn't good for the boy. Papa hardly ever sees anybody but his family anymore, Anna thought. She found it less regrettable that he avoided the literati and their scene than that he had shed all his friends. The extraordinary reading two years previously hadn't given him back his self-confidence; the consequences of his little swipe at the regime were an enduring sign that the ice age was not yet over. Viktor Tsazukhin had reminded the members of the Writers' Association that he was a recipient of the Order of the Fatherland, that he had spoken before large Party gatherings and been invited to receptions. How long ago had that been? Twenty years? Basically, Anna knew of her father's significance only from pictures she'd seen and things she'd heard. As a little girl, she'd been told who the people with Viktor Ipalyevich in the framed photographs were, and she knew where the fancy presentation edition of *The*

Red Light stood on the bookshelf. More than his early work, however, she loved the poems he'd written in recent years, poems that remained unpublished. As the man with the peaked cap grew sadder and understood less and questioned more, Anna found herself drawn all the more strongly to his shorter, smaller pieces. Instead of lengthy evocations of the human spectacle, his current output was characterized by instantaneous sketches, a couple of stanzas about a misunderstanding at a bus stop, lines that distilled several weeks' work. His poetry described the people of Moscow, not so much their utopian dream as their actual present; his verse shined a light on their everyday lives, captured certain moments, dedicated itself to a feeling of disappointed hope for the unattainable. Yes, Anna loved her father through his poems.

"How's your husband?" the plasterer asked, tearing her from her thoughts.

"He's good. He likes it where he is." To all who knew of it, the fact that Leonid had been transferred without explanation necessarily seemed like a punishment, and as for the real reason, Anna couldn't reveal it to anyone. She screwed the cup back onto her thermos bottle and climbed up her scaffolding.

The following morning, Petya's fever had increased. Anna swapped shifts with a colleague, dressed the boy so heavily that only his eyes and nose were visible between his scarf and his fur cap, and set out with him for the polyclinic. Along the way, she gave Petya some white lozenges to suck—they didn't help, but he liked them. When he announced that he was feeling better, she knew that he was scared of the treatment that lay in store for him. Not even six months had passed since they'd been to see the doctor about his earaches. The doctor, a woman, had pulled his earlobes, and when Petya cried out loudly, she'd diagnosed an infection. She'd prescribed drops, which indeed deadened the pain, but the inflammation grew worse. Petya had whimpered for an entire night and fallen asleep at dawn. When he woke up, Anna had discovered a yellow stain on his pillow; his eardrum had burst and pus had run out of his ear while he slept. From then on, the boy had felt better, even though he was deaf in that ear for weeks. At the follow-up examination, the doctor had proudly announced that the membrane was going to heal.

The freshly painted outpatients' clinic impressed Anna; the work on the window frames and ledges had been skillfully carried out. Inside the clinic, the gray, oil-based paint remained unchanged. Petya was breathing in brief gasps and could hardly keep himself upright. In order to reach the children's department more quickly, Anna carried him piggyback up two floors, only to find a disappointingly long line of people waiting to see a doctor. The queue stretched all the way out to the stairwell. Automatically, she asked who the last person was, and when told, she said, "Then I come after you." The other mother nodded. She was handsomely dressed, with a tailored jacket and a black cap. The little girl she was holding by the hand turned toward Petya. At this distance from the treatment rooms, there were no chairs or benches, and so Anna spread her coat in a corner of the stairs to give Petya something to sit on. A nurse hurried past them, muttering something about a "Gypsy camp."

The morning was almost gone when they were called. The lady doctor sounded Petya's chest and back, determined that he was suffering from a catarrh, and said that such a condition was standard in wintertime. Anna described his leaping fevers and his breathing difficulties, his frequent coughing and streaming eyes; the doctor assumed that they were all connected. She stuck to her diagnosis—a feverish cold—and prescribed a dose of ultraviolet therapy and an inhalant. "It's winter, that's all," she said, waving the next patient in. "When spring comes, you'll see . . ." She returned to her desk.

In spite of the transfer form she'd been given, Anna and Petya had to wait another forty-five minutes before he was summoned to the radiation room. While the boy was inside, Anna went over the course of the next few hours in her mind. She visualized the trip back home, the shopping she'd do on the way, the ride to her worksite. Because she'd swapped shifts, she had some unexpected free time, several hours' worth. She wanted to get something out of the day, to wrest a little enjoyment from it while she still could. She called Rosa Khleb from the nearest telephone.

"I'm taking my lunch break at twelve noon," said the pleasant voice at the other end of the line.

"The thing is, I'm not dressed for going out to eat," Anna answered. "And at three o'clock, I have to catch the workers' bus on Durova Street."

"You've got enough time," Rosa said, and when Anna hesitated, she added, "Don't worry about your clothes—you don't need to dress up for this place." She named an address, and Anna rang off.

Petya left the radiation room happy, declaring that he was warm all over. On the way back, he stopped several times to talk about the magic light he'd been shot with; the light, he said, had made the nurse's white coat shine blue.

When she saw the line in front of the pharmacy, Anna lost patience. With a tight grip on Petya's hand, she pulled him past the waiting customers to the entrance. "It's an emergency," she said to the protesting women and gave the gaunt pharmacist an imploring look. If he wished to, he could banish her to the end of the line.

"What does he need?"

Ignoring the murmurs of disapproval around her, Anna took out the prescription.

After a scant look at it, the pharmacist said, "We don't have that. I can give you something similar." He turned to the storage drawer cabinet behind him. "But it'll cost more."

"The doctor said . . ." Anna tapped the prescription.

"Yes or no?" With a jerk, he pulled out a drawer.

"I'll take it." She removed from Petya's grasp the plastic sign advising customers that they could have only one prescription filled per day.

The substitute medicine was three times as expensive as the one originally prescribed, but the growing ill humor of the people waiting in line induced Anna to pay without further delay. Taking her boy by the hand, she stepped out into the cold.

When they got home, the apartment had been tidied up and Viktor Ipalyevich, dressed in the jacket he wore around the house, was sitting at the table. His composition book lay in front of him, and next to it, a writing pad with notes. The glass beside him was empty. Anna laid her hand on the samovar; whatever Viktor Ipalyevich had been drinking, it wasn't tea. His cap was pulled down to his eyes, as if he wanted to shut out the visible world. His pencil hung motionless over the paper.

"Would you like beef in pepper sauce for lunch?" Anna asked as she passed him on her way to the kitchen. She'd put the fatty meat in a marinade the night before and needed only to cook it. Petya took his book from the sofa, pulled the curtain to one side, and threw himself onto the bed.

"I swapped shifts with Svetlana today. Will you fix Petya's dinner?"

The figure in the black woolen jacket didn't move. While sautéing the garlic, Anna read the little leaflet that had come with Petya's medicine, set some water on to boil, and prepared his inhalant. She squeezed tomato paste out of a tube, stirred it into the pot, and added the meat. Then she went into the other room and sat down across from her father. He didn't look up. There was writing on the page in front of him, but an eraser lay close at hand. In order to save paper, Viktor Ipalyevich would make repeated revisions of a poem on the same sheet, until it was gray and worn from erasures. Anna started telling him about her morning at the clinic, heard the water boiling, rushed to the kitchen to fetch it, stirred the meat as she passed, and carried the steaming pot into the room. She called Petya, who laid his book aside, grumbling a bit, and trotted over to the table. She poured the required amount of the inhalant into the water, put a cushion under the boy, told him to lean over the pot, and spread a towel over his head and shoulders. He gasped for air and started struggling; his mother stroked his back. If he was a brave boy, she told him, he'd start feeling better that very day. Gradually, the little fellow under the towel began to breathe evenly.

"How's it coming along?" Anna asked her father.

"Nothing's coming anymore. I've been aware of it for a long time." He looked at her with watery eyes; his homemade liquor was having its effect. "The spring has dried up."

"But you were writing well just yesterday."

"One can always write *something*." He turned over the page and showed his daughter that he had torn out all the preceding pages. "Worthless stuff. I sit there from morning till evening and tell myself I'm practicing a craft." He threw his pencil across the table. "An idler, that's what I've become. Nobody needs what I produce." He laughed grimly. "I haven't met my quota. The committee will scold me."

Anna said nothing and contemplated the carpet hanging on the opposite wall, her only wedding present. While Leonid was still living with them, Viktor Ipalyevich had done better at keeping his drinking under control; it was embarrassing for him to let himself go in front of his son-in-law. Anna's eyes wandered to the shelves where her father's books stood. Above the shelves hung the wall light in the gilded sconce, which had its own odd history. She gazed at the rusty radiator and the velvet cloth that hid the sleeping alcove. She'd neglected to wash the curtains in the fall; now, yellowish and heavy, they'd have to wait until spring.

"Lunch is almost ready," she said. When she stepped past Viktor Ipalyevich, she could smell his rotgut liquor. In the kitchen, she turned off the gas, put the meat and sauce on a platter, and carried it and the plates into the other room.

"Will you clear the table?" Without waiting for her father's consent, she clapped his notebook shut. His gloominess took her breath away, and she could hardly wait for her appointment with Rosa.

"How long do I have to stay down here?" Petya asked, coughing as he spoke.

"Just a little while longer." Anna served her father and herself and started eating. "For the most part, the beginning of a poem comes to you fairly easily. And you write the ending quickly, too." She pointed to the closed composition book. "It's just in the middle where you have problems, isn't it?"

"What do you know about how a poem gets written?"

"Nothing." She chewed slowly. "I know nothing about it."

"Then don't tell me anything about it, either." He picked at his food. "How often is Petya supposed to have these inhalation treatments?"

"No more!" The red face appeared from under the table. "I just had one, I don't have to do it anymore."

"Again before he goes to bed," said Anna. She put some food on the boy's plate and took away the pot of water. "You'll feel better tomorrow," she told Petya, looking at the kitchen clock. "Does the brave boy want a treat?" She returned to the room with a cookie in her hand. Then she put on her scarf and grabbed her coat. "Errands," she said, answering Viktor Ipalyevich's questioning look.

"You've hardly eaten anything."

"Put it in the oven for me." She was already out the door.

The bus took Anna from west to east. She got out at the Lubyanka Theater stop, took longer than she liked to find the right street, and stopped to stare in amazement at an old man who had piled bundles of dried green twigs against the wall of a building. He turned his sign—OAK 50 KOPECKS, BIRCH 45 KOPECKS—so that she could see it. She shook her head, thanking him, and looked for a spot where she could wait undisturbed. Ten minutes passed. Rosa's tardiness annoyed Anna, and she resolved to give her friend five more minutes before she went off to have a glass of tea on her own.

Rosa Khleb had turned out to be the most refreshing and, at the same time, the most disastrous acquaintance that Anna had made in recent years. She couldn't imagine a more interesting friend, but Rosa was also a she-devil who often made Anna wish that they had never met. Two years previously, in June, around the time when her affair with Alexey had begun, Anna had gone to buy bread at a bakery on Kalinin Prospekt that offered five different kinds. In no hurry, she'd moved forward in the line, mentally going over her remaining errands.

"But it's back there," she heard a man at the counter say.

The girl behind it held out a loaf to him.

"That's at least five hours old. I'd like some of the fresh bread back there on the trays." He pointed toward the ovens.

"Next in line."

"Wait a minute, *I'm* first!"

"You want some bread from *back there*, right?" said the shop assistant, imitating him. "That'll be available in an hour." Disregarding the man's protests, she signaled to a woman with a child to step up to the counter. The woman wasn't choosy; she took the proffered loaf and thrust it into her shopping bag. Furious, the man pushed his way out of the crowded shop.

Only then did Anna notice the pretty woman standing in front of her in the line. She was wearing a striking summer dress, dark blue with a light-colored pattern. No dye could have produced the natural color of her shoulder-length blond hair. She might have been around Anna's age, but her bearing, her self-confident air, suggested a woman in her thirties. When the blonde's turn came, she didn't make her choice hastily, as the other customers did; she took the long-handled spoon from the counter and pressed the metal into the loaves that were on offer. By the fourth, the people behind Anna began to grow restless. "They're all the same!" one cried out.

The shop assistant nodded and said, "They all come out of the same machine."

"How old is that one?" the blonde asked.

"It's fresh." The girl tried to hand her the loaf, but the customer decided on another one. "That man who was just here was right," she said without emphasis. "You ought to put out your newest loaves. This bread's already getting hard." With that, she took the loaf and went to stand in the line in front of the cash register. Very soon, Anna was behind her again. It had grown dark outside, a draft of cool air entered the bakery, and thunder crashed over the rooftops.

"Oh no, not now!" a woman cried. She quickly counted her kopecks, dropped them on the cashier's counter, and ran out in an attempt to beat the coming storm. The next woman in line was equally hurried, but not the blonde. She calmly opened her shopping bag, let the cashier peer inside to see whether there was anything there besides a loaf of bread, took out her purse, and started looking for the correct change.

"It's going to be pouring in a minute!" a man barked.

After paying, the blonde ambled past the line of customers to the exit.

Anna paid in her turn, put her change in her pocket and her loaf under her arm, squeezed through the door, and stepped out. The air was green, there was a smell of sulfur, and lightning and thunder were following each other in rapid succession. She was surprised to find the blond customer still standing in the entrance, apparently having trouble with her umbrella. The rain was coming down so hard that two men who were running for the bakery collided just outside the door. Laughing, they hastened to take refuge inside. From one second to the next, the street was swept empty. Anna decided to wait out the heaviest downpour and leaned against the wall. As the pretty woman was still struggling with her umbrella, Anna offered to help and opened it with two swift movements.

"Where do you have to go? I can take you part of the way."

Had Anna been able to imagine the consequences of this offer, she would have run out into the rain without replying. Instead she gazed at the lovely things the blonde was wearing. "You'll ruin your dress," Anna said.

"I want to go to that café." Arm in arm, protected by the umbrella, and running in step, they set out.

When they reached the door of the bar, the unknown woman asked, "Shall we go in and have some tea?"

Anna, breathless, stood there without speaking.

"Without you, I would have got soaking wet," said the woman, smiling. "And by the way, my name is Rosa."

The meeting that took place one week later marked the first time that Anna stepped into the trap. For a long time, her family had enjoyed a privilege: During the 1940s, when Viktor Ipalyevich was at the height of his fame, he had purchased a grave in one of Moscow's central cemeteries. And so Anna was among the few who, when they visited their dead, could do so inside the city; most people had to go to the urn graves located on the outskirts. On that particular afternoon, having picked up some spike broom and some forget-me-nots, Anna had passed through the cemetery's main portal and watched the crows, which seemed to be attacking the graves. It was hot and sunny. Many visitors were kneeling on the marble gravestones, scrubbing them with brushes or putting plants on them. Anna reached the grave that was her goal and greeted a couple who had set up a table on their son's gravestone and were having lunch.

"We've brought Sasha some of the things he used to like." With a gesture, the father invited Anna to share their meal: *pirozhki*, hard-boiled eggs, pickled mushrooms, and fish. Regretfully, Anna pointed to the neglected adjacent grave and held up a hand rake. "First I have to tidy up Mama's place."

"The winter made a real mess." The neighbors kept eating.

Anna went down on her knees. Her grandparents' marker had been moved farther back, and in the middle stood a stone of polished granite bearing a picture of her mother. The photograph showed a pretty woman with her hair pinned up high on her head. The look on the youthful face gave Anna a pang; in reality, Dora Tsazukhina had been a slight, inconspicuous woman, somewhat shorter than Viktor Ipalyevich. She'd worked for the Writers' Association as one of a hundred typists and had met, at a reception, the poet whose work she'd revered even as a girl. Viktor Ipalyevich was divorced, and he enjoyed being revered by women for his poetry. He'd seduced Dora that very night and visited her a few times after that at the Writers' Association, but without considering the matter very important. Soon afterward, a lover of many years' standing left him for a sculptor who won the Lenin Prize. Finding himself empty-handed in every way had dealt a sharp blow to Viktor Ipalyevich's self-confidence. As chance would have it, the editing of his latest volume of poems had recently been completed, and Dora was typing up the revised manuscript, so that the two of them had professional reasons for spending time together. The poet had instinctively understood that in securing Dora he would be drawing to his side a lifelong admirer, someone who would always subordinate her existence to his needs and who (this consideration was not to be disdained) earned a respectable income. Dora and Viktor were married during a heavy March rainstorm; at the end of November, Anna came into the world. "She'll be an idealist," her father had declared, and he'd given her the name of the protagonist in Tolstoy's famous novel. The allocation of a larger apartment was achieved without difficulty, and Viktor, Dora, and the infant moved into their new home near Filyovsky Park. Dora wasn't robust, but nobody found her delicacy worrying; for Viktor Ipalyevich, all it meant was that he would go on his long hikes through the hills around Zagorsk alone or choose easier routes. On one such excursion, Dora had slipped and, although she didn't fall, broken her shinbone. The fragility of her bone structure aroused surprise; a medical examination revealed that she had cancer of the bone marrow. At the time when her mother was hospitalized, Anna was a fourteen-year-old Pioneer Girl. For three years, Dora had fought her illness with a determination that commanded Viktor Ipalyevich's deepest respect; in the final months, however, both he and his daughter had wished that the sick woman's ordeal might be over soon. Anna's mother died in the household; outside, as on her wedding day, there was a terrific downpour. The normally complacent Viktor Ipalyevich had mourned his wife's death more deeply than Anna would have thought him capable of doing, and during this period he'd produced his most beautiful poems: not elegies, but vibrant declarations of love to Dora. Shortly afterward, Anna had left school and accepted a trainee position in the building combine.

Now she knelt at her mother's grave. While casting hungry glances at her neighbors' picnic, she'd dug little hollows in the soil and planted the forget-me-nots in a circle around the gravestone. Then she'd swept all the blackened leaves off the grave and polished its brass ornamentation, and as she was kneeling there quietly for a moment, a cloth pattern came into her field of vision—a summer dress that Anna recognized. It was the same woman she'd met during the cloudburst outside the bakery.

"Anna?" the woman asked warily, as if she weren't sure of the name.

"Rosa!"

"What a coincidence!" the woman said, laughing. Her hair shimmered in the midday sun.

"Who do you have in here?" Anna asked, tamping down the earth around the forget-me-nots.

"My paternal grandparents." Rosa pointed to the cemetery's main avenue.

"My mother," Anna said, pointing to the photograph.

"You look like her."

"She died when I was seventeen."

"I'm doubly happy to see you again," Rosa said, extracting her wallet from her purse.

Anna remembered how embarrassed Rosa had been in the tearoom. She hadn't had enough money, and she'd been unable to pay her share;

Anna had even been obliged to lend her subway fare. "Forget it," Anna said. "It was my treat."

Rosa insisted on immediate reciprocation. She accompanied Anna as she poured stale water out of a vase, carried the vase over to a faucet, and filled the vessel with fresh water. When she placed the spike broom blossoms behind her mother's picture, flowers surrounded the gravestone like a yellow corona. Then Anna and Rosa strolled away together down the central avenue of the cemetery, followed by the curious eyes of the old couple.

"Just a moment," Rosa said, slowing her pace. "If you don't mind, I'd like to . . ." She pointed to the little church that gave the cemetery its name, and Anna realized that the cross around Rosa's neck was no mere adornment. They both covered their heads with scarves. It was cold in the chapel, and the space was filled with the singsong prayers of some old women. Rosa bought a candle, took out a small piece of paper, and wrote the names of her dead on it. After a short prayer, she laid the chit on a stack near the altar. Anna watched these proceedings with sympathy, which she was only later to understand was exactly what Rosa had wished to elicit. By performing a reactionary act in Anna's sight, she was giving her friend a sign of trust.

In the tearoom after the earlier cloudburst, Rosa had mentioned that she worked as a journalist for the English-language daily, the *Moscow Times*. Now, as they left the church, she told Anna of a telephone call to the newspaper that morning: During some demolition work in the Arbat quarter of Moscow, an old storeroom, unopened since the war, had been discovered. Her editor, Rosa said, had assigned her to report on this discovery, and she invited Anna to accompany her on the assignment.

The building complex was on the boundary of the Arbat quarter. At first glance, the high fence surrounding the complex made it seem inaccessible. The photographer, a stout fellow with curly hair, was already waiting. He yanked two boards aside, allowing the women to enter the worksite. The converted lobby, its windows blacked out by decades of dust, was on the second floor. When the photographer opened the iron door, Anna just stood there, speechless. She felt as though she'd entered some monumental film like the ones that used to be shown to her and her fellow Pioneer Girls. The gray concrete ceiling was thickly hung with huge crystal chandeliers that sparkled in the light of a heavy-duty, upward-pointing halogen lamp. The sight before Anna's eyes surpassed everything that she'd been taught about the wasteful extravagance of the feudal barons. Who had possessed the resources, not to mention the room, required to hang such luxury from their ceilings? For whom had workers' hands suspended countless rhinestones from little wire hooks and assembled chandeliers as tall as two stories in a modern building? Hesitantly, as if she might be called to account for every step, Anna entered the scene, while Rosa questioned the worker who had come upon the hidden treasure. The photographer worried about the quality of the light and shot pictures from every possible angle.

The report on "Stalin's Lamp Shop" had never appeared. Those who knew about the collection had preferred to help themselves to it. With a smile, Rosa had assured the head of the demolition firm that he'd be compensated for his discovery if he conducted himself appropriately. Even so early on, it should have made Anna suspicious to see a young woman, a journalist, in a position to make such an offer. Blinded by the hanging splendor, Anna had looked on, and the question never crossed her mind.

"Which one do you like?"

Anna's eyes had wandered to a wall chandelier with a gilt arm; Rosa had nodded in agreement. Once, some time later, Rosa had told Anna that the small lamps, the ones that could be carried off in a crate or a box, had disappeared soonest. For the middle-sized chandeliers, trucks with their tailgates down had pulled up in the parking area; the monsters, the largest of the treasures, had hung there for some time, and then someone had decided to dismantle them and sell their individual parts.

That was the day when Anna accepted the first gift, the first time she associated herself with someone she barely knew in order to obtain some benefit. Much later, a good while after the two had become the closest of friends, Rosa admitted to Anna that no member of her family had ever been buried in the Vaganskovskoye Cemetery.

"You look like an illegal street vendor," Rosa Khleb said, snatching Anna out of her memories. "Why didn't you wait inside?"

"There's . . . nothing there," Anna said, pointing in the direction she'd come from.

Rosa took her friend's arm, and together they turned back to the man with the bundled twigs. She was a head taller than Anna, and she was wearing a fur-trimmed coat and black leather gloves. She bought two bundles, one oak and one birch, and entered the passage that led to the building's inner courtyard. There was a cashier in one of the rear stairwells.

"As a club member, I'm allowed to bring a guest," Rosa said, paying for them both.

"What kind of club is this?" Anna followed her inside through a normal apartment doorway.

"You'll like it. Every now and then, when I have more time than I do now, I stay here for a full three hours."

The dressing room smelled as though sweaty laundry were being boiled somewhere nearby. Rosa surrendered her watch, her briefcase, and a gold bracelet to a woman in a white smock. Anna hastened to put her own things in the woman's hands. She received their coats and hats and handed them two tokens.

"The second one is for the towels," Rosa explained.

They entered a room whose elegance had faded. A carved mantelpiece crowned the walled-up fireplace. A sleepy old woman was sitting in front of a massive mirror; a copy of the house rules was fastened to the mirror's frame with thumbtacks. One of the regulations stated: "Anyone seen consuming alcohol must be reported at once." The woman showed them to a changing room. The coat hangers, the benches, and the shoe racks, but above all the moist, warm air, made it clear to Anna what sort of place they were in. Rosa loosened her hair and began to get undressed; Anna admired her ivory-white underwear.

"What are you waiting for?"

Anna let her pants, sweater, and shirt fall to the floor. When she was naked, she covered herself with the bath towel.

"I have to sweat out yesterday's office party," Rosa said, going ahead of her. "A couple of our correspondents were still going strong at dawn. Good thing we publish only twice a week—otherwise, there would have been no edition of the *Moscow Times* today."

Once they were through the next door, the temperature and the humidity rose sharply. Several women stood under showers and soaped themselves. For a long moment, Anna felt inhibited among strangers; at the washstands in the building combine, people rarely appeared unclothed.

"I thought you didn't have much time," Rosa said to encourage her. Anna stepped under the jet of lukewarm water.

"Prepare yourself for feudalism in its most horrible form!" Rosa said, indicating with an outstretched arm the steam bath's inner sanctum.

They entered a room whose contours could only be guessed, because it was full of steam. Along the wall, Anna could make out slabs of black marble for reclining, and in the middle of the room a bathtub that seemed to have been chiseled out of a single block of stone; two women were sitting in it, chatting. On the marble slabs, too, women were sitting and talking. Water and sweat ran along their shoulders and breasts and dripped onto the floor.

"Are you ready for the gallery?" Rosa smiled in a way that made Anna curious. They approached the last door together. A wave of hot, moist air took Anna's breath away and scorched her lungs. A lightbulb illuminated the square room, in which there were three tiers of benches, the highest tier right under the ceiling. In this chamber there was only one other person, a woman of extravagant proportions, snoring in her sleep. Anna and Rosa chose the middle tier and sat there for a while in silence, trying to get used to the climate.

"So how are things going for you, Comrade?"

Anna waited until the moisture on her nose formed a droplet and fell onto her knee. "I miss my husband."

"How much time does he have left?"

"You say that as if he were serving a jail sentence."

Rosa lay down at full length on her stomach. "I say that because I know you know the exact day when his time is up."

"His year on Sakhalin ends in March. Then he gets a six-day vacation." Anna leaned back against the stone wall. Her towel slipped off her breasts, and Anna spread it out under her.

Rosa put a hand on Anna's thigh. "Look at it this way: At that point, your situation will be settled. Leonid will get an official right of abode for Moscow, and you'll finally be allocated an apartment."

"Papa will be happier than anybody else when we leave him in peace inside his own four walls."

"Without you, your father wouldn't have any more walls at all. And furthermore, his books would be—"

Knowing what was coming next, Anna interrupted her with a gesture. "Viktor Ipalyevich isn't a nanny. He needs concentration for his work."

Rosa grinned. "Is there a selflessness medal? If there is, you ought to get nominated for it."

"I'm not selfless," Anna replied. "I'm anything but that."

The pipe behind them roared and steam, coming from the opening in bursts, enveloped them. The fat woman heaved a noisy sigh, rolled off her bench, and disappeared outside. The bath attendant passed with a small bucket and sprinkled water on the hot stones.

"And how is the Deputy Minister?"

Anna watched the attendant until she was out of sight. Then she said, "Alexey is wrestling with his ghosts."

"Which ones this time?"

"The demons of the Five-Year Plan. The Deputy Minister finds the figures that the CC plans to publish . . ." Anna waved one hand, slowly. "Too optimistic."

"Who believes figures? Everybody knows they're a fetish with Kosygin. He'll just give a pretty speech." She leaned forward, spread her legs, and slid to the step below her. "If that's all Bulyagkov has to worry about, he's in an enviable position."

Anna said softly, "He hates his job."

This remark made Rosa sit up and take notice. "What makes you think so?"

"He's never told me a single pleasant story about the Ministry. You know, the sort of thing you hear on the news. He's got the power to influence the scientific life of our country, and it doesn't seem to mean anything to him."

Rosa sat in pensive silence for a few seconds. Then she said, "He's like all men." She smiled. "When they go home in the evening, they like to gripe to their wives about their work. Bulyagkov, apparently, does the same thing with his lover."

Anna shrugged her shoulders.

"I think you're just about hard-boiled now, my dear. When I came here for the first time, I couldn't take more than five minutes in the gallery."

Rosa was dripping out of every pore, Anna noticed, while her own skin seemed only a little damp. She said, "Those of us in construction are used to tougher conditions than you in your chic editorial offices. In summer, I often have to work for hours in attics and dormers where the temperature must be one hundred and twenty degrees."

Rosa took up one of the bundles of twigs, signaled to Anna to turn over, and struck her, first gently, then harder and harder, on her back and her legs. Anna flinched at the initial blow but quickly began to feel an agreeable tingling and closed her eyes. After a while, she rolled onto her back, and Rosa continued the procedure. It didn't bother Anna to feel her friend's eyes on her body. Eventually, Rosa dropped the twigs and lay down on the stone herself. Anna seized the bundle of oak twigs and brought them down sharply on Rosa's posterior.

"Harder."

Anna struck harder. A while passed in which the only audible sounds were Rosa's quickened breathing and soft groans. Anna brushed the twigs over her friend's flat belly, over her muscular thighs and calves.

"Star-Eyes wants to see you," Rosa said. The bundle of oak switches stopped in midair, shivering. "I was going to call you today. You beat me to it."

"About what?"

"Your report."

"But just last week . . ." Anna laid the twigs aside.

"He has questions." Rosa sat up. "You behave like somebody afraid of failing an exam. Star-Eyes is satisfied with you."

"Where?"

"You'll learn that later." Rosa licked her lips. "We should have brought something to drink. They sell bread and chicken in the foyer." She stood up and wrapped the towel around her chest. "How would you like a bottle of beer?"

"Isn't alcohol prohibited?"

"For a Russian, you know surprisingly little about the difference between utopia and reality. They sell vodka in half-liter bottles, too, and with any luck there will even be some lemons."

Anna watched Rosa disappear into the steam and then followed her, as though walking into clouds.

THREE

Anna stopped in front of the Pushkin monument. During the day, the sun had melted the snow on the pedestal, and now the stone looked clean. She sat down. She still had errands to run, soon the shops would close, and yet she lingered on the dark stone. She couldn't yet bring herself to enter the building on the quay and go up to that eighth-floor apartment where everything appeared normal and logical and was in fact the opposite. Anna needed more time.

Suddenly, she heard a woman's voice: "My sweetheart, you poor little thing, you must be all worn out, and so tired, so sad. Come on up."

Pushkin's bronze trouser legs concealed the speaker. Anna leaned over, propping herself on her elbows, and saw a heavily dressed woman with a knitted scarf on her head. She was bending forward and helping someone to climb up beside her. Anna thought she might be a grandmother on an outing with her grandson, but in the next moment a mongrel dog leaped into sight, his hind legs slipping helplessly on the smooth stone.

"That's too high for you, all stiff and frozen as you are." The woman grasped the dog's chest with both hands and pulled him up. "I'm helping you, look, I'm helping you, my little friend." Befuddled by his new vantage point, so high above the ground, the dog shook himself and looked at the old woman. She stroked his head between his shaggy ears, opened her cloth bag, and took out some food scraps. Anna watched as the woman, chattering nonstop, fed the dog bread and cold potatoes.

"You've found yourself a good spot, at the feet of the great philanthropist. Nobody wants to act heartless here. You'll find compassion here, little one, yes, that tastes good, doesn't it?" As the old woman took another potato out of her bag, she noticed that she was being observed. "My Tasha died," she went on, as if she'd included Anna in the conversation right from the start. "A female poodle, she was. I made lots of pretty things for her—I didn't want my Tasha to be cold, ever. All the same, she often got sick, her eyes never stopped running. She died from something else, though." The dog gave the woman a nudge, because she'd forgotten to keep feeding him. "I don't have any more," she said, patting him hard on the head. "Tomorrow there'll be a little canned fish. Are you coming again tomorrow, my little friend? Well, I am, too, so we have a date, right?"

"Does he have a name?"

"We're seeing each other for the first time today." The old woman snapped her bag shut. "And he surely won't be here tomorrow." She looked at the dog reproachfully. "Street mutts are faithless." She scooted clumsily to the edge of the pedestal. "The dogcatcher may pick him up before morning. Right, sweetheart? If you don't watch out, you'll wind up in some research lab where they'll operate on you and stick tubes in you." The dog wagged his tail attentively. "At least you've had enough to eat this one time." She jumped down from the pedestal, pulled her bag after her, and disappeared into the foggy darkness. The mongrel didn't follow her; he laid his head between his paws and had a digestive nap.

The statue loomed blackly above Anna. It was high time for her to leave. She thrust her hands into her sleeves and tried to count the lighted windows in the apartment building across from her; like a trellis of light, they rose up out of the darkness and cast shadowy reflections on the frozen river.

Anna didn't want to deceive Alexey; the shamefulness of it festered in her like an ulcer. A solution would require but a single step: She would have to leave him. For doing that, she could have named a hundred reasons, among them the truth. In the beginning, she'd believed that time was on her side; everything had seemed amusing and easy at first. Anna tilted her head back.

She hadn't fallen in love with Alexey, she didn't lust after him, and yet the evenings she spent with him felt to her like excursions to an exotic island. Once a week, usually Thursday, she was picked up by Anton and brought to the Drezhnevskaya apartment. It was as if Anna were going out to a play in which she had the main role. They would always start by chatting about everyday things over a drink or two; eventually, Anna would go into the bathroom, undress, and return naked to the living room, where Alexey would already be stretched out on the sofa. He'd tell her of his travels, and thus she heard about remote regions of the Soviet Union, about people whose way of life differed utterly from that of the Muscovites. Once Bulyagkov evoked a happy memory, an incident from his childhood in rural Ukraine, and his tale made Anna think of one of her father's poems. Since she didn't know it by heart, she paraphrased some of the verses in her own words. Alexey liked this and asked her to do it on other occasions, turning the play of her thoughts into a game. Under normal conditions, she would have found it ridiculous to speak in images and to invent individuals and circumstances that didn't jibe with reality. But Anna was naked, she was a nymph in summer, improvising for the delight of her listener. Wearing an open white shirt, Alexey would loll on the sofa, sipping his drink and watching her as she darted around barefoot, took a book from the shelf, gazed at pictures, tracked the sun's path over the rooftops. Sometimes Anna would sit down beside him and he'd lay his hand on her hip or grasp her knee and lavish her body with loving gestures composed entirely of words. During their erotic fantasies, they'd remain completely serious, which aroused Anna all the more. They escalated into wild and lusty orgies that the aging man and the house painter would scarcely have been capable of carrying off in reality. Alexey told Anna that he seldom slept with Medea, not because of aversion or habit, but as one might forget something that had never been important. Anna asked whether he'd entertained other women in that apartment, and Alexey did not deny it. On those Thursdays, Anna's life was carefree, filled with a lightheartedness she'd never known before, something simultaneously lascivious and innocent. Those had been wondrous weeks, they had made the summer pass swiftly, and little by little, Anna had admitted to herself that she felt a deep love for Alexey. She recognized that the evenings with him were what she yearned for most, that the course of her week was directed toward them, and that in the hours before Anton picked her up, she could undertake nothing of any importance. She took great care to be assigned to the early shift on Thursdays, she got home with time to spare, and she made sure she looked her best.

"An entire bottle of shampoo in a month," Viktor Ipalyevich said one day. "Good thing I'm bald. Otherwise, our family collective would be given a deadline and ordered to justify this extravagance." When Anna only laughed, he spoke more pointedly: "How handy for you that Leonid spends so many nights in his barracks." Her answer was a scared look, to which he replied, "Leonid's not dumb, you know. And he loves you to boot."

"I love him, too," she said.

In actual fact, Anna wasn't unfaithful; she and Alexey didn't sleep together. However, the rules of their society forbade what they *did* do: They constructed a private dream, an individual world. Their conduct was "unidealistic" and "morally defective." When a man like Bulyagkov, who had access to all privileges, engaged in such behavior, it didn't have the consequences that would threaten a working woman. Toward the end of that summer, Anna had for the first time imagined the day when Alexey would drop her. The following Thursday, he found her uneasy; when he asked her why, she made no secret of her fears. They were drinking port wine, and Anna was fully dressed. Alexey took the glass from her hand, drew her head close to his, and kissed her for the first time.

"I love you," he said, as naturally as if he were asking her to open the window. "You have nothing to fear from me, not now, not ever. And if, in spite of that, you decide to break it off someday, I'll accept your decision."

"Why don't you sleep with me, Alexey?"

"So we can be like every other couple? So we can finally have a normal affair?"

"No. Because you love me."

They went into the bedroom together. As always, the bed was unmade. "I hadn't expected to adopt such concrete measures," he said.

"Makes no difference," she replied, pulling him onto the mattress.

Anna had seduced him and enjoyed it, but at the same time, she'd felt that she was ruining something. She'd gotten closer to the man, but she'd let the keeper of the dream escape. She'd allowed everyday air into their rarefied world. They had lain beside each other on the bed, naked. Horsehair protruded from the mattress here and there. The Deputy Minister had liver spots; his legs were sinewy and marked with blue veins. Afterward, Anna had grown sad. She'd felt that, instead of strengthening their relationship, she'd made its end more palpable. While she was in the bathroom, Alexey had put on a record; it was Shostakovich, somber music that sounded to Anna like a reproach. She'd taken her leave earlier than usual and—with her eyes—begged Alexey to pardon her.

Anna stood up and walked away from the statue. It had begun to snow; ice crystals smudged the points of light in the windows across from her. She moved toward the building with slow steps. Her affair with Alexey had endured for a year and nine months already, longer than many marriages. And for almost that entire length of time, her "relationship" with the other older man, the one who wore the dark green suits and the eyeglasses that twinkled like stars, had been in existence as well. When they met for the first time, she thought, how paternally he'd acted toward her.

It had been in August of that first year. On her way to meet Rosa in Arkhangelskoye Park, Anna had descended from the street into a low-lying garden, where thickly blooming flower beds and dwarf palms enlivened the grassy space. A man in a summer shirt was tearing roses off a climbing bush; on the pond, a woman was sitting in a boat and reading a closely printed manuscript. The summer was almost over, and anyone with sufficient time had hastened to the park in order to take in as much as possible of what might have been the last of the long, hot days.

Rosa and Anna had arranged to meet near the children's playground, where children were climbing through brightly colored pipes and whirling around on a wooden disc. The woman whom Anna sometimes thought of as "the Khleb," wearing a short red dress, came walking down the promenade.

"Which of them is Petya?"

"I didn't bring him," Anna replied in surprise. "I thought you said—"

"Oh, right. You shouldn't have taken that so seriously." Rosa took her arm. "My girlfriend has two of these little monsters. When they're around, there's no way to have a rational conversation with her."

While Rosa chatted, Anna wondered why someone like Rosa Khleb would want to be friends with her. What could she tell a journalist about? There was nothing special about her life; every day, she stood on her scaffolding, painted walls, hurried home, cooked meals for her father, son, and husband, if he was there, and got a little fatter, because she couldn't pay attention to her figure. What was so interesting about Anna that Rosa devoted so much time to her?

When the two reached the triple-spiral staircase, like a colossal braid linking the upper and lower levels of the park, Rosa stood still. "That can't be . . ." she said. She took a lateral step, and Anna followed her eyes to the profile of a gentleman in his fifties who was sitting at a table and drinking lemonade. Long after this meeting, it would occur to Anna that all the tables around him had been empty.

"Do you know him?"

"My teacher." Rosa had lowered her voice, as if she didn't want to disturb the lemonade drinker. "He hardly ever comes to Moscow."

"Don't you want to say hello to him?"

"Not now. We have an appointment later."

Rosa wanted to go on, but Anna held her back. "Go ahead, we've got lots of time."

"Kamarovsky doesn't like surprises."

It was the first time that Anna had heard this name. In her memory, it seemed to her that she herself, not Rosa Khleb, had instigated the meeting. "Go tell him hello." She'd led her friend into the park café and over to the man, who'd looked up only when the two women were standing in front of him.

"Rosa." He hadn't seemed surprised in the least. Sparks flashed from his eyes; the lenses of the glasses he was wearing had been ground and polished repeatedly.

To Anna's amazement, Rosa didn't explain that they had been walking there merely by chance. Instead, she took a seat next to him. "This is Anna," she said.

He gestured toward the chair across from him. Anna sat down and introduced herself with her full name. She'd expected that student and teacher would have things to talk to each other about, but he appeared to be interested only in Anna. "I take it you're married," he said.

She wore no ring; was it so easy to spot her as a wife?

"Anna has a five-year-old son," Rosa interjected.

"So he'll start going to school this autumn."

Anna acknowledged the truth of this observation and answered further questions, all of them courteously posed; and yet she found that

Kamarovsky's behavior went beyond a stranger's common curiosity. "You were Rosa's teacher?" she asked.

"Is that what she says?" His glinting glasses hid his eyes.

Anna wondered whether the man had been Rosa's mentor in journalism school or at the newspaper. She said, "I don't know anything about the newspaper business."

"And what do you know something about, Comrade?"

"Lime," she replied. "Emulsion paint. Oil paint. I'm pretty familiar with undercoat plaster and finishing plaster, and I even know how to do marbling."

"Have you seen the big hall in the Ostankino, which has just been reopened?"

"Only in photographs. I've never been there."

"During the restoration, it was discovered that the painters who decorated the hall a long time ago had used an unknown binder, and their pigments were considerably brighter than the ones used today. The chemical composition of the old pigments was studied in the laboratory, and they were found to include linseed oil, aluminum oxide . . . and animal urine." Kamarovsky nodded, as though he'd delivered some significant news.

"Are you an art historian?"

"In a former life. What else occupies your time, Anna?" His tone of voice had grown warmer. "What does your husband do?"

"He's a first lieutenant in the army."

"Stationed in Moscow?"

Anna named Leonid's unit and said where it was based.

"And you live with him and your little boy?"

"We live with my father."

"Right." Kamarovsky emptied his glass. "Your father is Viktor Ipalyevich Tsazukhin."

Anna's blood had shot into her cheeks. All at once, it was clear to her: This was an arranged meeting. She and Rosa had not just happened to pick Arkhangelskoye Park, had not randomly chosen the path to the steps; the man in the dark green suit wasn't sitting here in the sun for no reason; and above all, he was more than a teacher.

In the same soft voice as before, he'd asked, "Does your father know you're committing adultery?" And when Anna made no reply, he added: "You allow yourself to be seduced by the Deputy Minister for Research Planning."

"No, *I* seduce *him*, Comrade," she'd said. She didn't know where such cheekiness came from; she knew only that she didn't want to be interrogated anymore. The interrogator made a sign, and the waiter hurried over to their table.

"Lemonade?" Kamarovsky inquired, as though Anna had passed the first test. A couple who'd been strolling around the terrace tried to sit at the next table, only to be told that it was reserved. Anna gradually realized that Rosa had maneuvered her onto an island. She tried to look into Rosa's eyes, but they remained impenetrable.

"Why have you gotten involved with Bulyagkov?" Kamarovsky had asked. "Is it his position? Do you hope to obtain privileges through him?"

"No."

"It can hardly be his charm."

"I got involved with him because he asked nothing of me."

"Alexey Maximovich is in the public eye. Special security precautions are taken for him, measures intended to preserve his personal safety as well as his reputation." The waiter brought Anna's drink, and Kamarovsky paused.

"May I ask who you are?"

"We'll get to that later." He invited her to taste her drink. "Does your husband have any inkling of your relationship?"

"No."

"Then can you explain why he chooses to spend his nights with his unit, even though maneuvers came to an end some time ago?"

Anna had certainly noticed that Leonid wasn't coming home three or four nights a week. She'd consoled herself with the thought that comradeship had always been important to him.

"Leonid is either too proud or too cowardly to talk to you about all this," Kamarovsky said pointedly.

She hadn't mentioned Leonid's name, so she assumed the man in the green suit must know him. "Have you spoken with Leonid?"

"We won't intrude upon your married life unless it becomes necessary to do so. What we're interested in is the Deputy Minister's reputation."

"Alexey's careful."

"That's not the point." Kamarovsky gripped the side of his eyeglasses. "Alexey Maximovich Bulyagkov is a bearer of the Soviet Union's state secrets. Therefore, it matters with whom he speaks, whom he meets, with whom he sleeps. In order to ensure his safety, Alexey Maximovich must be kept under surveillance." He lifted his glasses. "Do you understand, Comrade?"

Warm and at the same time penetrating eyes were directed at Anna. Age had dimmed their brightness, and the glasses had left marks on the bridge of his nose.

"Do you understand me?"

"Not entirely."

"Once a week, you're alone with the Deputy Minister. You share intimate moments with him, and you learn what he thinks, what burdens weigh on him, what dangers he sees for himself."

"We've never spoken about anything like that."

"We can protect Alexey Maximovich only when we know his fears, only when we know where he expects danger to come from. It's the same in a doctor's office," Kamarovsky added. "If the physician knows where the trouble is located, the cure is easier."

"What do you want from me?"

"Inform us." For the first time, he'd included Rosa in his meaning. "Tell us about your meetings with him."

"He doesn't tell me any secrets!" Anna cried, deeply agitated.

"Oh, you can't know that." He put the glasses back on. "A remark, perhaps, a swipe at his colleagues, a political observation—all of that can be helpful in keeping trouble away from Alexey Maximovich."

Anna had said nothing—because she understood. Because fear of the unseen overcame her. She'd stepped into the trap that made an undisturbed life impossible. She'd caught the attention of those whose interest one must never under any circumstances arouse. "I don't think I can be of any use to you," she'd said. How weak her attempt to resist had sounded.

"You underestimate yourself," Kamarovsky had replied. "And you haven't yet recognized the advantages that such cooperation will bring you."

"Advantages?"

"Your father's poems are being examined by the Glavlit. If you were to help us, I feel certain that the examination could be expedited. Viktor Ipalyevich would have really deserved no less, and it's time for a new volume of his work to appear." Kamarovsky leaned forward. "Naturally, your husband's ignorance of your relationship will continue to be tolerated."

Anna's eyes had shifted from the table in the park to the water, where the woman, still sitting in the boat, was conversing with a younger man on the bank. She handed him the manuscript, and what she said about it seemed to please him.

Pensively, Anna stepped into the building on the quay. The elevator wasn't working; she took the climb to the eighth floor as an opportunity to warm up. At the top, she paused to let her breathing slow down. There was no nameplate to reveal who or what might be behind that door. She rang—one quick, sharp note—and Kamarovsky used the control in the living room to buzz her in. Anna hung up her coat and hat, cast a glance at the mirror, and walked to the end of the hall. The raffia lamp over the piano was hanging too low, and Anna ducked as she entered the room. Instead of lounging on the carpet-covered sofa as usual, Kamarovsky was standing at the window. The television set was on—pictures, but no sound.

"How are things in Perovo?" A. I. Kamarovsky asked without turning around.

"The combine is currently working in Karacharovo," Anna said, correcting him even though she knew he knew exactly where her worksite was located. "Interior finishing work in complex two hundred and fifteen."

"And how far along is complex two-one-five?"

"We're ahead of schedule."

"New living space for eight thousand comrades." He made a sign, and Anna stepped closer. "Until the triumph of socialism, our architecture was either backward or derivative." The warm air from the radiator next to Kamarovsky stirred the curtains. Anna loved this view. The apartment building stood at the foot of the Kalininsky Bridge; she could see the frozen river and behind it the Comecon building and the Hotel Ukraina, mysteriously grandiose in the winter fog. Anna could smell the moth powder on Kamarovsky's suit. He must have been outside; now the snow on his shoulders was melting and causing the musty odor. Had he been watching her while she sat under the statue?

"These days, our master builders no longer imitate the architecture of the West. Moscow has become an international city with its own unique character." He still hadn't looked at her. "Comrade Stalin had the court chapel in the Kremlin demolished. Do you know why?"

"Because it was a building associated with the clergy . . ."

"No." Kamarovsky gripped the side arm of his glasses. "Because it was ugly. It looked like a bunker gone wrong. By the time it was completed, the English had already built Westminster Abbey, and the influence of the Renaissance was spreading across Europe. Only in Moscow were the princes still putting up wooden buildings." Without having altered the position of his eyeglasses, he lowered his hand to the seam of his trousers. "Stalin just wanted to get rid of the ghastly thing."

As though signaling that the architecture lecture was now over, Kamarovsky closed the door to the balcony and walked past Anna as though she weren't in the room. He gestured to the visitors' chair and turned on the lamp. Cold light fell on her shoulders.

"Your report, Comrade." Kamarovsky remained on his feet.

Brezhnev's image appeared on the television screen, speaking urgently to the members of the Central Committee, who nodded like schoolboys. For a moment, Anna was distracted.

"Do you think that Alexey Maximovich will stab his boss, the Minister, in the back?"

The question took Anna by surprise. "No," she said. She turned her eyes away from the television. "He's simply having trouble making the situation clear to the comrades from the northeastern oblasts."

"And why do you think the Deputy Minister is having so much trouble communicating a decision made by the CC? Does he think it's wrong? Does he criticize it?"

"I don't know," Anna replied, her back stiff.

"Or might Alexey Maximovich see himself as the Minister for Research Planning?"

She recognized the fine line this question made her walk. "I can't draw that conclusion from anything he says. He's never suggested that he's unsatisfied with his position."

"But wouldn't it be only natural? In the research field, Comrade Bulyagkov, who was educated as a physicist, is more competent than the Minister himself."

Anna remained silent. Alexey had told her that he'd broken off his scientific studies decades ago, but he'd never mentioned the reason why.

Kamarovsky gave her a friendly look. "How ambitious do you think Alexey Maximovich is?"

She thought about Alexey's disparaging remark: *We're just puffed-up bureaucrats.* There was no ambition in that, only resignation.

When her silence persisted, Kamarovsky leaned down to her. "What do your feelings tell you about that, Anna?"

His use of her first name frightened her. "I have no feelings for such things, Comrade Colonel."

"Spoken like an agent for internal security."

"I'm not an agent."

"We don't let our emotions guide us," he said, ignoring her remark. "We take advantage of other people's emotions."

"I don't believe I would be in a position to take advantage of Alexey's emotions."

"Of course not. You provide the Deputy Minister with support, just as we do." Kamarovsky pointed to her dress. "What is that, Comrade?"

She looked down her front; he was referring to a slimy stain on her left breast. "That's . . . oh for goodness' sake . . . it's phlegm. It's been happening so often lately I hardly notice it anymore." Before she could try to remove the spot, Kamarovsky said "Please wait" and went over to the sink at the far end of the room. He ran water on a towel and brought it to her.

"Dawn patrol," Anna said, rubbing the spot. "Petya has fever, along with a deep cough." She held the fabric of the dress away from her body and rubbed some more. "When he wakes up, he's so short of breath . . . I don't know what to do."

"What does the doctor say?"

"Nothing that helps." For a second, their eyes met and held. "It's a woman doctor. She says he's got a catarrh and prescribes an inhalant the pharmacy doesn't have."

"Have you tried another doctor?" He took off his glasses and held them against the light.

"Not yet," Anna said cautiously.

"In your place, that's what I would do." Kamarovsky breathed on the lenses.

"To tell you the truth, I don't know . . ." She left the sentence unfinished.

"I've heard about someone." He put the glasses back on his face, reached for his pen, took a sheet of paper, and wrote a note three lines long. Anna held her breath, as though the slightest sound might deter him from what he was doing. The pen hovered over the paper for a second, and then the Colonel signed it with his initials. He took out a rubber stamp, stamped the paper, and, with apparent indifference, pushed the sheet over to Anna. "The man's supposed to be good. Maybe he can help Petya."

"This is very kind of you." She made an effort to hide her great joy, her hope for Petya.

"Kind? Not at all. I have an assignment for you, and I don't want your concern for your child to have an adverse effect on your performance." As though writing the note for Anna had reminded him of something, Kamarovsky opened the top drawer of the desk and took out a small box containing tablets. He pressed one out of its packaging and swallowed it without water.

"An assignment?" Carefully, as if it were an important document, Anna folded the paper and laid it on her lap.

FOUR

The next day was a Sunday, but Anna, anxious and worried, checked her mailbox downstairs in the lobby. The letter had been delivered by a messenger; she noticed the special stamp on the envelope right away. She stood with bowed head, reading the letter. It bore the signature of her building combine's secretary and informed Anna that she had been chosen out of thousands of Soviet women to take part in an educational trip for the benefit of proven and tested former Pioneers. Lost in thought, she climbed back up the stairs.

"An educational trip?" Viktor Ipalyevich asked. "It's been ten years since you were in the Pioneer Girls." He screwed up his eyes. "Do you by chance have an admirer in high places?"

Anna jumped at how unerringly her father had guessed the truth. His work folder was already closed for the day, and he'd been perusing a novel. Now he stood up, switched on the samovar, and cast a glance out the window. "Pretty unusual, to go on such a jaunt at this time of year." Gray snow hung on the window ledges like wads of dough, and a ladder of ice led down from the roof. "Where are you supposed to go on this trip?"

"Dubna," Anna replied, without enthusiasm.

"They're sending you all to the physics city?" Perplexed, he scanned the opening lines of the letter and then read aloud: "Religions dissolve like fog, empires collapse; only the works of science survive over time."

It was the motto of the trip. The guests from Moscow were to visit the facilities in Dubna, a center of Soviet research, and receive instruction in its latest achievements during colloquies with scientists. "That certainly beats me," Viktor Ipalyevich said, turning the letter over as though there might be an explanation on the other side.

"It has to do with the celebrations for the twentieth anniversary of the science city," Anna explained. Given her way, she would have torn that letter to shreds, burned the shreds, and forgotten about her assignment. She pretended to have urgent business in the kitchen; once she was on the other side of the door, she took several deep breaths.

Viktor Ipalyevich followed her. "Foreign diplomats, high officials of the Communist Party, and members of the nomenklatura are allowed to go to Dubna. And now, my daughter!"

"Why not?" she said curtly, letting herself be provoked despite all her scruples. "I have the same right as anyone else to be informed about scientific progress."

"Politicians' platitudes," he said, laughing, but he gave way before her angry look: "Of course you'll go on the trip, Annushka, don't worry about a thing, it'll do you good."

"Three days. Can you look after Petya for such a long time?"

"Haven't I always?" Viktor Ipalyevich opened his arms. "Come here, Pioneer Girl, let's drink to your trip." Knowing there was no use in opposing him, Anna got out the little glasses.

That night, she tossed and turned as she lay beside Petya. The boy's breath rattled in his throat; his head was nestled against one small hand. Anna drew the curtain aside, lifted her feet out of the alcove, and crept through the room. On the sofa, Viktor Ipalyevich slept without a sound, as if death had surprised him in his sleep.

She went into the kitchen, sat beside the stove, and lit the gas. The heat in the building was turned down so low at night that a film of ice had formed on the water in the sink. She lifted her legs, clasped her thighs at the knees, and held her feet near the flame. Shooing away the confused thoughts of half-sleep, she undertook some sober reflection. Was Alexey really behind her invitation, as Kamarovsky had tried to make her believe? Or was the Colonel merely using this as a pretext to lull her into a false sense of security? She recalled her conversation with him. "Bulyagkov himself set up the whole thing," Kamarovsky had said. "Obviously, he wants to have a romantic encounter with you outside Moscow, and so he sees to it that you win an educational trip."

"And suppose Alexey suspects something? Suppose he wants to put me to the test in this unusual situation?"

"When you're a member of the visitors' delegation, don't do anything that might make him suspicious."

Anna's eyes glided over the window joints; the cracks in the cement were stuffed with newspaper, but still there was a draft that fluttered the blue flame on the stove. She put her feet back down on the floor. Her soles felt a little singed, yet at the same time her whole body was shivering with cold. I must see Alexey again before the trip, she thought. I must know whether his suspicions have been aroused. A sound from the living room indicated that the urge to urinate was about to awaken her father. Anna turned off the burner and groped her way through the dark apartment to the sleeping alcove. As she pushed the curtain aside, she realized that she had never, in the year and a half since her affair with the Deputy Minister began, contacted him on her own initiative. He'd always gotten in touch with her, either in writing or through Anton; but this time, she would have to break the ritual order of things. She lay down next to Petya and drew the curtain closed. Immediately afterward, her father got up and shuffled sleepily toward the bathroom.

If the building hadn't stood opposite the Lenin Library, she would have overlooked the address. There was no nameplate, nor the smallest sign to reveal to the uninitiated that one of the special institutes was housed behind this smooth facade. Anna looked up the front of the multiple-story building. She exhorted Petya to behave particularly well and pushed open the iron door.

The policeman looked up from his papers. He wasn't the usual badly barbered kid with the carelessly knotted tie and worn shirt sleeves; his uniform was meticulously turned out and the sides of his head completely shaved. "Wrong door, Comrade," he said, not in an unfriendly way, but as if no one had ever contested that sentence.

"I'm coming from . . ." Anna unfolded Kamarovsky's note and approached the policeman's table.

"Step back." With an outstretched finger, he motioned her to stay behind the line painted on the floor. She obeyed, pulling the confused Petya with her. The policeman bent over a document. Then he said, "What do you have there, Comrade?"

She hesitated again, until he invited her closer with a patronizing wave. She carefully laid the piece of paper on the edge of his table. The policeman picked it up as though it were one of hundreds like it he received daily, most of which failed to pass his inspection.

"This isn't an admission certificate," he said without looking at it. Anna hunched her shoulders, as though expressing sorrow for troubling him with her request. The policeman held the writing up to his eyes. She watched as the fingers gripping the paper stiffened and slowly lowered it to the desk. "Why didn't you say so at once, Comrade?" His smile uncovered a golden tooth. "You have to understand, many people try to get in without authorization, and it's my duty . . ." He returned the paper to her, stood up, and showed her the way to the stairs. While Anna held her boy's hand, the policeman pushed open the swinging door and let mother and son pass through it.

In the next moment, her surroundings were transformed. No more flaking paint, no more diffuse light from weak bulbs; here everything gleamed. A line of halogen torchères extended along the corridor, and the comforting green walls shimmered; the synthetic floor covering appeared to have been wiped clean minutes before. A nurse seated behind a semicircular window raised her head.

Anna presented her piece of paper. "Is there any chance of seeing Doctor Shchedrin?"

Under any other circumstances, she would have had to reckon with an unfriendly, condescending, or in any case negative reply. The nurse checked the authenticity of Anna's note of recommendation, picked up the telephone, and informed someone that a patient was on her way to consult Doctor Shchedrin.

Anna corrected her: "I'm not the one who's sick—it's my son."

"The doctor has time for you." The nurse directed her to the third door in the adjacent corridor.

"Is that the waiting room?" Anna asked, taking Petya by the arm.

"That's Doctor Shchedrin's office." The nurse waited until she was sure the visitor had entered the right door.

It was a friendly room, with a medicine cabinet, plants in stone planters, and a large assortment of children's toys. There was a door in the opposite wall, and through it came a physician out of a picture book. His coat was fitted at the waist, and under it he wore a woolen suit and a bow tie. He looked comparatively young—there was only a little gray at his temples. A red fleck in the corner of his mouth indicated that the doctor had just been eating. He greeted Anna, bent down to Petya, and gave him his hand.

"How can I help you, Comrade?"

Encouraged by all the unusual friendliness, Anna told the story of Petya's affliction: the early shortness of breath, the frequent attacks of dizziness and weakness; then, starting a few months previously, the coughing; and now, for the past several weeks, the constant fever. By way of ending her account, Anna started to repeat the diagnosis pronounced by the doctor in the polyclinic, but Shchedrin stopped her with a wave of his hand and swung Petya up onto the examination table. He did not ask the boy to stick out his tongue, nor did he have him undress; Doctor Shchedrin merely examined Petya's eyes, pulled his eyelids down, and told him to look in all directions. Finally, he took hold of Petya at the point where his spine joined his skull. As he did so, he asked Anna, "Has he ever been tested for allergies?"

"We've always been told it was a cold, a catarrh," Anna stammered, as though she'd committed a sin of omission. "Is it bad?"

"Not yet." The doctor reached behind him and handed Petya some brightly wrapped candy. "In any case, until a year ago, he would have been too little to have the tests."

"Tests? Does that mean a serious illness?"

"First we have to find out Petya's secret," Shchedrin answered. "Then we'll do something about it. And after that, I promise you, Comrade, your boy will be considerably better."

She felt such a sense of relief that she stood up and strode toward the doctor, but instead of falling on his neck, she embraced Petya. "Did you hear that? You're going to be well soon!" The boy nodded.

Shchedrin leaned toward the intercom. "I need a full blood count." He turned around. "You look like a brave boy."

Petya darted a look at his mother. "Why?"

The doctor took out a case and opened it. It contained many little bottles, all of which looked the same. "Lay your arm on this cushion," he said, pushing it under the boy. "Now I'm going to make thirty-three marks on your arm. And then we'll see what happens."

"Marks that hurt?"

"You know how it feels in the summer, when you get a mosquito bite, don't you?" Shchedrin smiled. "It itches a little, right? But it doesn't hurt."

"A wasp stung me once. That hurt a lot."

"Compared to a wasp sting, this is nothing." The doctor took out an indelible pencil. "I have to number the marks so I can tell them apart later." He began to write little numerals on Petya's arms, one to twenty on the left and twenty-one to thirty-three on the right; next he opened a sterile package and extracted a tiny knife. Then, taking the first vial out of the case, he said, "And now we start." Holding Petya's arm still with one hand, he sought out a spot above the wrist and made a scratch in the skin. Petya's eyelids twitched, but he made no sound.

"Was that bad?" The doctor daubed a drop from the little bottle onto the wound.

"What kind of allergy could it be?" Anna asked, watching as her son's arm was covered with precisely placed drops.

"There are many possibilities, almost as many as the marks I'm going to make." Shchedrin threw the small knife into the trash basket and pulled out a new knife. "Grasses, flowers, dust mites. Moscow air isn't good for our lungs. It's particularly hard on children."

Anna had never heard anyone say openly what everyone knew: that the air pollution in the capital was harmful to your health.

"I can't change the air," Shchedrin went on, "but we should make sure that Petya doesn't come into contact with irritants. In addition, there's a new medication available. If the tests show what I think they will, I'll give him a prescription for it."

Anna gazed at the doctor with warmth that bordered on affection. Medicine that really helped? It was too good, too rare, to be true. Her gratitude extended to the man who had made this happiness possible, to A. I. Kamarovsky, who'd done nothing but write a note.

A nurse brought the instruments for the blood test. Before she left, she asked Anna, "Would you perhaps like some tea, Comrade?"

Anna nodded gratefully. Doctor Shchedrin took the next little bottle out of the case.

FIVE

The earflaps of Anna's fur hat were down as she approached the six-story building. She had left Petya with his grandfather and set out on her search, beginning behind Red Square. After a whole day of thawing, sleet had fallen that morning, and pedestrians were stalking along the walkways as if they had artificial limbs, slipping and sliding, clinging to walls and traffic signposts. Anna had to laugh at the crazy ballet being performed by people around the Central Committee building, who danced with their briefcases pressed tightly under their arms. The weather was Anna's ally. Everyone was concentrating on reaching his goal without falling down, and nobody observed the young woman who was visiting, one by one, the six entrances to the building complex. The gates were made of steel, the underground levels protected by concrete ramps. Anna's attention was directed toward the vehicles that approached the CC complex and disappeared inside or stopped nearby. Without exception, the automobiles were black, with license plates that began with the letters MO. The Volgas and Chaikas aroused no interest in her, but if a ZIL drove by, Anna made an effort to get a look at the back of it. She reached the windowless annex to the main building; there were many ZILs parked outside, one behind the other. Struggling to keep her balance, Anna moved along the pavement, looking at the limousines' ice-covered rear ends and rectangular taillights. Her eyes were seeking a broken brake light with a dent in its metal housing. The damage had been done during her last ride in the car. More hastily than usual, Anton had turned off the Mozhaisk Chaussée and failed to notice a concrete pillar. There had been an unpleasant crunching sound, and Anton had leaped out with a flashlight in his hand and run to the back of the car. "They'll be laughing at me in the garage," he said when he got in again. "I'm the driver with the most accidents." He winked at her in the rear-view mirror. "I'm not going to take it to the repair shop just for a dent. Don't give me away, Comrade."

Since the announcement of the Five-Year Plan would be made very shortly, Alexey had to go to the Central Committee every day, and right about this time, too; Anton must park the car somewhere around here, she thought. At the third ZIL, Anna hesitated and bent down for a closer inspection. It wasn't a dent, just the remains of some ice still clinging to the rear fender. The security officer on duty at the gate noticed her and approached. Anna pretended to straighten her cap, using the car window as a mirror, and skidded away. When she reached the main entrance for the second time, the number of policemen there had doubled; one of them pressed his walkie-talkie to his ear. The steel panels of the gate parted, the policeman stopped the ordinary traffic, and a convoy of four limousines appeared, their rear-window curtains all closed. The first car drove into the inner portion of the complex, followed by all the others; none of them slowed down. The gate closed, and the policemen disappeared back into their sentry boxes. Anna imagined that she had seen Brezhnev himself being driven to work. Since the assassination attempt on him a few years before, it was said that the General Secretary always traveled in a convoy so that nobody would know which limousine he was riding in. Anna looked over the square. She could have been watching the arrival of any CC member, she thought; what difference did it make?

After an hour, she admitted to herself that with so many ZILs about, it was naive of her to think she'd be able to find the very one that Anton drove. In the end, the weather and the chaos on the streets made Anna give up and sent her on her way back to the bus stop. Later, loaded down with purchases from various shops, she entered a telephone booth and dialed the number of the apartment on Drezhnevskaya Street. As she had expected, there was no reply. It was clearer to her than ever before that the Deputy Minister could get in touch with her at any time, but the reverse was impossible.

Some days later, Anna was informed that the visitors' committee was having a preparatory meeting. Its purposes: introduction to the work of the science city, illustration of the basic concepts of physics, distribution of informational material.

After the early shift, Anna set out for a meeting house of the Moscow City Soviet. There she was given a laminated card that declared her an official member of the "Dubna Visitors' Committee." In an overheated room on the fourth floor, most of the other members of the delegation were already present, among them a young woman who was a budding Aeroflot pilot, the forewoman of a factory that made finished building parts, a slender blonde in training to become a peace ambassador of the Soviet Union, a schoolgirl named Yelena, and a cashier who'd attracted notice because of her unusual mathematical abilities. Among the men, there were two Irkutskians from the International Friendship Club, a young farmer from Karabanovo, the director of a Moscow orphanage, and a producer at a radio station. Anna presented herself with her job title, and a woman with dyed black hair stepped forward and shook her hand. "I'm Nadezhda from combine four-four-seven," she said. She had small eyes, and her face appeared to be stamped with a permanent grin. "So you're the girl who's going with us instead of Raisa." Nadezhda took a seat in the middle of the first row and offered her colleague the place next to her.

"What happened to Raisa?"

"She was replaced all of a sudden. No reason was given." Nadezhda gazed mockingly at Anna. "Have you come directly from work?"

Someone came into the room. His shirt and tie looked new, and there were sharp creases in his trousers. "Good day, comrades. I am Mikhail Popov, group leader for our three-day excursion to Dubna," he said. His voice sounded like a sewing machine.

The members of the delegation interrupted their conversations. Popov draped his overcoat across the back of a chair, stepped to the podium, and opened a document folder. "The acquisition of knowledge requires human courage," he began without a transition. "The Soviet scientists chose a deserted area, a marsh, as the place to build the biggest research center in the world. It serves exclusively peaceful purposes." As he read, he held a finger under each successive line. "The city of Dubna is surrounded on three sides by rivers—the Volga, the Dubna, and the Sestra—and on the fourth by the Moscow Canal. These waterways were of the utmost importance for the transport of heavy equipment. The land where laboratories and apartment houses now stand was originally under water; the engineers took boats to the various worksites."

When Popov turned the page, it sounded like a whiplash. He looked up, and his eyes met Anna's. She nodded, showing her interest, and at the same time wondered whether he might be the minder whom Kamarovsky had certainly assigned to her.

"On the fourteenth day of December 1949, the synchrocyclotron began its work. The main building required more than seven hundred thousand cubic feet of concrete; the walls are more than one hundred feet high; the ceiling alone weighs ten thousand tons." Mechanically, as though trained to do so, Popov tilted his head to one side. "Imagine a magnet that weighs seven thousand tons. Three Volga limousines could comfortably park on each of its poles." He responded with satisfaction to his audience's mild tittering; yes, his look seemed to say, science has its lighter side, too. Then he went on, describing the efforts made by the building collective in 1949 to fulfill its duty of putting all machines in operation before the government's stipulated deadline. "Enthusiasm and the creative spirit of the Soviet engineers led to success." At this point, Popov began to read a list of technological research achievements that had been produced in Dubna.

Anna stretched her back—her shoulders ached. The substance of Popov's lecture would surely be in the materials up there in the box, ready for distribution. She looked behind her, and she had the impression that most of those present found nothing new in his revelations. The pilot was playing with a button on her jacket; the peace ambassadress, lost in thought, ran her fingers through her hair; only the forewoman was leaning forward with her elbows on her knees and listening. Anna was sure that Kamarovsky had smuggled in another "member of the delegation," someone tasked in his or her turn with reporting on Anna's conduct and methods. She knew that she was starting to judge reality according to a scheme learned from the Colonel. She'd grown adept at machinations, she was acquainted with the means of gaining advantages for herself, and she was preparing to use people the way Kamarovsky did. Wasn't she even making use of Kamarovsky himself? Hadn't she foreseen that he'd be able to find her and her son a decent doctor? It had cost him nothing and made Anna happy. She thought of the little presents for Petya that Anton had picked up in specialty shops; now they were probably lying on the backseat of the limousine. Anna was afraid of her own hedonism, but at the same time, she didn't know how to curb its growth. She'd already taken on too much. With a sigh, she slumped against the back of her chair. She'd lost the thread.

SIX

The following day, she urged her father not to forget to call Doctor Shchedrin that Wednesday, when the results of Petya's tests would be in. She admonished the boy not to make things difficult for his grandfather and implored Viktor Ipalyevich to keep television watching within reasonable limits.

The bus stopped on the Kutuzovsky Prospekt, about a ten-minute walk from Anna's apartment. The checkered travel bag bounded off her thighs as she walked. She hadn't had enough sleep and felt generally confused, troubled by her vague sense of what lay ahead. When she reached the square, it didn't take her long to find what she was looking for. The banner was legible from far away: WELCOME PIONEERS! OFF TO DUBNA, THE SCIENCE CITY! The words covered the whole side of the bus. Anna chose a window seat and wedged her bag into the space beside her feet. The orphanage director sat across the aisle and wanted to chat; Anna's answers were so meager that he gave up. Most people climbed into the bus during the last ten minutes before its departure; the Aeroflot pilot was even a little late. With the help of her bulky bag, Anna kept the seat next to her empty. She wanted to sleep, she wanted to reflect, and she had to get busy with the book Kamarovsky had sent her.

It was still pretty dark outside—full daylight was a long way off, but some dawn grayness filtered through the window. The bus had hardly started moving when Anna laid her head back and closed her eyes. In a last flash of awareness, she recognized that they were swinging onto Dmitrovsky Chaussée; from there they would access the expressway and head north. The roar of the traffic was transformed into the shrieks of birds, ugly creatures that fluttered and flapped around her; their cries sounded like accusations. Although dozing, not fully conscious, Anna was nonetheless aware that an argument had flared up around her. The forewoman was of the opinion that Soviet science was ten years in advance of the Americans. When the orphanage director pointed out that the researchers who'd won the Nobel Prize in recent years had come overwhelmingly from the West, the slight fellow stepped into a crossfire aimed at him by the others. Wasn't he aware that Stockholm was situated in the West? Had he ever taken a close look at the members of the Nobel committee? A person would have to be blind not to notice the tendency toward provocation in the selection of winners. And besides, as early as 1945, the Americans had started recruiting Nazi scientists, regardless of whether they were war criminals or not. "U.S. technology is nothing more than Nazi technology in its mature form," the forewoman said, summarizing her position. "Soviet achievements, on the other hand, are a real result of cooperation among socialist states."

The orphanage director was so bold as to observe aloud that in Dubna, despite the many socialist nations with scientific programs, the percentage of researchers from the DDR was disproportionately high. "I would assume that these people also worked for Hitler in the old days."

There was something decidedly physical about the storm of objections to this remark. The members of the delegation crowded around the orphanage director, giving him pieces of their minds. When the bus unexpectedly turned off the main highway and came to a stop, the squabblers thought Popov had ordered the halt by way of calming things down. But this was, in fact, the first item on the day's program: "Breakfast in Dmitrov, City of the Revolution."

On the double, the former Pioneers were led into an unprepossessing wooden house, which accommodated a nursery school. Two rows of little children, wearing heavy clothes and holding hands, formed a guard of honor for the guests from Moscow. Inside, the headmistress of the school greeted them and invited them to sit at tables already prepared for their visit. The coffee was fresh, and the bread was still warm. Everyone tucked in hungrily; Anna refilled her coffee cup twice. As the guests ate, the headmistress explained that they were on historical ground: Prince Peter Kropotkin, an eminent forerunner of anarchist communism, had chosen this simple house for his residence when he returned to Russia from his long exile abroad. The guests hardly had time to finish their meal; still clutching their cups, they were escorted into Kropotkin's study, which had been preserved in its original condition. Group leader Popov expressed his thanks in the name of the delegation, and everyone walked out past the guard of freezing children and climbed back aboard the bus.

The travel time to Dubna had been given out as an hour and a half, but Popov called for a second halt along the way. In a thick fog, they had to get off the bus and clamber up an unreal hill. "We are now on the outskirts of the industrial city of Yakhroma," he declaimed. "Do you see that railroad bridge? It marks the farthest point that Hitler's soldiers reached. The Germans were less than seventy miles from Moscow, but they underestimated the striking force of the Red Army, and in their plans of conquest, they had made no allowances for the pitiless Soviet winter!" The place Popov pointed to could have been anything at all; except for swaths of fog, nothing was identifiable. Nevertheless, the little gathering lingered there, gazing in silence, and nobody spoke on the way back to the bus. They drove along slowly; the bus was now traveling through a thick, milky fog its headlights could barely penetrate.

The blacktop road ran alongside the railroad line, bridges of various types crossed rivers and marshy areas, and, as scheduled, the group reached the city shortly before noon. At the city line, a banner greeted them: THE ATOM IS A WORKER, NOT A SOLDIER! The flags of the nations that were members of the Institute were flying above the hotel entrance; Anna could identify most of the flags, but the orphanage director had to help her with Albania and Vietnam. The bus turned ponderously around the circular flower bed in front of the hotel. A man in a fur coat was waiting for them; he greeted Popov but didn't offer him his hand.

"Czestmir Adamek," Popov said, presenting him. "Our scientific guide. When you have questions, you will address them only to him, and he will relay them to the Institute worker. In this way, we can prevent unqualified questions from stealing the researchers' time."

"Comrade—Comrade—Comrade—" The fur-clad man nodded to each of them as they stepped out of the bus; he took a moment longer to assess the women.

In the entrance hall, there were two stairways and an elevator with paint flaking off its metal doors. The reception desk was raised, offering an overview of the lobby, and the front desk manager was waiting at his post with the room keys lined up on the counter in front of him. List in hand, Popov stepped up to the desk and organized the distribution of rooms. He began in alphabetical order: "Armiryev, Butyrskaya—"

The front desk manager interrupted him: "Is there a Comrade Tsazukhina among you?"

Anna needed a moment to react to her father's surname, even though Anna Tsazukhina was what she'd been called when she was a Pioneer Girl. Her first thought was of Petya. Were his test results so bad as to necessitate a telephone call to Dubna? She pushed her way through the group.

"You're Comrade Anna Tsazukhina?" the uniformed manager asked, holding out an envelope. "This was left at the desk for you." Having turned over the envelope, he began to compare Popov's list with his own and to hand out the keys.

Avoiding the eyes of those around her, Anna retreated to a chair near a window. She opened the sealed envelope, which bore her name, and unfolded the sheet of paper inside. "Welcome, Pioneer Girl," she read.

The words were written in the Deputy Minister's sloping hand. "Your program ends today at nine. Anton will be parked at the rear entrance."

She turned around. Couldn't everyone see how the hot flush spread over her face?

Nadezhda approached her. "Something unpleasant?" she asked.

"On the contrary." Anna quickly shoved the note back into the envelope, picked up her bag, and returned to the waiting line. At that moment, though she could not have said why, Alexey's lines made her unspeakably happy, so much so that her eyes became moist. She forgot the delegation, her new surroundings, even Kamarovsky's assignment. She was going to see him again, Alexey, her big, clumsy wolf; somewhere in this settlement in the woods, he was waiting for her with cooled wine and some delicacy to eat. His simple message proved to Anna that it had really been his idea to fetch her to this place. He missed her; for the sake of her company, he'd organized a complicated process and used his influence, just for two nights with her. She stuffed the envelope into her coat pocket. In a year and a half, she and Alexey had never yet spent an entire night together, and Anna was looking forward to the experience. At the same time, it made carrying out her assignment even more repugnant. She stood there, deep in thought, surrounded by the other "distinguished visitors," who were comparing their room numbers, stowing their baggage, and making plans for lunch. Popov, standing on the stairs and speaking loudly, informed them that their first activity would be a visit to the synchrocyclotron.

"Tsazukhina," the receptionist said, holding up the key to room number seven. Anna nodded and took the key. This time, she permitted the orphanage director to carry her bag.

The main course had just been served when Czestmir Adamek entered the dining room. The scientific guide spotted Popov at the Aeroflot pilot's table, slipped past the other tables, all of them occupied by members of the visiting delegation, and hissed something in the group leader's ear. Popov wanted to finish his meal, but he rose to his feet when Adamek gestured toward the clock on the wall.

"Everyone listen up!" Popov said. He informed his group that the sightseeing tour had been rescheduled. "We meet at the bus in five minutes." Popov wiped his hands on the tablecloth, assumed that everyone would comply with the new instructions, and hurried to the exit. When he looked back, he saw that only the bus driver had stood up.

"You're not at some coffee klatch!" Adamek cried out. "The science center is a high-precision operation. Every man-minute costs the State a million rubles. Your conduct is harmful to Soviet research!"

As though they were puppets on a string, the members of the delegation stood up and pressed toward the door. No one thought about their coats; dressed as they were, they rushed through the dining room and into the open. Because of the cold, the bus wouldn't start right away, and the driver kept looking apologetically at Adamek and pleadingly at his dashboard. At last, the diesel engine sputtered to life, and the bus swung away from the hotel and onto the main road. The snow lay a yard thick on the roofs of the Institute. Something was glinting among the bare larches; Adamek confirmed that the Volga, at that time of the year still covered with thick ice, was what they were seeing through the trees.

They reached a complex that looked like a factory building; as they got closer, it became clear that the structure was about one hundred feet high and entirely of concrete. The Pioneers sprang from the bus and followed Adamek through a steel door, into a stairwell, and up the stairs, their boots resounding militarily in the narrow space. In an anteroom, Adamek had everyone stop and pointed to a radioactivity-measuring device set in the wall. The needle was at rest in the green area.

"We're taking advantage of a pause between two work processes to view the accelerator. We shall move in an exactly straight line, very close together. There will be no talking." Adamek pressed a button, the door clattered, and a high-pitched acoustic signal sounded; some visitors held their ears. An Asian man in light gray overalls and a close-fitting hood that left only his face uncovered was awaiting them. He distributed caps and overshoes, all of the same white, synthetic material.

"The air around the accelerator is purified," Adamek explained. "Hurry up and put those things on. Work time on a synchrocyclotron is worth more than gold."

The Asian shoved a box toward them. "For the watches," he said.

Adamek was the first to remove his from his wrist. "The magnetic field hasn't been neutralized yet. The mechanism of your watches would go crazy in there." At the next door, he stopped yet again. "The nuclear spectroscopy section has just completed a test. You will observe how the researchers dismantle their target, which has just been bombarded with protons. From this point on, there must be absolute silence." He entered and stood next to the door until Popov had ushered the group inside.

SEVEN

Anna was in her hotel room. She'd locked the door, and now she was staring out the window. The streetlights dyed the terrain a dismal orange. She was disillusioned. Certainly, the platform and roof of the accelerator were colossal in size, extending for hundreds of feet, but in the center all that could be seen was a control console, set in concrete, with dials and instruments whose illuminated arrows quivered in different positions. All at once, loud detonations like gunfire had sounded from down below, and everybody had flinched. Discharges, Adamek had explained. While the electromagnetic bursts followed one another more and more closely, a team of researchers had come out onto the platform. They were wearing protective suits that covered them completely, including their faces, and they carried a cloth about ten square feet in size, mounted on supports. An unscientific observer might have thought that the researchers were bringing in their dirty laundry to be cleaned. Before they reached the control center, Adamek had already ordered his group to leave. Inaudible in their synthetic slippers, the visitors had hastily marched to the exit; in the passage, the Asian had given them back their watches.

Anna was exhausted. Since early morning, she and the others had been bombarded with impressions, had seen things the likes of which few Soviet citizens would ever get to see in their entire lifetimes. Despite her weariness, she sat at the table and took from her bag the book she'd brought along. It was a standard text in theoretical physics for students in their first semester.

"In the condensed phase, matter appears as either a solid or a liquid. Free atoms form a crystal, producing a binding energy of an order of magnitude equivalent to . . ."

Anna considered the sequence of signs that followed and then read them aloud: "A hundred kcal divided by mol equals one hundred times two point six times ten to the twenty-second power divided by six times ten to the twenty-third power eV . . ." It was the first formula in the book, and one of the simplest.

"The empirical fact that the band structures of free electrons diverge shows that valence electrons are only weakly scattered on ionic cores."

Discouraged, Anna slammed the book shut. Reading it was pointless. Even if she were to get close to the physicist who was the subject of her assignment, even if she should manage to have a conversation with him, she wouldn't understand the information she obtained! She paced helplessly around the room: wallpaper, closet, bed, her bag, and, outside, the silent street. She felt dead tired and, at the same time, exceedingly nervous. From childhood on, she'd been taught this principle: Every individual must undertake and carry out tasks assigned by the Party. Today, however, Anna wanted to slip out of her otherwise so reliable skin and admit to herself that there was no coping with her present assignment.

Sounds from outside her door indicated that dinner was imminent. She felt hungry, but when she looked at the clock, she realized that it wasn't worth the trouble to go to the dining room, because Anton would be picking her up very soon. Anna opened the closet; the short dress would be inconspicuous under her coat. She undressed and washed her face in front of the mirror.

Punctual to the minute, the black ZIL turned into the rear courtyard. Anna was waiting on the steps. The kitchen was at its busiest, the windows were open, but no one observed the member of the visiting group who slid onto the backseat of the limousine and pulled the door shut behind her.

"Today we don't have far to go," said Anton, nodding to her in the rearview mirror.

They drove past two blocks of houses on the main street, turned into the riverfront promenade, and stopped in front of a one-story villa.

"Who lives here?"

"The house belongs to a member of the Academy who's seldom in Dubna." Anton got out, opened the gate, and drove onto the grounds.

Alexey received Anna neither outside the house nor at the front door. Curious, she stepped into a comfortable room; there was a wing chair close to the fireplace. Alexey sat in the chair with one hand pressed against his forehead and the other raised in a formal gesture of greeting. Anna laughed—Alexey was imitating a famous painting of Stalin. "Little Father, how are you?" she asked, giving the Pioneers' hand signal and stepping before the Great Leader.

"One grows old, Comrade," he answered in the familiar rasping intonation. "It does one good to see you young activists, your fresh faces." Bulyagkov sprang to his feet. "And your splendid bodies!" He took Anna in his arms and stroked her hair. Composed as always, Anton brought in a load of firewood and disappeared.

"So this is the way our worthy Soviet scientists live?" she asked, looking around.

"This is the way I live when I visit our worthy Soviet scientists." Alexey went to the table, a cork popped, and Sovetskoye Shampanskoye—Soviet Champagne—sizzled in the glasses. Anna knelt down and felt the fine, silvery threads of the carpet. Alexey brought her drink; still kneeling, she clinked glasses with him and watched his bobbing Adam's apple as he swallowed.

"How wonderful that you're here," he said, sinking down next to her. His belly spilled over his belt. "Were you surprised when you got my note?" She embraced him; his stubbly beard scratched her. "It's a good thing you got something to eat in the hotel," he said over her shoulder.

"Why?"

"The Dubna grocery warehouse was already closed. Not even my influence could make it open again this evening." He shrugged. "I dined out with the physicists."

Anna thought about the pike in aspic that was being served in the hotel dining room, and her mouth watered. "You mean you don't have anything at all here?"

"Don't they give you enough to eat in the hotel?"

"I just thought . . . because otherwise, this bubbly will go to my head."

"What if it does?" He poured her some more from his glass.

"Tomorrow I have to understand some really difficult things."

"Who cares if you don't understand them?"

Alexey's dismissal of the official reason for her sojourn as unimportant infuriated her. "I want to take advantage of the opportunity! This is a fabulous place, and I want to learn as much as possible!"

"And so you should," he said, appeasing her. "So you should, Annushka. During the day, I'll leave you to the protons and the transuranic elements. But in the evening, when the researchers are dreaming about discovering number one hundred and fourteen, you belong to me."

"A hundred and fourteen?"

"Didn't you know that most of the elements after the hundred and second were discovered here in Dubna?" He leaned back, propping himself on his elbows. "A hundred and three lived practically forever, a full eight seconds. His brother a hundred and four disintegrated after only three tenths of a second." Alexey nodded sadly, as if he'd lost a beloved relative.

Anna's assignment sprang into her mind. "Is that why you're here? Is some new discovery about to take place?"

"No. The accelerator and its successes are the Minister's department. My area of responsibility concerns the theoreticians."

"You understand their research? You know what it's about?" The bubbly wine made her bold.

"Of course not. Since my student days, a revolution has taken place in this field. It's fascinating—I wish I had more time to look into it."

At that moment, he looked quite young to Anna; all the heaviness seemed to have fallen from him. She asked, "What part of it fascinates you the most?"

"The language of mathematics! It contains the only truth known to me, the only one I revere."

"Why didn't you become a scientist?"

"Had my life run in a different course, nothing could have prevented me from becoming a scientist." He refilled their glasses. "I'm afraid, though, that I wouldn't have been more than mediocre at doing science."

Anna tried to imagine him as a young man. What ideals had he followed? What had he looked like as a boy? He never spoke about his past; their common ground was limited to the present. After the next glass, she went looking for the bathroom, undressed briskly, and lay down naked on the carpet next to him.

"How warm it is," she said with a smile. "Is that all from this fire?"

Alexey looked into the flames. "This house has thirteen radiators. Otherwise, in your present condition, you'd get chilblains." He nestled against her breast.

Anna awoke in her hotel room. There was a sound of hurrying footsteps in the hall; she'd overslept. She felt hot and nauseous, and when she stood up—too quickly—everything spun. Bent over from the waist, she waited until the room slowed down and stopped. The sweet, fizzy wine—Alexey had insisted on opening the third bottle, too—and then the vodka . . . she retched, but she had nothing to throw up. I need a piece of white bread, she concluded, and got dressed in spite of her trembling limbs. Alexey had informed her that some physicists were coming to breakfast; Anton had driven her back to the hotel in the dim light of early dawn.

Everyone was in good spirits in the dining room. The members of the delegation had used the preceding evening to get to know one another better. The peace ambassadress allowed the nice kolkhoz farmer to pour her some coffee; the Aeroflot pilot had changed seats, and she was now in conversation with the radio producer. Looking offended, Adamek was sitting at a small table, alone. Anna swayed a bit as she headed for her seat; when she tuned in to the ambient conversations, she heard people calling one another by their first names. The orphanage director wanted to know where she had been the previous evening. When he started to serve her some ham, Anna waved it away and asked for tea and white bread. She sipped the hot drink and hoped for relief. Soon Adamek announced that it was time to go. Without argument, the whole company made for the bus. Popov ate a buttered roll as he walked.

After they were under way, Adamek announced that they were going to have a chance to admire an innovation of worldwide significance, the completion of a unique research instrument. The bus passed a flat-roofed building located behind some bare shrubs. "Which institute is that?" she asked. The hoarseness of her voice scared her.

"That's where the international collective of theoretical physicists works," Adamek answered, visibly pleased that someone was showing interest in his explanations.

"When will we visit it?"

"You'd be disappointed," Adamek replied. "There's nothing there but blackboards, mainframe computers, and thinking cubicles for the comrades."

"Who's the head of the institute?"

"Nikolai Lyushin. His name isn't as well known as the names of the scientists who work with accelerators, but their successes are often based on his theoretical insights."

Anna let herself sink back in her seat. For the first time, someone had named the man who was the subject of her assignment. The bus swung into the next curve, and the flat-roofed building vanished.

Not long afterward, the group was watching the presentation of a device that bore some resemblance to an orange. This instrument, which was used to examine the radiation spectra of short-lived isotopes, was an "iron-free toroidal beta spectrometer," but Adamek affectionately called it "our citrus."

Standing before a schematic depiction, Adamek gave a lecture. "All nuclear energy is based on Uranium-235," he said. "A tiny amount of U-235 is present in common uranium, but supplies are dwindling, and uranium mining is becoming more and more expensive. The starting point of the series of tests that we're going to see is the bombardment of depleted uranium with proton bundles, whereby some of the uranium is changed into plutonium, the basic material of our nuclear power plants."

An hour later, they were still listening to their scientific guide, who was discoursing upon a shadowy green point that was visible on a monitor. In her weakened state, Anna found the lecture fatiguing. She leaned against the wall and struggled against her nausea, which wasn't going away. Surprisingly, Adamek announced that they would now have lunch. Asked about the unusually early hour, he explained that the delegation would have the honor of dining in the physicists' cafeteria, but that the visitors would have to be finished with their meal before the scientists arrived; the capacity of the cafeteria's kitchen was limited.

The radiators in the ground-level dining room were covered in dust, the ceiling lamps flickered, and there was nothing to suggest that every day, the most brilliant minds gathered to eat in this place. The women in the kitchen served the members of the delegation a dark stew that the menu called "Rabbit Ragout." Anna's stomach wasn't yet up to that, so she sipped her tea and looked around. A bald man was lighting his next cigarette with the end of his current one; a woman with her hair in a bun hesitated, obviously wondering whether or not to sit at his table, because his expression said that he wanted to be left in peace. Three female scientists came in wearing classic white lab coats. A pin on the chest of one of the three began to blink; she turned around, put her tray back in the rack, and left the room.

During the meal, Adamek announced a change in the afternoon schedule: The Neutron Physics Laboratory, he said, was under too much pressure at the moment; therefore, the group would go for a walk along the Volga. Almost all the delegates were relieved at this news, with the sole exception of the Aeroflot pilot, who complained. "First we're dragged to lunch at eleven in the morning," she said, "and now we're sloughed off for some free time on the riverbank." She had the impression that the visitors' program had been inadequately prepared. "I think Dubna is marvelous," she concluded, appeasing the wounded Adamek, "and so I want to see as much of it as possible. For example, the Institute for Theoretical Physics—why can't we get to see the source, the place where all the research projects originate?"

Anna observed the slender woman from one side. Could she be the second horse in Kamarovsky's stable? Could she, like Anna, have an assignment?

"The program has been set for weeks and cannot be changed," Adamek replied.

The swinging door in the entrance opened and in came two men. The younger one wore a white shirt, black jeans, and light shoes. His blond hair hung down to his collar, and he had a weather-beaten face. The other man, who was speaking to him very intently, was Alexey. They sat at the first table they came to, but the younger man immediately sprang to his feet and dashed to the counter. In front of the menu board, he flung his arms in the air and began abusing the cooks. "You can eat this shit yourselves," Anna understood him to say. "Do you hate hungry people, or what?" The server dished him up some vegetables. He took a bottle of beer and went back to his table, where he realized that he'd forgotten to open the bottle and, without further ado, knocked off the cap on the table edge.

All conversation among the members of the visiting delegation fell silent; everyone was observing the scene. Bulyagkov, who'd ordered some wine, took a sip, made a disgusted face, and moved the glass some distance away. His blond companion laughed gloatingly. "Can't your department do anything about this? All we get to eat here is shit." He noticed that they were being stared at. "Research tourists from Moscow," he grumbled, turning his back on the delegates' table.

The Deputy Minister let his eyes pass over the other people in the room. No expression on his face revealed that he knew Anna. When he spoke again to his companion, he used his first name: Nikolai. Electrified, Anna sat up straight.

"Are you trying to suck it out of my brain?" the younger man asked. "Well, my friend, there's nothing there!" As he ate, the Deputy Minister watched him pensively. They continued speaking, but with much more restraint. Soon the blond laid down his knife and fork and left. Bulyagkov, who'd eaten nothing, followed him.

"Does he look familiar to you?" Adamek asked. "That was Nikolai Lyushin."

The novelty of having just seen both a member of the Central Committee and a leading physicist was enthusiastically discussed. The critique of the visitors' program was forgotten; everyone had the impression that the place they were in was very important. Anna ate a few bites, found the rabbit ragout good, and emptied her plate.

The Volga was so wide in that stretch that you could see the curve of its surface. Like schoolchildren who had left the duties of lesson learning behind, the members of the delegation skated onto the frozen river, held hands, formed a chain, and hauled one another over the ice. Adamek maintained the dignity of his office but let himself go so far as to sit on the riverbank and smoke an old-fashioned pipe. Group leader Popov folded his arms behind his back and described a great circle in the middle of the river. The ice sighed under his blades, and Anna's eyes searched for dangerous cracks. The orphanage director glided up to her from one side. "Supposedly, you can go skiing over there," he said, pointing to the hill on the opposite bank.

"How do you know that?" she asked as they returned to the group together.

"The nickname of that spot is 'Dubna's little Switzerland,'" he replied. Ice crystals trembled in his hair. "They even have a cross-country course with floodlights. Do you ski?"

She shook her head. He said, "Well, that's too bad, but we don't have enough time for it anyway."

Anna wondered whether the orphanage director was flirting with her or trying to tell her something.

Nadezhda, cheeks aglow, came charging up to her two colleagues. "We're going to have an ice race! Will you two be partners?" The members of the visitors' delegation were dividing up by twos. The women were to hang on to the coattails of the men, who would act as carthorses.

"I don't know," Anna said. She looked over toward Popov, who by then had almost reached the opposite bank.

"You've been keeping to yourself the whole time, Princess," Nadezhda said snidely. "Grab onto this guy and race with us!" She went back to her partner, the handsomer of the two Irkutskian delegates from the Friendship Club, and prepared for the start of the competition.

Anna said to the orphanage director, "Looks like you're going to get your exercise sooner than you thought." They lined up with the others, and the radio producer gave the signal.

Right at the beginning two couples collided, cursing as they fell over one another. Yelena, the schoolgirl, was so light that her partner was able to pull her into the lead. The kolkhoz farmer's coat ripped, leaving the peace ambassadress helplessly holding the loose tails in her hand; without hesitating, he lifted her to his shoulders and carried her in the direction of the finish line. Because there were an insufficient number of men, the cashier and another, younger woman, a college student, had banded together. They proved to be a strong pair, and they gave Yelena and her partner a run for their money. The orphanage director was frailer than Anna had expected; when he stumbled near the halfway point, she changed roles with him and hauled him behind her. They were the last to cross the finish line, their breath like white clouds around their heads, but for the brief duration of the race, Anna had forgotten her assignment and the impossibility of carrying it out. The others were already conjecturing about where they could get alcohol to toast the winners with.

Adamek joined the group, smoke billowing from his pipe. "Time to go," he said. "They're waiting for us in the Neutron Physics Lab."

Arm in arm and giggling, the members of the visitors' delegation returned to the bus. Popov's absence was noted; a long, sustained whistle informed him that departure was imminent. Then they saw him, a small gray point in the distance, hurrying over the ice.

EIGHT

Anna spent the time after the tour of the laboratory in her room. She could hear some of the others changing for dinner, and in the room next to hers, the fellow from Irkutsk was visiting Nadezhda. They spoke softly for a while, but then their conversation fell silent, something struck the wall, and there was a cry, followed by tittering.

I'll acknowledge my failure, Anna thought. *Comrade Colonel, it was not possible for me to acquire the information without arousing suspicion,* she said to an imagined Kamarovsky. Then she sat down on the bed, somewhat relieved. But her comfort didn't last long, for soon her inescapable sense of duty announced its presence. She'd be in Dubna that night and the following day; she still had time to act. Should she, on her own initiative, simply go back to the physicists' cafeteria in the hope of finding Lyushin there a second time? She remembered the remark the orphanage director had made on the Volga, the reference to the area dedicated to winter sports on the opposite bank of the river: Would that be where she could find the opportunity she was looking for?

These and other speculations made Anna so nervous that she leaped to her feet and changed—for the second time—the blouse she intended to wear to dinner. But then she opened the physics textbook again. She chose a chapter on quantum mechanics and tried to concentrate. Why am I kidding myself? she thought, her eyes still fixed on the text. I'm a house painter, the daughter of a poet, the wife of a soldier. I could have a delightful stay here, I could enjoy the nights with Alexey, but instead I'm trying to be a spy! I must be crazy, I should be punished, and one day I will be, too! She commanded herself not to waver, read the introduction in one go, and was surprised to find that she vaguely understood it.

How does Leonid put up with all this? Anna wondered as her finger slid down the page. How has he been able to keep silent for so long in the face of such cheating? Why has he decided to close his eyes to the obvious? The more intense Anna's affair became, the more often her husband spent the night in his barracks. He assiduously overlooked every change: that she spent more time on her appearance, for example, or that she came home with things they really couldn't afford.

One evening, after Anna had settled into the backseat of the limousine that would transport her to Alexey, she'd noticed Leonid stepping out of the shadow of an archway just as the big car was pulling away. She'd expected her husband to make her explain herself later that night, but when she came home, he was already lying in the sleeping alcove with his face turned away from her. Anna could tell by his breathing that he was still awake, and when she got into bed, she'd pushed herself under his arm. Without a word, he'd stroked her hair and then turned away. When she woke the following morning, he was already in his uniform, sitting at the table next to Petya and cutting the boy's bread into bite-sized pieces. Leonid had stayed with his unit for the rest of the week.

He's not a weak person, Anna thought; he knows how to assert himself, and within the limits of his possibilities, he's single-minded. She turned the page pensively. What he was lacking was passion. The only devotion he showed was in his love for Petya. And yet, Anna would have found intolerable the unresolved condition in which Leonid had voluntarily remained for months.

Rosa, that witch, as if she were capable of gauging Anna's desperation, had offered her help precisely when Anna had been on the point of chucking everything. She'd decided that she was willing to accept any consequences rather than to go on living a life of double deceit. And at that exact point, Rosa had proposed a meeting.

"Doesn't it bother you, constantly having to lie to Leonid?" she'd asked innocently, but at the same time so empathetically that Anna had shared her feelings with her. Then, on the very next day, Anna had been ordered to appear in Kamarovsky's office, and the Colonel had presented her with his plan. He'd explained that officers from Moscow who volunteered for service in inhospitable parts of the Soviet Union might hope for special privileges upon their return. "It wouldn't be for a long time," he'd said. "But I think it would be best for us to avail ourselves of this expedient."

She was so far gone in deceit that Kamarovsky could allow himself to make her such a proposal, Anna thought fearfully. Shouldn't she stand up to him, once and for all? Anna didn't want to lose Leonid, and she didn't want to lose Alexey. Confounded by her dilemma, and full of shame at herself for taking up Kamarovsky's offer unresistingly, Anna had asked, "So where would he get transferred to?"

The Colonel had pulled over a map that showed the locations of the various army units and tapped on a position in the Northeast.

"Siberia?" she'd whispered. "No, I can't do that . . . you can't ask that of us."

"How long has your husband served as a lieutenant?" After Anna told him, Kamarovsky had sat there with an impenetrable expression on his face, as though, first of all, he had to consider the matter. Then he said, "A promotion might be possible. Naturally, your husband would have to apply for his captain's commission himself."

She'd stared at the map and tried to comprehend the incredible distance that lay between Moscow and *there*. "What guarantee do I have that Leonid will be allowed to come back home?"

The Colonel's silence had made it clear to her that haggling with him was a foolhardy undertaking. Then he said, "I'm not in command of

Leonid's army unit, but should he decide to go along with a transfer, the circumstance will be taken into account, and it will be borne in mind that you both have cooperated with the security forces."

This answer was too vague for Anna. "When will he get an irrevocable right of abode for Moscow?"

"In a year, or at the latest, a year and a half."

"I'll consider it."

While showing her to the door, Kamarovsky had reiterated, "It wouldn't be forever."

That evening, Anna had initiated the overdue conversation. She and Leonid hadn't been so honest with each other in years. They'd admitted that their only remaining interaction involved organizing the day: Who was bringing Petya to the doctor, who was picking him up from school, when would his grandfather have to lend a hand? They'd calculated how long it had been since they'd made love. Anna said it was because they slept in the same room with Viktor Ipalyevich. They'd hugged and petted each other, not with passion, but rather as though each sought protection in the other. Finally, since the subject lay close to hand, Anna had indicated that there was someone else; nothing serious, she'd explained, but nevertheless, not something she could end overnight.

Even then, Leonid had shown no interest in hearing reasons or learning names; he'd even told her he trusted her! Furious, she'd moved away from him on the sofa and told him to his face that she was having an affair with a member of the Central Committee. "And I'm being required to continue it, too!"

Leonid had been neither wounded nor outraged, but merely alert. Without Anna's mentioning the KGB again, he'd wanted to know if their conversation was being listened to. She'd laughed, but with a glance at the familiar objects around her, she'd nonetheless admitted that she'd never considered such a thing even as a possibility until that moment. Since the name of her control officer had also been dropped, Anna considered that the moment had come to present Kamarovsky's proposal. Once again, Leonid's reaction had been not reproachful but practical. "Ever since I became a commissioned officer, I've been allowed to serve in Moscow. But no one who doesn't belong to the nomenklatura can get out of serving in the provinces at some point." He stood up. "That means that they would surely transfer me eventually, sooner or later. Why not now?"

"Do you know what that means?" She'd taken his hands and named the place in Siberia. For the first time in a long time, she'd noticed how sinewy his lower arms were. "Nine months of winter."

"We have a big, glorious country. Why shouldn't I get to know more of it?" He'd gone over to the bookshelves. "We don't have a single book about Siberia."

Not long after that, Leonid had taken matters into his own hands. He'd started bringing home books about the North and cutting out every newspaper article he saw that described the beauty of Siberia. Anna had distrusted his optimism, thinking it was just for show, and she'd read aloud to him reports stating that the ground in Yakutia never thawed out. The houses there, she read, were built on concrete pillars to keep the heated rooms from warming the soil and causing the whole building to sink into the resultant mire. Nevertheless, Leonid's willingness to make the move remained constant, and one morning after night duty he'd told Anna that he'd decided to try for a transfer to Minusinsk. His application was already being considered.

"Why so far away?" Anna had asked. Strangely enough, she'd felt rejected.

"Does it make a difference?"

It had been a long time since she'd seen him so self-confident. He'd looked up the place in the atlas and determined that there were five time zones between Moscow and the city on the Yenisei River. "After this, I'll be an expert in coal mining," Leonid had said with a laugh, reading her a statistic that estimated the coal reserves in the area at 450 billion tons.

At night, Anna had wondered how she'd let things go so far. Wasn't her situation beyond all reason? In order to maintain an illicit relationship, she was standing idly by and watching while her husband let himself be exiled to the other side of the socialist world. She understood Leonid's motives less and less. Instead of asserting his rights—hadn't Anna secretly hoped he would?—he was falling in with Kamarovsky's perverse proposition, and he was prepared to relocate at a great distance and without resentment. She almost envied him his eager anticipation at the prospect of getting to know some of the Soviet Union's outlying regions.

In the days after her husband's decision, Anna's image of him had changed more and more starkly. How generous and spontaneous Leonid was! In their thoroughly muddled situation, he remained composed and kept his sense of humor. Unexpectedly, he'd become again the person whom Anna had once liked so much. She'd even told him that, had even sought his affection, but Leonid had rejected her advances. She'd tried to give him an idea of the barren wastes he proposed to enter and asked him whether he wouldn't curse her for having driven him into exile, and he'd responded by chiding her for being such a romantic. It was then that Anna had admitted to herself that her feelings for Alexey were fading.

Simultaneously with Leonid's promotion to the rank of captain, the news had come that he would be transferred not to southern Siberia but to Sakhalin Island, in the easternmost part of the Soviet Union. He'd reacted calmly even to this change and explained that the pay for duty on Sakhalin, because of its extreme location, would be double what he'd been expecting, and besides, frontier troops were given preferential treatment. When Anna checked on the distances this time, she found that Moscow and the island were separated by eight time zones.

"I'll never get so close to Japan again," Leonid had said with a smile. "The strait between the island and Japan is barely thirty miles wide."

He'd made an unemotional decision to go to the East, and his departure had been equally serene. He'd inculcated in Petya the notion that he must now represent his father as head of the family; with deadly seriousness, the boy had accepted the charge. When Leonid thanked his father-in-law for his support, Viktor Ipalyevich had maintained a grim silence, just as he'd done throughout the preceding weeks in the face of all the changes he found reprehensible but couldn't comprehend.

At the last moment, Anna had felt suddenly afraid and implored Leonid to reconsider. Tears weren't appropriate for their situation, he'd replied amicably; they would see each other again in a few months. Assailed by the thought that she'd made the worst of all possible choices, Anna had watched in panic as her husband picked up his suitcase, threw his better uniform, still on its hanger, over his shoulder, and left the apartment. An army police vehicle had taken him to the airport.

During the first days, Anna had received no news of him; all she knew was that the journey took thirty-six hours and that he would have changed planes in both Omsk and Khabarovsk. She had felt as though she were paralyzed; she'd cursed Kamarovsky's plan, but most of all, she'd cursed herself, and she'd canceled two dates with Bulyagkov.

After nearly a month, she'd received an enthusiastic letter from Leonid. Sakhalin lay in the same latitudes as the Mediterranean Sea, he told her, but the climate was incredibly harsh and unpredictable; for the first time in his life, he saw himself completely at the mercy of Nature. He'd done some reading about the time before the Revolution, when Sakhalin was the worst penal camp in tsarist Russia and millions of people had literally rotted there. Today, he pointed out, it was the site of a first-class fishing industry, and the military bases were well organized. He went on to say that the civilian population living on the island was made up mostly of women, because the men were off working on the mainland or had simply cleared out for good. When Anna read that, her loneliness had been augmented by jealousy. The whole time, she'd looked upon Leonid as the one who'd been cheated on and treated like dirt; now, in her mind's eye, she saw him as a brand-new captain in a snappy uniform, cruising an island full of women!

Anna had spent a sad winter. Bulyagkov, sensing that she was at her wit's end, had behaved with surprising consideration. For even though Leonid's departure had technically simplified the affair for Alexey, something fundamental had changed, and the two of them had reverted to the earliest form of their relationship: dinner and chatting on the corner seat. During the course of these conversations, strangely enough, the Deputy Minister had given Anna advice about her marriage, pointing out to her that longing was the strongest engine of any passion. And so it was Alexey, the cause of all the confusion, who gradually helped her to get over it. The spring had turned lush and heavy. When Anna turned out the light in Moscow, for Leonid, six thousand miles away, it was time for morning roll call.

Anna lurched upright and listened. No more sounds came from the neighboring room. Resolutely, she clapped her physics tome shut, washed her face, brushed her hair, and went to dinner. The atmosphere in the dining room was as relaxed as it had been at lunch. Anna took her seat between the orphanage director and the blissful Nadezhda. Dinner consisted of pork and potatoes, and someone had scared up some red wine. Anna drained her glass in one gulp and accepted a refill from the orphanage director. The Aeroflot pilot had successfully insisted that the radio be taken from the lobby and set up in the dining room; the Irkutskians quarreled over the station of choice. Anna had received no message from Alexey and didn't know whether or not Anton was waiting for her outside. Eating calmed her nervousness, the wine made her weightless; she began to enjoy herself and kept on drinking. In the meanwhile, the peace ambassadress was dancing with the kolkhoz farmer, and

Nadezhda fetched her Irkutskian and laid her arms around his neck. The next time Anna looked up, the tables were empty, and everybody who had a partner was swaying to the music.

"You look like you're somewhere else," the orphanage director said. "Why are you always so aloof?"

"Leave me alone," she said, slamming her glass on the table.

"Come on," he said, and stood up.

"Shit music." She shook her head.

"As loaded as you are, what difference does the music make?"

Anna felt that she was being helped to her feet. The man who'd seemed so frail to her grabbed under her arms and pulled her around the table. "If you don't watch out," she said, "I'm going to throw up on your shirt."

"Just as long as you're having a good time." He put his arm around her neck. Her feet slid across the floor. She sank against the male chest and stopped thinking altogether.

Anna knew neither how long she'd danced nor with whom, but in the end, she must have wound up in Popov's arms, because she remembered that the group leader had seen her to her room. She'd dropped her blouse and skirt near the bed and slept in her underwear.

That morning, Anna's hangover, oddly not as bad as the one the previous day, faded quickly after some coffee and salted herring. The group breakfast was a rather silent affair. It was obvious that not one of the delegates felt the slightest desire to visit the day's main attraction, the phasotron. Even Popov had exceeded his limit the night before and made no attempt to hurry the group along. Only Adamek's appearance set everyone in motion.

Pallid and gray, the members of the visiting delegation stared out the bus windows while being driven to the other end of Dubna. Anna's head bobbed up and down with every bump. It was clear to her that she'd let the entire evening slip by without doing anything to carry out her assignment. The visitors were led into a large shed, where protective goggles were distributed to them to shield their eyes against the dazzling light radiating from the welding torches in the main hall. The reactor was not yet finished, Adamek said, which meant that they had a unique opportunity to peer into the bowels of the gigantic machine. The Aeroflot pilot found it disappointing to be presented with a worksite instead of particles in rapid motion. The others trotted along behind their scientific guide, who introduced them to a female scientist named Stretyakova, the designer of the complex.

"In a few weeks, particles will be hurtling through these channels at close to the speed of light," she said in a high-pitched voice that seemed incongruous with her stout physique. The delegation stared into open tubes with pipes that could just as well have been connected to the sewage system. "Anyone who gets dizzy easily should stay down here," Stretyakova declared, and then she started to mount a narrow ladder that led to the ceiling of the reactor hall. Given their weakened condition, each of the visitors, as individuals, would have declined to participate in such a climbing party, but no one wanted to be shown up in front of the others. And so they made an orderly ascent, first the peace ambassadress, then the Irkutskians, followed by Nadezhda, and so on until Adamek, who went up last, his eyes unobtrusively fixed on Anna's rear end.

When they had gathered on the circular steel walkway, the visitors were shown the reflector and the yard-thick concrete wall that provided protection from radiation. Leaning far over the railing, the scientist pointed out the bottomless shaft into which the control rods would be inserted. "Below us, it's ninety feet straight down to the zero mark."

Most members of the group believed her without staring into the abyss.

"With the help of decelerated-neutron irradiation chambers, one can see through living cells without harming them," explained Stretyakova. For the first time, therefore, high-speed neutrons were going to be used in biological research.

The group was spared the climb down the ladder; they were released through a door into the open. A blast of icy air struck them as they emerged. They went down the exterior steps to the foot of the reactor and walked beside frozen bulldozer tracks to the laboratory huts.

"I thank you for your attention, and I wish you a good trip home." Stretyakova's lecture passed so seamlessly into a farewell that even Adamek took a few seconds to understand that they were being dismissed.

"We thank the Comrade Doctor for her precious time," he said, led the members of the delegation in a brief round of applause, and then signaled to them to bestir themselves. The bus driver had not been informed of their movements, so the little group had to make their way to the parking area over icy sand heaps and through defoliated undergrowth. During the ride back to the hotel, the atmosphere was tense; Popov's expression showed that he was ashamed of his team.

A message from Alexey was waiting for Anna at the front desk. He complained about having been stood up the previous evening and ordered her to come to lunch at his borrowed house. Anton had another errand to perform, he said, so she must come on foot. Anna was none too pleased at the prospect of this visit. Flustered and sleep-deprived, she hurried to her room, showered, and—without informing Popov—set off on her walk.

The way was unfamiliar in daylight; all the houses on the riverfront promenade looked alike. In the end, she found the villa only because Alexey was in the garden.

"I wanted to split some firewood," he said as he pulled open the iron-barred gate. "But there's not an ax to be found anywhere on the premises."

She went ahead of him toward the house. He caught up with her on the shoveled path. "Where were you?"

"I got no message at all from you."

"Am I supposed to send you a love letter every evening?"

"I didn't see the car." As she spoke, she hung up her coat.

"It's too bad the evening was spoiled."

"Yes, it is," she said, closing the subject.

"Wine?"

"I'd rather not." She turned off the harsh ceiling lights and sought out a spot in the dimly lit alcove.

"You look pale." He remained in front of the cold fireplace.

"We've got a pretty hard-drinking delegation, you know."

"You were partying while I sat here bored?" He was obviously in a complaining mood, but after keeping it up for a bit, he eventually went into the kitchen. "Would you like something to eat? Anton picked up some cold cuts."

Anna greatly needed something warm. "Do you have any eggs? Shall I fix us some eggs and sausage?"

"Will you do that?" he asked, suddenly the mildest of men, and showed her the pantry. Then he waited in silence while Anna rummaged around.

"I'm awfully tired, Alexey," she said over her shoulder. "These scientific lectures . . . can we sleep a little?"

As though she'd spoken a magic word, he hugged her from behind and pressed his unshaven cheek against her ear. "Yes, let's sleep, Annushka, I'm tired, too . . . God, am I tired."

"First we eat," she said, pushing him aside. The sausage had a strong smell.

When they were seated at the table, she asked, "How much time do we have left?"

"My work in Dubna is done."

"Our group still has to visit . . ." She wiped the egg yolk from her plate. "I have no idea what we're going to visit."

Anna left half of her meal untouched and went into the bedroom. Alexey followed her, pulled his suspenders off his shoulders, and watched Anna slip into the bed in her underwear. "Oh, this feels good," she said. She turned on her side and drew up her legs.

"Shall I set the alarm clock?" Unable to bend over and untie his shoes, he sank down onto the edge of the bed.

"I don't care."

"Some Pioneer Girl you are." Still wearing his shirt and pants, he lay down, got under the covers, and stretched out his hand until it came to rest under Anna's thigh. Then everything grew still.

Even in her dozing state, Anna's sense of duty tormented her. Could she in good conscience waste her last hours in Dubna sleeping? She saw herself standing on the mighty reactor's cover plate, surrounded by scientists with masks covering their noses and mouths. The roof began to shake, then positively to rattle, but nobody seemed to take this state of affairs at all seriously. *Don't you hear that?* Anna cried. *Can't you feel it, any of you? Everything's exploding!* She opened her eyes and saw that Alexey was on his feet. "But we haven't been in bed five minutes yet," she whispered.

"Someone's here." He stepped to the window and pushed the curtain aside.

No reason on earth could give her the strength to sit up. "Is it Anton?"

"Good God," Alexey growled. "Him, of all people."

She rolled over onto her back.

"You stay in bed," the Deputy Minister ordered her. "Don't make a sound. I'll get rid of him as fast as I can."

"Who?"

"That madman Lyushin."

The bedroom door had not yet closed when Anna sat bolt upright. Sleep filled her head and made her limbs heavy; nevertheless, she forced herself to think clearly. If she still had one chance left to tackle her assignment, that chance had now come. Anna threw off the blanket. Her thighs, white and widely spread, lay on the sheet; her feet were covered by blue socks. By then, Alexey had admitted the visitor. She hurried into the bathroom to wash the sleep from her eyes. There was a broom leaning behind the door; she saw it too late. It slid along the door panel, crashed against the wainscoting, and made a bright, sharp sound when it struck the tiled floor. She stood stock-still; the conversation in the neighboring room had ceased. "No listeners," someone said, and the bedroom door was yanked open.

From close up, Nikolai Lyushin seemed smaller. He hadn't taken off his overcoat, under which he wore no jacket, only a white shirt. The hair on his temples was damp, as if he'd been running.

"Oh," he said. "Well. Good day, Comrade." He turned back into the living room. "I'm sorry, Bulyagkov, really. Don't be angry."

Anna waited for Alexey to appear in the doorway—she was standing in the bathroom, and Lyushin just outside of it—but nothing stirred. She took the woolen blanket from the bed, wrapped it around her shoulders, and walked past the scientist into the living room.

Alexey was sitting in his armchair. "As you see, we'll have to have this conversation another time," he said.

"Please introduce me," Lyushin said, stepping in behind Anna.

"The comrade is part of the group that's visiting from Moscow."

"Nikolai Lyushin," the blond man said.

"The quantum physicist?" she asked, looking at Alexey.

"You know who he is?" Bulyagkov seemed more curious than surprised.

"How do you know me?" Lyushin came so close to her that she could smell his aftershave lotion.

"From the material they handed out to prepare us for our study trip."

"And you are what . . . a student?"

"I'm a house painter." She noted the exchange of glances between the two men.

"I'm afraid I may be intruding," said Lyushin, as though it weren't obvious.

"We were trying to take a nap," Anna said coolly.

"How about something to drink?" Before Bulyagkov could stand up, Anna had already grabbed the bottle from the shelf; the blanket slipped off her shoulder.

"Let's sit down." He poured the drinks, and Anna slid onto the settle.

Lyushin remained on his feet while he tossed back his first glass. "My place isn't so comfortable," he said.

"That's because you've got skis standing around everywhere." Alexey clinked glasses with Anna. "Professor Lyushin was the Soviet champion in the triathlon."

"In the days of my youth." Without hesitation, he sat next to Anna.

"Where do you ski?" she asked, although she guessed the answer.

"Across the river." Lyushin indicated the direction with his head. "There's a first-class cross-country course. You can even ski it at night."

"I thought scientists were on the whole . . . unathletic people."

"Stupid prejudice. Most of the ones here are ace athletes. You should see the river in summer. Covered with sails, and water-skiing is the latest rage." He poured himself another drink. "We even have a soccer team. They have a game soon against the atomic city of Novosibirsk."

"In summer, it's really . . ." Alexey sought the right word. "It's really idyllic here. Twenty years ago, this area was uninhabited."

"Why was Dubna built here, of all places?" Anna was conscious of the unreal situation. The nuclear scientist and the Deputy Minister were sitting on either side of a woman wearing a woolen blanket. She nodded to one and then to the other, as her two male companions took turns telling the story of Dubna's early years. The place called Novo-Ivankovo lay in the area later to be submerged when the "Moscow Sea" (the Ivankovo Reservoir) was filled. Novo-Ivankovo was torn down and rebuilt stone by stone next to Dubna; after that, the waters that would form the reservoir came pouring into the valley. Today, the reservoir's gigantic power plant provided electricity to the capital as well as Dubna itself.

"The people of Moscow were nervous," Lyushin said. "In those days, not very much was yet known about the power of the atom." He tilted his head to one side. "For reasons of radiation safety, Dubna had to be sufficiently far from the capital, which is why they drained the swamp where the city now stands." He asked Anna what facilities the delegation had visited; Anna named the cyclotron, the nuclear spectroscopy laboratory, and the worksite where the phasotron was being built. Then she asked, "Why can't we visit your department?"

"We're the ugly ducklings of scientific research," Lyushin said, wheeling his glass on the table edge. "Nothing radiates where we are; no circulating particles approach the speed of light. We just sit with our slide rules and try to get our teeth into the uncertainty principle."

"You can imagine it in more modern terms," Alexey said to Anna. "These days they use big computers instead of slide rules."

"Otherwise, however, little has changed since Bohr and Heisenberg," Lyushin insisted.

"What are you working on?" The question was out before Anna could consider the consequences. The two men looked at each other. She expected to hear something about state secrets and security regulations.

"The probability that nucleons will be present in a localized region of space," said Lyushin, as naturally as if he were giving out a cooking recipe. "If e is smaller than v, then the probability of presence tends toward zero. Therefore, the kinetic energy would be negative and the speed imaginary, which is of course nonsense, and nevertheless, the energy values are positive."

"All right, now we know," Bulyagkov said with a smile. "And now you understand why your bus keeps driving past the theoretical physics building without stopping."

"It's too bad, all the same," said Lyushin. His face lit up. "We have a beautiful new coffee machine. That alone would be worth a visit."

"I'd like to learn more about the subject," Anna said, her back turned to Alexey.

"Do you have some understanding of quantum mechanics?" Again, the men exchanged surprised looks.

"I've read about electron diffraction."

"Tell us." It wasn't so much an invitation to take a pop quiz as the expression of a specialist's amused curiosity at the prospect of having a conversation about his chosen field with a half-naked woman. Anna searched her memory for whatever fragments remained from her perusal of the physics textbook.

"Under certain circumstances, electrons behave as though they're not particles of matter, but waves."

"So far, so good," Lyushin said, nodding.

"But one can't predict whether they'll appear as matter or as waves."

"Sometimes the damned things behave like both at once," Lyushin agreed.

"And therefore quantum mechanics can only determine the probability of a particular event, it can't offer a precise result."

Lyushin smiled at Bulyagkov. "First semester theoretical physics, passing grade," he said. They clinked glasses together.

Strangely enough, being consigned to a marginal role in the conversation didn't seem to bother Alexey. He didn't play the master of the house, nor did he encourage the uninvited guest to leave, but rather stood up and fetched another kind of vodka. Meanwhile, Lyushin talked about the angular momentum of composite particles and the quasi-stationary state of neutron spin and ended with a reference to his current work, which concerned the uncertainty principle and perturbation theory. "An exact solution to the Schrödinger equation can be found only for a few very simple cases," he said, tousling his hair. "Most problems lead to series of equations so complicated that they can't be solved exactly. We think approximate calculations are the only way to reach a result, and therefore lower-order terms must simply be left out." His straw-colored hair was now standing up in all directions.

"And does that work?" Anna posed the decisive question as though it were one of many.

He exhaled forcefully through his nose. "Do you know what the scientist's three capital Fs are? Failure, failure, and failure." He sighed and leaned back.

"Have you failed, Professor Lyushin?"

The blond-haired man gazed at her. "It looks that way at the moment."

Anna felt Alexey freeze beside her.

"My department must retreat several steps," Lyushin continued. "All the way back to an equation that we developed a year and a half ago."

"That's no failure. It's just a backward step." She pulled the slipping blanket higher.

"But it costs money," he said, smiling at her. "Money that the Ministry for Research Planning doesn't want to make available." The scientist looked over at Bulyagkov. "Is she really a house painter?"

"You're surprised?" Alexey asked, grinning. "She represents the general cultural level of our working men and women!"

Anna stood up and went to get dressed.

"Do you have to leave very soon?" Lyushin called to her. "I wanted to show you our coffee machine!"

"We're going back to Moscow today. I really can't stay any longer." She closed the bedroom door and slipped quickly into her clothes. Lyushin offered her a ride back to the hotel.

"I'd better not accept," she said. She gave Alexey a regretful look, expressing sorrow that their last date had taken such an unusual form, and put on her coat. "It would be better for me to show up unaccompanied."

The two men followed her to the door. "Thanks," she said as she took her leave. "Today's lecture was certainly the most interesting of all." She gave her hand to Lyushin and a fleeting kiss to Alexey, whose relaxed cheerfulness persisted undiminished.

Anna stood in the snow. Then she walked slowly to the gate, but as soon as she was through it, she hurried along the riverfront promenade and the main street, broke into a run at the sight of the flags over the hotel entrance, ignored the front desk manager's look, and rushed up to her room. Her hand flew over the page as she jotted down as much as she could remember, making a special effort to record technical terms. When she laid down her pen, she heard the members of the delegation hurrying down the hall outside her room. Suitcases were being shifted, doors were slamming closed; their departure was imminent. Anna considered what excuse she might use to soothe Popov, who would want to know why she'd been absent from the official farewells. Before tossing the physics textbook into her bag, she gave the volume an affectionate pat.

NINE

"Personally, I don't like the Moskva swimming pool," Kamarovsky said, turning to Anna as though he expected her to agree.

"Why not, Comrade Colonel?"

"Because it's on the very spot where the Palace of Soviets was supposed to be built."

Kamarovsky's window offered no view of the pool, yet he spoke of it as though he had the ground plan of the city in his head. "Le Corbusier had been hired for the planning. Think about that: an international ambassador of communism. His towers would have been overwhelming—I'll show you his drawings for them sometime. What a victory we could have celebrated for revolutionary architecture."

Anna was standing behind the Colonel. As was the case with all her visits, this one had begun with a lecture on recent Soviet building design. There was a bowl of various citrus and tropical fruits on the table; she couldn't decipher the composer's name at the top of the musical score that lay on the open piano.

The drive home from Dubna had passed in silence. The bus riders turned their thoughts to the demands and requirements of their ordinary lives, from which they had been removed for three whole days. The driver stopped for gas only once; nevertheless, Anna thought the return trip longer than the outward journey. She'd never left Petya alone for so long. Viktor Ipalyevich did what he could, but he was old and unpredictable. Had he bothered to call about Petya's test results? How serious was his condition? Did he need prolonged treatment? Who was going to pay for his medicine? As Anna's concern grew, she began to find every mile too far, and the distance to Moscow interminable. As on the original trip to Dubna, the orphanage director had sought to engage her in conversation, and she'd pretended to be asleep. When they reached the city limits on the Dmitrovsky Chaussée, the members of the group had assured one another that they would meet again; numbers were exchanged and suitable meeting places suggested. Nobody alluded to the fact that half of the delegation was scattered over the whole country. Anna had let the orphanage director get her bag down, nodded when Nadezhda referred to the monthly gathering of the building combine, and climbed out of the bus. She'd crossed Kutuzovsky Prospekt; the weather was colder than in Dubna. It had been after midnight when she'd finally reached the apartment. The first thing she'd done was to listen hard, trying to hear whether Petya was sleeping. She'd been relieved at the sound of soft breathing behind the curtain. Viktor Ipalyevich was not on his sofa but clattering around the kitchen. She'd put down her bag, greeted him, and put on some tea for her father and herself.

"Child's play" had been his answer to her series of worried questions. "I don't know what's supposed to be so hard about bringing up kids. You make sure they have enough to eat, you help them with their homework, you tell them when they're supposed to go to bed and when to get up, and you take them to school." From all appearances, Viktor Ipalyevich had been in a fine mood, and although he rarely displayed any of his official decorations, he was wearing one pinned to his lapel.

Anna had not been taken in by her father's glib attempt to gloss over the past three days. "How late did you two stay up playing chess?" she asked. "Did you let him drink beer? Did he take a puff on your cigar? Did he change his underwear?"

"Why are you on about his underwear?" Viktor Ipalyevich had pushed his cap back, revealing his forehead's white skin. "We washed his hair. He let his cloth fish go for a swim—the poor little thing didn't survive."

"What did Doctor Shchedrin say?"

"I didn't reach him right away."

"You forgot!"

"No," he said, defending himself. "I called three or four times. I had to speak to three women before I could finally get your doctor on the line."

"When?" Anna had impatiently snatched the tea caddy from the shelf.

"This afternoon."

"And?" She'd stood perfectly still, with the raised teakettle in her hand.

"It's complicated. You have to take Petya to see him again."

"In his office?"

"In Shchedrin's clinic."

"In the hospital?" Anna had forgotten to pour the tea.

"He sounded friendly," Viktor Ipalyevich had said soothingly. "You know yourself what a blessing it is just to be allowed to speak to such a physician." He'd raised his arm. "And I don't want to know how you were able to contact him—I don't want to know!"

"When's the appointment?"

"Tomorrow. I made sure it wouldn't interfere with the shift you're working. Tomorrow at eleven." Anna had looked up into the rising steam.

As though he wished to shut out the architectural transgression, Kamarovsky pulled the curtain halfway across the balcony window. "There were seven years of negotiations over Le Corbusier's sketches, but then, in the end, water-based recreation got the nod. Now, right in front of our building, we have a paddling pool!"

"Comrade Colonel, I wish to inform you that I have failed," said Anna, a little too loudly. "As an informant, I'm a bust. My services can't be of any further use to you."

Kamarovsky smiled at her, as indulgently as a doting uncle. "Impatience is mounting everywhere," he said mysteriously. "That's because of the spring. Everyone's longing for it, even though we all know we're going to have to wait two more months before it deigns to come." He did not follow his usual custom of directing her to sit at the desk to give her report but instead escorted her to the sofa. For himself, he chose the chair facing her; behind him, the soundless television screen showed a roundtable discussion, six men and a woman.

"You completed the entire three-day visit?"

Anna nodded. She was wearing black; in front of the mirror, she'd thought it looked like the proper outfit—black conferred strength on her.

"Dubna's impressive, isn't it?" Anna answered this question, too, in the affirmative. "Which excursion did you like the best?"

The amusing afternoon on the Volga came into her mind, but instead, she said, "The synchrocyclotron. It was impressive to see the scientists at their work." She pulled her turtleneck collar up under her chin. "Comrade, I'm asking to be discharged," she continued. All too aware of her tendency to vacillate, she wanted, this time, to be the one who initiated the change of direction.

"Did you meet Lyushin?"

"On the last day," she answered, convinced that he knew about her meeting in any case.

"Were you able to speak with him?" She nodded. "Therefore, you fulfilled the first part of your mission." He turned and faced the television screen.

"Our meeting took place because of a coincidence."

"A coincidence?" He snapped his head around, eyeglasses flashing.

"We did have a discussion, but I don't deserve the slightest credit for having brought it about." Anna stood up. If he keeps deflecting the conversation like this, she thought, I've lost. Speaking as though the man in the chair were not her case officer but rather a sympathetic advisor, Anna explained that she was beginning to confuse intrigue and reality. She sometimes caught herself acting a lie as though it were the most natural thing in the world, she said, and even though this was all in the service of a good cause, she recognized that she was the wrong person for the job. She'd served the KGB for a year and a half, she'd never refused an order, she'd tried as hard as she could, but now, she was begging him—here Anna stood in front of Kamarovsky, who was still seated—to release her and to let her go back to living a normal life.

Kamarovsky, too, rose to his feet, and their clothes were momentarily in contact. "This day comes for everyone," he said. He went over to the television set and changed the channel. Pensively, he watched some little birds bathing in a soup bowl. "For everyone who works on the *outside*. It's the hardest thing of all, Anna. Please take your seat again."

He rarely called her by her first name. She couldn't let herself be lulled, but she obeyed him, grateful that he was taking up her subject. He approached the sofa from the side and placed one foot on the armrest; he was wearing lined slippers.

"You think we people on the inside have it easy. If we need information, we give someone an assignment, and then we evaluate the results." He made a gentle pause. "I used to be on the street, too, Anna, working on the outside. It sharpens your discernment, but it simultaneously makes you lose focus. Who's an agent, who's just a fellow human being, who's an informer, who's simply telling us something? Back then, I lost my capacity for chitchat, would you believe it? In the evenings, when we'd have a few drinks and the others would make small talk, I couldn't stop looking for what lay behind their words and analyzing their characters. I eavesdropped on my friends, and I wouldn't have hesitated to make use of the information I had on them. It was during that time that my wife left me." He gave Anna a warmhearted look.

"So didn't you think of quitting then?"

"Once or twice. Yes, I wanted to put an end to it, because I felt that my work had turned me into some kind of freak. Life had lost all normality as far as I was concerned." He lowered his head, and the glint of his spectacles struck her eyes. "At the same time, I realized that the decision wasn't up to me. I trusted my case officer; I trusted the Party."

Anna's heart sank. Kamarovsky's last words hung over her like a neon sign. She understood that he'd told her his—or someone else's—story just to keep her up to the mark. That meant that he wouldn't simply let her go.

"There's one thing I've never forgotten, even in my moments of doubt," Kamarovsky said, removing his foot from the sofa. "My occupation is not a job, it's a struggle whose purpose is to combat our society's enemies and to protect its representatives. Therefore how I feel is unimportant; there can scarcely be anything less significant than how an individual feels while the battle is raging. The only thing that matters is the outcome, the result, which justifies all misgivings, all doubts, and every other human emotion. Those are subjective feelings; the Party, however, thinks objectively, and it acts exclusively in the interest of society. To subordinate yourself to the Party's insights must necessarily be for the benefit of all and therefore for the welfare of each individual."

As though he wanted to assure Anna of his accessibility, Kamarovsky sat down next to her. "Your case is different," he said in a suddenly changed voice. "You're not made for such a life, Anna. I know that."

The shift in tone rendered her speechless. In some confusion, she stared at his white-tipped hairs, his fine nose, his slightly mocking mouth.

"You have some feelings for the Deputy Minister. At the same time, you believe you're deceiving him. Moreover, you have to hide your actions from your husband and your son, and you even lie to your father."

It seemed to Anna as though she were sitting with the Colonel in a movie theater where the film of her life was being shown. Kamarovsky spoke softly, as though he didn't want to disturb the other people in the audience. "I don't shy away from calling things by their names," he said, "because I know that your mission will soon be concluded. We're just about ready to close the Deputy Minister's case."

"Case? I thought I was doing all this for his protection."

"Of course you are." Kamarovsky made a soothing gesture. "The aims we're pursuing will enable us to avert a specific danger that threatens Bulyagkov. Soon, very soon, Comrade. And that's why your report is of such great significance."

He pressed a hand against his brow and fell silent for a moment, during which Anna watched his head sink. His hand fell, too, and landed as though lifeless on Anna's thigh. It looked to her as though Kamarovsky had dozed off in the middle of his explanation.

"Comrade Colonel?"

His breathing appeared to have stopped. Then, as though he'd suddenly regained consciousness, Kamarovsky jerked his head up and heaved a deep sigh. When he noticed his hand on the young woman's leg, he stiffened his fingers and got immediately to his feet. "You were saying that your conversation with the leader of the theoretical physics section came about by accident." He reached the desk in three steps, leaned on its edge, and opened a file. "How so?"

A rush of blood flooded Anna's face. From one second to the next, the Colonel had yanked her into the place where he wanted her. She said, "Because I didn't find Lyushin, he found me."

Kamarovsky unscrewed the top of his fountain pen and gazed at the nib. "I had the information that Lyushin likes to ski at night passed on to you. Why didn't you act on that tip?"

Finally, Anna had the solution to the mystery of the second agent: The skinny orphanage director, so intent on ingratiating himself with her, had been on the job. He, at least, had carried out his assignment brilliantly.

"I considered it unlikely . . . actually, I thought—"

"You didn't act purposefully because you had a bad hangover," he said, interrupting her. "You needed to be clearheaded, and you weren't." In the light of the desk lamp, Kamarovsky looked older. His eyes blinked behind the lenses of his spectacles. "Please describe your meeting with Lyushin in detail."

As an outward sign that she was ready to give a sober report, Anna left the sofa and sat in her usual place. She outlined the situation on the afternoon in question and described Lyushin's sudden appearance in Bulyagkov's borrowed house.

"Did you have the impression that the relationship between the two is of such a kind that would permit unannounced visits?"

After a brief hesitation, Anna answered that the situation had not seemed unusual to her. The two men had quarreled the previous day, and she'd looked upon Lyushin's appearance as an offer of reconciliation.

"In your opinion, what was the quarrel about?"

"Money. Lyushin referred to setbacks in a research project. He wants more money so that the research can continue."

"Setbacks?" The nib of the fountain pen was pointing at her. "Are you completely sure about that?"

"That was the word he used."

"How did you come to be talking about that?"

Anna recalled the crazy afternoon, remembered how she'd sat there in her underwear with the scratchy blanket wrapped around her shoulders. "I had done a little research and learned something about the basics of quantum mechanics," she answered. "Lyushin was quizzing me. It was a kind of teacher-student situation." Aided by her notes, she gave an account of the conversation, used Lyushin's own technical language to describe his problem, and ended with a reference to the series of equations in which the scientists proposed to achieve greater accuracy by leaving out lower-order terms. "At this point, Lyushin conceded that he had been forced to take some steps backward." Anna lowered her notepad. "His department must revise their work all the way back to an equation that was constructed a year and a half ago."

The Colonel nodded. "Lyushin's Stationary Law," he said. "A fabulous breakthrough, or so it seemed at the time." He turned to a fresh page and wrote a few lines. "How did Bulyagkov react to Lyushin's revelation?"

"He knew about it. Apparently, the main issue was the continued financial support."

"And the lost time." Kamarovsky licked his lips like a thirsty man. "Dubna is dependent on Lyushin's results. There's a whole series of construction projects in the works, all based on his revolutionary methods."

He stopped talking and opened a drawer. She expected him to take something out of it, but he laid an empty hand on his writing pad. "I'd like to thank you, Comrade. You've fulfilled your assignment more thoroughly than you seem to know. For several reasons, we've had doubts about whether or not the theoretical physics section was being cagey about its successful results. Your information, Anna, gives us concrete clues."

She responded to his unexpected thanks with a nod and shoved her chair back, thinking that her report was at an end.

"I've had this on my desk for the last two weeks."

Looking up, Anna saw that Kamarovsky was holding a document in his hand. "I wanted to give it to you personally." He inverted it and pushed it over the desk to Anna. The document was entitled "GLAVLIT—Summary Decision."

"I acknowledge that it's taken a long time, but the result warrants the delay."

Her eyes flew over the printed lines. She couldn't immediately grasp the sense of what she was reading, obscured as it was by convoluted official language.

Kamarovsky ended her uncertainty: "It looks as though we shall soon be holding a new volume of Viktor Ipalyevich Tsazukhin's poetry, fresh from the press," he said. "The committee has arrived at the view that the submitted poems are morally and politically conducive to the formation of the Soviet character and to the elevation of the citizens' social consciousness. The committee accordingly authorizes without reservation the publication of the collection and undertakes to have the volume printed by the government press with the help of public funds."

Anna kept her eyes fastened on the paper. It was dazzlingly clear to her that she was, once again, on the point of letting herself be bought. Her first reaction was the wish that the price would be sufficiently high. Her words of gratitude were succinct, she rose to go, and the Colonel accompanied her to the hall stand. While she slipped into her coat, she asked, "How did you get over it when your wife left you because of your work?"

"Ah, that." He turned toward the piano and smiled. "I still had music. It unites the things we've been talking about today. It's analytical in construction, yet it makes an immediate connection with our emotions."

"Do you play often?"

"Every free minute I have." He walked her to the door.

As A. I. Kamarovsky listened to the sound of Anna's footsteps fading away down the stairs, he imagined what she would say if she knew that there had never been a Mrs. Kamarovsky. The Colonel was sure: The subtle affliction that would bind Anna to him from that day forward, his tragic submission to his sense of duty, and his calculated display of an almost erotic relationship with the Party would serve to motivate this particular female agent. His lie, therefore, was in a good cause. He sat at the piano and clumsily played a few bars. Neither his abilities nor his strength sufficed for more. He felt the vague presentiment returning, and this time, concentrating on music making wouldn't help him out of the crisis. Breathing heavily, he closed the score and waited. He was waiting to see whether the atonic seizure would set in a second time and overcome him before he could do anything about it. When it failed to materialize, he dared to stand up and move toward the desk with cautious steps. As he did so, he made sure not to come too close to furniture and other objects. He opened the drawer, took out the little envelope, suppressed his horror at verifying that a single tablet was all it contained, and swallowed the tablet. In the interval before the medicine began to take effect, he sank down onto the chair and concentrated on the thing lying closest to hand, which was Anna's report.

TEN

In the morning, mother and son snuggled behind the curtain for a long time. Petya told her about a new teacher who was in the habit of sitting on her desk; when she did so, you could see under her skirt. Anna listened to the sounds he made when he breathed, checked his eyes for redness, and asked when the last time he'd taken his temperature was. Eventually, she made breakfast. The boy liked having a holiday from school; he got dressed cheerfully and was eager to go outside.

They reached the building across from the Lenin Library right on time. The policeman on duty told Anna how to get to Doctor Shchedrin's Institute for Histamine Determination. The receptionist there explained that the doctor was with another patient and suggested that she and Petya have a seat. With every minute that passed in the pretty waiting room, Anna's fears grew. She let Petya play with a toy tank.

"I'm sorry, my treatment room is still occupied," Shchedrin said by way of greeting. His white coat was buttoned up, and he'd been to the barber since their last consultation.

"Does Petya have to go to the hospital?" Anna blurted out.

"Only for the adjustment," the doctor said, nodding. "Please follow me."

"What adjustment?" Taking Petya's hand, Anna went with Shchedrin into the little kitchen that adjoined the waiting room.

"As you see, we're overbooked." He closed the door. The windowless room gave Anna the impression that she was about to receive some news of a particularly confidential nature.

"Your son has asthma," the doctor said. "The original cause may have been the carbon monoxide pollution in the capital, but that alone wouldn't account for his most recent symptoms. Petya's suffering from a very strong reaction to a particular allergen."

Since the muscular structure of the bronchi in children is not yet fully developed, Shchedrin explained, asthmatic symptoms can arise, and he would give Petya medicine to remedy those; it was more important, however, to identify what was triggering the boy's attacks. "In your son's case, it's a question of dust allergens, so it may be difficult to restrict his contact with them."

"How do you mean?" Anna asked. She was sitting on a stool and holding Petya on her lap.

"Dust is an integral part of daily life." Having searched the cabinet in vain for a clean glass, Shchedrin rinsed out a used one and poured himself some tea. "Do you have rugs on the wall at home?" he asked. Anna nodded. "Take them down," he said, wrapping his aristocratic-looking fingers around the hot glass. "Pictures, knickknacks, mementos are all dust collectors. Keep them away from Petya. How about books?"

"My father . . ." She interrupted herself, thinking it unnecessary to mention that she lived with a writer. "We have many books."

"Put them in the cellar. Along with stacks of newspapers, decorative cushions, horsehair mattresses, embroidered tablecloths, and woolen blankets."

She was surprised to hear him describe her apartment so precisely.

"Even if it means a big change for you, get yourself some smooth, synthetic materials. They aren't very popular with dust mites." Shchedrin drank and grimaced. "When will they finally learn to make tea in this place?"

Anna considered how she ought to inform her father that his four walls, the very walls within which he'd so generously welcomed her and her family, were partly responsible for Petya's illness.

"Still, there has to be something else," Shchedrin said, pouring the rest of his tea into the sink. "You told me that Petya's condition gets worse when he's asleep. There must be an allergen source in the immediate vicinity of his bed. Do you have down pillows or duvets?"

What he meant was suddenly clear to her. "A year ago, we . . . my father, Petya, and I sleep in the same room. For the sake of privacy, we've hung a velvet curtain in front of the sleeping alcove."

"Velvet!" Shchedrin exclaimed, laughing. "The dust mite's paradise, the allergy sufferer's hell!"

Petya understood that the conversation was about him but gradually lost interest in it; Anna looked around for something he could play with. Shchedrin showed the boy into the children's waiting room and stepped out into the corridor with Anna. He announced that he would start treating Petya's asthma with medication to dilate his respiratory passages. No medicine could cure the dust allergy itself, he explained, and therefore a gradual desensitization would be necessary, which Shchedrin would initiate with allergen injections.

While he was explaining his diagnosis and the treatment he proposed, Anna became increasingly aware of a nagging discrepancy. On the one hand, merely gaining access to such methods had to be considered practically miraculous; on the other, it entailed a new dependence. "Doctor," she began. Through the open door, she could see her son. "I don't know how I can pay for all these things."

"That's the least of your problems." He nodded to a nurse who was calling him to the telephone.

"What does that mean?"

"It's already taken care of." The nurse held out the receiver to him. "Everything's been arranged."

Observing the doctor's composure as he spoke on the telephone, Anna wondered what kind of agreement Kamarovsky and Shchedrin had reached. A little later, as she and Petya were heading for the exit, she had the Colonel's image before her eyes. Despite Anna's confidence in the physician, Kamarovsky's involvement in Petya's recovery filled her with anxiety.

On the way home, she considered how she should reveal to her sensitive father the special privilege Kamarovsky was granting him. Father and daughter's pact of silence, Viktor Ipalyevich's resolute overlooking of the obvious, required a complex ritual, with whose help he was able to justify to himself his double way of thinking. Anna bought meat, vegetables, and—even though it exceeded her household budget—a can of peaches in syrup.

"I have a pork shank for us," she called out when she entered the apartment. "I'm going to cook it to celebrate this day." She went into the kitchen and set about putting her words into action.

Although Viktor Ipalyevich had contempt for the economy of privilege in a state whose foundation was equality, he accepted Anna's privileges, through which he lived a comfortable life free from material cares. He smoked cigars that couldn't be found in any ordinary Moscow shop, and he wore arch supports in his shoes; under normal circumstances, he would have had to wait until his splayfeet became chronic before his application for such a luxury as shoe lifts would have been approved. The box of pills that Anna had obtained from Shchedrin's private dispensary was not a mere convenience, it was a distinction; such a gift couldn't be dismissed as a bribe, like real coffee or cotton towels. Her little boy's life was about to undergo a vast improvement.

Now Viktor Ipalyevich started trying to figure things out: It was an ordinary weekday, and in a few hours, his daughter's afternoon shift would begin. There had been nothing in the mail that could explain

Anna's words. What reason was there to celebrate? He went through the family birthdays; none of them fell in March. "So what's the occasion?" he asked, as mildly as possible.

"Be patient!" Anna called out, relieved to find that he was playing along without resistance, but still searching her imagination for a way to avoid bruising his class warrior's pride. She boned the meat, tied it around a bundle of herbs and vegetables, seasoned it, browned it with garlic and onions, and put it all in the oven. After scrubbing the onion smell off her hands, she took the bottle of Soviet Champagne out of her shopping bag and gathered up two large glasses and a shot glass for Petya.

"That's all for today," she said by way of inviting her father to remove his writing materials from the table, which she then began to set.

"Smells great," Viktor Ipalyevich declared. He went to the sofa, sat down, and paged through his notes, all without looking at her. After she returned to the kitchen, he followed her movements through the open door. She added tomato puree and caraway seeds to the roasting meat, cuddled with Petya, who had come running into the kitchen, sat him on the work surface, and let him watch as she cut up the pork. After arranging it on the porcelain dish with the violet pattern, she called to her father to open the Champagne. Viktor Ipalyevich popped the cork. The wine spilled over the rim of Petya's little glass, and the boy contorted himself to lick it.

"To the health of a distinguished poet—my father."

"I'm not going to respond to you until you explain the reason for this mysterious announcement."

She served father, son, and herself some meat, put the rest on the stove to keep warm, and came back into the room with one hand behind her back.

"You've got mail, Papa." She laid the Glavlit decision on the table next to his plate.

For a moment, he considered challenging her lie—he knew their mailbox had been empty—but his curiosity was too great, and it was followed by disbelieving amazement. With his fork in one raised hand and the document in the other, the poet read the news of his pardon.

"This is almost three weeks old," he said, pointing to the issuance date and trying to cover up his emotion by being gruff.

Anna, too, had noticed that Kamarovsky had apparently held on to this reward for her work until he thought the proper time had come to reveal it. "You know how bureaucrats are," she said.

"Good God," her father murmured. He pressed his lips together, but his agitation, hot and irrepressible, overcame him. He stood up, laid the document on the middle of the table, and took off his cap. Gray, frizzy hairs stuck up in all directions, and his white pate contrasted with the brown skin of his forehead. Shaken, his shoulders slumping, the poet stood over the table, supporting himself on its top and muttering while a thread of saliva dripped from his mouth. His grandson gave Anna a perplexed look as his own small lips began to tremble. Happy though she was, Anna wouldn't give in to sentimentality; instead she cried, "But that doesn't mean the food should get cold!"

Viktor Ipalyevich sank down onto his chair as though a hand had been laid on his shoulder. He cut himself a bit of pork and took a bite. Tears ran down his cheeks. After a while, he spoke. "I must . . . before anything else, I have to . . ." he said. "The proper sequence!" He raised his head. "The proper sequence is very important. Will you help me, Petya?"

"With what, Dyedushka?"

"We have to get our poems out. We'll look at every single one of them—no, even better, you'll read them to me. What do you think? And after that, we'll decide which one should come first, which one second, and so on. And in the end—you understand, Petya?—we'll have a whole book full of poems."

The boy nodded and said, "I'll read them." Then, to give himself strength, he said it again: "Yes, I'll read them. When do I start?"

"This very evening!" His incredulity mingling with the recognition of what a profound and thorough change that piece of paper signified for him, Viktor Ipalyevich renewed his assault on the pork, chewed a mouthful, and emptied his glass in one gulp. In his excitement, he dunked one corner of the Glavlit document in tomato sauce.

Anna recalled that there was something else she'd intended to do that evening. The reason behind her intention lay in the last question Shchedrin had asked her: "Has there been any family incident that might have distressed Petya?" As she sat there in confused silence, the doctor had explained his query: "Allergy sufferers need a calm, secure environment. Distress or anger can intensify their allergies or even cause allergies to break out. Have you and yours undergone some sort of change that has disturbed Petya? It could be something that happened months ago."

Anna had begun to perspire, and the floor had seemed to be shaking beneath her. "My husband's a soldier," she'd answered. "He was transferred out of Moscow almost a year ago."

"Did father and son have a good relationship?"

Anna had done some mental reckoning: Petya's symptoms had manifested themselves after Leonid's departure. The relationship between the two of them was not merely good, but intimate, playful, filled with deep trust. One heart and one soul—that's what they actually were. A telephone call is expensive, Anna thought, basically beyond our means, but this evening, she would call Leonid and tell him about Petya's illness. She'd put the boy on the telephone and let them chat with each other. It was the least she could do.

ELEVEN

Leonid hung up. For a long moment, he stood still, his back to the desk in the military guard post. The soft voice still sounded in his ears. It was eight o'clock in the morning, and therefore midnight in Moscow; if Anna let Petya stay up so late, the thing must mean a lot to her. Leonid thanked the sergeant for having notified him, buttoned his overcoat all the way up, and left the central barracks. The windstorm was so strong that it pressed him against the wooden hut's exterior wall. Leonid pulled down his ear flaps and fastened them under his chin. Bent forward, holding his arms tightly to his sides, he struggled on. There was nobody else on the parade ground; most of the barracks had wooden planks across the windows, screwed into place to keep the gusts from bursting the glass panes.

Leonid shivered. In this weather, he was supposed to assemble a technical squad and see to the cutter that had gone aground with its cargo of scrap iron during the night. Here, at the southernmost point of Sakhalin Island, most ships anchored at a respectful distance from the coast, for the sea was treacherous. The Three Brothers, three jagged reefs thrusting up out of the water, became invisible in heavy seas. The coastline consisted of dark inlets whose rock formations had formerly been exploited for their coal beds. In the winter months, the sharp-edged forms were veiled by storms and snow flurries, and the cold temperatures burst the sewer pipes that emptied into the sea at this point. Waves as black as night broke over the decks of the patrol ships; that morning, they had been unable to sail because the cutter was blocking their passage.

"How did the boat even get into the prohibited area?" the major had asked Leonid at morning roll call.

"The southwest drift turned east overnight," Leonid replied. "When the ship became disabled, the captain let it be driven into the bay and stranded so it wouldn't sink in the open sea."

"Check the ship's papers, the nationalities of the sailors, and their Party membership, if any, and examine the bill of lading and the cargo," the major had ordered. "I don't want to be fooled by some damned Jap."

"The cutter sailed from Vladivostok three days ago."

"How do we know she didn't make an intermediate stop in Japan? Pay close attention to the tachograph." With this final instruction, Leonid was dismissed.

When he got close to the crews' quarters, the one-story building, anchored to the ground with steel cables, protected him from the wind. Now able to walk upright, Leonid continued on. The major was well aware that the freighter, which had picked up its cargo of scrap iron along the coast of the Sea of Okhotsk, was no spy ship. The reefs off Korsakov had brought many a vessel into distress, either because the ships lacked the necessary navigation equipment or because they were overloaded and could no longer be steered. By this time of year, it was possible that the sea a few hundred miles to the north would be unnavigable for a vessel without ice-breaking equipment, so the stop in Korsakov was to have been the last for the cutter with the scrap-iron cargo before her return journey; but the Three Brothers had seen to it that this would be the freighter's last journey of all.

The technical section's offices were located off to one side of the post. The advantage of this position was that the soldiers of the unit could guard their camp themselves. Had the guard detachment been under company command, it wouldn't have been long before individual pieces of equipment started to appear on the black market. The disadvantage of the little cluster of huts was that they stood so close to the edge of the cliff; one false step or strong gust of wind, and one could vanish into the void. Leonid grasped the steel cord that served as a handrail and moved along it, hand over hand, taking care to avoid the slippery seaweed that the storm tide had washed up three hundred feet high.

The technical service considered itself an elite unit. Its personnel, exclusively seamen, had managed to acquire, piece by piece, the most modern equipment for their detachment. The fact that Leonid, the landlubber, was their commanding officer had to do with the death of Captain Ordzhonikidze, who'd fallen off the cliff during a risky operation; the search for his body had only recently been called off. The Korsakov military base was chronically understaffed, it hadn't been possible to mobilize a specialist from any other garrison, and so Captain Leonid Nechayev had been transferred there, temporarily, it was said. Leonid knew that such temporary arrangements sometimes lasted until the soldier in question retired from the army.

The transfer to a unit that actually had a mission was a surprise and even an irritation to him. Monotony had been the most characteristic feature of his previous years of service. While many officers suffered from such a state of affairs, Leonid had found it to his liking. Not out of dullness or laziness, but because symmetry, equilibrium, fascinated him. Even though he didn't think in terms of such comparisons, he experienced the daily repetition of life as a monkish activity and the barracks as the scene of a cloistered existence: the early morning siren, like a gigantic rooster; the men standing shoulder to shoulder and washing themselves; the indistinguishable, dull gray, badly shaved faces in the mirrors; the preapportioned breakfasts. The sausage rounds on each plate were as identical as the men who swallowed them. At morning roll call, officers stood on one side and men on the other, but these could not exist without those, and vice versa. There were indeed differences in the work—one man sat in the supply room, another was assigned to the paymaster or performed guard duty—but, strictly speaking, what did they do? They punched holes in papers and filed them away in pasteboard binders, or someone drew up lists, another checked them, and a third checked the checker. Lunch, dinner, latrine break one hour after each meal, Party indoctrination in the evening, close of duty, taps: The same sequence was followed today, as it would be tomorrow and the rest of the week, of the winter, of the year. Even the nightly booze-up brought the day to an end in friendly monotony; everyone drank his half-liter bottle, became mellow and jovial, spoke sentimentally, and fell onto his bunk in a daze. It pleased Leonid to see so many men, different in age, temperament, and nationality, welded together into a single cohort. Their thoughts and hopes—pay, women, leave, family—resembled one another like eggs in a basket. Everywhere outside of the army, results had to be achieved and plans carried out; jobs were specialized and required individual commitment. The Red Army defined itself through its steadfastness. Its task consisted in being monolithic, in raising the unchangeable to the level of a principle. Should the army one day give up this position, it would be all over with security, and, above all, with the security in people's heads.

Leonid had never wished for challenging work. With his qualifications, he might possibly have joined the army engineers or become a pilot—but he didn't *want* to. Leonid Nechayev was twenty-nine years old, athletic and fit in appearance, with test results that demonstrated his intelligence; he was popular with his men and considered an agreeable subaltern by his superiors. But there was one quality lacking in his personal inventory: ambition. He'd reached the rank of second lieutenant effortlessly and had been promoted to first lieutenant when his turn automatically came up. His captain's commission, the single unforeseeable turning in his career, had brought him freedom and anxiety in equal measure.

He recalled his telephone conversation with Anna. He'd recognized from the beginning the potential for problems with such a woman, but all the same, recent events had surprised him. His Anna was proud, filled with the highest ideals, and she dreamed of accomplishing something that would benefit society. He hadn't imagined that she'd cheat on him, but rather that she'd want to give her life a mission. Her father had probably laid those qualities in her cradle; to be the daughter of an important Soviet writer entailed obligations. When Leonid had first met Anna, she was already a house painter, but in his view, her profession had represented nothing more than an intermediate stage on the way to something else. He could imagine the sacrifice she'd made by giving up school after her mother's death, but readiness to make sacrifices was also an essential part of her character; her important father must be enabled to go on living his poet's life. Leonid prized books that dealt with interesting subjects; he was suspicious of poems. In Leonid's eyes, someone who took weeks to get a couple of verses down on paper was a parasite.

As for the separation from Anna, Leonid was able to cope with it. Their relationship had never been particularly passionate. Of course, going so long without seeing Petya caused him pain—in fact, it was a source of deeper regret than he'd imagined himself capable of. For Leonid, his son's welfare was more important than anything else. Now Petya was ill, seriously ill, and Leonid, six thousand miles away, felt helpless to do anything for the child. Taking early home leave was out of the question. His garrison was small, the number of officers limited, and the duty arduous. He and his comrades represented Russia's last bulwark against the imperialistic world; just beyond them lay Japan.

The abyss was now so close that the sea-spray struck his face like a steady drizzle. The final feet had to be crossed without the help of the steel cord. He narrowed his eyes, wobbled forward, and entered the office of the technical unit like a shipwreck survivor. Except for the private first class on telephone duty, the office was empty; the rest of the men were in the workshop, preparing their mission.

"They'll be ready soon," said the private. His rolled-up shirt sleeves revealed a pair of powerful forearms.

"Before we begin the operation, we have to do a security check." Leonid removed his coat, which was soaking wet, and took his foul-weather gear out of his locker.

"High tide's in an hour," the telephone man said. "After that, we won't be able to do anything."

"Major's orders," said the captain, his voice grating. "We start in ten minutes." He went into his room. Formerly, he'd never had to speak sharply to his men; he'd been on good, even familiar, terms with them. These lads, however, were falcons, overqualified, ready for anything, and often bored by the endless, dark days, on which nothing happened. It was hard to keep them under control, especially since Leonid was their professional inferior. For these men, it was a joy to board a light boat and head into the breakers, but Leonid hated the entire process. Mostly, he held on tight to whatever he could while the others sat insouciantly on the sides of the boat. The spray blinded him, and he feared that one of the three-foot-high waves might sweep him into the sea.

He kicked off his boots, pulled the oilskin over his pants, and slipped into the black waterproof jacket that bore the insignia of his rank on its lapel. This little scrap of material gave him the power but not the qualifications to command. He sank down slowly onto a chair; the oilskin made an unpleasant sound. Outside Leonid's window, the storm was howling with such force that rational thinking was scarcely possible. Nature burned a single thought into his brain: Sakhalin was an isle of madness. Before he left Moscow, he'd read Chekhov's travel report, but the reality of the island was worse and could hardly be described in words. From January to March, cyclones blowing up from the Indian Ocean raged over Sakhalin. Between July and November was typhoon season; the last of those had caused more than a hundred million rubles' worth of damage. Seaquakes regularly flooded the eastern portion of the island; because of the incessant tremors, large and small, no house with more than one story could be built without proper anchoring. The temperature often sank below minus sixty degrees Fahrenheit, and the men were frequently shut up inside their garrison for weeks because of snowstorms. After two sentries were snowed in and nearly starved in their guard post, subterranean passages between the barracks had been dug. Normally, the harbor wasn't navigable at that time of year, and the patrol boats stayed in a cove protected by concrete walls. So far, it had been an unusually mild winter; it was already March, and still no avalanche had blocked the roads or severed energy connections. The technical unit helped earthquake victims, towed ships in distress, and set up new seismographs around the mud volcano's crater in order to predict its next eruption more precisely.

While Leonid was looking forward with trepidation to the upcoming mission, he reflected that only a word, only a signature would have sufficed for him to be transferred to some other location in the Soviet Union, to some quiet one-horse town in the Russian provinces, say, where time would have passed gently, shortened by little amenities. Why hadn't he taken that path?

The invitation had reached him through the mail. With mixed feelings, he'd gone across town to the Lubyanka and approached the ominous building from the side. In the square, the monument to Dzerzhinsky was shining in the sunlight, but even on that fine, bright day, the headquarters of the state security agency had looked gloomy and menacing to Leonid. Instead of being subjected to the usual stringent controls, he hadn't had to wait so much as a minute before being shown directly into the Colonel's office. Kamarovsky was sitting behind a metal desk. His uniform was made of fine wool, the epaulets embroidered with "gleaming gold thread," for which officers had to pay out of their own pockets. His decorations included the Order of Lenin and two badges identifying him as a Hero of Socialist Labor. When Leonid entered the room, he'd wondered why the curtain was half closed on such a beautiful day before realizing that the Colonel preferred to sit in shadow while every visitor was obliged to stand in the light.

After the exchange of salutes, Kamarovsky had asked, "Are you familiar with this?" and pushed a book with colorful binding across the desk to the lieutenant. "Informative, enlightening, and entertaining, all at the same time."

Secret Front was the book's title, white letters on a red background, under them a sword, a yellow shield, and, in the center, a red star, the emblem of the Committee for State Security, or KGB. The author of the book was Semyon Tsvigun, whom Leonid knew by name as the Deputy Chairman of the Committee. Leonid asked, "What's it about?"

"About the Soviet citizen's need for vigilance against imperialist undermining." Kamarovsky had pushed up his spectacles and massaged the bridge of his nose. "The bookstores can't keep up with the demand for this volume. Keep it, Lieutenant."

"Many thanks, Comrade Colonel." As though wanting to take no chances on forgetting the book, Leonid placed it on the edge of the desk.

"Vigilance." The Colonel offered him a seat. "An important quality in the service."

Leonid was of one mind with the Colonel.

"So you want to leave Moscow?" Kamarovsky was holding a form that Leonid recognized as his own application for transfer.

"Temporarily," he hastened to reply.

"What led you to request Minusinsk, of all places?" The Colonel's finger ran along the lines of print.

"I'm interested in geology. The bituminous coal mined around Minusinsk is unusual and valuable, and the mining methods—"

Kamarovsky raised his hand. "You're serving with the armored infantry. What do you care about mining?"

Minusinsk was said to be a pretty town with a mild climate, and the company stationed there had a reputation for informality. "I've read that soldiers are brought in to work the seams when there's a personnel shortage in the mines," Leonid replied. "That was my motivation."

"Ah, I see." The Colonel laid the paper aside. "I spoke earlier of vigilance. What would you say to an assignment in that field?"

Leonid made no reply. In itself, his transfer was a routine army matter, involving nothing of necessary interest to "competent organs."

"Minusinsk is in an exposed position," Kamarovsky said into the silence. "Any infiltration must be prevented. Our vigilance not only preserves the integrity of the regiment stationed there, but also thwarts industrial espionage in the mining areas. It's important to identify anti-Soviet elements both among the soldiers and among the local civilian population. Such elements are troublemakers and enemies of the people."

"What form would such an assignment take?" Leonid's eyes fell on the book *Secret Front*. The title took on a new meaning.

"Your rank would entitle you to live in the quarters reserved for higher-ranking officers and to eat in their mess hall. That's an important advantage. The assignment would also entail a flexible allocation of your duty time. And of course, your special field of activity would have a positive effect on your pay."

"I mean the practical part of my work." Tension made Leonid sit there stock-still with his knees pressed together.

"This intelligence work requires you to select an internal staff of collaborators, whose task it is to provide you with information. You draw the necessary conclusions, write up reports, and forward them to us."

From the day when Anna revealed to him that she was working for the state security agency, it had been clear to Leonid that, sooner or later, he'd be drawn in, too. He didn't condemn her, but he couldn't forgive her for not having told him sooner.

"I'm grateful for the honor of having been taken into consideration," he said formally. "However, I find ordinary regimental service sufficiently demanding. More difficult assignments would be beyond my capabilities at this time."

"Ah, well, we don't want to rush into anything," Kamarovsky replied affably. "It's an unexpected offer. I understand that. You should give it some thought and—of course—consult with your wife." His smile was so insolent that it infuriated Leonid.

"Thank you, Comrade Colonel. I'll think it over," he said. When the Colonel nodded, Leonid rose to his feet, saluted, and made an about-face.

"Lieutenant." Leonid, heading for the door, heard the voice behind him. "You've forgotten your book. I shall expect your answer in a week."

Leonid had neither spoken to Anna about this conversation nor reported to the Colonel after the week had passed. He'd simply kept silent. His transfer to Sakhalin had come through a month later in the form of marching orders passed on to him without explanation. Leonid had never again heard from Colonel Kamarovsky.

There were sounds outside, and then men entered the building. Before the knock on his door, Leonid was on his feet, clad in his weather gear and ready to go. The first man to enter his office was Staff Sergeant Likhan Chevken, the alpha male among the men and the only Nivkh. As a member of one of the indigenous peoples of Sakhalin, he couldn't become an officer in the Red Army, but he was the person best qualified to command Leonid's frontier troops. Chevken had served in the company the longest; he was a soldier, mechanic, sailor, and medic, all in one person. He was familiar with all of Sakhalin's natural phenomena and spoke all the dialects of the island. Chevken was short and round; his dexterity, tenacity, and fighting spirit were not immediately apparent. At the same time, he was the personification of gentleness, the only man in Leonid's troop who didn't make him feel that he wasn't entitled to lead it. "So we're doing the security check first?" Likhan Chevken asked in a tone that implied the existence of a better solution.

"What do you suggest?" Leonid asked.

"Maybe we could work in parallel," the Nivkh replied. "Three men can inspect the cutter while the others prepare for the salvage operation."

Leonid didn't act as though he first had to ponder Chevken's suggestion; the man was always right. The captain divided his men into groups and gave the order to move out.

The men left the barracks ten at a time, bracing themselves against the wind. It looked as though they were about to stagger straight to the edge of the abyss, but in reality, they were heading for the elevator that was hidden behind a rock overhang. The steel cables sang. The mounts for the guide rails had been driven into the stone a yard deep, yet Leonid got nervous every time he had to descend into the void that lay beneath the veils of sea-spray, fog, and drizzle. He stood as far to the rear of the elevator cage as he could, clinging to the grille. Before Chevken, the last to enter, stepped inside, he used a remote-control device to start the diesel motor, which was located in a bunker at the base of the elevator. The gears engaged with such a jolt that Leonid was afraid they were in free fall, but the metal cage slowly went into motion and slid down the face of the blackly gleaming cliff. When, after riding down in silence, they arrived at the bottom, the men dashed out into the storm and began running around busily. Since the elemental roar made speech impossible, they communicated with hand signals; like a bunch of deaf-mutes, Leonid thought, as he struggled toward the last of the three boats. He'd already been through the procedure: The first of the inflatable dinghies carried a load of steel cables, which would be transported to the site and made fast to the cutter; men from the second boat would mount balloons, which after being inflated by remote control would lift the grounded vessel's cargo and hold it in equilibrium. Leonid would sit in the third boat, which served as a backup in case something happened to one of the other two. He felt for the weapon under his oilskin. In spite of the ice storm, a smile crossed his face; he wouldn't be so careless a second time.

Having ascertained with relief that Likhan Chevken would steer his boat, Leonid helped drag it into the water. The sandy fairway had been artificially constructed; other than that, the only land feature far and wide was sheer rock. The breakers immediately buffeted the light boat, yanking it away from the land, but Chevken gripped a line, held it steady, and motioned to Leonid to jump in. Irritated by his own clumsiness, Leonid awkwardly took his place amidships and held on with both hands. Chevken and another man sprang nimbly into the boat, paddled like mad, and started the outboard motor as soon as they reached the proper depth. When Chevken set the dinghy on course, a mighty wave plunged under it, thrusting its nose perpendicularly into the air; but the wonder of those boats was that they always stayed on top of the water. For a few daredevil seconds, the dinghy balanced on the crest of the wave and then rushed down helter-skelter into the next black trough. Leonid tightened his stomach muscles—a vomiting skipper was out of the question. He hoped with all his heart that the first salvage attempt would be successful; otherwise, they would have to launch the crane ship, a nearly impossible undertaking in such a turbulent sea. Leonid knew his men. They'd work until they dropped to remove the obstruction from their harbor. In the worst case, the cutter would have to be blown up.

While Leonid was squinting against sleet and spray, Likhan Chevken, barefaced and open-eyed, drove the boat out of the cove. Already the leftmost of the Three Brothers was coming into sight; Chevken skillfully steered around the sharp-edged, jagged rocks. Beyond them, the scrap-iron cutter appeared, lying aslant like a rusty arrow thrust into the seabed. The other two dinghies were bobbing toward the freighter, but they yielded the right-of-way to the commander's boat. Chevken fired off a flare, which was answered by a flashing signal from the cutter, inviting them to come aboard.

A rope was let down from the stern into the water. The storm lifted the rope and flung it against the ship's side. Chevken cast out a boathook and maneuvered his vessel alongside the ship. Leonid peered into the raging sea-spray. The distance between their boat and the grounded ship looked immense; however, he stood up, grabbed the auxiliary rope, and swung one leg onto the rung; the other leg was still standing in the inflatable boat. Chevken called out, "Now!" and already the wave was upon them, driving the boat toward the open sea. Leonid made a false step, slammed against the ship's rump, and sank up to his hips in the water. The icy cold robbed him of breath; he pulled himself up the rope ladder with both arms, found a rung, and started to clamber, uncomfortably aware that the arrival of a Soviet frontier patrol officer ought to have looked different.

It was a pretty good bet that the cutter was carrying not only scrap iron but smuggled goods; the reception its crew might give their rescuers would not necessarily be friendly. Leonid made sure that his men were close behind him, reached the lopsided railing, and pulled himself on board. In such weather, every formality was dispensed with; the ship's mate led the way for Chevken to follow. Leonid wiggled his toes in his boots, which had taken on a quantity of ice water. The bulkhead leading to the wheelhouse opened, and a cold gust of wind blew the visitors inside.

The captain of the cutter was a bearded man with Kyrgyz eyes. "You're bringing some shitty weather with you," he said to Leonid by way of greeting.

"You're in a restricted area," said Leonid, disinclined to make small talk. "Your ship is blocking the entrance to the harbor," he went on, as if he were telling the captain something he didn't know.

"I radioed to say we'd sprung a leak."

"The harbor entrance must be cleared as quickly as possible. We're initiating a salvage operation." Seeing only two others in the room, Leonid asked, "How many men do you have on board?"

"Fourteen, Captain." The commander of the freighter put on a show of obsequiousness.

"Call them together," Leonid ordered. By then, the third member of his group had also arrived. "I'm going to inspect the ship. Bill of lading and logbook, please," he added, a little more courteously. "Tell your people to have their papers ready. Any foreign nationals?"

The captain shook his head. "All Soviet citizens."

"Soviet citizen?" Leonid pointed to the helmsman, whose skin was almost black.

The mate answered for him. "He's a Tuvan from the Yenisei valley."

Leonid placed himself in front of the captain. "Open your cargo hold."

"As you wish, Comrade." The captain took some keys out of a metal box. "One bulkhead, however, is sealed."

"According to your radio message, you're carrying only scrap iron. Why the sealed bulkhead?"

"I couldn't say. The stuff was brought on board and sealed as per the shipowner's instructions."

Leonid turned to Chevken and asked, "Do we have the Geiger counter with us?" The Nivkh nodded. Leonid then ordered the third man to begin salvage operations. The man took out a walkie-talkie. Leonid didn't feel that he was under any threat from the crew, but the sealed bulkhead made him uneasy. It wasn't unusual for shippers to enhance the market value of their freight with contraband. The captain of the cutter couldn't have given much thought to the possibility that his ship would get into distress, and he would try to prevent the confiscation of his cargo. Leonid's hand rested on his holster. Although he'd never had to use his service weapon while on a mission, the pistol was the object of his special care. The reason for his attention lay half a year in the past.

Shortly after Leonid's duty on Sakhalin Island began, the garrison was struck by a severe earthquake. The tremors started after midnight. Jolted out of sleep, Captain Nechayev didn't figure out at first what was happening. His iron bedstead was vibrating and the lamp above him swaying back and forth as though someone had given it a good push. Leonid turned on the light. Shadows flitted over the walls and the furniture. The quarters he was in had been built at ground level without any special anchoring. It was late summer, and the weather was pleasant; Leonid looked outside and saw soldiers in their underwear and others with their pajamas tucked into their boots. Wearing his uniform trousers and a pair of slippers, he left the building and watched from the parade ground as the trembling earth sent the wooden barracks into strange convulsions. Here a window burst into pieces, there a roof crown fell off or a wall collapsed outward, exposing the interior like rooms in a dollhouse: bunk beds, chairs, tables with liquor bottles rolling off of them. Leonid hurried to a briefing with the major, who ordered him to have his men fall in properly. Leonid, who hadn't yet been assigned to the technical unit, passed the order to his sergeants. A few minutes later, the platoon under his command had fallen into line as directed. Leonid allowed the men some time to sort out their equipment, and while they were doing so, he realized that he'd forgotten his own military belt, complete with sidearm, in the barracks. He dashed back and found his leather belt and holster, but his service pistol was gone. Recently—only a few days ago—he'd taken it out to clean it, and so there was only one possibility: His pistol had been stolen. Leonid put on the rest of his uniform, including the empty holster. While he inspected his troops, he tried to determine from their faces which of them might be the thief. Officially acknowledging the theft was unthinkable; a soldier could be guilty of few faults worse than getting his service weapon stolen.

The next morning, while the cleanup was under way, Leonid spoke to the most senior of the sergeants and asked him how one could replace stolen pieces of equipment. "Buy them," the fat man said. His face looked as though it were set in aspic. Leonid knew that the black market was illegal but tolerated, since officers, too, profited from it. Proceeds were distributed from top to bottom.

So what did the captain need, the sergeant wanted to know. Leonid named a hard-to-find sanitary article and was handed a piece of paper. The address written on it was in Yuzhno-Sakhalinsk, the island's chief city.

"People who aren't in uniform get better prices," the fat sergeant counseled him. "The man to talk to is Yevchuk."

After going off duty, Leonid changed his clothes and took the bus to Yuzhno-Sakhalinsk. Some men from his company, also on their way to town, inquired whether the captain was looking for a good time. For appearances' sake, he asked them to recommend a nightclub.

Yuzhno-Sakhalinsk was a town that had sprung up quickly, with the usual mixture of four-story apartment buildings and ground-level wooden houses. The administrative centers of the state oil and gas holding companies stood out like palaces in the cityscape. Leonid bought some smoked fish from a street vendor, and as he ate it, he was struck, as he'd been when he first arrived, by how many Koreans he saw, visible proof that Asians had decided to remain in the Soviet Union after Sakhalin was liberated from Japan.

The address the sergeant had given him wasn't far from the train station. When Leonid got there, dusk was already falling. The building he was looking for took up the entire block and seemed, at least outwardly, to be a large store that sold seeds and fertilizer. Leonid looked around the official stockroom and said to the only clerk that he'd heard one could also buy spare parts for toilet facilities there.

"We're about to close," the man said gruffly, taking off his work smock.

"Is Yevchuk in the building?"

The clerk looked the visitor over, found him unobjectionable, and acknowledged that he himself was Yevchuk. "What do you need?"

At first, Leonid stuck to his story and inquired whether the store carried a certain kind of ball valve.

"Maybe so, maybe no," said Yevchuk. Then he led Leonid into the real stockroom. "You have to look for it yourself."

Leonid was ready for anything; nevertheless, the size of that warehouse amazed him. He saw displayed, on some five thousand square feet of floor space, all the basic necessities that were in such short supply elsewhere: dishes, housewares, canned goods, furniture, entire bathrooms, closets, even musical instruments. The largest section contained automobile parts. About twenty people were rummaging around in the items on the display tables; some customers clutched exhaust pipes or generators or dashboards in their arms. Yevchuk led Leonid to the toilet section, which wasn't so well stocked—cracked toilet bowls, rusty pipe couplings. Relieved at being unable to find what he wasn't looking for, Leonid casually asked what the weapons inventory was like.

"Who did you say recommended this place to you?"

The captain in civilian clothes named the sergeant and declared, in plain language, that he—Leonid—was looking for a good pistol.

"Don't have any."

Leonid had expected this response and indicated that he was prepared to pay a premium to anyone who could help him find what he wanted, but it was only when he pulled a small roll of ruble notes out of one trouser pocket and thrust them in the other that Yevchuk decided to take a chance. "In that case, we have to go down one floor." He opened a door, made certain that nobody was following them, slipped in behind Leonid, and locked the door from the inside. Saying, "Our rifle selection is bigger," Yevchuk turned on a light and presented the armory.

Leonid concealed his amazement. The weaponry on offer before him would have sufficed to arm an average-sized company: everything from assault rifles, sorted according to their year of manufacture, to component parts for light artillery pieces. The items displayed for sale were all in excellent condition, not damaged or substandard goods but modern equipment that was missing from the military's inventories.

"Pistols are over there."

Leonid went to the display table. After a brief glance, he knew his weapon wasn't on it. "These seem positively antique," he said, not looking at Yevchuk. "Don't you have anything newer, anything that's come in recently?"

"New acquisitions must be treated first."

"Treated?"

"You don't want to buy an item that can be traced."

Leonid understood. "Ah, the serial number."

"Our weapons have never had such a number," Yevchuk said with a smile.

"I'm kind of in a hurry," Leonid said, unrelenting. "What would it cost me to buy a pistol with a serial number?"

"We've never had such a case." Yevchuk's suspicions had immediately reappeared.

"Please do me this favor." Leonid extracted his money roll, peeled off a bill, laid it next to a revolver, and turned away. When he looked at the table again, the banknote had disappeared.

"I'll see what came in yesterday," Yevchuk explained. "Wait here."

He wasn't gone five minutes before returning with a cloth bag that contained two weapons. Yevchuk placed them on the table for Leonid's inspection. He recognized his pistol at once.

"This one's an ornamental piece," Yevchuk said. "It belonged to a colonel. You see the initials on the barrel? And that's a one-aught-six, standard issue for the armored infantry. It's got a good feel in the hand."

Leonid's pistol had been unloaded. He patiently let Yevchuk explain to him the workings of his own weapon, seemed to hesitate before his two choices, and asked about the price of the colonel's pistol. Yevchuk named a sum that was unquestionably too high.

"In that case . . ." Leonid put the colonel's gun aside. "I'll take this one, then."

Yevchuk offered a price break for the more expensive pistol, but Leonid didn't waver. They haggled a while longer. In the end, Leonid bought his weapon for the equivalent of a month's pay.

"We could still file off that number real quick," Yevchuk offered. His customer thanked him but declined, asked if he could have the cloth bag for carrying the piece, and left the store as quickly as possible.

Relieved at having evaded disagreeable consequences, Leonid examined his surroundings. The streetlamps were just coming on. This part of town was quite lively, with people going in and out of the little bars around the train station. Leonid decided to take the late bus back to Korsakov, stuffed the cloth bag containing his recent purchase into an inside pocket, and strolled off into the evening. The soldiers he saw were wearing linen uniform jackets, which were a rarity on Sakhalin even in summer. A couple was having trouble with their motor scooter; to save face, the young man had his girlfriend sit on the scooter and started pushing both machine and girl up a hill.

Leonid felt like having a drink. He made sure the pistol was securely stowed away and stepped into a corner bar. It was furnished in the style of a yurt: Larch poles ribbed the ceiling, giving the impression of a tent; pelts and art objects adorned the walls; only the bare concrete floor broke the illusion. The waitress, who was wearing a yellow silk jacket, offered the guest a seat at a table already occupied by a family. Leonid wanted to sit by himself and said that he'd be glad to wait until one of the smaller tables was free. There was no bar, so he leaned against the wall and ordered vodka; then, sipping his drink, he looked around him.

Although it was a workday, people had dressed up for their restaurant visit. There seemed to be about as many Nivkhs as nonnatives of the island; at one table, for example, there was a Russian family, and some Koreans were sitting at the one behind it. An older man turned his daughter's wheelchair around and pushed it toward the exit. Leonid signaled to the waitress that he'd take over their table, but just as he reached it, he collided with someone who'd had the same idea. It was a woman, and she was rubbing her shoulder.

"Forgive me, I didn't see you."

"I've been waiting longer than you."

"Certainly." He turned away.

"Is anybody with you?" Leonid shook his head. The woman pointed to the only other chair. "Well, then . . ."

She looked older than he and was wearing black trousers and a red jacket with darts that combined with her pinned-up hair to produce a somewhat insolent effect. He noticed the man's wristwatch on her arm. They took their seats, and Leonid looked around for a menu. "There are only three dishes," she said. She opened her jacket, revealing a collarless lab coat underneath. "Smoked fish, smoked meat, and smoked whale. Everything's too highly seasoned, but it's edible."

"You come here often?" The pistol was pressing against his chest, but he didn't trust himself to transfer the weapon inconspicuously to another pocket.

"When I have to eat fast. The hospital's only a block away."

"That's where you work?" The lab coat wasn't right for a nurse.

"Alas, it is." She looked over at the waitress, who came smiling to their table. "The Number One," the woman said.

"For me, too," said Leonid, falling in with the company. "And tea."

"How do you know what the Number One is?"

"Well, you surely didn't order whale, did you? What do you do in the hospital?"

"I'm a butcher," she answered, adding, when he stared at her in surprise, "under the circumstances, what I do can't be called surgery."

"You're a surgeon?"

"A visiting surgeon. In a few months, I can go back home."

"Where's that?"

"Yakutia."

"In eastern Siberia? And you're looking forward to that?"

"It's cold," she said, "but our hospitals aren't as prehistoric as the ones here." She exchanged her knife and fork. "In Yakutsk, I work as a doctor should. Here I'm glad for a day when chickens don't stray into the operating room."

Their food arrived. When the woman tucked in hungrily, Leonid saw that she was left-handed. "You're not from here," she said.

"How can you tell?"

"You have the big-city look."

He cast his eyes down. "What does the big-city look like?"

"It looks like you know better. About everything." She chewed. "Moscow, Leningrad?"

"Moscow. You're eating too fast."

"I know, it's not becoming." She drank some tea. "I'm Galina Korff."

He took his first bite. "An unusual name."

"Believe it or not, my grandfather was the last governor-general of Sakhalin."

"So how did you wind up in Siberia?"

"How, indeed. We had a revolution. After that, governors weren't very popular." She looked at her watch. "My whole family was exiled."

"You were allowed to study at a university even though your grandfather was a counterrevolutionary?"

"Only a smug, arrogant Muscovite would ask such a question." She wiped her mouth. "Incidentally, what you're eating there is whale meat." She stood up. "I have to get back."

He put down his fork. "You perform operations at this hour?"

"The electricity's more reliable at night." She buttoned up her jacket. "During the day, the lights flicker constantly. Sometimes we have to run the heart-lung machine by hand."

"You're exaggerating, right?"

"Of course. What's your name?"

"Leonid Nechayev." He pushed his plate away. "Are you here every evening?"

"Why do you ask that? You want to flirt with me?"

He wiped his greasy mouth on the back of his hand. "What makes you think that?"

"You're the type," Galina said. "What do you do?"

Leonid noticed that the people at the next table were pricking up their ears. He reached the waitress before Galina did and paid the check. "If you permit me, I'll walk along with you," he said. They left the eating place together. It was a friendly night, and contrary to his usual custom, the captain felt lighthearted. "Which direction?" he asked.

Galina stood still and said, "First you have to tell me what you are."

"I'm an army officer. Stationed in the south, in Korsakov." He scrutinized her to see whether this admission put her off.

"You're wearing a wedding ring, Leonid," Galina said, and started walking up the hill. He remained at her side. With every step, the pistol beat against his chest.

Metallic noises indicated that the men outside were busy with the salvage equipment; a steel hawser was being secured to the cutter's hull. Captain Nechayev's hand was still on his weapon. He wanted to hold Galina Korff's face in his memory, but try though he might, it faded. In his imagination, Galina's features were replaced by Anna's—her cheekbones, her nose. Galina's lips were more scornful, her eyes more mysterious.

They went down the ship's rope ladders. Leonid had Likhan Chevken go first; behind them, the third man in their team provided security for the inspection. They reached a bulkhead with a sign that read CARGO HOLD. NO SMOKING. Leonid wondered what could be flammable in there. Peering through the hatch, he saw that the storage space contained scrapped motors; diesel oil and gasoline formed shiny puddles. The last bulkhead was locked with steel wire and the room sealed with a leaden plate.

"According to your bill of lading, you're carrying nothing but scrap metal," Leonid said to the ship's captain. "Why is this area locked up?"

"That's how the shipowner wanted it."

"I'm officially breaking this leaden seal." Leonid told Chevken to approach; the Nivkh was holding a bolt cutter at the ready.

"Without my consent."

"Your protest is duly noted." Leonid gave Chevken a sign. One clip sufficed to sever the wire, and the sergeant opened the bulkhead.

"After you," said Leonid to the captain. The latter made no move to turn on the lights. Leonid asked Chevken for a flashlight and stepped through the doorway. This hold smelled not of iron and oil but of wet newsprint. He switched on the overhead lights. Except for three pallets stacked with cardboard boxes, the room was empty.

"That's all there is, Comrade," said the captain, trying to play down the discovery.

"Open them."

Chevken unclasped his knife and cut through the straps around one of the boxes. He pulled out an illustrated magazine and handed it to the captain. The magazine's name wasn't written in the Cyrillic alphabet; a girl lounged under the letters. A quick flip through the magazine left Leonid in no doubt as to its contents. He found a red and blue pennant on the back cover.

"From Denmark," he said, as if that explained everything.

The ship's captain reiterated his assertion that he'd had no knowledge of the content of those boxes and that they were the shipowner's responsibility. Leonid chastised the captain for neglecting his oversight duties and called upon him to follow along voluntarily to the commander's office; otherwise, Leonid said, he would have to place him under arrest. The contraband would be confiscated. In his secret heart, Leonid regretted not having brought more men with him; in the face of any genuine resistance, he and his team would be seriously outnumbered.

He heard the sound of footsteps on metal, and the officer who was directing the salvage appeared in the hold. Leonid was informed that the cutter had been tied up and made fast, and that the operation must begin at once. Leonid left a man behind to guard the contraband and, accompanied by the captain, left the bowels of the ship.

The sky had cleared, but the wind was blowing as hard as ever. The cutter was surrounded by inflated buoys, and his men were circling it in their rubber dinghies.

"We have to start! The tide's lifting the ship!"

And in fact, with a harsh, grating sound, the cutter went into motion. Although she seemed at first even closer to capsizing, she quickly righted herself, and her dripping bow sprang out of the water. The dinghy drivers sped toward the cutter's stern. Leonid saw one of them bellow into his walkie-talkie; three hundred feet away, somebody started the winch. Thick steel cables rose slowly through the sea-spray, winding around the hull from both sides, stiffening, and pulling taut. The cutter was shaken by tremors, there was a shrieking and roaring of metal, but nothing moved.

"Hold that tension!" shouted the man in the dinghy.

"Two more waves," Chevken said to Leonid. "Look over there—the Brothers are already going under."

In fact, only the noses of the black, ship-wrecking rocks could still be seen. The cutter settled down, the vibrations slowed and dwindled, and ropes and air cushions produced stability.

"Here she comes!" Leonid heard someone cry out. "She's climbing, climbing . . ." The rubber dinghy drove off, made a loop, and approached the stern again. Many voices shouted, "There it is," and at the same time, the dinghy driver steered his boat back around to avoid being rammed by the upward-lurching cutter.

Chevken came up to Leonid as he leaned on the railing. "We're afloat."

"Well done!" Leonid shouted before turning around. Just as he did so, the captain of the cutter tried to make his way to the helm stand. "Where do you think you're going?" Leonid asked.

Chevken stood in Leonid's way. "He has to take the helm," the Nivkh explained in an undertone. "He can use the rudder to help us with the salvage." The cutter was shaken by a jolt as the winch pulled her in the desired direction. "We still have to get through the Brothers without wrecking the ship."

"Shall I start the engine?" the sea captain asked. He waited until Leonid took his hand off his weapon.

"Start it," Leonid said. Then he turned to the rail and cursed the day when such a landlubber as he had been saddled with such a command.

TWELVE

Leonid and the major were leaning over the opened box. "What shall we do with the contents?"

"Get rid of them," said Leonid's commanding officer, lost in thought.

Leonid noticed a mended area on the shoulder of his superior's uniform. Did the major do his own sewing? "Get rid of everything?"

"What do you mean?"

"We let the men divide up one of the boxes of Japanese belt buckles we seized. And the same with the razor blades."

The major went to his desk. "But this stuff isn't razor blades or Malayan whiskey."

"So we burn it?"

"I wonder . . ." The major pulled his uniform straight. "Do you know the little teahouse on the road to Kholmsk?" Leonid had heard of it. "Have you ever been there yourself?" The captain answered in the negative. "Many of the men drive there in the evenings. That has to stop."

"You want us to close the teahouse on the road to Kholmsk?"

"A teahouse is a teahouse. On the other hand . . ." The major sat down with a sigh; the complexity of the problem exhausted him. "Prostitution is forbidden. Pornography is likewise forbidden. I wonder which of them does more harm."

"There have been several accidents on the way back from Kholmsk," Leonid replied. "The road goes through the mountains, and the men are drunk when they drive home."

"Exactly." The major's face lit up. "Do you think the men would go to the little teahouse less often if we . . ." He waved his hand toward the box. Leonid's expression indicated a cautious affirmative. The major raised his chin. "Place a box next to the drink machine. Make sure that each man takes only one magazine. I don't want anybody trafficking in this stuff. And now send me the captain." He took hold of the cutter's documents and extracted her commander's identification papers. "A Kyrgyz. I could have guessed."

Back in his office, Leonid gave orders for the deployment of the forklift truck. The pallets, together with their load of boxes, were transported from the ship to a land carrier, handed over to the members of a second unit, and by them conveyed to the incinerator. Leonid had his men cast every box, except for one, into the fire. Before anyone had taken a look inside the boxes, they disappeared into the flames and were burned up within minutes.

After lunch, the sergeant informed him that the surviving box had been placed, as ordered, next to the drink machine, and that an hour had passed before the first soldier noticed it. Shortly after that, the sergeant reported, the "special consignment" was completely depleted. He inadvertently gave himself away when he declared he hadn't expected Danish girls to be so scrawny.

Leonid concluded that this was the right evening to take another trip to the island's capital city. Since his meeting with Galina, he'd been in the yurt-restaurant twice and waited for her to come in, but in vain. By now, almost half a year had passed; the surgeon had probably completed her work in the hospital and gone back home.

Leonid reserved a vehicle from the motor pool. It had been dark for a long time when his duty day ended. He brushed off the better of his two uniforms, put on a clean shirt, and polished his boots. He agreed to take along two soldiers on the condition that they would have to get back to the base on their own. The two young fellows were eagerly looking forward to the binge they were about to embark on. The weather was horrible; some lower stretches of the road were mud wallows, and at higher elevations, in the mountains, it was snowing hard. As they were finally descending into the valley, Leonid almost drove into a stalled truck. The driver was trying in vain to lever his vehicle's wheel and axle out of the mud. The captain, delighted not to be carrying a towing rope—soiling his going-out uniform was not to be thought of—happily offered the driver a ride to Yuzhno-Sakhalinsk.

He dropped off his passengers in the vicinity of the train station and parked his car in the neighborhood where the little eating and drinking places were. Unhurriedly, he entered the yurt-restaurant and drank a glass standing up. Then a table came free; Leonid ordered whale meat with rice and ate slowly, drinking tea between mouthfuls. When he stepped outside again, he found that an ice storm had swept through the streets and covered the pavement with a layer of reflective film. Amid pedestrians who were holding tightly to one another, falling, and laughing uproariously, Leonid groped his way up the hill. Eventually, he reached the Yuzhno-Sakhalinsk Hospital, walked across the dimly lit lobby, and asked at the reception desk for the Department of Surgery.

"You're in the Department of Surgery," the nurse replied. She wore a cylindrical cap on her head.

"May I speak to Doctor Korff, please?"

"I'll see if I can reach her," the nurse said, picking up the telephone.

In excited anticipation, Leonid paced a little, careful not to make any noise. Placards in display cases urged compliance with the rules of good hygiene.

"Here at the front desk," he heard the nurse whisper into the phone. "No, he's alone."

Not a minute later, a swaddled figure came barreling around the corner: blue lab coat, blue pants, hair confined under a bonnet, white surgical mask covering mouth and nose. "You?" Galina Korff put her hands on her hips. "You're scaring my girls!"

Leonid waved his arms in irritation. "How?"

"You come in here wearing your parade uniform, you march up and down. A person might think the army was occupying the hospital."

"I wanted . . . no, please, I'm not here on duty," he babbled, turning toward the nurse.

"So what do you want?" Galina's eyes flashed up at him impatiently.

"I've been looking for you."

"Are you ill?"

"No."

"Lonely, then." She smiled under her mask.

He didn't want to have such a conversation in the nurse's presence. "Any chance you might have a minute later?"

"Cases are waiting for me: one internal bleeding, one severed thumb." She pointed to the row of benches that was screwed into the wall. "If you're willing to wait that long . . ."

"How did the thumb accident happen?"

"Circular saw in the fish factory."

He shook off the bloody image. "Won't you be too tired after all that?"

"That depends on you." She pushed her bonnet back and scratched her head. "See you later, then."

Leonid nodded to her departing shape, and only then did he become aware of how weary that day had made him. I talked to my son on the telephone, he thought; I didn't perform too hopelessly during the salvage operation, and I confiscated some dirty magazines. Now I'll be happy to sit here without having to *undertake* anything. He watched Doctor Korff disappear through the next swinging door.

THIRTEEN

Usually, Petya had long been asleep by now, but not this evening. Viktor Ipalyevich had turned on all the lights in the apartment and taken out the folders containing his work of the last many years. Table and sofa, shelves and windowsill were covered with pages of poetry, some typed on thin paper with the poet's old typewriter, but most handwritten on sheets torn from pads of graph paper. As Anna dried the dishes, she cast an occasional glance at the show. Grandson and grandfather were shuffling around the room, pausing often to stand still and admire, like visitors gazing devoutly at the memorabilia in the Museum of the Revolution. They stopped in front of the radiator, and the old man pointed to a sheet. The boy read aloud,

Uncoil your march, my lads!
Up, Blue Shirts! Storm the ocean!

Viktor Ipalyevich clicked his tongue, as though he were tasting wine. "No, that's not it," he said. He pointed to another poem. Petya got up on tiptoe so that he could see it better. He read,

I can't cast off the unmoored boat;
The shadow's step eludes my hearing.

"I like that one especially!" Anna called from the kitchen.

"You do?" Her father was already in the doorway. "Do you think it would be a good idea to open the cycle with it?"

Anna dried the carving knife. "No. Too mellow, too playful. For the beginning, you need something militant."

"Just what I was thinking!" He disappeared. "Come on, Petya, the fighting poems are on the sofa."

Several folders were searched through and the collections *With Prometheus' Hands* and *Spare Us the Eulogies!* taken out. The boy began to read one poem after the other, but his grandfather wasn't satisfied. "Old-fashioned," he growled. "The war was still going on when I wrote that." He nervously ran his hands over the table. "We need . . . it should be . . . damn it, I ought to write a new one!"

Petya yawned and tried to turn the page, but the old man prevented him. Viktor Ipalyevich glanced at the poem skeptically, read it in silence, and laid the page on the table. In the kitchen, Anna listened to his voice:

Where does Russia begin?
In the Kurils, or on
Bering Island, or at
the Kamchatka Peninsula?
Russia begins in her goodness,
her truth, her perseverance.
There is the source, and it flows
not from her mountains
but from her great works.
Friend, it flows from you!

Anna waited for his commentary, sure that he'd find something to criticize here, too, but silence reigned. Then she heard Petya jumping on the sofa. Curious, she turned the water off and stepped into the room, where she found her father standing with his hands on his hips and gazing down at the poem. "Not bad, I have to say. After so many years, still . . . not bad." It had been a long time since Anna had last seen him smiling as he was at that moment. "Petyushka, this will be our first poem," he said, nodding thoughtfully, as though his own judgment were not absolutely trustworthy. "Come on, we'll put it in a new folder."

He received no answer. The boy had curled up among the papers like a puppy and fallen asleep. Anna wiped her hands off, picked up Petya, carried him to the sleeping alcove, and undressed him.

"I'm going to see about getting a new curtain tomorrow," she said, touching the place where the culpable curtain had formerly hung. Her father was sorry that he would soon have to put an end to all sound and movement in the living room. On tiptoe, he continued his journey through his own verse. The two of them, father and daughter, performed an odd ballet: Viktor Ipalyevich stepped mincingly to the radiator, while Anna dodged him in order to bring Petya to the bathroom. When they returned to the room, her father retreated from the sofa and let her pass on her way to put the boy to bed; then she went to the kitchen, where she turned off the light. Viktor Ipalyevich was going through a bundle of papers, his back to her, as she undressed and threw on her nightshirt. Then she slipped past him and sat down in the alcove.

"We did right to throw away that dusty thing. I believe Petya started sleeping better already last night." She gazed at her son, who'd wasted no time falling asleep again; his head rested on a freshly washed towel, which Anna, in accordance with Doctor Shchedrin's instructions, had spread over the boy's pillow. "Would it bother you if I did a few more things in the kitchen?"

Viktor Ipalyevich didn't lift his eyes from the pages before him. "Of course not," he said. Seeing him so happy and hopeful gave Anna a satisfaction she had long gone without. She glided barefoot over the floor.

It had been only a week since Dubna, but her impressions of the place were already fading away. The ice race on the Volga came into her mind. She thought about the fork-tongued orphanage director, and about Adamek and his pipe. Would Nadezhda and her Irkutskian ever hear from each other again? As for the scientific achievements she'd been granted the opportunity to marvel at, Anna scarcely gave them a thought. In retrospect, it was hard to comprehend the time and effort it must have cost Alexey to smuggle her into the atomic city. They had been together one evening and one drowsy afternoon; wouldn't they have been able to accomplish that more comfortably in Moscow? And why doesn't he get in touch with me, she thought fretfully. She had something of great importance to tell him. During the morning shift, while she was perched high up on her scaffolding, Anna had decided to make a full confession to Alexey; he must know everything. It would be up to him, and not to Kamarovsky, to decide how things would proceed. As she was loading a trowel with mortar, this solution had suddenly seemed utterly simple to her, and the freedom of her decision had made her completely euphoric.

From an inner corner of the sleeping alcove, Anna watched the poet as he gathered his folders together, made sure that he was also bringing tobacco and liquor, and disappeared through the kitchen door. With the velvet curtain gone, Anna could hear all too clearly every sound coming from the kitchen. Her father banged open the ashtray's metal lid. When he struck a match, it was like a whiplash. She turned off the light and got under the covers. Since Petya was taking up most of the bed, she lay on her side. Was she just telling herself that he was breathing more freely, or was it actually the case? Tomorrow, she'd continue the cleaning operation. Now that she knew the cause of Petya's suffering, she saw dust traps everywhere, in every cushion, in the window curtains, in the tablecloths.

From now on, she'd sweep the floors and wipe off the windowsills every day and dust the radiators once a week. How wonderful it was that her boy was not terribly sick but only allergic; she felt capable of overcoming his affliction by dint of her own efforts, and it was a good feeling. She curled up her legs and intertwined them with Petya's little calves. From the kitchen came the breathy murmur of her father's whispering:

He ended up a thousand versts deep into foreign territory,
Where a bullet struck him down.

Anna was surprised at how much there was to know about dust. For example, she'd discovered that dust wasn't as dry as it was reputed to be; in fact, dust mite larvae throve best in a moist atmosphere. She'd learned that dust was indifferent as to whether it lay on cheap or costly material, but that expensive velvet welcomed dust and therefore dust mites, whereas cheaper synthetic fabrics hindered the proliferation of the little beasts. Leather was an enemy of dust, and wool offered itself as a hatchery. In winter, the mites procreated more slowly, because the air was so dry. Soon, however, when the temperatures were rising and water returning to its liquid form everywhere, breeding season for the dust creatures would begin.

The next afternoon, Anna incurred her father's displeasure by opening the window in the living room for several minutes. "Stale air can lead to mildew formation," she declared, repeating a principle enunciated in the book that Doctor Shchedrin had given her.

Not for the first time, Viktor Ipalyevich watched loose pages of his poetry fluttering around the room and sent Petya chasing after them. He was putting up with the dismantling of his familiar surroundings, but in his view, the comfortable living room had already been stripped bare. At the moment, his daughter was cleaning the back side of the radiator; she'd tied a brush to a long stick and was on her knees, stubbornly scrubbing away. After her return from the early shift, she'd taken an old toothbrush to the spaces between the floorboards, removed the newspaper from the broken window panes, and covered them with plastic film. Now, as she was about to take down the wall rug, he voiced his objection: "That's enough!"

"I'm going to put it in the cellar."

He pointed to the homely piece and asked, "How long does it have to stay in exile?"

"Until Petya moves out of here," she answered vaguely.

"I gave you that rug as a wedding present. The pattern of interlocking circles was supposed to be a symbol of your enduring love." Viktor Ipalyevich insisted that the rug should remain where it was until a substitute wall adornment could be found.

Showing that she was ready to discuss the matter, Anna asked, "A picture, a map, a poster?"

"Something beautiful! There's nothing left in this apartment worth looking at!" With outspread arms, he gestured toward the dust-free wasteland around him.

"I'll think of something," Anna said. Then she turned her attention to pulling out the first of the nails that fastened the rug to the wall.

"The rug stays there."

"For Petya's health!" she cried out.

"Petya's temperature is back to normal, and his eyes are clear." Anna's father took up a position in front of the wall rug, as though he meant to defend it. "By the time the spring's over, he'll be playing soccer!"

Anna decided not to defy his prohibition. After all, he was right: Shchedrin's diagnosis was proving to be accurate, the medicine was starting to work; she simply couldn't believe in Petya's miraculous transformation, not yet. She'd become cautious insofar as good luck was concerned. Anna put her tools in a box and stowed it under the kitchen sink. In the living room, her father turned on the television.

". . . The crucial aspect of matter is not its materiality, but the fact that it consists of a number of miniature processes that stand in mutual reciprocity with one another."

Anna straightened herself and pricked up her ears; she knew that voice.

"Matter does not 'be'—it *happens*."

Where had she heard that sneering inflection before? She was in the living room in two steps—and she hadn't been wrong. The program was *The Open Ear*, the woman who hosted the show was moving slips of paper about, and across from her sat Nikolai Lyushin, casually dressed in a suit but no tie. Anna stretched out her hand in surprise.

Viktor Ipalyevich raised his head. "It's some physicist," he explained.

Lyushin's name appeared in a graphic. In her next question, the interviewer mentioned the atomic city. Anna crouched down beside her father.

"Do you know him?"

"I may have seen him in one of the institutes."

Lyushin told the interviewer about a research study undertaken by colleagues from Vietnam and the German Democratic Republic, working under his direction.

"Vain fop," said Anna's father. "Will you look at how affected he is? Watch him reach for his glass. He's positively basking in his own significance."

That word *vain* opened Anna's eyes. Vanity. Lyushin was good-looking, intelligent, and witty, but his vain attitude negated everything else.

"Overbearing jackass." Her father stood up to change the channel.

"It's almost over." She wanted to watch the rest of the interview.

Leaning with one elbow on the television set, Viktor Ipalyevich remained still. The interviewer regretted that her time was just about up. Lyushin seemed indignant at being ushered out so soon. "You referred to the enormous amount of resources that a complex like Dubna swallows up," he said, interrupting his hostess. "Let me assure you that the fundamental research will pay for itself. In my Institute, we have assembled the greatest collective of theoretical physicists in the world. Because one thing is certain: There's nothing more practical than a good theory." He smiled into the camera and tossed his hair off his forehead. Then, quite concisely, the hostess thanked him. The program's theme music drowned out her closing remarks.

"It's been a long time since I've seen such a popinjay," Viktor Ipalyevich said, changing the channel. Some light entertainment program was announced, and he sank back into his chair. Anna remained silent as she stepped to the window. In Dubna, Lyushin had impressed her as an eccentric genius; in the television appearance she'd just seen, he'd exposed himself as a narcissist. Strange, she thought. Logically, you'd figure someone whose profession required him to look into the very deepest parts of things would be a profound person himself. On the television screen, a pop duo, tightly entwined, sang a hit tune.

FOURTEEN

Anna's patience was tried for six days before the Deputy Minister contacted her. During that period, she cast aside her decision several times, mostly at night, when the reasons for her proposed course of action seemed dubious. She told herself that Alexey would repudiate her as soon as she revealed the whole truth to him. But by day, her plan regained strength. Alexey was a tactician—wouldn't the possibility of a double game appeal to him? Deceiving Kamarovsky was what frightened Anna the most. He gave her the inexplicable impression that he was omniscient. Hadn't he expressed his benevolence toward her by the pardon—no other word would do—he'd procured for her father? Anna had the impression of moving through a minefield. The feeling that had gradually come to predominate in her was revulsion at her double-dealing. Alexey treated her obligingly, affectionately, and he seemed sad and sometimes lost. There was nothing in his character that justified Anna's betrayal of his trust.

Surprisingly, the location he chose for their next appointment was not his apartment but the Proletarskaya subway station, near a busy marketplace and the bustling Volgogradsky Prospekt. Alexey's message was so spontaneous that there was no time for Anton to pick her up; Anna had to take the subway.

"Things are difficult at the moment," Bulyagkov informed her by way of greeting. He was wearing his jacket open, a rare thing for him to do, as he was always fearful of getting a cold. "The Twenty-fourth Party Congress is pure chaos." He pointed to a narrow passage behind the station, and they went toward it.

"The leadership opened Pandora's box when they raised the minimum wage. If they institute the new rate in Central Asia, the comrades in the Far East will want the same thing. If we yield to them, then we'll have the Kazakhs and the West Siberian raions on our necks." He took Anna's arm. "Kosygin knows that, of course, but he's ready to screw everything up for the sake of his pretty balance sheets. And so he appeals to every department to see whether it can make still more cuts and save still more money!"

The unusual location of their rendezvous and the short notice she'd been given unsettled Anna, and so did the Deputy Minister's chattiness. He seemed merry and nervous at the same time. Before they reached the market, they passed a group of young men who were standing around a monument. Each of them was looking in a different direction.

"Shall we?" Alexey guided Anna toward the group. As he'd expected, they were selling books, which were spread out on the monument's pedestal. While Anna merely glanced at the covers of the books, Alexey rummaged around in them with obvious pleasure. For the most part, they were works of tsarist literature, their ornate leather bindings inscribed with golden letters, along with books by ostracized authors.

"Well, what do you know . . ." Alexey said, brandishing a small, well-thumbed volume: *Freedom Comes Naked.* Grinning with pleasure, he opened the book and showed Anna a photograph of a considerably younger Viktor Ipalyevich. "These people act as though they think your father's some kind of forbidden, esoteric figure." He handed the book to her. "Here, it's a gift."

She accepted, letting him have the pleasure. He complained about the price to the vendor but was unable to reduce it by so much as a kopeck. When he reached for his wallet, he discovered that he'd forgotten it and waved to Anton, who was hovering about unobtrusively.

"I don't much like taking you to such a place," Alexey said. "But believe me, Annushka, this is the only way we could see each other."

A furious hissing interrupted him, and he leaped aside in fright. Anna laughed; a gander was flapping around the Deputy Minister. The fowl, attached by one leg, was yanked back in midflight and landed on its belly. It screamed and stuck out its pointy tongue. Suddenly, as though some magic had transported them to another world, Anna found herself surrounded by hundreds of animals. Just ahead of them was the cat section: predominantly newborn kittens curled up in cardboard boxes.

A boy noticed Bulyagkov's searching look and sprang over to him. "These are all house-trained," he declared, opening the sales dialogue. He lifted up a cat's tail with one finger and proudly pointed out that the animal was a first-class tomcat. Bulyagkov waved him off. "Black cats with white checks are rare," the boy said, determined to hold on to his potential customer.

"I don't need a cat." Alexey declined the invitation to pet the animal and pointed over to the market's main alley. "There," he said to Anna.

First they had to walk past hundreds of dogs. A litter of Ovcharka puppies was crawling around the sawdust-covered bottom of a crate; only their drooping ears bore any resemblance to the full-grown sheep guardian. Black terriers barked. Smiling, Bulyagkov indicated a basket with Tsvetnaya Bolonkas, which were on offer in four different colors. Their owners extolled the value of their wares: "The tsar's lapdog," they said.

The air was filled with puling and whimpering, and the vendors' stands were surrounded by Muscovite women on the point of yielding to temptation. Every cardboard box belonged to a cute little girl who swore she'd let her darling puppies go only if they found a good new home. In the next section, ornamental fish stared out of plastic bags, and a mountain of squirming worms awaited the next fishhook. In the end, when Anna and Alexey were simply surrounded by howls, whimpers, and the frantic beating of wings, he explained to her the reason for this visit to the market.

"Isn't that more like a gift for a child?" Anna asked.

"Medea wants a living creature in the house." Alexey stood in the midst of innumerable cages and looked around. "As I said, I know I'm not being very gracious, taking you along with me to buy a birthday present for my wife. She wants someone to be glad when she comes home. Since that someone's obviously not me . . ." He was drawn to the bright, colorful parrots. "Medea's afraid of dogs, rabbits shit everywhere, and so I was thinking about a bird, maybe one like this." He waved a finger at a red bird with a black beak, which bent down from its perch and snapped at him.

"And who's going to take care of it, then? Animals need attention." An affectionately mocking look from Bulyagkov spurred Anna to defend her point of view. "If you're never home and neither is Medea, that's animal abuse."

"Then I'll get a pair." He took a few steps to where the songbirds were. Green, yellow, and white, many with raised crests, they sat in their cages.

"I've heard those are illness-prone."

"So why are they singing in the cold?" Bulyagkov inquired about the price of a pair of young woodcocks, but in the end he opted for two nondescript canaries because the vendor threw in five packages of birdseed. Anton paid, picked up the cage, and followed Anna and Alexey as they continued to stroll around the enormous market. They passed paddocks with sheep and goats; a young elk was on display as an attraction. Anna was beginning to fear that she'd never have a chance to speak about the real reason for their meeting when Alexey took her hand. "How much time do you have?" he asked. "Shall we get something to eat?" He turned to Anton: "Do you know a restaurant around here?"

"I'd like to speak to you in peace," Anna said.

"You can't do that while we eat?"

"Couldn't we sit in the car?"

"Then Anton will have to pick up something for us," Alexey said, grumpily complying with her request. "Where did we leave the car?"

Anton went ahead of them, clasping the birdcage to his chest. The black ZIL was parked in a side street.

"Make sure you get some shashlik," Alexey said to Anton as Anna climbed into the limousine. "And beer would be a good idea, too."

Anton put the birdcage on the front passenger's seat. Suddenly plunged into semidarkness, the birds fell silent. The Deputy Minister sank down on the seat next to Anna, and the door closed. "These Central Committee sessions are killing me," he muttered. "I never used to be affected like this. I could work night and day when we were preparing a Five-Year Plan." He turned his head. "Can you tell me why I'm so tired?"

"You eat the wrong things." She noticed how heavily he was perspiring and pulled the scarf off his neck.

"I've done that forever. It's never hurt me."

"When the Party Congress is over, you should go out to the dacha and take some time off." Anna was nervous; one ill-judged word in the beginning could ruin everything. "Spring's coming," she said, stroking his temples. "Maybe what you've got is springtime lethargy."

"In March? That would be strange."

Anna made a first, oblique attempt to steer the conversation: "Have you ever hinted to Medea that you see other women?"

"Why should I?"

"You mean you've never had the urge to tell her the truth?"

He raised his head. "And who'd be served if I did that?"

"Isn't the truth desirable in itself?"

"In most cases, the truth hurts. It can only benefit the person who tells it."

His sober tone unsettled her, as did the way he suddenly started scrutinizing her.

"It takes strength to keep quiet, Anna." He drew her to him; her head sank against his shoulder. "Maybe keeping your mouth shut is a stupid male virtue, but it's a virtue all the same."

She was tempted to leave it at that. Why did she want to ease her conscience? Because she was hoping for Alexey's forgiveness. Would she actually be telling him anything new? Of what use would it be to him to know that Anna reported their conversations to the KGB? And yet, it didn't make very much sense to keep up a lie just because the truth was unattractive.

She tried another tack: "The only person I ever see around you is Anton," she observed. "Don't you have any protection besides your driver?"

"How do you mean?" He smiled, but she could sense the alertness in his gaze.

"I never see any security people around you."

"Do you have the impression that I'm in danger?"

In the long silence that followed this question, Anna realized that the time for innocent chatter had passed, and that she couldn't go back. "After all, you're . . . you're an official of the Soviet Union, a bearer of state secrets."

"I was in danger once upon a time, many years ago now. And ever since then, everything that's come afterward has seemed harmless." He undid the top button of his shirt. "I've never told you about my family."

His offer to talk about himself was so unexpected and direct that Anna could muster only a mute nod.

"My father was a civil servant in Kharkov, in Ukraine. He carried out the land surveying for the kolkhozes in an enormous area between the Donets and the Don. His frequent travels and his influence as a survey official made him a prominent person. He was a veteran member of the Party and presided over the provincial government." Alexey looked outside, where a group of young people was strolling toward the limousine. Not imagining that they were being observed through the window, the youths stopped right in front of Bulyagkov.

"Then came the time when Vradiyev's show trial was being prepared. He'd been relieved of his positions as premier of the Ukrainian SSR and chairman of the Economic Affairs Council, accused of nationalistic deviation and factional activity, and called upon to perform unsparing self-criticism. Our family had the bad luck to be related to Vradiyev on my mother's side. At every show trial, care was taken to produce a series of subordinate accomplices who were prepared to testify against the main defendant. My father was assured that the Party was aware of his achievements and that the court would declare a verdict in appearance only; as soon as the dust settled, he would be granted a pardon. When my father declined to take part in the deception, he was arrested."

Alexey kept his eyes fixed on the window, so that he seemed to be telling his story to the young people outside.

"My father was chained hand and foot and put in an underground cell. His jailers pumped in cold water through the ventilation flaps and threatened to drown him. There were other tortures, and he held out against them all for three months before he signed the first confession. In the meantime, we had no news of him. My mother asked all his old Party friends for help; they either remained silent or pretended they were out. She received a single letter from the prison. The handwriting was my father's, and the letter stated that he wasn't afraid. He was a true communist, he wrote, and as such had nothing to fear from the state security agency, which was the iron fist of the people's democracy and struck only its enemies. When she read that letter, my mother knew he was lost. She sent my sister and me to an uncle who lived outside Ukraine. Because my uncle forbade me to show myself in public until everything was over, I had to break off my pursuit of a degree in physics." Alexey turned to Anna. "For a whole year, I did nothing but wait."

"What happened to your father?"

"He had to go through the whole procedure. Right on cue, before the trial began, the state security headquarters turned into a convalescent home; the accused were given medical care and nursed back to health.

In the meantime, a committee of experts had underpinned the vague accusations against Vradiyev with technical details. He was now accused of economic sabotage. The defendants who'd been selected for the show trial were assigned teachers, with whose help they learned question-and-answer texts and—above all—their confessions, verbatim and by heart. The same scripts were distributed to the judges. The trial took place in the Great Hall of the People's Army Retirement Home in Kharkov. The only spectators allowed in were dependable factory delegates, people from the kolkhozes, and some selected journalists. The proceedings were broadcast on the radio."

Outside, one of the young people inadvertently bumped against the window. His friends suggested that he should watch what he was doing and pulled him away in the direction of the market. Meanwhile the impact had awakened the birds, which ventured a duet of tentative peeping.

"First, Vradiyev's prestige was dragged through the mud," Bulyagkov went on. "He was 'convicted' of being a separatist of long standing who'd collaborated with fascist stool pigeons in the early forties. But before he admitted his guilt and requested the severest penalty, the squad of co-defendants had to perform. My father spluttered during his confession and lost his power of speech. The court was obliged to have the confession that had been tortured out of him read aloud."

The two birds were now merrily chirping away; inside the automobile, their singing sounded unusually loud.

"Vradiyev was sentenced to death by hanging. Many of the others received a sentence of life imprisonment. My father got twenty years of forced labor." Bulyagkov leaned toward the cage and tapped its bars with one finger.

"And then?" Anna gazed at the white nape of his neck.

"It was a good year, nineteen hundred and fifty-three," he said, smiling and turning around. She didn't grasp his meaning right away. "On the fifth of March, nineteen hundred and fifty-three, Stalin died. The following December, my father was rehabilitated. Not long after that, in an anti–show trial, the Ukrainian chief prosecutor, as well as the head of the secret police, was condemned and executed."

"And how about you?" she asked, touching his shoulder. "Did you go back to Kharkov?"

"I went to Moscow with my uncle."

"Why? I don't understand . . . When did you see your father again?"

"We buried him a month after he was set free."

The birds had fallen silent; tilting their little heads, they stared at the big human finger that was stroking the bars of their cage.

"His back was completely crooked, he had a broken thigh bone that never healed right, and he couldn't digest solid food anymore. He died from a rapidly spreading deterioration of his mucous membranes. Soon after his funeral, my mother and sister left Kharkov, never to return."

Anna removed her hand from his shoulder and leaned against the car door. "Why are you telling me this, Alexey?" She examined the man beside her: bent forward, sweat running down his temples.

"To make it clear to you how much better everything is these days. Up until the end, my father remained a fervent member of the Party, because he believed in its self-healing powers. Today, things like what happened to him don't happen anymore. Checks on governmental entities are strict and correctly applied. Such an arbitrary power apparatus would be impossible in our Soviet Union."

Anna nodded, but the situation made her uneasy. She'd wanted to make a confession and unexpectedly found herself listening to his. The shadowy, enclosed space, the frightened birds, and Alexey, divulging incidents that, in current practice, remained unmentioned . . . Why this sudden openness? What was his purpose in revealing himself to be the son of a convicted enemy of the people? Back at their first appointment, Alexey had suggested that he'd climbed as high in the nomenklatura as a non-Russian could. Didn't his story throw a different light on his career? Anna sat there, rigid with concentration, while a silhouette approached the car.

The front door opened and Anton climbed in. He was balancing two paper plates of shashlik in one hand.

"No beer?" Bulyagkov asked.

Anton handed them the food and then pulled two bottles out of his overcoat pockets. "There aren't any glasses."

The Deputy Minister thanked Anton and told him to drive off; they'd eat on the way, he said.

"Careful, hot," said Anton, then he closed the door and started the engine.

FIFTEEN

March was uncommonly mild. Now that it was getting dark later and later, Anna found her workdays longer than usual. She caught herself holding a dripping brush in her hand and gazing out of the window openings of her worksite, searching the treetops for signs of the first green fuzz. A long spring lay ahead of her, followed by a difficult summer, and an interminable stretch of time would pass before the leaves would begin to change color again. In the bus on the way back, she enjoyed the last rays of the sun and told herself as persuasively as she could that something had to happen during the coming season, something that would steer her life in a new direction. But didn't everyone wish for that at the beginning of every spring?

When she got home, she didn't feel like cooking, so she put some bread and sausage on the table. Petya was having an afternoon nap. As though they were on a picnic, Viktor Ipalyevich took out his clasp knife and started cutting the sausage into thin slices.

"Do you remember the show trials?" Anna asked as she stirred the buttermilk.

"What put *that* in your head?" He looked at her with red-rimmed eyes; since his volume of poetry had started to take shape, he often worked until dawn.

"What was it like, when they were going on? I really don't know anything about them."

He peeled back the sausage casing so that he could cut more slices.

"You were a prominent person. Weren't you ever called before any of the tribunals?"

"Who would want to question a poet?"

"You were the 'Voice of Smolensk,' the 'Conscience of the Comintern Youth,'" Anna said, quoting from the inscriptions on his decorations. "Your testimony carried weight."

"I'd like to know what kind of significance that still has today," he said, instinctively lowering his voice.

She poured out the buttermilk. "Who else can I ask, Papa? Nobody talks about those things."

"What would be the point? That's all in the past. The Party healed itself from within a long time ago." The sausage slices were getting thinner and thinner.

"Politicians' platitudes," she said, teasing her father with one of his own favorite expressions.

"I never gave testimony at any trial." Viktor Ipalyevich thought for a moment and then added, "However, my doctor was arrested."

"What do you mean, your doctor?" Neither of them had yet touched any of the food on the table.

"Doctor Mikhoels. He removed my ganglion." Viktor Ipalyevich showed Anna his right hand. "It was on my middle finger. I could hardly hold a pen. The doctor was pretty arrogant, but a good surgeon. It was the only time I was ever questioned." He held up a slice of sausage to the light. "Respected physicians were accused of forming a conspiracy. It was said that their goal was to poison the Party leadership."

"Why in the world would they have wanted to do that?"

"It's hard to understand without some historical context. The fact that they were doctors wasn't really the point." Viktor Ipalyevich took a bite and chewed it. "In 1948, the Jewish Anti-Fascist Committee was dissolved. From that time on, *Pravda* referred to Jews as 'rootless cosmopolitans.' Of the thirteen physicians who were arrested, eleven were Jews. Doctor Mikhoels was among the accused."

"And did you testify?"

He shook his head. "That wasn't required of me. There were plenty of others available for that."

"What happened to Doctor Mikhoels?"

"He remained alive, but he had to leave Moscow. They took him somewhere."

"But . . . haven't you ever wondered . . . ?"

"No." He threw himself against the back of his chair. "I'm an artist. I represent my own minority."

"What happened to Doctor Mikhoels's family?"

"I have no idea. His family—what does that matter to you?"

"Were they deported, too?"

Her father was getting exasperated. "The man operated on my ganglion! How should I know what happened to his family?"

Anna spread butter on a piece of bread and cut it into small pieces. "If a non-Russian had a family member who was convicted in one of those trials, what would have been his lot? The survivor's, I mean. What do you think would have happened to him?"

"A non-Russian? No, no. Most of the Jews who were executed were native Russians."

"But let's suppose a Hungarian—or a Ukrainian, say—had someone in his family who—"

Viktor Ipalyevich laid both hands noisily on the table. "Enough. I don't know where we're supposed to be going with all this. Let's eat, and then Petya and I are going for a walk."

"What's a Jew, Grandpa?" The gentle voice came from the depths of the sleeping alcove.

"That's what you get," Anna's father grumbled to her. Then he called out, "If we come across one, I'll show him to you."

The small, tousled head appeared. Petya climbed up onto his chair, and his mother served him his bread and butter. "How are you today?" she asked, stroking his head.

"I feel good. Can we go to the park?" he asked Viktor Ipalyevich.

"Sir, yes, sir!"

"I think I'll have a bath today." Anna examined her fingernails. If she soaked in the tub long enough, the paint spatters would (she thought wistfully) go away.

A short while later, she heard the two walkers heading down the stairs. Anna was glad to have some quiet minutes alone in the apartment. The water wasn't as hot as she'd hoped; she heated some in the kitchen, added it, and dropped her clothes. Although the bathtub was too short, she lolled in the water as best she could. Her plashing echoed from the tiled walls, and she quickly grew weary. She soaped her hands and laid them on her stomach. What if—she wondered—what if Alexey made his confession to forestall mine? The thought was there suddenly, as if it had arisen from the steam. Anna breathed more slowly. Had he figured out what she wanted to confide to him, perhaps because he'd *known* it for some time already? She raised her head, and water dripped from her hair. The idea seemed so ridiculous that she laughed out loud. Why the devil had he told her about his father's trial? Alexey Bulyagkov was a Deputy Minister: For the first time, Anna pondered why, when he actually made more decisions concerning research planning than the Minister himself, Alexey was still that Minister's deputy. Did the reason have to do with his family background, with his father's long fall from grace? A non-Russian, she thought: a Ukrainian. When she was a Pioneer Girl, she'd been taught the doctrine of the different national paths to socialism. In her workaday life, she'd realized that the lovely theory she'd learned had been supplanted by the concept of Russian primacy. Even in such a subsidiary structure as Anna's building combine, the nationalistic hierarchy was unmistakable: Although Valdas, the Lithuanian, coordinated every building project the combine undertook, the Russian, Yarov, remained the foreman. When the materials elevator broke down, it wasn't the Russian women you saw hauling the heavy buckets, it was the Kazakh women. In the light of this observation, Anna found it remarkable that a foreigner, a Ukrainian who'd fled to Russia, had made it all the way into the Central Committee's inner circle.

She noticed the wrinkled skin on her fingers; her bath had cooled. Since she couldn't get any warmer water to flow out of the faucet, she reached for a bath towel. She'd just finished drying her legs when the telephone rang. Of late, most calls had been for Viktor Ipalyevich; the government press had questions about setting the poetry volume, and the poet was under pressure to deliver the completed manuscript. Expecting that she would have to apologize for her father, she picked up the phone.

The man at the other end of the line spoke Anna's name without introducing himself. "I'm in Moscow," he said, as though this piece of information alone sufficed to explain his call.

Had she not seen that television program a few days previously, she wouldn't have had the remotest chance of identifying the caller by his voice.

"Don't you know who I am?" Nikolai Lyushin asked, practically insulted.

"How did you get this number?"

"You can figure that out yourself, Comrade." He laughed harshly. "I know hardly anybody in Moscow, and I have no plans for this evening. Therefore, I'm taking the liberty of inviting you to come out with me."

"Why would you ask me out?"

"During our little quantum chat, you showed that you were a gifted student. And so I thought you might wish to delve into the subject a little more deeply."

The safest answer would have been a no, but Anna's time in Kamarovsky's service had taught her to sense, behind every event, the presence of another event. Lyushin's proposal had a deeper meaning, and it was her duty to fathom that meaning. Therefore, she said, in a slightly friendlier voice, "It's already pretty late."

"Don't they say that the Moscow night never ends? I'm sitting in the Ukraina hotel, and I'm bored to death. Just a little drink, Comrade—what do you say?"

"I have to wait until my son comes home. Can you call back in half an hour?"

Delighted by her apparent change of heart, he said, "I'll reserve the best table!"

She stood before the sofa, lost in thought. Although the floor was wet under her feet, she didn't go back into the bathroom, but instead opened her telephone book. There was only one person she could ask for advice. Anna looked up the number of the *Moscow Times*. She hadn't talked with Rosa since Dubna, and so some flowery greetings would have been in order, but Anna skipped all courtesies and went directly to Lyushin's offer.

Rosa asked, "Has he said what he wants?"

"At first, I thought he'd come here on account of this television program, *The Open Ear*. Don't you and your colleagues know why he's in Moscow?"

"So Lyushin turned on the charm for you, did he?" Rosa asked, ignoring Anna's question. "But he knows about you and Bulyagkov."

"Should I turn down the invitation?"

"Well, he can hardly start fumbling with your underclothes in the restaurant of the Ukraina hotel."

"It's not so far from the restaurant to his room."

Rosa laughed. "You mean you'd like to go there?"

The question was a provocation, and still it caught Anna off guard. At that moment, it became clear to her that she had a real desire to put a few scratches on Nikolai Lyushin's dandified facade. She asked, "Shall I inform Kamarovsky?"

"I'll take care of that," came the immediate reply. "You should go to the Ukraina. Wouldn't you enjoy turning one of the most brilliant heads in Russia? Order the most expensive things on the menu, bleed the fellow dry, thank him for a pleasant evening, and leave the restaurant." She hesitated, as if there were still something she wanted to say. "Call me up afterward, no matter how late it is."

While Anna, now dressed in a bathrobe, was wiping up the wet floor, she heard the light footsteps and the heavy footsteps mounting the stairs together. She went to the little vestibule, opened the door for father and son, and looked for her blue dress in the wall closet. Petya told her about a dog that had almost been run over. When Viktor Ipalyevich saw that Anna was making preparations to go out, he turned ostentatiously to his poems.

SIXTEEN

The physicist was wearing a light gray suit inappropriate to the season and a blue shirt that set off his burnished hair. He'd secured one of the much-requested alcove tables. As Anna approached, he stood up and offered her the seat next to his on the upholstered banquette. She noticed that he had unusually small ears and a liver spot on his chin. Anna sat on the wooden chair across from him.

"The band's behind you if you sit there," he said, trying to change her mind.

She looked over her shoulder. The little stage was empty. "How did you get my telephone number?"

He laughed. "The hotel in Dubna keeps complete lists of its guests. There was only one house painter in your delegation. Riddle solved."

Although a glass of wine was in front of him, Anna got a whiff of stronger liquor. She spread her napkin on her lap.

"It's wild game week in this restaurant. They have Manchurian venison. Or would you prefer capercaillie, or maybe some hazel grouse?"

"What are you having?" she asked, ignoring his display of esoteric culinary information.

"We could start with snipes' eggs. The red wine is outstanding."

She consented to the wine but wanted no appetizer. There was noise behind her as the musicians came back from their break and took up their places. Their stage was a semicircular platform thrusting out from the back wall and festooned with flower garlands. Above the stage hung a chandelier.

"Tell me about your father," Lyushin said, opening the conversation. "What's he writing at the moment?"

"How do you know who my father is?" Anna had been happy to learn about the hotel guest list, because it meant that Alexey had nothing to do with Lyushin's information, but now mistrust was reawakened.

"You gave yourself away!" Lyushin plucked happily at the corner of the tablecloth. "Your name was on the delegation's list as Anna Tsazukhina. Even in Moscow, Tsazukhin's a rare name. Can we expect a new volume of verse from your father soon?" he asked, raising his voice to be heard over the music, which began as he was speaking.

The band launched into a lively tune, and the sudden volume of sound put an end to the conversation. The waiter came and took their order, bending down and bringing his ear close to Lyushin's mouth. "We'll have Manchurian venison," the physicist said. Then, addressing Anna again, he asked, "Did you by any chance watch *The Open Ear* the other afternoon?"

They discussed the broadcast and the interview until the waiter brought a new carafe of wine and filled their glasses.

"You have a perfect neck," Lyushin said. As he leaned forward, she smelled the alcohol on his breath again. "I'm glad you came."

She drew away from his touch and asked, "What brings you to Moscow?"

"I have an appointment with the Minister tomorrow," he answered. His casual tone failed to mask his desire to impress her.

"Are you going to meet Bulyagkov, too?" Now that Lyushin had brought up the Ministry, Anna was certain that Alexey knew he was in the capital.

"Of course. Without your friend, no research project gets off the ground." He clinked glasses with Anna and drank.

"Will the Ministry give you the resources you need?" she asked, daring to probe a little deeper.

"I like to think about our afternoon in Dubna. When you were wearing nothing but a woolen blanket." His hand played with Anna's knife. "You were a joy to behold. For those of us who live in barren isolation, such sights are rare." Seeking an excuse not to look at him, she turned around and faced the bandstand, where the portly fiddler was beginning a passionate solo. "What shall we do afterward?" Lyushin asked. "Will you show me Moscow?"

"I work the early shift tomorrow." Even though Anna hadn't expected anything different, she was disappointed at the predictable course the encounter was taking. How nice it would be to be cuddled up with Petya in their sleeping nook right now, listening to Viktor Ipalyevich's sardonic commentary on the television offerings. She drank some of the heavy wine and let her eyes wander over the room, where every table was occupied.

"Is this your first time in the Ukraina?" Lyushin asked, interrupting her gazing. "Frightfully baronial, but still impressive, don't you think?"

All of a sudden, the situation appeared so grotesque to her that she stood up and excused herself. On the way to the ladies' room, she crossed paths with the waiter, who was bringing Lyushin's order of snipes' eggs. She hurried past the band and up some stairs; the female washroom attendant eyed her, calculating what sort of tip she might be likely to give. Anna leaned on a sink, stared at her reflection in the mirror, and washed her face with cold water.

A strange scene awaited her upon her return. Something had flown into the violinist's eye. He stood at the front of the bandstand, helplessly holding his instrument at arm's length, while his colleagues tried to remove the offending speck with their handkerchiefs. Entranced, the diners stared up at the stage, as though they were watching a group of acrobats performing a difficult trick. The fiddler cried out in pain and begged his comrades in God's name not to be so rough; then he sprang backward, fending off the others with his bow and shouting that he required medical attention. After a moment, he stepped forward again and began to speak, just as if his speech were part of the performance. "Please excuse me, but my pain is too great," he said. "Is there a doctor in this esteemed audience?"

Nobody responded to the violinist's appeal, whereupon he actually bowed and then, with both eyes tightly shut, staggered off the stage. The bassist took over as announcer and informed the public that it would unfortunately be impossible for the group to continue without a violin. The members of the band formed a row, faced the audience, bowed as their injured colleague had done, and left the bandstand, accompanied by irritated applause. They marched past Anna, who then returned to her table and found Lyushin eating with apparent delight.

"Most delicious," he said, holding out a skewered snipe's egg to her. A half-full glass of vodka was on the table in front of him; between bites, he tossed down the remaining half. "It's not only poets who are poetic," he declared in a surprisingly loud voice. "Some sort of lyricism is granted to every creative person. We scientists, for example, possess as much imagination as writers do."

The waiter brought another glass of vodka.

"How else could we have named the streams of cosmic elements 'proton showers' or 'electron sheaves'? In order to characterize the quantum numbers of particles that have existed only in theory until now, we ascribe *magical* properties to them. Theoretical physics is the poetry of the sciences!"

Anna looked on as her companion got steadily drunker.

"The poetic in us is the longing to see into the depths of things, to comprehend their connections, to call out to the passing moment and say, *Stay awhile!* Do you understand that, Anna?" It was obvious that he needed no encouragement to go on. "And I have succeeded!" He reached for his glass. "I *have* brought the moment to a halt. And I needed no Mephistopheles to help me do it!" He spoke the last words so loudly that a couple at a nearby table turned around. "Similar projects are under way in Japan and the States," he continued more softly. "But they haven't got as far as we have. Not even close. They can't come up with any conclusive formula." He pointed at himself with his fork. "I can."

Anna's initial irritation had turned into amusement, which now gave way to curiosity. "The last time I saw you, you said you'd failed."

"It depends on how one fails," Lyushin said. He pushed his plate away and treated himself to another swallow of vodka. "I need more time, more time! But the dogs are breathing down my neck. They're after me like hyenas."

"Who's breathing down your neck, Professor Lyushin?"

A man in a black overcoat approached the part of the restaurant where gilded columns screened off the recesses containing individual tables from the rest of the dining room. His upper body leaned forward from the waist as he headed toward his goal. Anna noticed him first. While she was still wondering why he hadn't handed in his outer garments at the cloakroom, he entered the circle of light shed by the chandelier. With his hat on his head, Alexey looked to Anna like a Party leader from the provinces. In the shadow of the hat brim, his eyes were invisible, but his nose and cheeks were red from the cold.

"Well, this is certainly a surprise," he said, coming to a halt in front of the table.

At first, Lyushin had trouble reconciling Bulyagkov's presence with that time and place. Holding his glass in his right hand, he pointed at the newcomer with his left as if he'd forgotten the newcomer's name. "What are you doing here?"

"That's what I was about to ask you," Bulyagkov said to Anna.

She felt as though she'd landed in a scene from some anachronistic farce. There sat Lyushin, the charmer, too drunk to function; there stood Alexey, the lover, who seemed to have caught Anna red-handed; and here she crept, the crafty serpent, getting what she deserved.

"How did you find me?" Lyushin asked.

"My Ministry pays your expenses," Alexey answered.

"Let's drink to that!" With irrepressible self-assurance, the physicist gestured toward an unoccupied chair.

"I must speak to you alone," Bulyagkov replied, glancing sidelong at Anna.

"Don't we have all day tomorrow at the Ministry for that sort of thing?"

"I was just about to leave," Anna interjected.

"Imagine, this is Comrade Anna's first time in the Ukraina," Lyushin said, switching to a conversational tone.

The waiter appeared behind Bulyagkov. "Your coat?"

"I'm not staying," the Deputy Minister replied.

A second waiter came up, pushing the serving cart. A silver platter was laden with steaming slices of meat, dressed with a greasy sauce and garnished with bay leaves and bilberries. The waiter began to distribute the portions.

"I'd rather not eat," Anna said.

The waiter paused with uplifted serving utensils.

"Please fetch the comrade's coat," Bulyagkov said, indicating Anna.

Whatever was behind Alexey's sudden appearance, she didn't like the way decisions were being made on her behalf. "Maybe I'll have a little taste, after all," she declared.

The waiter placed a plate in front of her, and for the second time she laid her napkin on her lap. Then she cut herself a piece of meat.

"We were discussing *The Open Ear*, the TV program," Lyushin said, trying to get a conversation going. "A nerve-racking interview. The subject was too much for the woman who moderates the show. She was in over her head."

Upon hearing this assertion, Bulyagkov took a seat. "You talked about your project on television?"

"Perhaps a bit, in a popular-science sort of way."

Anna saw the two exchange looks.

"The Minister will want to hear details from you tomorrow," Bulyagkov said.

"I have the documents with me." Lyushin stabbed his fork into a morsel of venison, brought it to his mouth, and chewed. Meanwhile, Anna, inexplicably ravenous, cleaned her plate.

"I'd like to go through the papers with you," said Bulyagkov, unbuttoning his coat and leaning back.

"Now?" Lyushin patted his forehead with his napkin.

"How are you getting home?" Alexey asked, tapping the back of Anna's hand.

"On the subway, naturally."

"Don't be silly. Anton will give you a ride."

"And what about you?" She didn't understand his sudden change of mood.

"I'll be here for a while yet. I've got some things to do."

"The three of us!" Lyushin said with a laugh. "Like the Three Musketeers! We should all go to a bar."

Bulyagkov gazed at him with cold eyes. "Comrade Anna surely has to get up early. And as for you, Nikolai, you'd best go to bed soon so you can sleep off your liquor."

"I find Moscow even more provincial than Dubna," Lyushin said with a sigh; however, when Anna stood up and accepted her coat, he didn't protest. "It was a pleasure, Comrade," he said. "Too bad we didn't have more time together."

"Thanks for the invitation." She wrapped her scarf around her head.

After he'd walked a few steps with her in the direction of the exit, Bulyagkov observed, "I believe you should thank the Ministry for Research Planning."

"I'd rather go home on the subway," she announced. The moment alone with him was disagreeable to her. Halfway to the door, he took her hand, squeezed it, and turned back without a word.

As she hurried over the richly patterned carpet, Anna tried to make sense of her departure. Had Alexey, insulted and offended at having found her with Lyushin, thrown her out? Had he turned up at the Ukraina only to speak to Lyushin, or had someone tipped him off about her? Anna went through the revolving door and into the cold night air, which hit her like a blow.

When Alexey returned to the table in the alcove, Lyushin was studying the dessert list. "Let's go."

"I've got a craving for something sweet—"

With unaccustomed violence, the Deputy Minister struck the menu out of Lyushin's hand. "You've had enough sweets for one evening." Like a dog only now perceiving the possibility of a beating, the physicist rose to his feet. Bulyagkov made for the steps to the mezzanine, where the elevators were. By the time the double doors split open, Lyushin had caught up with him, and they stepped into the elevator together. "Have you completely taken leave of your senses?" the older man barked as soon as the doors shut. "I don't care whom you choose to meet. But inviting Anna to this place was stupid and dangerous!"

"You can't believe that I asked your girlfriend here—"

"Shut your mouth." With a gesture, Bulyagkov directed Lyushin to push the button for his floor. "What did you tell her?"

"Nothing! In any case, nothing that she could have understood."

"So you told her something!"

"No, I didn't, I swear!"

"She's Kamarovsky's informant." Bulyagkov stepped closer.

"Then why didn't you get rid of her long ago?" Lyushin hissed.

For a moment, the Deputy Minister seemed about to punch the suntanned face beside him, but instead, he thrust his fists into his pockets. "I thought you understood the game. If you hadn't played Don Juan tonight, Anna would still be our best camouflage."

"I gave away nothing. What do you think I am?"

"I think you're someone who acts like an idiot whenever his dick takes over. Anna will report to Kamarovsky . . . she has to! And the old devil will draw his own conclusions." Bulyagkov smoothed his hair back and put on his hat. "Where are the papers?"

"In my room." Lyushin was holding tightly to the rail that ran around the elevator car.

"In the safe?"

"No, in the . . ." He paused, realizing that he'd made yet another mistake. "In my suitcase."

"I'll take them away with me tonight and put them in a more secure place."

The elevator doors slid open, and Lyushin staggered out first. "Please, believe me, I had no designs on Anna. I . . . I don't know anybody in Moscow, and she's such a charming person."

"The crucial question is whether Anna will continue to believe your story." Bulyagkov watched pensively as the other unlocked his door.

They entered the dark hotel room. Lyushin hurried to his bag and pulled out a briefcase. "There," he said, handing it to Bulyagkov. "You see, there wasn't anything to worry about."

The Deputy Minister turned on the lights and examined the combination lock. "Most of the time, the Minister limits his questions to the bare essentials. Speak only when you're called upon to do so." He held out the briefcase to the physicist and said, "Open it."

Lyushin dialed in the combination and took out two apparently identical folders.

"Which is which?"

"That's the folder for the Minister. And this one's for you."

Bulyagkov opened the folders and paged through the documents, comparing them. "Good." He thrust the folders under his arm. Lyushin lay collapsed on the sofa. "You'll come to the Ministry tomorrow at eleven o'clock sharp," Bulyagkov said. "We won't see each other again until the appointed time. When you arrive, I'll be with the Minister, and we'll be expecting you." He turned to the door. "And no more bars tonight, you understand?" He left without waiting for an answer.

SEVENTEEN

Anna didn't call Rosa Khleb that night, or the following morning, either. As she did every day, she took the building combine's special bus to Karacharovo, put on her work overalls, and together with her colleagues—all women—began her shift in the shell of the twelve-story building. She felt safe on the scaffolding. Here, there was no telephone; here nobody asked her to explain herself. Anna applied a coat of fine-grained plaster to the ceiling. *You have to call Rosa,* her sense of duty reminded her; hesitating any longer would arouse Kamarovsky's suspicions. Anna had no illusions about why she was stalling instead of following the usual procedure: She couldn't decide how to report Lyushin's drunken performance. Had he really given something away, or had it all been mere boasting? It seemed obvious that he was putting off the Ministry in order to gain more time and increased funding for his work. Fame and success were of great importance to him, and if he was withholding the results of his research, he must have reasons for doing so. Suppose Anna were to express her suppositions; who would benefit from that? Certainly not Nikolai Lyushin. Wouldn't his conduct be classified as irresponsible and harmful to the State? It's not your job to analyze information, she told herself. So why was she toying with the idea of portraying her date with Lyushin as an innocuous encounter? Basically, there was only one person toward whom she felt responsible: Alexey. As Lyushin's superior, it was he, first and foremost, who was being traduced.

She spread the plaster over the ceiling with circular movements. Although droplets of the stuff were sticking her eyelids together, she worked on, lost in thought. At the end of her shift, she locked up her tools, changed into her street clothes, and was bused back to the center of Moscow.

After getting off at Durova Street, she took the subway for two stops and went into a small notions shop near Gorky Street. Anna wasn't shopping for cotton or woolen fabrics, which was what most of the establishment's customers required; she was on the lookout for synthetic material. Before long, she found what she wanted: a slick blue fabric, which though unpleasant to the touch was made entirely from a fiber described by its manufacturer in Omsk as indestructible. As Anna lifted out the bolt of material, she flinched from the discharge of static electricity. She asked for a length of twenty feet, chose a tape, paid, and left the shop.

When she got home, instead of climbing to her fourth-floor apartment she knocked at a door on the first. The door opened, slowly and hesitantly. "I'm glad you're home, Avdotya," Anna said, greeting the shape in the semidarkness.

"Ah, Anna, well, well. I thought you were the mailman!" Avdotya said, shouting because she was hard of hearing. Anna, who had no desire to listen to the Metsentsev story, strode briskly and purposefully into the apartment. "I have something for you." She turned her head toward Avdotya so that the older woman could read her lips.

Next to the window stood the symbol of Avdotya's craft, the pride of her life: her own sewing machine. At the end of her long and meritorious service in the garment industry, the company had rewarded its retiring forewoman with the gift of an obsolescent model. As a consequence, Avdotya had been the recipient of a virtually unbroken series of commissions ever since her retirement. Since Metsentsev, the Party secretary for that district of Moscow, was also one of her customers, things went smoothly for her.

Anna laid her packet of material on Avdotya's table and said, "I need a curtain!"

"What?" Avdotya closed the door.

"A curtain, little mother!"

"I couldn't possibly start making it before next week!"

"But this is only Tuesday!" Anna unrolled the fabric.

"I have to turn the cuffs on thirty shirts. Then Ryukhin on the fifth floor wants me to alter his suit, and the Perth family has ordered a wall hanging!"

"My Petya needs the curtain!" Anna acted distressed. "He's sick, he's really sick. He's got some kind of nasty allergy. If I don't keep everything that sets it off away from him, then my boy can't get any air! This curtain will let him breathe freely!"

The old woman picked up the material and examined it with an expert eye. "Loosely woven," she muttered. "I'll need to make a double stitch."

"But look how smooth." Anna spread out the piece of fabric. "Three panels every six feet. How much work can that be?"

"What about the tape?"

Anna took it out of her bag. "It won't take you even an hour, Mother! And you'll be helping Petya breathe at night! Besides, the curtain will muffle Papa's snoring."

She negotiated the price in the same tone of voice, and Avdotya determined that Anna should check back with her in two days to see when the work would be finished. Relieved, Anna left the ground-floor apartment and mounted the stairs to her own. Halfway up, she stumbled and spent a few moments wondering about her lack of strength; then she realized she hadn't had a thing to eat all day long. She closed her eyes and leaned against the banister. When she felt better, she walked up the rest of the way, took off her scarf as she entered the apartment, and hung her coat on the hook.

"You're late." Viktor Ipalyevich looked up from the table. "I couldn't give your lady friend any information about when you might come home." With a movement of his head, he indicated the sofa. In front of the wall hanging sat Rosa Khleb. A stack of Anna's father's poetry collections lay on Rosa's lap, and the top volume was open.

"Good evening," she said. "With Comrade Tsazukhin's poems to read, the time flew by."

Speechless at this "house call," Anna looked from one of them to the other.

"She didn't want anything to drink," said Viktor Ipalyevich, by way of excusing himself for the fact that he had a cup of tea in front of him while Rosa had nothing.

Anna turned her head toward the sleeping alcove. "Petya's playing in the courtyard with the others," his grandfather explained.

"I never tire of reading the poems in *The Red Light*," Rosa said, holding up the battered volume.

"May I offer it to you as a gift?"

"What have I done to deserve such an honor?"

"I rarely meet any of Anna's friends." He looked at his daughter. "You usually get home at five."

"I bought the material for Petya's curtain. Avdotya's going to sew it for us."

During this innocuous conversation, Anna tried to grasp the urgency that lay behind Rosa's unusual visit. Was Anna's delay in reporting really that serious? Should she have called Rosa last night, after all?

"Will you have dinner with us?" Anna asked, in an attempt to clarify her visitor's plans.

"I'm afraid I don't have enough time. I just wanted a chance to chat with you, Anna." Rosa briefly arched her eyebrows. "I waited so I could at least tell you hello, but now I must be off." She put aside Viktor Ipalyevich's books, except for *The Red Light.* "I accept this with humble gratitude," she said.

"Wait a moment, I'll write something in it." He unscrewed his fountain pen and formulated a dedication. Rosa watched him, smiling as she did so, but Anna could detect her impatience.

"I'll walk you to the bus," Anna said as her friend was putting on her cap.

"That would be nice of you."

"Will you go and call Petya in?" Anna asked her father as she slipped into her overcoat. "I'll fix dinner as soon as I get back."

Rosa exchanged farewells with Viktor Ipalyevich; then she and Anna left the apartment together and went wordlessly down the stairs. At last, Rosa broke the silence. "Your father's a very pleasant man," she said.

"He can turn his charm on and off, whenever he wants. Did you meet Petya, too?"

"Viktor Ipalyevich pointed him out to me from the kitchen window. A sweet boy."

The preliminary banter was over. "I couldn't call you last night," Anna said. "Petya was still awake, and Papa was working on his poems."

When they reached the second floor, Rosa stopped. "Where can we go?"

"I don't know. There isn't anyplace around here."

Rosa pointed downstairs. At the turning between the ground floor and the cellar, there was a sort of niche, an element of fanciful building design left over from tsarist times. "Let's sit down there. The place would appeal to Star-Eyes." Rosa began to descend again. "You know his fondness for architecture."

The mention of Kamarovsky made it painfully clear to Anna that the time for her to reach a decision had arrived. Rosa's coming all the way to Filyovsky Park meant that the department must be particularly interested in Anna's report.

They came to the narrow recess, in which residents of the apartment building used to sit and chat during the summer months. The built-in wooden benches were worn smooth, and innumerable steps had scratched the stone floor.

Rosa sat down. "Lyushin left the Ministry only a little while ago. The meeting lasted longer than expected."

Anna dropped down onto the bench beside her.

"How was your evening?" Rosa asked. "What was his reason for calling you up?"

"What you suspected. He wanted female company." Anna was speaking softly, and yet she thought she could hear her whispered syllables wandering around in the stairwell like ghosts. She reported what the physicist had eaten and how much he'd drunk, and she even related the stupid incident of the fiddler who'd gotten something in his eye.

"Did Lyushin mention his work?" Rosa cocked her head so that she could better see Anna's face. "Did he talk about why he'd be paying the Minister a visit?"

"He wants increased funding for his research. I've already given Kamarovsky a report on that."

"Considering Lyushin's vanity, I'm surprised he didn't try to impress you with his accomplishments. He made no reference—none at all—to his research project?"

I have *brought the moment to a halt*, Anna thought, remembering Lyushin's words. *And I needed no Mephistopheles to help me.* "He probably didn't have time to bring it up before Alexey's unexpected arrival," she answered.

Rosa Khleb nodded. "The meeting was arranged between the two of them."

"And you sent me to the Ukraina even though you knew that?"

"I didn't know it yesterday. We got a tip today from someone in the Ministry. How did Bulyagkov behave? Like a jealous bear?"

"He remained surprisingly calm."

"He's a politician," Rosa said with a little smile. "Maintaining the facade—that's what the gentlemen on the Central Committee are best at." She clasped Anna's hand. "Wait until the next time you're alone with Alexey. I'm sure he won't be so calm then."

A noise made the two women turn around. A few feet away, a door opened, and Avdotya started shuffling toward the mailboxes. She noticed the other two only when she was right in front of them. "Good heavens! Who are you?" the old woman shouted.

"It's all right, little mother! It's me, Anna!"

"And who's with you? Come out of there or I'll call the police!"

"This is my friend Rosa," Anna said. "And this is Avdotya, the seamstress."

"We were just chatting," Rosa said to the old woman. "Just chatting a little, that's all."

"In the dark?" Avdotya shook her head and turned toward the mailboxes.

Rosa led Anna outside, where they spoke a few minutes longer. In the end, Rosa seemed satisfied and with a brief embrace bade Anna farewell.

"We should do things like this more often!" Viktor Ipalyevich was standing in a part of the apartment where Anna had never seen him before, namely, in front of the mirror. He'd taken off his cap—a rare occurrence in itself—and was occupied with arranging his hair. With the years, it had retreated from the crown to the back of his head, but Viktor Ipalyevich was running his finger through it as if it were a thick mane.

"Do what, Papa?" Anna ascertained that Petya wasn't back yet.

"People!" He twirled a pathetic little tuft sprouting from the middle of his bald spot and tried to give the strands a specific direction. "We should surround ourselves with people again, the way we used to. This reclusive life isn't good for us." He looked at his daughter in the mirror as though she were chiefly to blame for his hermitlike existence.

"Didn't you say you were going through a phase that made it impossible for you to put up with the outside world?"

"How can you take my gloomy nattering seriously?" He laughed, displaying his high spirits. "It took a visit from your friend to remind me that Moscow is out there! What does she do, your friend?"

"She works for a newspaper."

"A colleague! A fellow writer!" Viktor Ipalyevich shouted. "And she didn't say a word about that! She talked about my work the whole time." He turned his back to the mirror and twisted himself in an attempt to see how he looked from behind.

"Why isn't Petya here? Why didn't you go down and get him?"

"Do you know what I'm in the mood for? A party!" The poet pointed to his notebook. "Don't I have a good reason to invite people over for a party?"

"What people?"

"Haven't they been wondering for a long time what their friend Viktor Ipalyevich is doing? And I'll tell them: He's working on a volume of poems, and it's almost finished! That's why he wants you all to gather around him and celebrate this great event!" Overheated, he pulled off his woolen jacket and hung it over the back of his chair. "Of course, your lady friend will be among the invited guests."

Anna interrupted his flight: "What about Petya?"

"It won't hurt him to stay up a little later than usual one night."

"I mean now!" She stepped in front of her father. "Do you want him to stay outside until he catches cold?"

"Right, I have to fetch Petya," the old man said, nodding absently. "We'll invite everybody, all right? Uyvary and Madame Akhmadulina and good old Lebedinsky and Vagrich . . ."

"Writers?" she asked, unable to believe her ears. "You want *writers* to set foot in this apartment?"

"But that's what I've been talking about all this time." He put his hands on his hips. "Will you cook for us, Anna? Will you do that? I'll pay for everything."

"With what?"

"With this, my dear child." All at once, he was holding a piece of crumpled paper on which there were some handwritten figures.

"They've paid you something?"

"For the first time in nine years." He nodded without emotion. "A princely advance. I don't know anyone they've ever paid so well."

"Since when do you have this?" Anna held the check under the lamp.

"Two days now. I wanted to wait for the best opportunity to surprise you with it. Do you think your beautiful friend will accept my invitation?"

"Rosa?" Anna frowned. "If she knows that a bunch of banned writers will be gathering here, I think she'll be only too happy to come."

"Really?" He grinned without understanding what Anna was alluding to. "So the only question remaining is what you'll prepare for our guests."

"No." She picked up her scarf again. "The only question is whether you're going to fetch Petya home for dinner, or whether I'll have to do it."

"Petya, yes, right, he must be frozen stiff!" The old man jammed his cap onto his head, put on his coat, and headed for the door. "Ah, Anna, I'm so glad, this is really a brilliant idea. We'll put some life in this musty old place!" As he was about to go out, he turned around again and said,

Come see us tomorrow, uplift and gladden us!
Today's rain refreshed us, and the forecast is glorious.
And should we want stormy weather,
We'll make some together!

And with that, he ran out of the apartment.

EIGHTEEN

Over the following days, Anna tried in vain to get in touch with Alexey. Only after a week had passed did he contact her and suggest a meeting. It was the first time she'd ever been obliged to turn him down; the date he proposed was the very evening on which Viktor Ipalyevich planned to throw his party.

Anna's father used the occasion as an excuse to resume his distilling operations. Turning a deaf ear to all her warnings, he took to leaving home early in the morning, scouring the city for the cheapest potatoes, and returning laden with twenty-pound bags. Then he'd peel and chop the tubers and place them in the boiling apparatus. The resulting mash would go through several distillations, at the end of which a stream of clear liquid flowed into Viktor Ipalyevich's funnel. The smell of liquor wafted through the apartment and the stairwell and even drifted into the inner courtyard. Anna searched the faces of her fellow residents in the building, trying to discern whether they found her father's illegal distillery a nuisance and were likely to denounce him to the authorities. But when even Secretary Metsentsev, who was picking up his laundry from Avdotya, ascended to the fourth floor to taste the Four-Star Tsazukhin, Anna abandoned her protest and let her father have his way.

"Now, that's what I call booze!" he called out as he emerged from the kitchen. "This batch gets five stars!"

During the same period of time, in addition to distilling, Viktor Ipalyevich had submitted the repeatedly revised manuscript of his poems to the publisher and was awaiting the first proofs. He confidently hoped to have them in hand by the day of the party, so that he could offer his colleagues evidence in black and white of his return to the literary scene.

Viktor Ipalyevich had expressed no particular wishes concerning the provision of food and drink for the occasion; he'd simply pressed a high-denomination ruble note into Anna's hand. She spent three days devising and refining a menu, but in the end, she rejected the whole thing and opted for a mixed buffet. She set out with a long shopping list, and to her surprise, she needed only two days to acquire every item on it. After that, the distillery was thrust into a corner and all work surfaces cleared for the preparation of the tomato aspic, the herring zakuski, and Anna's baked potato dumplings. When Viktor Ipalyevich saw the refined little morsels that resulted from his daughter's labors, he cautiously asked her to consider that a crowd of Russian writers resembled a swarm of hungry grasshoppers and suggested that she prepare something more substantial for their guests. Accordingly, Anna steamed leeks and yellow beets in salted water for an entire day, pressed them through a sieve, thickened the purée with a roux, and, aided by Petya, seasoned the whole concoction. Meanwhile, she pressured Avdotya in vain to produce the new curtain; the seamstress hunkered down behind allusions to commissions for high-ranking customers and postponed the time of delivery. The party would have to take place with the sleeping alcove exposed to view.

A few minutes before the arrival of the first guests, as Anna was putting on her green dress, she realized that she usually wore it only when she went to meet Alexey. The thought of spending an evening with him briefly awakened her longing, but joy soon returned, because Viktor Ipalyevich, at least for one night, was forswearing his reclusive habits, and the two of them, father and daughter, were really and truly giving a party.

"I slept with my censor," said the writer Akhmadulina, the first guest to enter the apartment. Her male companion uttered a brief, ironic laugh, to which her response was, "If I thought it would change anything, I'd really do it." She threw her scarf over a chair. "But when they're going to put you to work for the Censorship Department, I presume they cut off your dick first." She embraced Viktor Ipalyevich.

"I have no doubt you're right," the poet said, laughing. He'd buttoned his Russian shirt all the way up; instead of his customary suspenders, a belt was holding up his trousers; and he'd trimmed his beard and his eyebrows.

The younger Strupatsky brother arrived. "You made it all the way to the All Unions Ministry?" he asked Akhmadulina incredulously. "They rejected me even from the Cultural Committee of the Russian Republic." With his chestnut brown hair, amber eyes, and long eyelashes, Strupatsky was an extremely handsome man. Wherever he went, he nourished the hope that Moscow writers could be not only interesting but also good-looking.

Anna greeted Vadim Kozhevnikov, whom her father had designated as a materialistic, corrupt hack ever since his war novels and spy stories had made him a ruble millionaire. "Well, well, my friend, where have you parked your new car?" Viktor Ipalyevich asked mockingly, standing at the window and pretending to search the street.

"Good evening, my dear Viktor. How lovely to see you after such a long time," said the easygoing Kozhevnikov, ignoring his host's jab. The two men sported the same style of beard, but Kozhevnikov was portly, and his little goatee capped a double chin.

"Have you delivered another irrelevant, blood-soaked volume to the Glavlit?" Viktor Ipalyevich asked, needling his colleague even as he embraced him.

"These days, no one but you has the nerve to propose dissident poems," the bestselling author said, accepting a glass of Five-Star Tsazukhin. Chattering away, the two men retreated to the sleeping nook.

After eight o'clock, the apartment filled up quickly. The toothless Vagrich brought news of the person who'd been named editor in chief of *Novy Mir*. Amid general disappointment, the writers speculated that the new editor would toe the Party line even more assiduously than his predecessors. One of the younger authors said, "The days of Aleksandr Tvardovsky are gone forever."

"True," Akhmadulina agreed. "The magazine's been worthless ever since Tvardovsky got the ax. They don't dare attack anybody now, except the Chinese and the junta in Chile."

While Anna was rearranging some dishes, she identified the sensation she had—she felt like a stranger—and realized that she'd felt that way whenever her father had invited his literary colleagues into the Tsazukhin home. This time, too, was like being in the midst of a race of people who communicated in their own coded language. As for her, she hardly spoke during the party, except to respond to requests for her recipes or to describe her ongoing battle against Petya's allergies; she limited herself to providing fresh supplies of food and drink. This limitation didn't spoil the party for her, but it helped her see even more clearly that the man with whom she lived under one roof, day in and day out, belonged to a rare species. Tonight, among people of his own kind, he blossomed.

Rosa Khleb appeared, accompanied by a couple who were both actors. Anna had conveyed her father's invitation to Rosa halfheartedly and had secretly hoped that her friend wouldn't have time to attend the party, but there she was. Her companions were part of the Taganka Theater Company and had starring roles in Yuri Lyubimov's currently acclaimed production of *The Tempest*. Even though Viktor Ipalyevich evinced a lively interest in the arrival of these two artists, he was particularly electrified by the coming of the Khleb. "We meet again, sooner than expected!" he cried over the others' heads, pushed his way through the crowd, and kissed Rosa's hand. She'd chosen to wear her sailor outfit, which gave her (as many of her clothes did) the air of an adolescent angel. Anna was amazed at how young Rosa could look when she set her mind to it.

Word went round the gathering that a reporter for the *Moscow Times* had come to pay her respects to the poet, and soon the writers were crowding around Rosa. She'd read Strupatsky's latest collection of short stories and asked him some critical questions. The author gave evasive answers that were supposed to be funny, but Rosa laid him low with a few sentences: "Your ambivalent attitude toward the present is reflected in your book, Comrade. When I read it, I wasn't completely sure, because you're such a skilled craftsman. Unfortunately, meeting you in person has confirmed the impression of emptiness I got from your texts."

Anna admired Rosa for giving Strupatsky her frank opinion and inwardly agreed with her. In the course of the evening, Anna had heard nothing but self-adulation and general wound licking from her father's colleagues. They complained about the oppressive censorship, which made it impossible for them to write "the Truth." The experimental philosopher Vagrich even let himself go so far as to say that his work should be judged not by what it contained but by what it did *not* contain.

Returning from a brief stint in the kitchen, Anna found that a new energy had suddenly seized the company, with the result that the table and the sideboard had been shoved against the wall near the window and a half circle formed around the sofa. The guests in the front row were lounging on the floor; behind them sat those who'd managed to get a hold of chairs. Petya was perched atop the living-room cabinet, where someone had placed him. The actress assumed a feline attitude near the sofa, and her partner stood with his face to the wall and bowed his back. He was shaking, portraying a man racked by heavy sobs.

"Now does my power gather to a head," he recited through his tears. His partner replied, "You did say so when first you raised the tempest, sir. How fares the King and his followers?" Anna gathered from someone's whispered remark that what she was hearing was Shakespeare. Without a struggle, the acting couple had let themselves be persuaded to present a sample of their art, and the scene, in their performance, was filled with pain and hopelessness. They dashed around the sofa, hauling and mauling each other, until the actor, in indescribable affliction, uttered the words "And deeper than did ever plummet sound I'll drown my book," and pitched forward onto the actress's lap.

During the vehement applause, and while the audience was breaking up and beginning to discuss Shakespeare, "their contemporary," Anna noticed that her father was standing in a corner, looking gray and bitter. She couldn't figure out why until she spotted the folded manuscript pages in his hand. The poet had suffered a crushing insult. No one had asked him to read from his recent work; instead, the actors had put on their own show, and in his very home. Anna would have liked to bring the guests' discourtesy to their attention, but she didn't intervene.

The level of sound in the apartment rose. The radio was playing loudly, and Anna was glad that both the upstairs and downstairs neighbors were among the guests and thus prevented from complaining about their disturbed rest. The supply of Five-Star Tsazukhin was exhausted, and Anna brought out the store-bought vodka.

"Has Alexey contacted you yet?" Rosa asked behind Anna's back.

Anna looked around cautiously to make sure that nobody was listening to them.

"These stars of the poetical firmament orbit only around themselves," Rosa said with a smile. "They don't even notice us."

"So far, I haven't been able to meet him."

"You should. Star-Eyes won't like it if your brief evening with Lyushin has damaged your relationship with Alexey."

Anna nodded. "I'll make it up to him."

"Lyushin was granted the funding he wanted," Rosa went on. "When he left for Dubna, he was quite satisfied."

Anna was trying to fathom the meaning of this remark when she heard a familiar, drunken voice coming from someone in the crowd milling around the sideboard. "It's been years since the last time I read a Soviet author! I find you all so tame and domesticated I prefer to immerse myself in the works of the nineteenth century!"

It was Viktor Ipalyevich, getting even with his colleagues for not having asked to hear a sample of his poetry. "As I look around," he cried, "I remember how much more revealing the compositions of our classical authors are than anything any of you dare to write." He took a step toward the bookshelf. "All the Yevtushenkos, Voznesenskys, and Kozhevnikovs amount to but one thing: a dreary farewell to Russian literature!" With no less effect than the actors had produced, Viktor Ipalyevich flung out an arm and swept the topmost row of volumes from the shelf. They flew through the room, struck several persons, and landed with cracked spines at the writers' feet. Anna expected expressions of dismay or protests, but she was wrong. As though at the end of a successful performance, the playwrights and poets, the essayists and novelists burst into unanimous applause, praised Viktor for his revolutionary gesture, and received him cordially into their midst again. More surprising than his fellows' thick skins was Viktor Ipalyevich's own reaction: His face beaming, he snatched the cap off his head—his sweaty hair stood up in all directions—and bowed around the room. "And now, ladies and gentlemen," he said, compelling his listeners to fall silent. "I shall demonstrate to you what contemporary Soviet verse is!"

He took out the crumpled pages and, without waiting for his guests to settle down, began at once: *"On Good Fortune."* Approving whispers indicated that the subject was a welcome one.

Why pull the wool over your eyes?
I didn't leave my union card at home;
I threw it in the trash bin on the Petrovka.

A calm set in, a sign that the guests weren't at some ordinary party, but in the home of Viktor Ipalyevich Tsazukhin, the poet, who was still capable of snapping in all directions while others had long since grown toothless. He read without emotion and yet vibrantly; his verses enfolded his audience. He ended his poem on good luck with these lines:

All things pass. Even our Star will go out.
But human grief is as deep as eternity.

No one ventured to say anything until Rosa asked, in a refreshingly matter-of-fact tone, "And you got that past the Glavlit? I admire your courage, Viktor Ipalyevich."

He couldn't have received a finer compliment. The poet went down on one knee in front of Rosa and kissed the hem of her skirt. With some effort, and surrounded by laughter, he rose to his feet again. Kozhevnikov, profoundly moved, embraced him. "You are our most precious diamond," the million-selling author said before blowing his nose.

When two a.m. came and went and apparently no one had yet given any thought to leaving, Anna asked her neighbor if she could take Petya downstairs to her apartment and put him to bed. He protested, even though his eyelids were rapidly getting heavier, and he fell asleep on his mother's shoulder while they were still on the stairs. She laid him on the neighbor's sofa, covered him with a blanket, savored a few peaceful moments at his side, and went back upstairs.

Things gradually started to break up, including the apartment furniture. A chair was reduced to its component parts; five guests lay unmoving in the sleeping alcove. In the kitchen, the pall of cigarette smoke was so heavy that people had to sit on the floor in order to breathe. Anna pondered what method she could use to initiate the process of departure and settled on tidying up. This plan faltered because of the impenetrable juxtaposition of legs, bottles, and food scraps. An hour later, a place was freed up on the sofa; she sat down and closed her eyes. Words and sounds reached her from farther and farther away. She prepared herself to remain in that position until daybreak.

When she heard the steps on the stairs, she started awake immediately.

Surely no partygoers could be arriving at this late hour; the fun would never end. She must prevent them from entering! With leaden limbs, she rose to her feet and saw her father lounging against the windowsill; one of his hands was caressing the back of Akhmadulina's neck. Anna climbed over a group of guests who were spinning bottles and reached the apartment door. Someone really was coming up the stairs. She put on her most resolute face and slipped outside. The newcomer hadn't turned on the lights and seemed familiar with the steps. He climbed up slowly, like someone carrying a heavy burden.

At the next turning, his shock of hair appeared, as well as his brown overcoat. When he saw the woman standing one floor above him, he dropped his pack and charged up the last flight of stairs.

"Anna, you're still up!" Leonid said joyfully.

Without a moment's hesitation, she threw her arms around his neck.

NINETEEN

Leonid's memory of his first night with Galina—it had been, in fact, a morning—remained fixed in his mind. He'd waited five hours for her in the Yuzhno-Sakhalinsk hospital. During that time, several emergency cases had been admitted, and the friendly nurse had informed him repeatedly that Doctor Korff wouldn't be free for a while yet; wouldn't he prefer to come back another day? But Leonid had traveled to the capital city precisely in order to see the woman in question, Galina the severe, Galina with the scornful eyes. After midnight, when the ambulance sirens had finally fallen silent and the bustle in the hospital corridors gave way to an unreal calm, Leonid had stretched out on the row of three screwed-down chairs and fallen asleep.

When the scent of her perfume awakened him and he looked up, Galina Korff was standing over him. "Is this your idea of performing night duty, Comrade Captain?"

Leonid tried to leap to his feet, but his smooth boot soles slid on the synthetic floor covering; he barely stood up, and then he was lying down again.

"If one were to gauge the condition of our armed forces by your appearance, I should think the estimate of our military strength would be distinctly low."

He didn't know anyone who expressed herself the way Galina did. Leonid was used to the barking of the men in his battalion, who spoke a good deal but hardly ever said anything. Sometimes he even forgot that there were other ways of speaking Russian besides soldiers' slang.

"Well, what shall I do with you now, my stalwart drum major?"

He was upright again, but his head was still heavy with sleep. "So you were very busy?" It was all he could think of to say.

"Two premature births brought on by the mothers' overwork." She started toward the exit. "I was able to save one of the babies." She waited for him to push open the swinging door. "Then there was a thumb amputation, followed by a case I'd rather not describe to you if we're going to get something to eat."

They stepped outside. The streets of the capital were empty.

"Two-thirty," Galina said, looking up at the illuminated hospital clock. "We won't find anything open." Pensively, as if there were a range of possibilities, she peered down the street. "What do you say to the following option? I invite you to my place."

The night had turned a murky gray that the streetlights made even murkier. An icy half hour later, they were sitting at the cozy table in Galina's apartment, which would not have been out of place in a novel from before the Russian Revolution. The double windows had been handmade by joiners who'd skillfully fitted the component parts together without using either nails or screws. Leonid marveled at the construction of the inner sashes, into which a tiny, rectangular opening had been set for purposes of ventilation. The living room was paneled in a way he'd never seen outside of a museum. Within minutes, the small, coal-burning stove had diffused so much heat that Leonid removed his uniform jacket. "How did you find this jewel?" he asked.

"Find it? I rescued it." She brought beer, some green liquid, and water to the table. "The housing combine was just about to tear out all this junk, as they called it, and replace it with modern materials. I had to sign a statement in which I agreed to accept various anachronistic items."

She poured him a drink. “It breaks my heart to give up this apartment. I won’t find anything like it in Yakutia.”

“When’s your duty here over?” He watched as she diluted the green liquor.

“In four days,” Galina sighed. Noticing his curious gaze, she held her glass against the light. “The green fairy in absinthe. Have you never tried it?”

He took a sip and grimaced in surprise. The thought that this was probably their last meeting made him gloomy. “Where did you learn to talk like that?” he asked. “I don’t know anybody who gets so much out of our language. Who taught you that?”

“My head.” Galina sank back in her chair. The strain of a long day fell away from her.

“Your head may be the tool, but who sharpened it?”

“A dangerous counterrevolutionary,” she said with a smile. “At the time, he was already a very old man, and I was just a tiny little thing. My grandfather, the former governor-general. I learned everything about poetry and about our writers from him. My outlawed dyedushka even taught me the little I know about playing the piano.” She threw two lumps of coal into the stove. “I was born in Yakutia. By that time, my family had already come to the end of their odyssey. It had led them through several prisons and an eastern Siberian penal camp that must have been truly awful, because not one of my people ever told me anything about it. In the end, since my family had accepted everything without protest and Grandfather had affirmed from the bottom of his heart that the epoch-making, revolutionary changes that had taken place in our country were nothing short of fantastic, the powers that be apparently grew tired of punishing us for having been born with silver spoons in our mouths. My father was banished to the most desolate corner of the world and given an underpaid job, and there, finally, my grandparents were allowed to live in peace. Soon, however, the war broke out. It probably would have gone unnoticed in Siberia if the demand for coal hadn't doubled. And not long afterward, I came into the world."

She went to the kitchen to prepare some soup. Leonid stretched out his legs; it had been a long time since he'd felt so comfortable. The fog outside, the noiseless night, the woman busy at the stove—he got up and went to her, hugged her from behind, and clasped her breasts. She stood still for a moment before returning to her culinary activities. A little later, the barley soup was on the table. Galina put a spoonful of sour cream on each portion.

She stood beside his chair. "Well? That was all?"

He pulled her down on his lap, the spoon fell to the floor, sour cream spattered the floorboards. Galina kissed more wildly, more playfully than Anna; her mouth seemed to be everywhere at once. Her pelvis never stopped moving the whole time she was sitting on him, so he lifted her up and tried to carry her into the next room. But Galina insisted that they eat first; she wanted him to appreciate her soup.

"Take that off," she said, pointing to his wedding ring.

Their embrace was wonderful, weightless; their bodies intertwined in total intimacy and remained entangled long after they collapsed and lay panting. He'd often wished that something of the sort would happen with Anna, but it had seemed an empty fantasy, and he'd told himself that he wasn't capable of transporting a woman to such a height of passion. With Galina, everything had happened effortlessly. He couldn't stop caressing her; he'd had to travel five thousand miles from home in order to meet someone like this. Everything felt warm to him; it was as if he'd seen the pattern in this carpet or his toes at the end of this bed a hundred times before; even the way to the toilet seemed familiar. When Galina fell asleep in his arms and her breathing grew regular, he gave no consideration whatever to leaving and thought only briefly about the excuse he'd offer for having missed the morning roll call. Then, gently, he woke Galina up, and they made love again. When the inexorable brightness of dawn appeared, she pulled the thick curtains closed and announced with a sigh that now she must sleep for a few hours. Leonid got up. As he put on his uniform, he found every movement difficult, and the prospect of saying good-bye to her seemed impossibly daunting.

"Today's my birthday," he said suddenly, speaking into the chilled air of the apartment.

"Then you were born under the sign of the fishes," Galina murmured, already half asleep. "I'm a scorpion."

He pulled on his second boot, kissed her thick, naked foot, and left. He had breakfast in the city, followed by a shot of liquor for his birthday. Then he went back to the base. A long letter from Anna had come for him; in it, she told him how much she wished they could be together on that day. She'd enclosed a drawing, made by Petya, which depicted an oversized soldier on a tiny island. Only when Leonid washed his hands that evening did he notice that he'd left his wedding ring at Galina's. He knew the date when she was leaving, he was aware that he had only a few days to get the ring back, and yet he let the time pass.

Leonid spent the melancholy day of Galina's departure in his office on the edge of the cliff. As the hours passed, he came to the realization that his betrayal of Anna's trust meant nothing to him. He almost wished that Galina would take the ring with her to Yakutia.

One week later, a small package came to Leonid in the military mail. He assumed it was from Anna, but the return address was the hospital in Yuzhno-Sakhalinsk. He knew what the contents would be. *One does not forget such a thing, Comrade!* These words were written in a vigorous hand on the sheet of paper the ring was wrapped in. At the bottom of the page, easy to overlook, was an address: 119 Cosmonauts Street, Yakutsk. No salutation, no hopes to meet again; and yet, for Leonid, that address was the origin of a temptation that grew stronger and stronger with every day he spent on Sakhalin Island. Cosmonauts Street, number 119, was on the mainland, far away, yet it soon came to represent for him the focal point of his deepest longing; he would have preferred to die than never to see Cosmonauts Street. So when his turn to take home leave approached, it was only logical that he should put in for a week not in Moscow but in Central Siberia. The major asked no unnecessary questions and signed Leonid's pass.

A transport plane that picked up foodstuffs for Sakhalin Island brought him to Khabarovsk. From there, it was another fifteen hundred miles to Yakutsk, the capital and chief city of Yakutia, where he landed on a gloriously sunny morning. On the drive to the city center, he saw some of the so-called Yakutsk Cripples: houses whose heat had melted the ground under them. As a result, their cement piers had sunk into the mud, and the structures leaned in all directions. Only when he stepped out into the open air could Leonid feel how dry and cold it was; the first sign came from the tiny hairs in his nose, which froze at once and began to bend and crackle with every breath he took.

He'd sent Galina a letter a week before and waited until his departure for an answer, but in vain. From Sakhalin, a room had been reserved for him at the Red Army Officers' Residence in Yakutsk; he dropped off his luggage there and made inquiries in the motorized unit concerning the address on Cosmonauts Street. While speaking with the comrades, Leonid noticed that every vehicle in the yard had its motor running. "In the winter, they run twenty-four hours a day," a driver explained. "Sometimes we have to light a fire under the engine block so they don't freeze solid." He laughed merrily. "So what? We have more than enough oil around here."

One of the trucks was headed in the direction Leonid wanted, and the driver gave him a ride. The town looked featureless, he thought; all the architecture served but one purpose, namely, to keep the frost out. On the roadside, he saw cars whose tires had burst from the cold. The windshields of vehicles contained double layers of glass; house windows had triple layers. People on the streets were so thoroughly wrapped in warm clothing that only their eyes showed. At a mobile street stand, milk was being sold in frozen blocks; for easier transport, wooden handles were frozen into the milk.

"What I don't understand, brother," said the driver, yanking Leonid out of his contemplation, "is why a man on leave would come here, of all places."

"I'm visiting someone."

"A relative?"

Leonid nodded to forestall further questions. They turned into a wide, tarred road lined with apartment blocks. Leonid thanked the driver and jumped out. He'd been warned not to take leather boots to Yakutia, because leather freezes and cracks apart in extreme cold, so he'd had the wardrobe officer give him some felt boots. Shod with this ungainly footwear, he stamped down Cosmonauts Street. He had to walk a long way, because every building had only a single house number; 119 was almost past the city limits. By the time he finally reached it, his face had gone numb. The nameplates and doorbells were behind a protective door; in semidarkness, he searched for Galina's name. When he finally found it, a peculiar feeling of nervousness overcame him. He pressed the button, but there was no sound to indicate that his pressure had triggered a signal in one of the apartments. After several tries, he pressed the button next to Galina's. A female voice cautiously responded, and Leonid said that he wished to speak to Doctor Korff.

"Is it you who's running around on foot outside?" asked the voice in the loudspeaker, and before he could answer, a buzzer sounded.

On the second floor, a door opened as Leonid approached. "How can anyone be so reckless?" said a thin-faced woman. She was wearing so many layers of clothing that everything on her person flapped a little. "Comrade Korff doesn't sleep here very often," she said, offering Leonid a seat on a kitchen chair.

"Does she spend the night at a friend's place?" he asked. The thought had occurred to him before, but now, for the first time, he feared that his journey to Yakutsk had been a mistake.

"When she works late, there's no transportation available, so she sleeps in the hospital." Galina's neighbor shook her head. "You're a madman. At this time of day, most people are at work. You could have frozen to death with nobody around to help you."

"I don't find it so cold." Leonid put his fingers up to his cheeks but couldn't feel his own touch.

"People have died just from breathing. The moisture in their breath turns to ice, they swallow it, and it chokes them," the woman said. She poured him some tea. "Where did you come here from?"

"Sakhalin."

"Don't tell me fairy tales." She offered him sugar.

"Before that, I lived in Moscow." Even though Leonid was burning to see Galina as soon as possible, no matter where he had to go to do so, courtesy required him to satisfy the woman's curiosity about the distant capital.

"We're not barbarians here, either," was her reply after Leonid had described the theaters, movie houses, and nightspots of Moscow. "Our surroundings may be harsh, but we have culture." She showed him a monthly magazine, in which some dates were marked. "In April, the ballet is coming to Yakutsk, and our own symphony orchestra will perform the music."

"Yes, it's a big country," he replied, rather inconsequentially.

"And we're the biggest region in the biggest country on earth."

By this point, Leonid had completely thawed out; his cheeks and nose were burning, and he felt twinges in his fingertips. The neighbor lady explained to him where the hospital was but forbade him to set out for it on foot. She hung a red flag out of her window, and after that, they simply waited until a vehicle drove up to the building.

"That's the way we do it here when somebody wants to go somewhere." She accompanied Leonid to the door. "Say hello to Galina for me. And tell her I have some mail for her." The woman picked up a stack, and Leonid's letter was on top.

He walked outside and climbed into the car. The driver dropped him off near the hospital, and sooner than he expected, Leonid laid eyes on Galina. "I have to go away," was the first thing Doctor Korff said. She was so bundled up that he recognized her only by her voice.

"For how long?" His disappointment made him angry.

"Three days."

"Are you going far?"

"Six hundred miles." As she spoke, Galina checked the equipment that was being loaded into crates of some synthetic material. "Keep the ambulance warm," she ordered. "The instruments mustn't be allowed to freeze."

"Six hundred," Leonid stammered. "You're going to drive six hundred miles in an ambulance?"

"Don't be ridiculous. We're flying. The pilot knows the route, and the weather's supposed to remain good."

"Galina . . ." She was bustling here and there, but Leonid stepped in her way. "I have only four days' leave. Can't you wait until tomorrow?"

"If the woman isn't operated on today, she dies," Galina said, cutting him off. "There's room in the ambulance. Come on, you can ride with me to the airport."

More taken by surprise than persuaded, he agreed. They hurried to the entrance hall; the ambulance was waiting outside, its blue light turning and flashing.

Now that their brief reunion was about to come to such an austere end, the two of them sat unspeaking in their seats as the vehicle took them back to the place where Leonid had arrived only a few hours before. At last, Galina said in an accusatory tone, "You might have written."

"My letter's lying unopened in your neighbor's apartment." He told her of his visit to the apartment building on Cosmonauts Street. Then he asked, "Aren't there any doctors in the place you're flying to?"

She took off her hat. The look in her eyes struck him like a blow. "Have you looked at the Yakut Autonomous Soviet Socialist Republic on a map? There's nothing here. And this gigantic nothing is virtually uninhabited. It's less expensive to fly doctors to where they're needed than to station them in such extremely remote places."

The ambulance rolled into a sharp curve. The crates were tied down tightly, but Galina and Leonid were flung into a corner of the seat. She didn't seem to register their brief touch. Then Leonid spotted the turboprop aircraft, which was being towed with rotating propellers to the inspection building.

"That's one of *our* planes!" Leonid cried in surprise.

"Of course." She buttoned her coat all the way up. "Do you think physicians have private jets at their disposal? We almost always fly in military aircraft." She knocked on the interior window. "Get the crates inside the plane, fast!" While the turboprop and the ambulance were being brought as close together as possible, Leonid became aware of a huge machine that was also being rolled up to the airplane. Long hoses disappeared into the hatch, which a compressor was keeping warm.

"Galina!" Leonid jumped out of the ambulance after her. "I was looking forward so much to being with you!" The noise of three different engines made every word nearly inaudible. "I don't know . . . when we'll see each other again!"

"For an officer, you are remarkably out of touch with reality." Her hands, buried inside thick fur, reached for his.

"We're right here, right now! That's reality!" He tried to pull her against him, but Galina was inhibited by the presence of the workers. She ran toward the gangway that led to the airplane's passenger door. The pilot appeared at the top of the ladder to oversee the de-icing procedure. Galina clambered up beside the pilot, pointed at the equipment that was being loaded inside the plane, and gave him instructions. Leonid was freezing; the feeling of having no feeling in his face struck him as a metaphor for this brainless trip. All around him, the work teams were exchanging rapid handshakes in order to escape the cold as quickly as possible. The hoses were removed from the aircraft, the ambulance's rear doors were shut; Galina sprang from the gangway and went running up to Leonid.

"You're on active duty in the army! You can fly with me!" When he hesitated, she poked him. "What are you waiting for?"

"How did you do this?" he muttered, bewildered, as he returned the pilot's salute.

"I said you have relatives in Artyk!"

"Is that the name of the backwater we're going to? Artyk?"

Leonid saw the pilot disappear into the cockpit and followed Galina to the gangway. As he climbed up, he thought about all the service regulations he was in the act of disobeying. He couldn't immediately get his bearings in the dimly lit cabin; Galina pressed him into a seat. She pulled the hatch shut with one hand, gave the pilot a signal, sat down, and buckled herself in. The roar of the propellers grew louder, and then the aircraft started to move and rolled out to the runway. A few minutes later, the turboprop machine rose from the ground and climbed up toward the crystalline sky. Leonid watched the airport and the city disappear below him. He remained motionless for several minutes in his pod-shaped seat until he grasped his new situation. They followed the winding course of the river for a while and then turned toward the southeast. Except for the pilot, Galina, and Leonid, the eight-seater aircraft was empty.

"How long is the flight?" Leonid asked, calling to Galina from across the center aisle.

"Three or four hours. It depends on the wind." Galina unfastened her seat belt. "This box can't go faster than one hundred eighty-five miles an hour. You're on leave—relax and enjoy it." With that, she stretched out her legs on the seat beside her and folded her arms. "I spent half the night operating on people. Now I've got to sleep."

Leonid thought about home. Up until now, everything involving Galina had been spontaneous or even accidental: an officer in a strange land, a meeting with an unusual woman, a passionate night—sometimes such things happen. But from now on, he was cheating on Anna intentionally, with premeditation. This airplane was taking Galina and him to some remote spot, and even the pilot seemed like an accomplice. While Leonid watched the flatlands disengage from the mountains, he pulled off his wedding ring and casually stuck it in a pocket, as though hiding it from himself.

All at once, he choked a little and swallowed hard. Where was this sudden anxiety coming from?

"We're flying at twelve thousand feet. The cabin isn't pressurized." Galina sat up against the wall of the plane and looked at him.

A mountain peak appeared and disappeared beside the aircraft. "There are some thirteen-thousand-foot-high summits in this area," Galina said. "But the pilot's familiar with them." Abruptly, she got up from her seat and took the one next to him. "Isn't that wonderful?" She leaned against him, and they looked out. The rugged mountain crests stretched out to the horizon. "This is my homeland."

"Does anyone live here voluntarily?" Leonid's breath was coming in loud gasps.

"If you need oxygen, say so right away. A collapse is hard to treat when you're up in the air."

The conversation turned to normal topics. Galina confessed that the readjustment from Sakhalin to Yakutsk had lasted longer than she'd expected; he talked about his everyday army routine. He was mad to kiss her, but he hesitated on the incomprehensible grounds that he wanted her to make the first move. Eventually, the turning shadows signaled that they were changing direction.

"We're descending."

The pilot appeared in the frame of the cockpit door and explained that the weather at their destination was unfortunately not as good as in Yakutsk.

"Fasten your seat belt," Galina said, pulling hers tight.

"Why?" He hastened to clasp his buckle, too.

"'Not so good' means it's storming down there."

They flew into a gray wall. From one second to the next, the small aircraft was lifted and shaken, and then it began to lose altitude. The roar of the propellers changed pitch.

"Is that normal?" Leonid asked, emphatically calm. Down below, he thought he could make out snowdrifts, but they might also have been ice crystals. Soon afterward, visibility had been reduced by so much that the only thing he could see in the window was his own reflection.

"Do they have landing beacons down there in . . ." He'd forgotten the name of the place.

"Ar-tyk." The airplane was jolted mightily, and Galina's jaws snapped shut.

"But with a storm like this," Leonid said, clenching the armrests, "isn't the runway snowed in?"

"We have skis!" she shouted into the ambient noise.

Seeing that he couldn't do a thing to change whatever was about to happen, Leonid laid one hand on Galina's lap, leaned back, and breathed regularly.

They landed safely. The airport consisted of a single runway; since Leonid could discover nothing that looked like a landscape anywhere around, he thought that the snow must be piled up several feet high. Although still early afternoon, it was already getting dark.

"Artyk's population is only three thousand," Galina told him. All the equipment had been transferred from the airplane to an ambulance, and they were on their way to the center of the town. "There's no hotel, just a guest house." With unexpected tenderness, she leaned on his shoulder. "I have to go to the infirmary immediately."

"Shouldn't you get a little rest first?"

She shook her head. "They're doing the preoperative preparation now."

He pointed at the white storm outside. "What happens if there's a power failure?"

"The instruments run on diesel fuel." She stroked his cheek. "You make things comfortable for us. I'll come as soon as I can."

Three automobiles were at a standstill in the middle of Artyk's main intersection. The drivers, whose fur hats all looked alike, were talking emphatically to one another in the light of their headlamps. The ambulance driver tapped his horn; without haste, the three men climbed into their vehicles and cleared the intersection. At the entrance to the hospital, Galina and Leonid separated. While she was exchanging greetings with the local staff, he was asking the porter for directions to the guest house. The snow fell unabated; the snowflakes were fused into curtains by the driving wind. Leonid turned up his collar and struggled to make his way past a line of low-lying buildings. Only the roofs were visible on those structures whose walkways hadn't been shoveled clear of snow. Shortly before reaching his goal, the gusts became so strong that he had to turn his back to the wind and brace himself. He covered his eyes, because he was afraid they might freeze.

The illuminated roof sign that designated the house as a place that offered accommodations was frozen over; the letters glimmered faintly through the covering of snow. Leonid found a padlock on the front door and feared that he was going to have to find someone to open it for him, and in this weather. But the lock was only hanging loose, and he stepped into the creaking wooden house. An oil stove whose chimney pipe disappeared into the roof ridge was giving off so much heat that he removed his hat and scarf and unbuttoned his overcoat. There were two rooms off this central space, each with four beds, a bathroom, and a tiny kitchen. Leonid found some canned food and tea in a cabinet and set a water kettle on to boil. He pulled off the coverlet from one of the narrow beds and hesitated briefly as he wondered whether the invitation might not be too unambiguous; then he shoved two beds together and, with the help of every pillow in the room, made them as comfortable as possible. Without removing his boots, Leonid lay down and waited for the kettle to whistle.

TWENTY

She wasn't used to having a man in her arms when she woke up, or to warming the soles of her feet against his calves, or to hearing his deep breathing, so unlike Petya's soft, fluttering exhalations. Red wine had been spilled in the sleeping nook, so Anna had put fresh sheets on the bed.

It was a gray March morning, and there was no curtain to shut it out. She made an effort to keep her eyes closed so that she wouldn't see the chaos she'd spent the night in. Viktor Ipalyevich lay on the sofa, half dead from liquor and exhaustion; toward the end, he'd unbuttoned his shirt to the navel and done a dance, all the while shamelessly courting the chubby Akhmadulina. When Leonid arrived, the litterateurs who were still at the party hardly noticed. Eventually, when she was more than ready for them to leave, Anna had employed the only effective stratagem: She'd hidden the vodka and pretended that the last bottle had been drained. This drastic move had been followed by excessively drawn-out leave-taking, but gradually the last hats and coats disappeared and the sounds died out, until only Anna, her intoxicated father, and Leonid were left. He would have liked to see Petya there and then, but Anna hadn't wanted to disturb her neighbors again, especially not at that hour.

Her state of mind—her strong sense of relief—surprised Anna. She wasn't alone in the world. Her man had come home, her husband, Petya's father. Before his transfer, she'd often felt as though he were a stranger; the smells he'd brought home from the barracks were strange, as was the way the army barbers cut his hair. Leonid's laughter had sounded strange to her, to say nothing of the military jargon, the man-speak so ill suited to his personality. This strangeness might sooner or later have led to a breakup, but they hadn't broken up; instead, Leonid had gone far away. Since then, Anna thought, it had been left to her and her alone to cope with everything that needed coping with: her difficult father, Petya and his health problems, her morbid love affair, the furtiveness, the lies. All at once, however, on this unreal morning, her husband was lying beside her. Wouldn't it be only natural to find that strange, too, after so long? Leonid's limbs were heavy; when he rolled over, he nearly crushed her. Next to his, her legs looked as spindly as a child's. While she gazed upon him, registering everything, feeling his breath, touching the hair on his chest, Anna suddenly, physically realized how alone she'd been. She formed no illusions about the rekindling of love, but she felt the liberation of letting go, if only for a few days, of what she usually clutched with such an iron grip. Leonid was there, he'd take care of things, she could leave the decisions to him.

So there were many reasons why Anna didn't want to begin her day by cleaning up after Viktor Ipalyevich's party. It would take hours to make everything tidy again—but not today. Today, she'd let the apartment keep looking like a pigsty, let her father get the tomato sauce off the radiators and bring the glasses to the cellar and the tablecloths to the laundry room. Anna wanted an entirely happy day, a genuine Sunday. And after that, who knew, maybe the happiness would last; maybe their separation would even turn out to have been useful, and out of it a new togetherness might bloom.

She carefully detached herself from her sleeping companion, put her feet on the floor, and reached for her housecoat. First she'd go and fetch Petya, and then he could awaken his grandfather. Without risking a glance at the mirror, she walked swiftly to the foyer, ran her fingers through her hair, and took the key. Sunday silence reigned in the stairwell.

If it hadn't been for Petya, Leonid would have spoken before the night was through. But because of the boy, he wanted to be cautious, so he resolved to probe a little first, to find out how things stood. And since he was dead tired after his twenty-six-hour flight, Leonid had fallen asleep shortly after arriving home, but not so quickly as Anna. Her hair had tickled his nose, her body had seemed bulkier, and in his memory, her skin had not been so winter-white. They'd slept together every night for two years in that narrow alcove, but this time, anxiety made it hard for him to breathe. He'd always loved her "poetic" neck; on this morning, he couldn't find anything lovable about it. When he considered how little thought he gave to Anna's future, he had to admit that his lack of concern for her was strange in itself. His idea of Anna was that she could take care of herself, as she always had done, even when he'd been there; she'd never needed his help. And in the meanwhile, there was the KGB drama she'd gotten herself involved in. Fortunately, he'd been left in peace. He was an officer, stationed far away, but his "exile" from Moscow had proved to be a blessing.

That night in Artyk, Galina hadn't joined him in the guest house. Complications had prolonged the operation, and it had been hard to bring the patient back to consciousness. The surgeon had kept working in the little hospital until dawn. Leonid, in the meanwhile, had prepared some food, but in the end he'd eaten it himself, drinking an entire pot of tea in the process. At two in the morning, he'd started, fully clothed, out of a brief doze, undressed, and gotten into bed. Then, past daybreak, Galina had slipped in beside him. Sensing that she didn't want to sleep, he'd turned to her. This second time, unfolding between night and day somewhere in no-man's-land, their lovemaking had been so intense and beautiful that every individual moment remained vivid in his memory. He and Galina behaved as though that cabin, in the most godforsaken corner of the East, were their real home. She'd had to get up in a few hours to go and see how the patient was recovering from her surgery, but soon she'd returned with breakfast. They'd eaten it together, half naked, and then crept back into bed to make love and sleep. Leonid was so overwhelmed with tenderness that he could have cried, but instead he'd devoted himself to Galina with the ardor of a young lover. During the flight back, they'd sat with their arms around each other, and after they landed they'd gone immediately to her apartment. She'd read his letter, and then, after more passionate fondling, they had both suddenly grown serious. His three-day leave wasn't going to be enough for them. They acknowledged how hard they'd fallen in love with each other, and they saw their complete intimacy as something that must have consequences. Galina had said little, letting Leonid speak, and for the first time, he'd talked about his wife and son. In describing his situation, Leonid tried to make it seem—to Galina and to himself—that he and Anna were together only because she'd become pregnant with Petya years before. Then he'd confessed how much he loved Petya and stopped pretending that he was unhappily married. He'd kept quiet about the real reason for his transfer away from Moscow. Then Galina had abruptly announced that she would not, in any case, leave the region she considered her homeland, and here lay a decisive point: Where was the place where they could both live? Moreover, would a separation from Anna mean that Leonid would lose Petya? When his thoughts about insurmountable future problems became too much for him, Leonid had fled back into the moment with Galina.

He heard the door open and close. It was Anna coming back, he could tell, and the softer footsteps must be his son's. Leonid sighed. He'd returned to Moscow with specific intentions, but now everything looked difficult. "Petyushka," he whispered, feeling wretched.

Despite being half asleep, the boy jumped into the bed and sat on his father's stomach. Although Leonid knew how quickly young children changed, the sight of his son still took his breath away. In the space of several months, Petya's features had tightened; his eyes had grown more serious and his arms stronger. "When did you come home?" the boy asked.

"Very late," Leonid said. He was listening anxiously for telltale sounds in Petya's breathing.

"Why didn't you come and tell me good night?"

"Well, now I'm telling you good morning." Cautiously, as if unsure of what he was doing, Leonid petted his little man before finally drawing him into his embrace.

"Now you can't go away anymore," Petya whispered.

Leonid looked up at Anna, who was standing with her housecoat open in the midst of the ambient disorder. Her nightshirt swelled a little where her slight paunch pressed against the cloth.

"Just one more time." Leonid kept his eyes on Anna. "I flew halfway around the world to see you, my friend."

"Why do you have to go away again?"

"I'm protecting our borders." Tears welled up in his eyes. How stupid, how unsuited to the real purpose of his visit! Anna noticed and gave him a tender look, naturally misinterpreting his emotion.

"Why can't you protect the border here?" asked Petya, freeing himself from his father's arms.

"That's nonsense, Petyushka." Leonid pretended to rub sleep from his eyes. "There's no border in Moscow, is there?"

"The river," came the prompt reply. "People can't go back and forth over it, so it's a border."

"Do you remember when we looked at the map? Do you remember how big the Soviet Union is?" Petya nodded, unsure of himself. "In the East, where there's always ice and it's cold the whole year round . . ." Leonid hesitated. He could see Galina before him, in her apartment, in the hospital, in the airplane over the mountains of Yakutia, and the images threw him into confusion. Wasn't a confession called for here? Wouldn't he be doing the right thing if he admitted to his wife and son and—so much the better—the pigheaded old man, too, that he'd fallen in love with someone else, not that he'd wanted to, but these things happen? The very thought of such a confession was like a knife through his heart. The boy looked at his father, waiting for him to finish his sentence.

"There are cliffs three hundred feet high," Leonid went on, his head reeling. "And the country of Japan is only a few miles away. That's the border I'm protecting, Petya."

"Isn't your year on Sakhalin almost up?" Anna asked in surprise.

"Yes . . . that is, no. It's not yet decided."

"But you must know what your new post is going to be." She sat on the edge of the bed.

"Let's talk about it after breakfast." He lifted Petya from his lap, turned him on his stomach, and began to pinch and tickle him. It was a game they'd used to play for hours at a time. On this occasion, however, the giggling wouldn't start; the boy sensed that the game was a diversionary tactic.

"There's no way we can eat here." Anna gestured toward the general mess. "I don't have anything but the leftovers from yesterday." Reluctantly, she pondered whether it would be possible to make a breakfast out of those.

"We're off!" said Leonid. "Get dressed, Petyushka. We're going out."

"Yes!" The youngster's shout echoed around the room. On the sofa, Viktor Ipalyevich belched but didn't wake up.

More quickly than was his wont when getting ready for school, Petya threw on his clothes, even tying his own shoelaces, and stood at the door, wriggling impatiently while his mother packed the bare necessities for a Sunday outing. Although the wet, gray weather persisted, Leonid got his spring suit out of the closet. They left the apartment on tiptoe, as if anything short of cannon fire would have been capable of waking Viktor Ipalyevich. They didn't start to plan their excursion in detail until they were on the stairs. A trip along the Moskva River struck them as an unimaginative choice, and Krasnogorsk was too far away.

"I wonder if Vorontsovsky Park has thawed out yet."

Anna fell in with the suggestion immediately. "We'll certainly see the first flower buds there," she said.

The subway brought them to the train station. They drank cocoa with Petya and found an open bakery. The train was running late. By the time they got off a little south of the park, the sun had broken through the clouds.

"It's about time for spring," Anna said, smiling and taking Leonid's arm. Leonid relieved her of the bag she was carrying. It felt good to stand blinking in the sunlight. They climbed the hill where the pastoral landscape began. It was hard to believe that there was still frost within Moscow's city limits.

Anna was burning to learn where Leonid would be stationed next. She was sure he knew where he was going, even though he hadn't spoken of it; his reticence could bode well or ill, she thought. Maybe his transfer back to Moscow was a foregone conclusion, and soon they could start thinking about the apartment in Nostikhyeva.

Petya ran a little ahead of them, fell back, scampered about, but never got too far away—until the pond appeared. "Look, no more ice!" he cried, and then he dashed down the slope.

"Be careful!" Anna and Leonid shouted, as though with one voice.

A black dog, incited to action by the galloping youngster, left his owner's side and sprinted toward the pond, too. Petya noticed the dog in time and came to a full stop, but the animal rushed on and plunged without stopping into the water, spraying it in all directions. At first, seeing a vicious beast charging down upon their defenseless child, Leonid and Anna had sprinted side by side to the bank; now they were laughing with Petya and the dog's owner at the perplexed animal, which had rocketed out of the icy pond and stood some distance away, shaking himself and shivering frightfully. "He's harmless," said the man. He seized his dog by the collar and led the beast into the sunlight.

For no particular reason, Anna felt a sudden urge to make some sort of impression on her husband, the powerful man with the absent smile who'd come back to her, despite everything the past year had brought them. After making sure she'd brought a towel, she removed her jacket and sweater. "If a dog can do it, so can we," she cried out. She kicked off her boots, dropped her pants, and snatched off her shirt, and in an instant she was up to her thighs in the water.

"It can't be more than forty degrees in there!" Leonid yelled. Squealing for joy at the sight of his daredevil mother, Petya became so excited that his father had to make restraining the boy his first priority. The cold took Anna's breath away. So as not to lose her resolve, she leaped forward and disappeared into the brackish water. When she surfaced, she heard applause coming from the opposite bank, where passersby had stopped to watch. She paddled around in a circle, remembered the ice diver she'd seen in the Moscow River, and ended her swim as quickly as she could. As far as Petya was concerned, her ploy was a total success; he was thrilled by her exploit and described it as though no one had seen it but him. Shaking his head, Leonid held out the towel and rubbed Anna's shoulders.

"Now you need to swallow something hot," he said as Anna was fastening her jacket. Her teeth were chattering.

"There's only one place where we . . ." She clamped her shivering jaw shut and pointed in the desired direction.

They entered a gloomy establishment, whose proprietress looked as though Sunday walkers, like everything that had to do with the advent of spring, disgusted her. The menu was limited to red beet soup and bread with cheese. While they refreshed themselves and Anna warmed up, her impatience to learn Leonid's news grew. Eating made Petya sleepy, and when they went outside, Leonid had to carry him. They walked a short distance into the woods. In a clearing, Anna spread out the indestructible blanket that had served her and Leonid well the very first time they'd engaged in amorous play together, years before. The grass was still brown but dry. The sun glinted between bare birches and lit up the little hairs in Leonid's ears. He took off his scarf and opened his jacket and shirt. When he turned his head, Anna noticed the powerful tendons in his neck and realized how suntanned his face and chest were. Petya fell asleep at once. Anna propped herself on her elbows, breathed in the fresh air, and squinted at her husband.

"Did you miss me?" It sounded vain; she'd only wanted to say something that would show him how welcome he was. "I wish you didn't have to go back."

"Well, at least we have six days together," he said, keeping his face turned toward the sun.

His answer disappointed her. "Your year's just about over," she said softly. "We've made it through, you and I. Now everything's going to be normal again."

Her face looked relaxed, but one of her fists was clutching the blanket. He picked up a dead twig, broke it in half, and cleaned his teeth with it. "Normal?" His chest expanded, as though he wanted to go on talking, but no sound came from his moving lips. He poked at his gums until the twig was red with his blood. "Isn't everything normal?"

"We live six thousand miles apart." Anna leaned against his back. "Petya needs you." He froze, letting her know she'd chosen the wrong bait.

"I'll always be there for Petya." He looked over his shoulder to see if the boy was really asleep. Anna had brought up the unresolved issue, the question that Galina, too, had asked him again and again. How could a man be a father to his child if there was so much distance between them? Galina had been married before, but without children; because of her transfer to Sakhalin, her divorce had gone through without a hitch. It had been years, she said, since she'd wished for children; given her unpredictable profession, she probably wasn't cut out to perform very well as a mother, anyway. As for Leonid's performance as a father, he'd left his son in the hands of the boy's curmudgeonly grandfather for a year. Except his feelings for the child, what spoke for Leonid as a father?

Even if the whole mess had started with Anna's infidelity, he himself was acting a hundred times more irresponsibly.

"A possibility has come up." He had Galina's name on the tip of his tongue, swallowed hard, and threw the twig away. "There are still some things to verify." His gums itched; he spat blood onto the grass. "But the potential income is outstanding."

"Income." Her answer sounded flat and disappointed.

As he felt immeasurably in the wrong, Leonid began to speak with greater vehemence. "Just for accepting such a transfer, I get forty percent more than a captain's regular pay." After a cowardly few seconds, he turned to Anna. "And after six months, there's an additional ten percent bonus."

"Transfer to where?" Her voice was sad already; she'd understood.

"Probably Yakutsk." What was an optimistic way of pronouncing that name? "Maybe even farther east, on the Sea of Okhotsk."

"That's . . . I don't know where that is." Anna's Sunday was over. "For how long?"

"That's what I want to discuss with you." It cost him an effort to reach for her hand. "We'll see each other more often than we did this past year. I get forty days' annual leave and a round-trip ticket for my family to anywhere in the Soviet Union."

She thrust her fingers between his. "How long, Leonid?"

"If I sign up for five years, my pay is doubled."

"Five! Petya will already be in high school!"

"We're still young, Anna." Why was he trying to placate her? Why didn't he get it over with? On the flight to Moscow, he'd made a detailed plan: Petya would spend the warm months with him; the rest of the year, he'd live with Anna. Wasn't it desirable for the boy to get to know their great country at an early age? They wouldn't be the only couple that ever came to terms with such a compromise. Was Leonid supposed to live the rest of his life unhappily married to the wrong woman? After all, wasn't Anna really to blame for everything? Hadn't she driven him away?

"When do you have to decide?"

He stroked Petya's hair. Three days previously, he'd cleaned out his locker in the technical section's office on Sakhalin; his successor was already in place. His men finally had a genuine sea wolf for a commander. As an officer unattached to any unit, Leonid would have to persevere for another month on the island base; after that, the post in Yakutsk would be free. By coincidence—which he saw as destiny—the new barracks was only a few miles from Galina's hospital.

"As I said, they're checking my request," he murmured. "Above everything else, I wanted to see you and . . ." The words grew heavy on his tongue. "Isn't that unhealthy, to let Petya sleep for so long on the damp grass?" When Anna made no reply, he filled in the silence: "You know what I feel like doing? I haven't been in a movie theater since I left Moscow!"

Anna grasped at the straw and remarked that there were some interesting new films. On the way back, she said, they could pass by the Pushkinskaya Cinema. Then she remembered the chaos at home. "I'll be through cleaning up by this evening . . . yes, a movie's a good idea!" She tossed her hair back from her forehead. She felt that she had to be alone with him in pleasant surroundings. Six days weren't many, but they offered time enough for her to dissuade him from his plan. She'd prove to him that he didn't have it so good anywhere else as he did with her. Forget the higher pay and all the benefits! An apartment in Nostikhyeva was waiting for them, a new and better home. Anna resolved to go out there with him in the next few days and have a look at the ongoing construction. Leonid was a practical man; when all was said and done, he'd understand that Moscow was the only city where life was worth living.

TWENTY-ONE

There were two new movies showing in the big cinema on Pushkinskaya Square: *The Seventh Bullet* and a drama entitled *Without Fear*. Leonid and Anna were looking for lighter fare, so they moved on to two other theaters without finding a film they wanted to see. Dusk was already falling as they strolled past the Operetta Theater. The poster in front announced the comedian Yuri Nikulin's show *Attack on the Laugh Muscles*. The two turned away from the display cases.

Anna was exhausted. Although the family had helped with the cleanup operation, she'd wound up doing most of the work. The broken chair could probably be glued back together, but she'd had to throw away the floor lamp and the charred tablecloth. Eventually, the apartment had been returned to its former state, more or less, but as far as Anna was concerned, a kind of contamination remained, as if the place now bore a wound of indiscretion, inflicted on it by the Moscow literary world. Anna had put together an evening meal from the remains of the buffet. Viktor Ipalyevich, suffering the consequences of too much alcohol, had sought to regain control of his weakened body by moving very slowly and with great concentration. The poet was sincerely overjoyed at Leonid's return and curious to observe the affection between the father and son. When Petya learned that his parents were going out that evening, he'd started to whine, but he'd been consoled by Leonid's promise of a visit to the Red Army Museum.

As they walked down a winding street not far from the wall of the Kremlin, Anna and Leonid discovered a dimly illuminated sign for CINEMA UNDER THE ROOF and a poster that proposed *A Long Night: Sergei Bondarchuk's War and Peace*. A starstruck look came over Leonid's face. "Do you remember?" he said, as though speaking to himself.

The film was several years old but still popular, and Anna knew that Leonid had taken part in it—along with ten thousand other soldiers in the Red Army. They exchanged looks, and the decision was made. Since the showing had already begun, they had to ring a bell for the cashier, who graciously sold them two tickets. Every seat in the screening room, a reconstructed attic, seemed to be occupied; not wishing to disturb anyone by searching for their places, Anna and Leonid sat on the steps in the aisle. Leaning against each other, they let themselves be carried away by the large, colorful images.

Every hour of procrastination, every hour when he didn't say what he had to say, increased Leonid's discomfort. At the same time, he admitted to himself that the many long months he'd spent living in barracks had made him almost forget the comforts of family life. With Galina, passion had swum into his ken; now he was thinking that he'd also earned a bit of tranquillity. Accordingly, he'd wait for the right time to make his disclosure. It might, he knew, cause the edifice of his former life to come tumbling down, but even so, the upheaval should not occur wantonly or before its time. And until then, who could deny him the right to play the home-comer, the welcome husband and father?

Leonid loved Bondarchuk's *War and Peace*. On the screen, the first meeting between Prince Andrei and Natasha was taking place. The very young and beautiful actress Ludmila Savelyeva, in the part that made her famous, played Natasha. Then the director appeared, playing the central role of the noble Pierre. Leonid nudged Anna. "I know him."

She snuggled closer to him, knowing that she'd soon hear the old story. Even though the final decisions were made at the highest level, the soldiers from the chosen garrisons had scrambled to take part in the filming. The epic of their homeland, the mightiest novel of all time, was to be turned into a movie seven hours long—a prospect that made every Russian heart beat harder. Strictly according to regulations, the enlisted men had to play the foot soldiers, while Soviet officers were given costumes corresponding to their rank and identifying them as members of the staff of General Kutuzov, Napoleon's conqueror. Other Russian officers were assigned to wear uniforms of the French Grande Armée, but they refused and had to be replaced by actors.

Leonid had very much admired the director, Sergei Bondarchuk. With the help of dozens of assistants, he had made army groups move on cue, coordinated advancing cavalry units and pyrotechnics so that the trained horses would fall right in front of the camera, and in the end sent a thousand men marching into Napoleon's cannon fire. Leonid had played a Russian adjutant; his uniform was too tight, and the boots were missing altogether, but he'd been assured that the camera was going to shoot him only from the chest up. With a resolute look on his face, Leonid had harkened to his general's command and marched out of the frame a yard behind Bondarchuk.

He'd surely told this story a hundred times and seen the film a dozen. Nevertheless, the flickering images once again carried him away into the past, to the time when he'd met Anna, when they still had bold dreams. For the rest of his stay in the theater, Galina, icy Yakutia, and the great change hanging over him were forgotten.

They stayed until the end of the third part of *War and Peace*; it was already after midnight. Feeling good because of what she saw as the growing closeness between her and her husband, Anna strolled beside him to the subway and, soon thereafter, along the Mozhaisk Chaussée.

When they arrived home, they tiptoed past the sleeping Viktor Ipalyevich, climbed into the sleeping alcove, and put Petya between them without waking him up.

The following afternoon, as Anna was returning home from work, she started in alarm. Anton was in the ZIL, waiting for her. That could mean but one thing: Alexey wanted to propose a meeting. A hundred thoughts flashed across her brain. Her dearest wish was to make a clean break, and that would entail leaving Alexey. Leonid's presence positively compelled a separation! She'd give him a farewell gift, Anna decided, as she walked toward the ZIL; she'd tell him what she knew about Lyushin. Yes, that was how she'd do it: She'd go to Drezhnevskaya Street one last time, sit in the corner seat on the sofa, next to her dear old wolf, drink a little wine, and tell him the truth. Anna exchanged greetings with Anton and agreed to an appointment the following evening.

"Tomorrow I'm meeting that man for the last time," she began without prelude when she found Leonid alone in the apartment. She didn't carry her groceries into the kitchen; she had an irresistible urge to start talking honestly and immediately.

Leonid kept his eyes on the sheet of paper in front of him, scribbled a few more lines, and looked up. "Man? What man?"

Anna put out a hand to stop the bag of potatoes from falling off the table and answered that she was talking about the man from the Central Committee.

Leonid almost blurted out a question: Was he the reason she was meeting this fellow? He was downright fearful of the idea that Anna's CC contacts had something to do with him.

When he remained silent, Anna said, "It's the last time. I can't do it anymore, and I don't want to, either. I don't care what privileges come with it!"

She was in front of him again, Anna, who was filled with the highest ideals and at the same time caught in the web of necessity; Anna, who surrendered what she could to rescue her family's happiness. He laid an envelope over his sheet of paper. "Are you sure this is the right time to do that?"

His dispassion irritated her. Was he insulted to hear that the affair was still going on? Didn't he understand from her behavior that his homecoming had changed everything? Anna wasn't used to talking about feelings with Leonid. The signals between them had always been sent by other means—a good meal, a song on the radio, a smiling gaze at their son. Alexey, not Leonid, was the man who'd encouraged Anna to name her wishes and her fears. And now she was standing before her husband, unsure of how to proceed. She said, "I've decided, Leonid, and I know everything's going to be all right."

She moved toward him, the potato bag toppled over, and the first tuber spilled out, followed by several more. With his foot, Leonid prevented a potato from rolling under the cupboard. Anna knelt down. He didn't want to see his wife scooting around on the floor and bent to help her. They met in front of the sofa, still gathering up potatoes. Holding one in each hand, she crawled to his side, embraced him, sought his mouth, and pressed him against the sofa.

She couldn't understand why she was now wild for the very same man she'd scarcely desired during the course of the previous five years. What tricks emotions play on people, she thought; the Party was right to demand that individual passion be placed in the service of society as a whole. While Anna was considering what ideal she subordinated her own passion to and concluding that her attitude vis-à-vis politics was deficient, Leonid pulled his sweater off and unbuttoned his shirt. How simple it had been to live right when she was a Pioneer Girl: a camp filled with girls, a well-regulated daily routine, political instruction every morning and evening. Anna had known since those days that the Party's directives were like so many bridges and handrails that could assist a person in negotiating the complexities of daily life. The simplification of the data helped one to keep the goal in sight, to overcome setbacks, and to learn to deal with one's own demons. Meanwhile, things had progressed to the point where Leonid was sitting beside her on the sofa, half-naked, and she clambered over him. Despite her excitement, she couldn't ignore the musty old man's smell that emanated from the sofa cushions. It was as if Viktor Ipalyevich were there with them. Anna shut her eyes and caressed her husband.

The sight of the letter on the table a few feet away made Leonid feel ashamed. He'd hardly begun to write an amorous note to Galina, and now he was betraying his lover with his wife. Although he'd wanted to give his letter a simple opening, the first few sentences had turned out unusually ardent; Leonid didn't recognize himself as the author of such lines and couldn't imagine what had become of his vocabulary. The revival of his married life distressed him, and he'd felt the need to write straight from the heart, to cry out to Galina and implore her to return his love. If he didn't receive some sign from her, and very soon, he'd lose himself completely in his old life, and his psychological homecoming would be allowed to follow the physical one. Sex with Anna was unavoidable, but even after their long separation, sleeping with her brought him nothing more than ordinary pleasure. They'd never introduced much variety into their lovemaking; in the afternoon, the sofa had always been their chosen venue, so as not to rumple the freshly made bed. Leonid listened to the pitiful springs, doing their duty, and watched the lovely breasts, soft and full, bouncing up and down before his eyes. He tried to force himself not to think of Galina, as decency required, but his efforts failed. The images, the smell stole upon him, the inadvertence with which he'd thrown himself into her embrace, the intoxication that had sprung from it. He longed for Galina, right then, and his longing shamed him.

The sound came from just outside the door, and in the next moment someone entered the apartment. Before Leonid could snatch up his pants or Anna climb off of him, Viktor Ipalyevich was in the living room. Reflexively, with the movement of a character in an animated cartoon, he pivoted on his heel; the look of embarrassed surprise crossed his face only after his body had already reacted. He vanished as he'd appeared, with spectral swiftness.

"It's such beautiful weather," they heard him say in the foyer. "Why should we come back to this stuffy apartment so soon?"

"I'm hungry," the child's voice said.

"Is that a reason to stay inside?" There was a sound of rustling fabric, followed by the jingle of keys. "What do you say we go to the old Antler bakery and get some blini?"

"Blini?" the two on the sofa heard their son say. His grandfather's answer was overlaid by the closing of the door.

Leonid had a sudden mad desire to top off the already ludicrous situation. "So you're going to see that CC member," he said. "Where is it that you two meet?"

Anna, who'd been holding her breath, exhaled with a gasp. "Stop it, Leo," she said, jerking his head down to her chest.

"But it interests me." Now, he thought, I've got to ask some questions that have been unspoken for a year and a half. "How often have you two been together? All told, I mean."

Her upper body sagged. "I don't know how often." Like so many questions, this one couldn't be answered.

"Only once a week, or more than that?"

"Stop it! Stop it!"

"Would you say every three days?"

"He doesn't have much time," she let herself be coaxed into saying. "And he's married."

"So . . . once a month?" Why am I tormenting her? Leonid thought. Wouldn't this be the time for him to say, "I'm no better than you, I was lonely, and now there's this woman, and I want her. Unlike you, I can't say I'll never see her again, because I will. She's the reason why I applied for this new transfer"? Sensing that the interruption had incapacitated him, Leonid pushed Anna gently aside, stood up, and adjusted his clothing. She'd torn a button off his shirt; reproachfully, he showed her the spot.

She was as unhappy as she could be. Why couldn't she manage to convince him of her good intentions? From now on, all her efforts would be dedicated to the family; why wouldn't he believe that? She found the button and presented it to him as if it were a symbol of her honesty. Leonid gave her a fleeting kiss and sat down to his writing again.

"You must be hungry." She was concerned about reestablishing the good mood. "*I'm* hungry, in any case," she said with a laugh, gathered up the bag of potatoes, and sprang into the kitchen.

Leonid pulled out his partly written letter from under the envelope, read what he'd written, and felt the impossibility of writing anything more with Anna in the kitchen, just a few steps away. He folded the sheet of paper, slipped on his shoes, and announced that he was going out for cigarettes. On the way downstairs, he met his disgruntled son, who in the end had rejected all his grandfather's proposals and insisted on returning home. Leonid evaded the old man's knowing, fellow-male look, set the fidgety child on his shoulder, and brought him along on his cigarette-buying mission; Viktor Ipalyevich continued up the stairs to the apartment while father and son went galloping down. Petya squealed and dug his fingers into Leonid's hair. They ran outside into the bright daylight and reached the tobacco shop on the corner. When Leonid tore open the packet and put a cigarette between his lips, he remembered that what he'd actually set out to do was to finish writing his letter to Galina. He decided to put it off until that evening and offered Petya his hand. Smoking, he strolled with his son down the Mozhaisk Chaussée.

TWENTY-TWO

Anna could barely make out the sign for the narrow and dimly lit street: DREZHNEVSKAYA ST. She turned into it furtively, like an adulteress. She'd insisted that she didn't want Anton to drive her. She wanted to go to the meeting alone, say to Alexey what needed to be said, and disappear into the darkness again.

During the course of the day, familiar things had cheered her—the ladder, the paintbrush with the broken handle. She'd hung her bucket on a hook and painted the wall from top to bottom. By noon, three rooms were finished, and her shoulders ached from painting surfaces above her head. When her shift had ended, she'd been happy to be so exhausted; weariness reduced her nervousness.

She rang the bell. A while passed before the buzzer sounded. On the stairs, she considered whether there wasn't something she hadn't thought about. This would be their last time together; they'd drink a few glasses of wine, and she'd give Alexey her "farewell gift." Had the situation not been so dangerous, Anna would have found it more strange than anything else. She was acting like a double agent: Instead of reporting to her case officer with information, she was about to give it to the person under observation.

Although Alexey must have known that she was waiting outside his door, he didn't open it until she rang again. He looked haggard, his face was drawn, and he hadn't shaved for their appointment as he usually did. "There you are," he said. He sighed and without embracing her led the way into the apartment. She closed the door and took off her coat.

"Have I come at a bad time?" she asked, glancing into the kitchen, where this time no wine was standing ready.

"You're probably the only thing that hasn't come at a bad time today," he said with a tired smile.

"The Five-Year Plan?"

"It's finally concluded, over and done with." He turned to the glasses, and had Anna not sprung into action, his coattails would have swept the plate with the tsarina's portrait from the sideboard to the floor. Alexey took advantage of Anna's nearness to give her a quick kiss. "Excuse me—there are too many things going through my head." He opened the refrigerator, took out a half-empty bottle of white wine, and left it to Anna to bring the food.

"I've been doing a lot of thinking, too," she said, introducing her subject. She put the dish on the table and arranged the little sandwiches more attractively.

Alexey poured the wine, and they took their first sips.

"Leonid has come home," Anna said, sitting down across from Alexey.

He scrutinized her, not like the "other man" in her love triangle, but rather like a trainer wondering whether his fighter has the stuff to go the distance. "Has Leonid come home for good?"

"No." A cold spot in the pit of her stomach began to spread out. "He's trying to get transferred to Yakutsk."

Alexey's eyes narrowed. He wasn't prepared for such a conversation, and the prospect of it certainly gave him no pleasure, so Anna came swiftly to the point: "I don't want to lose him."

Alexey picked up his glass and made the liquid sparkle in the light. "Looks to me as though your captain doesn't exactly yearn to come back to you."

He made the remark jokingly, but it went through her like a knife. "For a year, Petya's had no father, and I've had no man."

"No man." They exchanged a brief glance, and Bulyagkov nodded. The lack of physicality in their relationship had never been an issue for them; now they were both thinking the same thing.

"We both knew we couldn't last the way we were. Something had to change one day." She put her hand on his.

"And now it's over?" Was his weird calm due to exhaustion?

"My love, my dearest," she said sadly. His sallow face, his disordered hair, the old eyes, and the melancholy that filled them combined to take Anna's breath away. "We were a good team."

"Are you breaking off our friendship, too?"

"Our friendship, never," she answered vehemently. He'd understood what she meant; why didn't she confess that she'd come expressly to break it off? "But I don't know where that will lead us. We were never what's called a couple."

"I suppose not." He leaned back with a look of serious consideration on his face. "I love you, Anna. Maybe I love you so much because we were never able to spend much time together. Maybe things were good for us for so long because there was always the temptation of thinking something more might come of them."

She thought about Kamarovsky, the other creator of this relationship, and about Leonid, who, this one time, knew where she was spending the evening. Alexey's woefulness overcame her, too.

"I've been saddled with taking a trip," he said in a different tone of voice. "I'll have to leave very soon."

"A trip? Where?" The change of subject had rattled her.

"Please let everything remain the same between us until I get back."

"Why? What's the difference if we say good-bye now or then?"

"A big difference, as far as I'm concerned." He rolled his wineglass around on its base. "Could you do that for me?"

"My husband's back at home, playing with our son. I want to straighten everything out." When he said nothing, she went on: "I can't do what you want me to do unless you tell me the reason for it."

Cautiously, as though he were afraid of breaking it, he placed the glass to one side. "I wouldn't like to cause Comrade Kamarovsky any unnecessary concern." The eyes of the Arctic wolf gazed at her.

The hanging lamp suddenly seemed to Anna like a sun shining in her face. Her mouth went dry. She stared at Alexey as though, in that instant, he'd been transformed into a dangerous predatory beast.

"Since when . . . ?" she whispered.

"Since when have I known?" He reached for her hand; she jerked it back. "Since before you knew, Anna."

In the silence, the room seemed to dissolve. "But then . . . everything was a game, a setup from the start?" She shook her head several times, as though trying to get an unpleasant sound out of her ear. "How could you love me, if you . . . ?"

"That's what's so marvelous." He reached for her hand a second time. "That first time, when I saw you on the ladder, in your overalls, with paint on your nose—that first time, you conquered me."

"Stop making jokes!"

"When it came to you, I was always serious." He kissed the base of her thumb. "At our second meeting—you remember, your father's reading—my heart was beating in my throat when I spoke to you. I was just an old guy, fat and worn out, and I had my eye on the beautiful, married house painter. I was in love for the first time in years, for the first time again, full of longing, and I felt so young it was mortifying even to me." With every sentence, he drew closer to her face. "Do you know how much I desired these lips, these eyes, your hair, every inch of your neck? It was childish and maybe unreasonable, but wonderful, too."

"But why . . ." She realized that she was incapable of doing justice to his passionate words. "Why didn't you ever want to make love to me?"

"That didn't mean I loved you any less." He stroked her cheek. "We *did* make love," he said with a smile. "I was embarrassed in front of you. I still am."

"And what about Kamarovsky?" she asked brusquely. Alexey's unexpected declaration had thrown her into total disarray.

"I knew the Colonel would set somebody on me."

"Why?"

"Because that's what they do to anyone who has a kind of power they can't assess. Science is such a power, Anna." He pondered for a moment. "But maybe my dubious past was reason enough."

"Your father?"

He shrugged. "I'm not a Russian. That's still a defect, even today."

Involuntarily, she moved closer to him. "Why didn't you ever say anything?"

"I didn't want to put you in a false position. It was obvious to me that if you knew what was going on, Kamarovsky would notice. He would have seen through you at once. Your ignorance was important to him." He added, lowering his voice, "And to me."

"You used me the whole time."

In the silence, they heard an automobile stop in front of the building. Alexey stood up and pushed the curtain to one side. "I hope we can do without reproaches. Couldn't you have said 'No' when Kamarovsky asked you to be his spy? You decided to do something for your father—and for Petya. I know very few people who would have refused."

Even though he was expressing what Anna had thought a hundred times, hearing it from him enraged her. "I can't go on like this. It has to come to an end today, right now. That's what I came here to tell you. Can't you just let me go?"

He closed the curtain. "All right. If nothing can dissuade you, it's over as of today."

Anna heard the car drive off. As the sound of the engine faded, Alexey picked up a sandwich and bit it in half.

She couldn't believe she'd gained his assent so easily. "Really, Alexey?"

He swallowed and took a sip of wine. "On one condition: Let's keep up appearances until after I return from my trip. I once told you that you'd never have anything to fear from me. Won't you just trust me?"

"How can I, after two years that were one big lie?"

Anna had never heard the doorbell ring inside the apartment. It was a loud, piercing sound, incongruous with this clandestine place. Alexey stood up and said, "Excuse me. This won't take long." He stepped into the hall and closed the door behind him.

Anna guessed that he'd been expecting this visit. She heard the front door open and listened in vain for words of greeting; there was only silence. What was going on? Why wasn't there the slightest sound of communication between Alexey and his visitor? Now she heard steps. She started to go into the next room, but the front door closed with a gentle click. She ran back and peered cautiously through the ornamental glass panes of the door to the hall. It was empty.

Precisely then, when Anna needed a clear head and all her reasoning power to consider the situation, her nerves gave way. Suddenly, everything she was going through seemed overwhelming, and she was racked by sobs that had lain silent in her for a long time, waiting to be set off. The hand she clapped against her mouth couldn't repress a gush of phlegm and saliva; she swallowed hard, coughed, ran stooping into the kitchen, washed her hands, and splashed water on her face. Her tears didn't stop right away, and as she stood there weeping, trying not to make any noise, she fixed her blurred gaze on the kitchen door.

Alexey had confessed his deep feelings for her and, in the same breath, revealed himself as a coldly calculating man. He'd taken a lover in the knowledge that such a step would drive her into the hands of the KGB. He'd been prepared to accept the breakup of her marriage and the ruin of her family in order to achieve a single goal: deceiving Kamarovsky. While Alexey voluntarily and apparently casually divulged to Anna information concerning the inner workings of his Ministry, he was providing the Colonel with facts whose analysis had resulted—at this realization, Anna caught her breath—in Kamarovsky's overlooking the *real* facts! Was it possible that the phlegmatic wolf had outsmarted the hard-bitten security officer?

Her weeping subsided, giving way to feverish cogitation. What sense could she make of all this? Didn't the high-ranking comrades all work in concert? Wasn't the KGB the Central Committee's instrument, its listening ear, its hidden eye, its torture tool? Hadn't Alexey himself asserted that the Party had abandoned its unjust practices and instituted stricter internal monitoring in order to eliminate the possibility of rule by individual diktat? Or was it naive to believe that the struggle for power within the walls of the Party's headquarters wasn't being carried on as fiercely as ever?

Anna's reflections went even further. If Bulyagkov had actually *staged* their entire time together, didn't that mean he'd brought her to Dubna deliberately? And could Kamarovsky really have failed to discern that the Deputy Minister for Research Planning had smuggled the house painter into the atomic city for other than romantic reasons? Had Bulyagkov, rather than Kamarovsky, intended for Anna to meet Lyushin?

"But why?"

She flinched at the sound of her own voice. She'd been staring at the enamel clock, whose ticking had never before seemed so intrusive. After trying for three days in Dubna, Anna remembered, she'd given up all hope of running into Lyushin again. And then, on the last afternoon, no less, mere hours before Anna was to leave Dubna and return to Moscow, the nuclear physicist had shown up in the very place where she was. Why hadn't Alexey made any effort to get rid of his uninvited guest? Because he wasn't uninvited! Nor had Alexey objected when she and Lyushin had a conversation about a field of research that was subject to the highest level of secrecy. Back on that afternoon, Anna had been proud of herself for understanding enough about quantum physics to follow what Lyushin was saying. But hadn't it been the other way around? Hadn't Lyushin kept his remarks as simple as possible so that he could be sure she understood? And if that was the case, it meant that *both* Bulyagkov and Lyushin had wanted Anna to receive some specific information, take it back to Moscow, and report it to Kamarovsky. In fact, she'd returned with only one piece of news, namely, that Lyushin's research project had failed.

She put her hand on the dripping faucet and turned it all the way off. The dripping continued; there was a washer problem here, too. Bewildered, she recalled that one purpose of her visit had been to confide to Alexey what she knew about Lyushin. She'd come within a hair of making a dangerous mistake. The less she knew, the less she said, the more dispensable she'd seem to the contending parties, and the sooner she'd get her wish: to be released from all this into the normality of her former life.

A glance at the hands of the clock showed Anna that only three minutes had gone by. She dried her eyes again, ran her fingers through her hair, and went back into the living room. Then she stepped into the hall and listened. Someone outside spoke, just for a moment, and then a key was thrust into the lock. Just as she closed the glass door, Anna thought she heard a woman's voice in the stairwell. Medea? Would Alexey's wife arrive here without notice? Anna dropped onto the corner seat, picked up her glass of wine, and drank half of it.

He returned with a little package. "My apologies," he said, and carried the package into the back room. "Are you hungry at all?" he asked from there.

"No omelet without eggs," Anna muttered. She wouldn't be taking his innocuous act at face value anymore.

"What?" He came back into the living room and closed the curtain.

"You can't make an omelet without breaking eggs." She stood up. "I have to go."

"Already?"

"Hasn't everything been said?" She was itching to dash to the window and see who was stepping out of the building at that very moment.

Alexey appeared to read her impulse and placed himself in the way. "You haven't given me your answer yet."

As he spoke, she sensed how dangerous he was, the man she'd seen so often in his homely cardigan, slightly tipsy or exhausted from work. One false word now and she'd be in danger. Apart from Anton, nobody knew where she'd gone, and nobody had seen her arrive. Who would ever think about looking for her here?

"Good," she said, apparently casual. "Let's leave everything where it is."

"Do you mean that?" It wasn't a question; it was, unmistakably, pressure.

"Yes." She turned toward the door, and he let her pass. "Will I see you before you leave on your trip?"

He followed her and helped her into her coat. "That would be lovely."

"May one know where you're going?"

He smiled thoughtfully. "A city where it's never hot, not even in summer."

Don't know, don't guess, Anna thought. As though she wanted to prevent him from talking anymore, she flung her arms around his neck, pressed herself against him for a long time, longer than usual, and ran out of the apartment and down the stairs without turning around.

TWENTY-THREE

The city looked strange to Anna as she made her way home, but she knew it was her and not the city; her perceptions were peculiarly heightened. She walked down the stairs into the Kurskaya Metro station. There were four ticket windows, each with a long line in front of it. Anna decided to try number three. After standing in place for ten minutes without moving, she stepped out and walked up to the front of the queue.

"So impatient, young lady?" someone said. "We're waiting, too."

The first person in line was a man whose hat was pulled down low over his forehead; a dog was sitting next to him. The man's face beamed with patience and serenity, and he seemed uninterested in accelerating the process. The ticket window was opaque, either misted up from the dampness or covered with dust—in any case, the person on the other side couldn't be seen. Anna spotted a small piece of paper stuck to the glass, with writing so tiny she had to stand inches away from it before she could read it. It gave notice that the window was temporarily closed. The behavior of the person who was first in line seemed inscrutable to Anna until she took a good look at his dog. It wore a white collar, and the leash the man was holding was attached to a long staff. Why hadn't the people behind him noticed that they were lined up behind a blind man at a closed ticket window? The second and third positions were occupied by a young couple, holding hands and whispering as they gazed into each other's eyes. Next came a stout woman, staring into space and talking to herself. Then there was a newspaper reader, followed by a listless Asiatic man who kept his eyes fixed on the tips of his shoes. Not a single one of them was interested in why the line wasn't moving; there they stood, acquiescing to their circumstances, while time rolled on by.

That's the way we are, Anna thought. Herd animals. We get crammed into situations where any people would protest, any people but Russians! We're content with a little reassurance, and we'll put up with anything. Nobody thinks to ask why window number three is closed! Window number three is closed everywhere in the country, but we don't want to know what's behind the glass or what takes place over our heads. We live like the bottom range of a pyramid, pressed down from above and bearing the entire burden. We've been told we're the most modern, most forward-looking society in the world. But what do we do? Stand in front of a blank window and wait. Surrender, accept, wait! "Window three is closed!" Anna cried, venting her rage.

Heads turned; people exchanged expressionless looks. Finally, they began to move, one by one, abandoning that queue to try their luck in the next. Anna informed the blind man that he had nothing to hope for from the window in front of him. He thanked her and, without losing any of his serenity, betook himself to the end of line number four.

Even if you shake people out of their apathetic acceptance, Anna thought, do they use the opportunity to give some thought to their situation? No, on the contrary; as quickly as possible, they look for the security of the familiar and start cooling their heels again somewhere nearby. And meanwhile—Anna's eyes turned upward—life presents itself in all its variety directly over their heads! Sometime in the past, before everything became so gray and resigned, revolutionaries built these vaults. Though a hundred feet underground, those men had been informed by the desire to make something beautiful, which Anna read as an outcry against everything deadening. High overhead, luminaires cast their gilded light into niches where amber statues stood, alert figures that seemed on the point of coming to life. A hunter urged his dog to the chase; a muscular woman offered the observer a plate; a student bent over his book. The early heroes and heroines of the Revolution *represented* the future for us, Anna thought; they made it into images that show us the way. But we stumble past them, vacant and blind. We're underhanded, corrupt, concerned only for our own advantage, and this miserable state of affairs is visible at every level. Kamarovsky distrusts Bulyagkov, Bulyagkov deceives Kamarovsky, Lyushin betrays the Ministry, the Minister neglects to question falsified reports.

Anna felt so beset by troubles that she could have screamed. She needed air; she rushed past the lines of gaping people, reached the steps, and ran up into the damp, cold night. Heading west, she hurried through the streets, stepping briskly past spires and domes, and burst into Red Square, the enormous center of the city, the illuminated monument of its past and, at the same time, of a glorious future. How could people who came to this place forget the purpose it served? How could they ignore the mausoleum of their greatest hero and disregard his principles? Did anybody gaze at the red star on the top of the tower or the flag flying over the Kremlin and not feel called upon to do everything he could to ensure that what those symbols stood for would become reality? At that moment, in the shadow of the brightly illuminated walls bordering Red Square, Anna would have given anything to have been one of the early revolutionaries, one of those who had made their way there in the old days to hear the speeches and see the personages, the builders of the new state founded on the principles of a brilliant theory.

After some minutes, during which she'd strolled along the brick walls to the mausoleum and then back to the cathedral, Anna grew calmer. She could distinguish individual faces again, not just the faceless mass. A skeptical-looking woman in a red, quilted coat, two Kyrgyz tourists in absurdly huge fur hats, a portly married couple making their way home after some last-minute shopping. In our hearts, we all want the same thing, she thought, soothing herself. It's just that many of us lack perseverance and patience, and we become fainthearted; we stop envisioning the goal. Anna felt satisfied to discover that a visit to this spot, where all the lines of the Soviet Union ran together, sufficed to restore her positive attitude.

She determined which Metro station offered the quickest way home and once again descended underground. When she got out at Filyovsky Park, she was filled with a sense of relief. The hardest step was behind her; she and Alexey had put an end to lying and reached a clear agreement. Now that she was confident of having removed the biggest obstacle standing between her and Leonid, she could imagine nothing better than spending the evening with her family.

The little apartment had rarely seemed so homelike to her: the old lamp, the books, Viktor Ipalyevich in front of the television set, Leonid snuggling with Petya in the alcove. Anna removed her shoes on the landing, and her thick socks made no sound as she slipped inside; none of the three noticed her yet.

"Can you imagine living in Siberia?" she heard her husband say.

"Why?" Petya asked.

"Just wondering. How would it be to take a trip away from all the bustle and noise of the city and go to a place where there's still a lot of land and wide-open spaces, where nature's vast and everybody can spread out?"

Anna noticed that her husband was keeping his voice down so that his father-in-law over in the TV chair couldn't hear him. She tiptoed nearer.

"How long am I supposed to be there?"

"Don't have a clue. I just want to know if it sounds like a good idea to you."

"Well, where is it, Papa?"

"It's in the East, far away. Everything there is different from here—it's much more extreme."

"What does 'extreme' mean?"

"It means only strong guys can survive out there. Guys like you."

Petya laughed and said, "And you!"

"We both have what it takes to make it there, right?"

"Right!"

Anna understood Leonid's effort to make his transfer something his son could grasp. She wanted to lie down beside her men and project the future with them.

"Maybe we could even live there for a longer time," Leonid went on.

Anna stood still.

"Then we'll be together always?" Petya asked.

"Well, you'll spend part of the time with Mama, naturally."

"She's not coming with us?"

"Sure she is." Leonid cleared his throat. "But she can't always be in Yakutia. She's got a good job in Moscow, and she won't want to give it up." Leonid rolled over, making the bed creak. "We'll just ask her when the time comes."

"Why hasn't the time come yet?"

"Because there's a lot of things I have to get straight. But I'm sure it won't be long now."

Petya seemed to ponder this. Finally, he said, "I wish we'd all stay together."

Anna felt that this was her cue. "Good evening, you two," she said, placing herself in front of them.

Leonid flinched. "Have you been listening to us?"

"I'm not supposed to know what you talk about in bed?"

"Mama!" Petya cried, laughing at her sudden appearance. "We're going to visit Papa in . . ." He couldn't think of the name.

"We were just kidding around," Leonid said airily.

"Not kidding around! Not kidding around!" Petya yelled jubilantly. "What's the name of the place we're going to?"

"Yakutia," Anna answered for Leonid.

"Yakutia!" She received a damp kiss, after which the boy threw himself on his father and hugged his neck. "Yakutia!" he cried again and again, until finally his grandfather sat up straight in his chair. "Can I watch this program in peace, or is the counterrevolution breaking out?"

Uttering the battle cry "Yakutia!" the child sprang out of the sleeping nook and charged his surprised grandfather.

"What's the meaning of this?" Viktor Ipalyevich said, protecting his cap.

"Yakutia!" Petya was not yet tired of shouting that name.

"Be quiet. That's the name of the most terrible place on earth, the coldest wasteland, the horror of every civilized person."

Confused, Petya fell silent, as though his voice had suddenly been taken from him.

"Are you a convict?" the grandfather asked, heightening the effect of his words.

"No, Dyedushka."

"Then what's all this uproar about? Only criminals get sent to hell on earth. Is that what you want?"

"No, Dyedushka."

"Well, then." With that, the old man lifted the boy off his lap and turned his eyes back to the television screen. It was as if he'd already forgotten the interruption.

Petya crept back to his parents. "Grandfather says—"

"Grandfather has his own ideas about that part of our country," Leonid declared. "But he's never been there."

"Have you?" Anna asked in surprise.

Glowing patches appeared on Leonid's skin. "Well, you see, the possibility came up. Flights between Sakhalin and Yakutsk—"

"So you didn't come home to talk everything over with me," she said, interrupting him. "You've already made your decision."

"How was I supposed to get an idea of the place without seeing it even once?"

Petya stared mutely from one to the other. Music played in the background; a speaker announced the next program.

"Is Yakutia really hell?" the boy asked his father.

"Of course it is," the old man said, intervening again. "What else would it be?" The three heard him get up and shuffle into the kitchen.

"That's not true," Leonid whispered. "And you know why not? Because there isn't any hell." He turned to Anna. "You're home already? Didn't you have a good meeting?"

She chose to ignore his sarcastic undertone. "Have you all eaten?"

"Just because you're not home one evening, that doesn't mean things fall apart here." He went to the bathroom.

"If we move to Yakutia, we won't be convicts, will we?" Petya leaned his head on his hands.

"No one's moving anywhere. You misunderstood. And now it's bedtime." She picked him up and put him down on the floor so that she could shake out the bed. "Time for tooth brushing," she said over her shoulder.

"Are you going to bed now, too?" The boy turned toward the bathroom.

"No, I'm going to sit in the kitchen with your papa for a while."

Upon discovering that the bathroom door was locked from the inside, Petya called out, "Tooth brushing!"

The latch was raised, the door opened a little, and the child slipped into the bathroom. When Leonid came out, his path and those of Anna and Viktor Ipalyevich all intersected simultaneously. The three of them stopped short. "Leo and I are going to talk for a little while longer," Anna said to her father.

"Not tonight," her husband contradicted her. "I'm dead tired."

Disappointed, Anna watched that evening's performance of the going-to-bed ballet. Her father prepared the sofa, Leonid undressed, and Petya entered from the bathroom with his pajama pants around his ankles. Viktor Ipalyevich gave his daughter a pointed look. Traditionally, he took off his clothes last, because not even members of his family had the right to see him in his underwear. But instead of tidying up the room and hitting the bunk, Anna went into the kitchen, closed the curtain, and started boiling water for tea. I can't go on like this, she thought. How were she and Leonid supposed to get back together when everything happened before the eyes of that bad-tempered old man, when Petya was constantly dancing around them? All her attempts to be alone with Leonid had fallen through; she hadn't been able to give their reunion the excitement and romance of a new love. When the kettle began to whistle, Anna could successfully ignore the sounds coming from the next room. She had a few days left. She had to find a way to bring Leonid back to her side.

TWENTY-FOUR

Two things perplexed A. I. Kamarovsky. The first was that the reports concerning Alexey Maximovich Bulyagkov had become so innocuous. Apparent normalcy was, in the Colonel's view, a sign that something extraordinary lay ahead. The commotion over the Lyushin project had died down. The Minister for Research had succeeded in embellishing the disappointing results in his report by correcting the date of Lyushin's expected breakthrough. After this cosmetic application, it seemed only logical that the Ministry should place additional funds at the disposal of the Institute for Theoretical Physics in Dubna. The Minister had signed the authorization, and Lyushin had returned satisfied to his backwater north of Moscow.

After the successful adoption of the Five-Year Plan, the hectic pace of bureaucracy had slowed down, and Bulyagkov once again applied himself to his usual work, shuttling between the Ministry and the Central Committee, receiving the representatives of the various oblasts, and giving them the opportunity to present their assessment of the technological progress achieved in their region. He commended the improved performance in pesticide development and labored in vain on promoting the field of petrochemistry. The newly opened oil fields along the lower course of the Ob River were ready for exploitation, but the physicists in Murmansk were still unable to deliver the desired capacities by means of bigger power blocks. The refining of crude oil remained the problem child of the Soviet economy, and even though research funding had increased enormously, there was still no breakthrough in sight.

In his private life, Bulyagkov moved between his residence in Arbat, where he and his wife, Medea, customarily stayed out of each other's way, and the scene of his erotic adventures on Drezhnevskaya Street. Although formerly the women booked to appear there had changed every few months, in the past two years Kamarovsky had learned of Bulyagkov's involvement in no amorous affair other than the one he was conducting with Anna Viktorovna Nechayevna, the daughter of the poet Tsazukhin. Anna's reports were unspectacular; however, Kamarovsky appreciated her collaboration. Unlike others, when she had no suspicious moments to describe, she didn't make up any. He often had to deal with reports turned in by ambitious agents who invented anti-Soviet activities for the persons they had under observation in order to further their own careers. During all their time together, Alexey and Anna's affair had remained an unruffled relationship.

Kamarovsky found all the more interesting, therefore, the fact that Bulyagkov's wife, Medea, who was Moscow's cultural secretary and above all suspicion, had now sued for divorce. For years, she and her husband had lived such loosely connected lives that the Colonel couldn't imagine any disruption that would explain such a step. The petition had been filed only a short time ago, but given the influence of both parties, it seemed likely that the case would be quickly settled. Yesterday, the practical first step had followed the official one. While Medea remained in the main residence, Bulyagkov had had some of his things brought to the Drezhnevskaya Street apartment, which was currently serving as his home. Kamarovsky found it difficult to believe in the so-called insurmountable antipathy that was supposed to have sprung up between the couple, but what he chiefly wondered about was why this was happening precisely *now*. As he saw no possibility of directly questioning Medea

Bulyagkova, he awaited all the more eagerly a visit from Rosa Khleb. She'd asked the cultural secretary for an interview. There was no reason to doubt the journalistic motives behind the request; after all, Mrs. Bulyagkova was a person of public interest, she coordinated every guest performance that came to Moscow from the Soviet provinces, and her picture was often in the newspapers. Rosa had announced that she was doing a feature for the *Moscow Times* and called on Medea in her office in the Cultural Center.

Kamarovsky was expecting the Khleb woman to arrive in ten minutes. It seemed improper to spend the intervening time idly, but he'd cleared off his desk so meticulously that he didn't know what to do during the rest of his wait. He sat down at the piano, played the five bars he'd mastered, and came to grief with the sixth. He improvised a little, letting his thoughts drift, remembering how smoothly his female trolley conductor had taken in the passengers' fares and returned their tickets and change, in spite of the lurching car. The mute Kremlin Bell, the biggest in the world, crossed his mind, and that sixteenth-century bronze cannon no one had ever dared to fire, for fear that it might explode. Kamarovsky strung together some melancholy chords, reducing the melody to the span of an octave. He wanted to play something more cheerful, something he could jiggle his knee to, but nothing of the sort occurred to him. At night, when everybody in the building was asleep, he'd sometimes sit at the keyboard and start banging away; he found it amusing that his neighbors in the adjacent apartments, who'd lived next door to him for decades and in that time had figured out what he was, didn't dare call the police. You're a fossil, Kamarovsky thought, born out of the fratricidal struggle between the Whites and the Reds; you think in terms of the old, long-outdated hierarchies. Look at the young people, how easily they move among our great accomplishments, how they take them for granted. They display no reverence for the privations that were the cost of every victory; they take the whole and shape it for themselves.

"The big Kremlin Bell," the Colonel murmured, lifting his fingers from the keyboard. The silence did him good. He knew what the true meaning of his words was, but instead of occupying himself with that, he returned to Comrade Bulyagkova's divorce. It was a private matter, so what was there to fathom?

Bulyagkov's career was the kind of success story you read about in books. After breaking off his physics studies, Alexey, a talented Ukrainian with dubious relatives, had met the pretty daughter of a good Moscow family. Through the girl, he'd gained admittance to the right circles; since her family recognized that she was going to marry Alexey in spite of all opposition, they decided not to exclude him, but to appropriate him. Medea's grandfather, the senior serving member of the Central Committee, had Alexey Bulyagkov's biography rewritten and his father recast as a staunch fighter against counterrevolution. After the wedding, important doors had opened to Medea's young husband, who wasn't shy about striding through them. His preparation in the natural sciences had predestined him for assignment to the research sphere. He'd climbed up the hierarchical ladder, step by step, until he'd reached the second rung, from which there was no further ascent. In addition to being an alcoholic, the Minister was lazy and erratic, and it had cost Kamarovsky a great deal of effort to suppress the evidence of his weakness for minors. Nonetheless, the Minister had the best connections; from now until his retirement, nobody would ever contest his position. Since the opening of the Bulyagkov dossier, the Colonel had sought to prove that Alexey Maximovich found his lot as Deputy Minister intolerable and would therefore engage in some maneuver to unseat the Minister. So far, Kamarovsky's efforts had failed.

And now, this unexpected divorce. What advantage would Medea gain from altering her status? She wasn't seeking to liberate herself so that she could be with some "other man"; culture had always been her only passion. In the course of the decades, Alexey had never eschewed cheating on Medea, but he'd always arranged matters so tastefully that she wasn't compromised. Bulyagkov was fifty-one, his wife marginally younger; what could either of them, at their age, do with their new freedom?

The big Kremlin Bell, the Tsar Bell, weighs two hundred tons, the Colonel thought. It had barely been hung when it developed an inner crack and had never sounded, not even once. Kamarovsky had had his daughter's graduation thesis, an essay on the Kremlin Bell, sent to his office and had read the document as though it were one of the many that constantly passed over his desk. The text, at once precise and patriotic, was written in a flowing style; with such a thesis, obtaining her diploma would be a mere formality. And so his daughter would complete her studies at the Polytechnic Institute a year early and begin working toward a degree in architecture at the university in the fall. Kamarovsky hadn't been in his daughter's company for eight years, nor did she attach any importance to a possible future meeting. Twenty years previously, her mother had informed him by post of the child's birth. How odd, to receive such a letter in the center of the state security apparatus. He'd offered his support, but the woman had never taken anything from him. She and, later, her daughter had been clever enough to keep themselves clear of power, knowing that it could be helpful in many instances, but that its bonds could eventually become too tight to shake off.

Now she lives with a fellow from Okhotsk, the Colonel thought glumly; he wished his daughter would get over this Greater Soviet flirtation and embark upon a relationship with someone from Russia proper. Then he smiled at his own chauvinism. It would have suited him to help her get assigned to a nice apartment. As it was, she and her friend were living with four other people in a low-rent pad in the suburbs. Kamarovsky had once driven past it. He'd wanted to arrange a little graduation party for her, but she hadn't even answered his letter. Sometimes, unbeknownst to her, he watched her from a distance; the library where she did her cramming was only a few blocks away. She's inherited my delicate bones, he'd say to himself, with crazy pride; she'll never have wide hips like her mother. Occasionally he'd dare to get a little closer to her, and he'd believe he recognized a kindred expression in her eyes.

Kamarovsky's head sank onto his chest. He jumped in fright. No, he couldn't have a seizure now, Rosa was arriving any minute! But the sudden release of his neck muscles was a sure sign. It must be the excitement, he thought as he stood up. The reflections on his daughter, the certainty that he'd never be more than an observer of her career—that had all contributed to putting him in the kind of emotional state he hated. He knew he wouldn't be able to stay upright long enough to make it to his desk, so he dropped to his knees and began to propel himself forward, a few inches at a time. If he could concentrate on something, however glassily, he might still be able to stave off the atony. However, it was a surer thing to . . . He raised his hand to the top drawer, where the little envelope with the tablets was always ready. He'd recently ordered some new ones; only two hours after his call to Doctor Shchedrin, a messenger had brought him what he wanted. On his knees, leaning his head against the cool wood of the desk, Kamarovsky pressed a tablet out of its packaging. The hand that was supposed to bring the medication to his mouth refused its duty and slid onto the floor. The Colonel stared at the useless hand. How ugly it was as it lay there; he didn't know how he could get it back. And then he let himself fall. A cheek and an ear slid across the drawer handle on their way down, and his head struck the parquet floor. Kamarovsky couldn't tell whether his hand was still holding the tablet; half fainting, he shoved his head to what seemed like the right spot. Seen from close up, the grooves between the floorboards spread out like lines of perspective and went on into infinity. He wondered why the technique for representing spatial situations, already in place by the time of the Romans' wall frescoes, had for centuries undergone no further development and had instead been displaced by symbolic perspective. The longer he jerked his head around, the smaller were his chances of coming upon the tablet. Then his ear felt, as though through wads of cotton, a small obstacle. Kamarovsky raised his head so far that his nose and mouth came to rest on the floor. Only with the help of his lips was he able to move forward. How heavy your skull could be when your neck muscles wouldn't play along. Kamarovsky pushed his open mouth over the pill. His tongue protruded and dropped downward, very slowly, until it felt the rounded shape, licked it, and gently raised it toward his mouth. The Colonel tasted dust and crumbs; when he closed his lips, his teeth grated on particles. He forced himself to bite down hard and worked his jaws to produce saliva. Then he swallowed and gagged until he was sure he'd managed to get all the medication down his gullet. Now there was nothing to do but wait. He could smell a faint scent of varnish, with which the floor had been sealed years before. He even thought he could smell his own sweat, the odor left in this spot by his feet.

By the time the doorbell rang, Kamarovsky was already capable of standing again. Groaning, though feeling steadily stronger, he rose to his feet and dropped into the chair. After the second ring, he stretched out his hand, just a little, and pressed the buzzer. Shortly thereafter, he heard the staccato sound of steps coming upstairs and entering the apartment. The Colonel made an effort to straighten his crooked spine. Rosa was wearing black; he nodded to her and motioned toward the chair across from him. She thanked him and took a seat, opening her portfolio on the way down.

TWENTY-FIVE

The most sensible thing she could do would be to hang the curtain. Avdotya had finally finished the job, and now Anna spread the blue fabric over the table to attach the hooks. The tape had been stitched across the top part of the curtain in an impeccably straight line, and the border, too, had been neatly executed. While she busied herself with the hooks, Anna became aware of an interior stillness; she wouldn't have called it calm. It wasn't the inner harmony that the performance of simple tasks sometimes produces, nor was it the peace of mind she longed for, but a void, like the grayness of the days that lay before her. Anna could do nothing but wait in anxious expectation for Leonid's decision, nothing but hang up the curtain.

She laid the fabric aside and sat on the sofa in her small apartment. Viktor Ipalyevich had gone off in search of cheap potatoes, Petya was in school, Alexey was probably being driven to some meeting, and Leonid was back on duty in the East. Suddenly, Anna couldn't help envisioning the whole country, like an enormous map, where people worked, argued, grew stronger, suffered pain. In many regions of the Soviet Union, spring had already arrived; in others, one couldn't yet begin to hope for it. The mental image of her dynamic homeland left Anna feeling empty and alone. She'd made the beds, and tomorrow she'd do so again. She was cooking something for Petya to eat, and she'd be cooking again that evening. She'd do the shopping and cleaning, as she did every day; she'd board the combine's special bus and start her shift. She did all this to feed her family, to go on living, to keep the whole thing running.

Leonid had gone back a day early. Forced to depart in advance because of weather conditions, he'd declared; spring cyclones were moving from the Sea of Okhotsk toward Sakhalin, and there was a good chance that landing an airplane there would soon be impossible. Strangely enough, Anna was convinced that he'd welcomed his early departure. He'd promised to give more consideration to his notion of getting a transfer to Siberia, but she had the impression he'd said that just to placate her so he wouldn't have to talk about it anymore. Five years, she'd thought in despair as she watched her husband going down the stairs with his bag slung over his shoulder. They hadn't told Petya that his father was leaving a day sooner than planned; Leonid had put him to bed with particular tenderness and held him in his arms during the night. Still half asleep, the boy had gone off to school in the belief that his father would be there to greet him when he came back home.

Now Anna was sitting there, on an afternoon like many others, and she didn't know how much time would pass before she'd see her husband again. Until very recently, she'd believed her life was safeguarded by a solid structure, which was now volatizing into an atmosphere of wan pointlessness. Hanging a curtain was the only thing to do. She adjusted the hooks and lifted up one corner of the fabric in front of the sleeping niche.

While Anna Viktorovna Nechayevna was inserting the hooks, one after another, into the rings on the curtain rod, the majority of those present at a meeting of the Central Committee's Department of Research were voting to accept the invitation of the Swedish Science Council. Even though the invitation came from a Western nation, the department was of the opinion that a scientific exchange would be advantageous in that it would demonstrate the open, international aspect of Soviet research. After this fundamental decision, the meeting proceeded to determine not which scientists would travel to Stockholm, but which Party officials would accompany them. The proposal that the Minister in person should head the delegation found general acceptance; Deputy Minister Alexey Bulyagkov would remain in Moscow for the duration of the visit. As the next order of business, the Minister instructed the Deputy Minister to draw up a list of eminent scientists, from among whom those most appropriate for the delegation would subsequently be chosen. It went without saying that a copy of the list would be submitted to the Committee for State Security, and that the Research Department would then have to wait and see whether the names on the list met with any objections from the KGB. There being no further business, the minutes of the assembly were turned over for transcription, and the Minister adjourned the meeting. The comrades made their way back to their offices or betook themselves to an early lunch. Although Alexey was hungry, he distrusted the special of the day—meat loaf—and limited himself to a portion of caramel custard and a bottle of lemonade. After lunch, he went to his office and made telephone calls for half an hour, dictated a few letters, and rejected his secretary's undrinkable coffee. He met with a ministerial colleague to finalize the wording of an obituary for a recently deceased cosmonaut and chatted in the corridor with a couple of old companions. Eventually, he sent word to Anton to pick him up at the rear exit.

The weather had cleared up, and the afternoon was inviting. Enjoying the drive, Alexey leaned back in his seat and gazed out the window. The melting of the last snow and the awakening of the buds went hand in hand, and water was gurgling in the roof gutters. Puddles stood in green spaces where the ground was still frozen.

All at once, Alexey changed his mind: "Let me out here."

Anton pulled over near Obukha Lane, so Bulyagkov could take a walk along a branch of the Moskva River. He liked to make decisions while out walking; in this case, he was thinking over the impending Stockholm trip and the task assigned to him in that regard. The accomplishments of Soviet scientific research could be seen most clearly in the chemical industry; therefore, chemists should form the main contingent of the visiting delegation: the ammonia experts from Severodonetsk and the synthetic-fiber developers from Nevinnomyssk. The distinguished collective of bone marrow specialists from Krasnoyarsk could be brought along to represent Soviet medical science. Of course, the Swedes were most interested in exchanges in the field of nuclear research, but here the Soviets would exercise prudence. There would be no risk in allowing Comrade Budker to go to Stockholm and present his work in aerophysics. Soviet study of laser–plasma interaction was old hat, Alexey thought; the Americans had long since outstripped everyone in that field. The delegation should include at least three scientists from the atomic cities of Novosibirsk and Dubna; Nikolai Lyushin had announced his interest, but sending him was out of the question. The man was too impulsive, unable to control his tongue, and inclined to boasting. Bulyagkov decided to anticipate the Committee's selection criteria and nominate only scientists who had families. Besides, everything had to move quickly; when it came to issuing visas, the folks in the Lubyanka wouldn't let themselves be hurried, and the trip was already set for May.

Bulyagkov left the embankment promenade and turned into the quarter that included, on its other end, Drezhnevskaya Street. The bushes were bright green, and he bent over to examine a twig. It's the most audacious leap of my life, he thought; I don't know anyone who'd take such a risk at my age. Above his head, some black and white birds kicked up a racket, zipping from branch to branch and celebrating the warmer weather. He looked up into the still-bare crowns of the trees and saw the sky through them, so brilliantly blue that it made his heart leap.

He thought about his last gift to Medea, the two canaries. In a queer way, the birds had now acquired a deeper significance: Only the cage had made them a couple; if you opened the door of the cage, each of them would fly off in a different direction. The separation from Medea was the most difficult ordeal on Alexey's chosen path. Respect and admiration had bound them to each other for half a lifetime. Everything he had been able to attain, he owed to her. The divorce hearing would take place in a week; Alexey wished it were over now. When the big guns started firing, Medea would already be a safe distance away.

Deep in thought, he reached the little street with the illegible sign. Entering the apartment house as the owner of a clandestine hideaway adjusted to suit the wishes of a succession of female visitors was different from entering it as a simple resident, walking up the washed-concrete stairs, and opening the heavily scratched door in order to spend the night here alone. In the foyer, Bulyagkov threw off his sports jacket. After his long walk, the apartment seemed overheated. Only then did he realize that he'd had scarcely anything to eat in the cafeteria at lunch and nothing since, and suddenly he was starving. He pivoted around toward the door, but the thought of the dismal neighborhood, where there was hardly a restaurant, made him change his mind. He'd eat at home.

During the moving-in process, Anton had seen to it that the refrigerator was filled with the bare essentials; a glance inside revealed to Alexey that he'd already eaten most of them. He found eggs, a moldy onion, and half a jar of sour cream. He disliked cooking and wasn't good at it, but he surrendered to necessity, grabbed the skillet, poured in some oil, and lit the stove. Then he cut the onion into thin slices. Alexey hated the life he was leading. His profession had turned out to be the opposite of what he'd had in mind many years previously, when he'd seized the opportunity to become an administrator of scientific research. He accomplished nothing more meaningful than the paperweight on his desk did. His contempt for the pencil pushers in his department struck him as increasingly pathetic with each passing day; he'd long since become one of them. The tool of his trade wasn't the microscope or the scalpel or the slide rule, but the rubber stamp.

Bulyagkov focused his mind's eye on the Minister, whose tactical shrewdness was exceeded only by his incompetence. He obediently distributed the funds in his budget in exact accordance with the capricious wishes of the Central Committee. Nobody thought in wide-ranging terms or made allowances for the decades-long continuity that was a necessity in complicated research work. Today the pharmacologists got the biggest chunks; tomorrow it would be the biochemists. Had the Minister not had Bulyagkov at his side, the cases of unwarranted favoritism, haphazardness, and corruption would have been past counting. At the same time, Alexey was aware of being merely tolerated: He was the troubleshooter for his clueless boss, the fixer for the Minister's mistakes. Despite his advancement, Bulyagkov had remained the fellow who did the dirty work, a second-class person, a man whose background barred him from ever really entering the nomenklatura. He'd always be the Deputy, surrounded by envy for his abilities and condescension regarding his past.

A crackling sound came from the frying pan, and the smell of hot oil rose to his nostrils. He quickly dumped in the onion slices and jumped away from the sputtering grease. Without Medea, I would never have come even this far, he thought, rolling up his shirt sleeves. The determining factor wasn't my qualifications, it was her contacts. If I hadn't let myself be blinded in my youth, if I'd gone ahead and finished my degree after all, maybe I would have been able to make the transition back into science. I could have returned to Kharkov and worked as a biophysicist; I would have had a real position in life. But for a young guy in Moscow, the allure of making a career there, Medea's charms, and the open-mindedness of her family were too tempting. In those days, Alexey had severed his roots; instead of the son of a Ukrainian renegade, he preferred being an up-and-coming nobody in the capital.

Bulyagkov stirred the sizzling onions, removed the skillet from the fire, added paprika and sour cream, and then broke a couple of eggs into the mixture. As he placed the pan in the oven, he tried to remember the last time Anna had fixed this for him. He'd explained that it was a dish from his homeland, and then she'd wanted to know what he'd been like as a boy. Happy, he'd told her. Yes, in spite of the war, he'd been happy back then. When the front moved near Smolensk, Alexey's father had taken them to Vyshnivets, a village deep in the forest, where one could hope that neither Germans nor Ukrainians would arrive. The land surveyor's family found welcome and shelter there for many months—indeed, for almost a year. Alexey's memories were of full days and protected nights. It was only after the victory that the hard times had begun, the stripping of his family's assets, his withdrawal from the university, the flight to Russia. He bent down and looked through the little window to see if the eggs had set yet. Too impatient to wait any longer, he snatched the pan out of the oven. Even through the potholder, the skillet was too hot, and he had to run the last few feet to the table, drop the pan on it, and blow on his fingers. He didn't really want to drink any alcohol, but he opened the bottle from simple force of habit and poured himself a glass. After fetching salt, pepper, a knife, and a fork, he sat down and ate from the pan. Never before in these rooms had he thought of himself as a single man, depressed, solitary, unable to cope with the silence. With the first hot forkful still in his mouth, he stood up again and turned on the radio. The music was pretty. Still chewing, he walked over to the window—daylight lasted so long this time of year! He would have liked to send Anton off to pick up Anna, yet he knew his longing was only an expression of his loneliness. He was going to lose not only Medea, but also Anna. He swallowed morosely, took in the next forkful while still standing up, and considered how he might get through the interminable evening.

TWENTY-SIX

The first month of spring brought snowstorms worse than any Leonid had ever experienced in Moscow in the dead of winter. The armored vehicles attached to his company dedicated the bulk of their time to such wintry duties as clearing the roads leading into the city. Yakutsk was almost cut off from the outside world, and food supplies were nearing exhaustion. At the hospital, Galina had the diesel generators running throughout every operation, because there was no counting on normal voltage levels. The storms piled up twenty-foot-tall snow cornices in many places; on some streets, residents had to leave their buildings from the third floor, because the ground was covered with snow two stories high.

Leonid and Galina spent more time together; however, the intense moments they'd experienced when their separation was imminent had been unique and did not come again. He'd thought that his transfer would bring tranquillity to their relationship, but Galina appeared to have her doubts about this unexpected togetherness. She figured her captain was just having a good time playing house with her, and she rejected any sentimental assessment of the matter, behaving as though she assumed that the arduous routine of daily life on the edge of the inhabited world would soon make Leonid reconsider his intention to sign on for five years' duty in Yakutia. Did he really believe he could be at home here? And if he did, why didn't he just sign the contract and be done with it? Why did he give such pathetic reasons for drawing out the process?

Leonid knew why. His sojourn in Moscow had left a sting in him, the pride of the formerly privileged man. What interesting lives Muscovites led, after all, what riches their city offered! Even though Leonid never visited a museum and went neither to concerts nor to the theater, he *could* have done so in Moscow, had he wanted to. If he lived there, he could participate in the big military reviews again, too; his former battalion of armored infantry traditionally formed the leading unit in the May Day parade through Red Square. Now May was near—spring in Moscow. The captain sighed, staring out into the driving snowstorm. He envied his comrades back home, polishing up the big machines, decorating the barrels of the guns, attaching the track protectors so as not to damage the streets of the capital. He'd always been happy on the days when they rolled the tanks off the base, drove the dozen miles into the city, and maneuvered into formation on the Leningrad Prospekt. As a young lieutenant, Leonid had scurried here and there among the steel treads with a tape measure in his hand, making sure the distances were correct to within a fraction of an inch. Then, when the tank command received the signal indicating that the fighters had taken off from Aerovokzal Airport, the armored unit would set out in a wide formation for the city center. Final alignments and adjustments would be made on Gorky Street, where they would already be surrounded by a sea of red flags. As they neared Pushkinskaya, the military music would begin to play, and then the convoy, its engines roaring, would roll into the square of all squares. The gunners stood in the open turrets, wearing their parade uniforms, while the drivers had to follow the spectacle through their observation slits. And for all, what an honor to be there! Leonid wasn't a man to whom pomp and ceremony meant very much, but for anyone who had ever experienced the scene, even if only once, the joyous cries, the luminous flags flying along the way past the Historical Museum, fluttering toward St. Basil's Cathedral, and up above, the comrades in their dark overcoats, standing on the platform in front of the Mausoleum and waving down, and then, at the beginning of the festivities, the bells pealing in the Spasskaya Tower and the fighter squadron thundering overhead—for anyone who'd witnessed that, patriotism had stopped being just a word, and the feeling of a common bond among all free men under the sign of socialism had become a reality.

One's duty to society could be carried out anywhere in the country, no matter how remote the spot, and yet Leonid was starting to get the feeling that he'd been lucky to live close to the heartbeat of Soviet life, and that he'd gambled that good fortune away. The pay he'd received while stationed in Moscow was far lower than what he got in Yakutsk, but what was a man supposed to do with his money in an icy wasteland? In the beginning, he'd given Galina presents—a bracelet with glittering pendants, which she never wore because it got in her way at work, an electric samovar, a new mattress—until she'd admonished him, telling him he'd do better to save his money for his son's future. Leonid had the impression, however, that Galina didn't care at all about Petya; it was more as if she were preparing him for the day when he'd realize that their time together was nothing but a stage in his inevitable return journey to his son and Anna.

Maybe that was the reason why Leonid started writing the letter. He wanted to do something that would make his purpose irreversible. You didn't reach a decision of these proportions and then overturn it because of a little misgiving. Leonid wanted to see himself as a man swept away from the fat life of the capital to the periphery of the Soviet world. Pioneers were needed here, men who were idealistic and serious. Deep inside, Leonid was aware that his idealism was a mere dream and his duties as an insignificant captain limited to office work. After the adventurous Sakhalin interlude, in Yakutsk his life had settled back into monotony. The sameness of the days was disrupted only by the weather and Galina's whims.

Her doubts also affected the passionate side of their relationship. As long as their time together was marked by the delirium of transience, Galina had been wild with desire; but now that Leonid treated her like "the woman at his side," her intoxication was a thing of the past, and their erotic life had become predictable. He wanted her every night, but she'd been turning him down more and more frequently, claiming that her work at the hospital left her exhausted. Leonid, however, was thoroughly committed to having made the right decision; he wanted absolute validation. He'd chosen Yakutsk for his future, and he wasn't about to let some initial difficulties push him into admitting defeat.

One afternoon when the sun was already going down outside and he was in the barracks, he began his letter to Anna. He placed his briefcase within easy reach so that he could slap it on top of the light gray letter paper quickly should his superior officer come in. The letter would close the door to Anna so irretrievably that Leonid would no longer have to fear his own fickleness.

Insensibly, the daily routine began to envelop Anna again. Petya's next visit to the doctor was coming up, and even though you needed only to look at him to see how much improved he was, Anna was anxious about the appointment. She very much wanted to bring Doctor Shchedrin something as a sign of her deep gratitude; she'd bought a bundle of palm fronds from a street vendor, but upon arriving home, she'd discovered that the man had cheated her. The furry buds had frozen in transport, and once inside the apartment, they'd fallen dead from their stems.

Help came to Anna in the form of a small package. Viktor Ipalyevich received it from the postman, laid it on the table, and eyed it suspiciously. Anna, resting on the sofa before her afternoon shift, raised her head and asked, "Why don't you open it?"

"Because I know what's inside." He stroked his beard.

"Who sent it?"

He held out the package, which was wrapped in brown paper. She was able to decipher the postmark: "State Publishing House of the Soviet Union." "Is this . . . your book?" She was already on her feet.

"They're not that far along yet. I think it must be the print proof."

"Open it!" she cried impatiently.

"I don't know . . ."

"What are you waiting for?"

"I'm feeling scared about the jacket design." He ran his hand over the package, as if the reason for his fear could be felt through the paper. "Open it, daughter, and tell me what you see."

With three steps, she was in the kitchen. She came back with a knife and leaned over the table.

"No, wait, I'll do it," Viktor Ipalyevich said. "I'll open it myself." Carefully, as though disarming a bomb, he stuck the knife into the package, drew the blade slowly through wrapping paper and glue, and exposed an inner package. He partially opened this one, too, saw something red inside, and hesitated. "You do it." He handed her the knife.

Anna cut the package open at once. The cover of the book showed a black sun; bright red birds flew out of its center and turned into a girl's hair. At first glance, the picture perplexed Anna, but she liked her father's name, printed in large white letters and taking up the top third of the cover.

"No dust jacket?" The poet was standing behind her with a look of deep disappointment on his face.

"What do you think?" Her eyes moved back and forth between him and the book.

"They're printing only a paperback edition."

"What's that supposed to mean?"

He snatched the book and flexed it vehemently with both hands. "It's cheap, don't you see! It doesn't lie snugly in the hand. It feels like some ephemeral periodical—like a magazine you flip through and throw away."

"Nobody would treat a book of yours like a magazine."

"It won't even stand up properly on a shelf!" He thrust the book into an open space between two others. The little volume sagged laxly to one side and then fell over rearward. "There you go, that's what my work's worth!"

"Papa, it's a volume of poetry. Of course it's thinner and lighter than a three-hundred-page book." She laid it in the center of the table.

"Precisely, and that's why it has to have a solid cover! Poems are the compressed experience of life. They should be in books you can carry around with you and take out when you're ready for them. But this thing . . . !" He opened it and immediately closed it again. "It looks like a map of the Moscow subway system!"

"You're exaggerating. See how good the title looks? They made a real effort." She pointed to the handsome, slanted script, the letters red against the black of the sun.

"The engraving's by Khlebnikov," he said, nodding gently. "I think he's the right choice. His art's harmonious with mine."

"What does it mean—the birds, the girl's hair?"

"What does it mean? Don't have a clue," the poet growled. "Khlebnikov always was a pretty woolly-headed artist." Viktor Ipalyevich picked up the book a third time, as if it were gradually gaining in value. "They've used high-quality paper." He ran his eyes over the imprint, the title, and the foreword, which had been written by the director of the Conservatory.

Viktor Ipalyevich Tsazukhin's legacy comprises thirty years of Soviet lyric poetry and is the expression of an epoch rich in hard-won victories as well as painful losses. Tsazukhin is a man pro-

duced by the Revolution; his striving toward the Soviet ideal, the longing in his work for justice and moral perfection, his fraught thought processes, which reflect his heart's joys and sorrows, and above all, the melody of his verses, which are attuned to harmonize with the times . . .

"When will the fellow finally learn how to construct sentences that make sense?" Viktor Ipalyevich flipped past the foreword, came to the first poem, read it in silence, and in the end held the book out at arm's length away from him. He said, "I don't know how much it's worth, but it must be worth something."

"Of course it is! My compliments." Anna removed the packing paper and as she did so discovered a second copy of her father's poetry volume. "Papa . . . ," she said, taking up this second volume. "You could do me a great favor."

Viktor Ipalyevich gladly accepted the idea of giving his poems to the physician who'd cured Petya. "I'll write a dedication, of course. I'll think it over tonight and inscribe the book tomorrow."

Satisfied with the happy solution to her gift problem, Anna departed for the afternoon shift. Interior work on the building in Karacharovo should have been completed long since, but nondelivery of materials had caused delays, and now there was an additional impediment: the impending ceremony to inaugurate the building. Since the date of the opening festivities couldn't be postponed, it was decreed that the workers would concentrate all their efforts on finishing the section of the building that bore the official memorial plaque, which was to be unveiled by the Party secretary for Moscow. In order to avoid detracting from the visual effect of this ceremonial act, all scaffolding had to be dismantled, removed, and then, immediately after the event, put up again—a piece of stupidity that was the subject of lively discussion on the workers' bus.

"Couldn't we just hang white tarps over the scaffolding?" a worker cried.

Another comrade answered her: "Where are we going to get white tarps from?"

"And would someone please tell me where we're supposed to hide the scaffolding so the Secretary won't trip over it?" said a third. Several of the women laughed.

The bus turned into the briskly moving traffic of the Garden Ring near Taganskaya Square, the city gradually sank behind them, and the suburbs came into view. Anna was sitting next to a male colleague, a friend of hers, reading over his shoulder as he perused his copy of *Izvestia*. When he came to the foreign affairs section, her interest was sparked, and she sat up straight. She'd spotted a picture of the Minister for Research Planning, surrounded by a group of smiling male and female comrades; Alexey was not among them. LEADERS OF SOVIET SCIENCE TRAVELING TO STOCKHOLM, the headline read. When Anna's friend started to turn the page, she asked him to let her finish the article. It declared that the Swedish Academy of Sciences was most eager to learn about the recent successes of its Soviet colleagues. Scientists from the fields of chemistry, medicine, and mathematics would form the main contingent, the article stated; the group of researchers would be completed by leading physicists from the atomic cities of Dubna and Novosibirsk. Anna tried a second time to find Alexey's face among all the strange heads. Hadn't he hinted at his travel destination? "A city where it's never hot, not even in summer." Wasn't that an allusion to Stockholm? Maybe, she told herself, the original plan had been that Bulyagkov would make the trip to Sweden as the leader of the scientific delegation, and then that plan had been changed. She read the next article, which described the icebreaker *Kalinin* as she sailed out on her maiden voyage. Anna imagined the ship on its long journey east and thought of Leonid, who was serving in the Siberian wasteland. After her friend turned the page, Anna raised her eyes and looked out at the impressive series of residential developments that had been produced in recent years, living space for some fifteen thousand comrades.

The bus's hydraulic doors opened with a hiss, discharging Anna and the others, who went to complex number 215 and took up their work. Why would Alexey announce that he was traveling to Stockholm and then not do it? During the past minutes, the question had kept itself hidden, but now it surfaced again and filled Anna with an uneasiness that wouldn't go away, not even when she bent over the bucket and stirred the thickened paint.

TWENTY-SEVEN

Anna handed her gift to Doctor Shchedrin in person and was disappointed by his reaction. Such a man, she'd assumed, would be able to appreciate contemporary poetry. However, Shchedrin held the book awkwardly in his hands and said he didn't have much time for reading. Even though the ensuing examination confirmed Anna's optimism as far as Petya was concerned, she was still disappointed to discover that the person to whom she attributed "the miracle" wasn't interested in anything outside of his specialized field. The doctor scrutinized the boy's eyes, fingernails, and back and was far from stingy with the candy rewards. And yet, Anna couldn't rid herself of the impression that the physician's interest was flagging; Petya, no longer a gasping, sickly child but a normal boy who was already participating in school sports again, had become for Doctor Shchedrin one patient out of many. He completed the examination quickly, lowered the dosage of Petya's medications, and dismissed Anna with the words "All's well that ends well."

She and the boy stepped out into the sunny April day. The trees in front of the Lenin Library were not only covered with green fuzz, they had also put out their first leaves, which quivered in the breeze. Petya's interest was attracted by the washed and polished limousines on the

Kropotkin Quay; the beginning of spring seemed to dip even the automobiles in brighter colors. A man in a dark green suit came walking toward them. Anna was about to cross the street, but something in the man's gait brought her to a stop. He raised his head, and his eyeglasses sparkled. Anna got a better grip on Petya's hand.

"Comrade Nechayevna?" Kamarovsky acted surprised, but Anna didn't believe for a second that this was a chance meeting. "Is this your little Petya?" the Colonel asked with a smile.

She encouraged Petya to give the stranger his hand, which the boy did without shyness.

"We should have another talk soon," Kamarovsky said. "Would tomorrow after work be all right with you?"

In that case, Anna thought, I'll have to fix dinner ahead of time. She nodded in assent.

"Good, then." The Colonel wished them a good day and walked on in the direction of the Lenin Library.

"Who was that?" Petya asked.

Anna made up a lie and set out for home, depressed. Her anxiety continued into the evening, while she sat silently on the sofa and watched the chess game between grandfather and grandson. It took her a long time to fall asleep. After the Colonel's announcement that the Bulyagkov dossier would soon be closed, and especially after her discussion with Alexey, she'd hoped that she was entering a final, calm stage, which would last until the men took up their inscrutable game again, but without her. In the darkness of the sleeping alcove, she thought about her meeting with her case officer, scheduled for the following day: For the first time, she would be reporting to Kamarovsky in the knowledge that Alexey, the man under observation, had turned the tables on the Colonel from the beginning. Even though the past two years had taught Anna to lie routinely and keep her camouflage in place at all times, she was afraid she might not be able to deceive Kamarovsky's searching eyes. She cast about for excuses not to go to the building on the quay, yet at the same time, she knew that such a move would only arouse the Colonel's mistrust. With a sigh, Anna put an arm around her sleeping child.

"For the mission I have in mind this time, I'm counting on your special intuition." In contrast to the other occasions when Anna had been in this apartment, for this visit the samovar was singing. Kamarovsky, who'd never offered her anything to drink before, busied himself with dishes, apologized for having only four sugar cubes in the house, and served her a glass of tea. Not immediately accepting his invitation to sit on the couch, she stepped over to the window and took a few sips. The room was flooded with light; for the first time since Anna had been making reports here, the curtains were completely open. The magnificent bridge soared over the black river, which was swollen by snowmelt and flowing with a mighty surge through the steel arches. The windows of the Comecon building reflected the sun in a rainbow of colors; the Hotel Ukraina was a gleaming silver tower.

"We need information about the Bulyagkov couple's divorce." The Colonel was standing behind her. His words penetrated Anna's consciousness so gradually that she held her breath for a moment. Kamarovsky stared at her attentively. He wasn't mistaken; Anna was surprised by the news. "So you didn't know?" he asked.

She slowly shook her head.

"He didn't drop any hints? Never talked about insurmountable difficulties at home? You never had to listen to the complaints of a frustrated husband, seeking solace with his young lover?"

Kamarovsky's sarcasm alarmed Anna; normally, he limited himself to asking questions and evaluating data.

"I can't believe he wants to separate from Medea," she said truthfully.

"I want you to get to the bottom of this . . . discrepancy." He was a dark silhouette in front of the glittering balcony door.

"What discrepancy?"

"Alexey Maximovich has a wife who's one of the most influential people in Moscow society, a woman to whom he owes his entire political career. How does he let her go? How, after so many years of reciprocal tolerance, have they come to a point where 'insurmountable obstacles' make it impossible for their marriage to continue?"

To avoid having to answer at once, Anna took a swallow of tea. "Maybe the divorce is to Medea's advantage. Maybe there's another man in her life."

He went to his desk and leafed through the notes that Rosa Khleb had turned over to him. The interview with Medea Bulyagkova had been unproductive. Moscow's cultural secretary had adroitly limited the conversation to cultural affairs and thoroughly described her concept for *Voices of the Soviet Republics*; in answer to personal questions, however, she'd added nothing to what was already in the mutual divorce petition.

"I need background material—some incident, some point of contention that makes this seem like a reasonable step."

"When it comes to love, not everything is reasonable."

How could she let herself be so carried away that she'd mouth a statement like that? Kamarovsky gave her a derisive look, whereupon she turned her back to the window and sat down.

"How's your husband?" the Colonel asked, unerringly.

"He's started his tour of duty at his new station."

"And how's he getting on there?"

"Well, I think."

"He applied for the five-year stipulation, right?" Kamarovsky leaned forward, hands on his desk.

"He did, but he hasn't signed it yet."

"How do you feel about this prospect?"

She shrugged.

"Five years is a very long time," the Colonel said. "And I want you to know," he added empathically, "we have nothing to do with it."

"What am I supposed to do with Alexey?"

"Meet him and talk about his divorce."

"With what justification?"

"You're the partner in Alexey Maximovich's longest-running affair." The Colonel tilted his head to one side. "Shouldn't you be getting your hopes up, now that he's going to be a free man again soon? In the meantime, he's moved out of the conjugal residence." Noticing that Anna's thoughts were elsewhere, Kamarovsky raised his voice. "We're interested not only in the reason but also in the point in time. As far as we know, there has been no recent occurrence in the Bulyagkov marriage that could explain this precipitous breakup."

"I met Alexey just last week." She got to her feet and placed the half-full tea glass on the desk. "What justification do I give for visiting him again?"

"You're right." The Colonel took care to see that the veneer wasn't suffering any damage from the hot glass. "So far, there's been no official statement about the divorce. So how could you have learned about it?"

Anna realized that, for the first time, she was a step ahead of Kamarovsky. Couldn't she go to Alexey and say, "The Colonel's doing a lot of speculating about your divorce. What would you like me to tell him?" At the same time, she was as baffled as Kamarovsky about what was going on. Alexey's revelation that he'd seen through Anna's double game from the beginning had sealed her eyes to whatever lay behind that disclosure: a second truth, a veil Alexey spread over his real motives. She believed his declaration of love, but she more and more doubted whether she had his trust.

On the way home, she thought about how adroitly Alexey kept the balance between trust and secrecy, how he gave the appearance of letting Anna in on his private affairs and at the same time measured out his truths in the doses that best served his purposes. What purpose was served, she wondered, by the announcement that he was going on a trip when he was apparently staying home?

She reached her building and slinked past Avdotya's door to avoid the seamstress's questions about the new curtain. Even though Viktor Ipalyevich came down for the mail during the day, Anna usually checked the mailbox. Winter hadn't done the lock any good, and she could barely turn the key. Inside was a letter from the building association; a renovation of the heating pipes had been pending for a long time. Also, there was something, probably an invitation, addressed to her father from the Guild of Young Soviet Poets; ever since the announcement that his volume of poetry was in line for imminent publication, Viktor Ipalyevich's social life had grown increasingly active. Oddly, the smallest envelope was the fattest. Who crammed so much paper into such a little envelope? When she saw the army postmark, Anna's face broke into a smile, and a glance at the return address confirmed her guess. A letter from Leonid was as rare as snow in August; it made her even happier to think that her husband had taken the time to write at such length. She attributed the letter's bulk to the barrenness of his surroundings, to the amount of idle time he had, and, above all, to the fact that he missed her. So the few, conflict-filled days of his home leave had eventually had the desired effect on him. How could a comparison between Moscow and Siberia turn out otherwise? As Anna thrust her finger under the seal, it occurred to her to let Petya open the letter. More quickly than they ordinarily did after work, her legs carried her up the stairs and onto the fourth-floor landing, where she immediately unlocked the apartment door. The place was unusually cold. Viktor Ipalyevich was wearing a thick sweater and sitting in the living room with a blanket over his knees, and a rustling sound was coming from the sleeping alcove.

"What's going on?" She hid the mail behind her back.

"The building management turned off the heat without saying why," the poet growled. "They could at least have waited until summer."

Anna pulled out the association's mimeographed letter, which informed residents that heat in the building would be temporarily shut off for maintenance work on April 11 and 12. She handed her father the letter. Without taking off her shoes and jacket, she went to the nook and bent over her son. "Look here, Petyushka," she said tenderly.

The dark-haired head emerged from the bedclothes, and then Petya shined a flashlight in his mother's face. "If I read under the covers, it gets warm right away."

She smiled at the flushed, childish face. "I think something's come for you," she said, presenting the letter.

"What is it?" He examined the envelope earnestly. "Who's writing to me?"

"To us, Petya." She laid the letter on his lap. "Papa's writing to us."

"Papa," he repeated with great reverence. "From Yakutia?"

She nodded. "This letter has traveled a long, long way to reach us. Would you like to open it?"

"Is he writing to tell us when he's coming back?" The child's finger traced the edges of the stamp. "Is he writing about the animals out there where he is? Did he put a present in with the letter?"

"Hurry up," Anna said with a laugh. "You remind me of old Avdotya, trying to imagine what Metsentsev's going to write to her about."

The child plucked cautiously at a corner. The paper didn't give way immediately, so he pulled harder and soon had several snippets in his hand.

"Stop," his mother said, laying her hand on his. "We don't want to tear it to pieces."

"In my day, we used letter openers," came the voice from the dining table.

"Very good idea." Letter in hand, Anna ran into the kitchen. She made one careful cut, and now she could pull out the pages—how many there were! She unfolded and smoothed them as she went back to Petya. "Now we're going to see how well you can read."

He scooted to the edge of the bed; Anna threw the blanket over his bare feet and sat next to him. Petya ran his tongue over his lips as though a hard task lay before him.

"'My dear wife. I'm sitting in the office here on the base and imagining you taking these pages into the kitchen and drawing the curtain across the doorway, curious to see what's awaiting you.'" Petya looked up. "Papa's writing to you, not me, just you."

"I'm sure he writes something to you in the next line or two."

"Besides, we're not in the kitchen, and we haven't closed the curtain."

"Then let's just close this one." She slipped off her shoes, knelt next to Petya on the bed, and pulled the blue fabric across the alcove. The gliding curtain made the lamplight dance on the pages; the ballpoint pen had been pressed deep into the paper.

"'I've been sitting on these lines for six days, dear Anna,'" Petya went on. "'My wastepaper basket is filled with failed attempts. I've never found anything so difficult.' He's not saying anything to me!" Petya scooted away from his mother. "What does that mean, 'failed attempts'?"

"That's when you first try to do something, before you know how it goes," she answered randomly. Her mind was focused on the reason behind Leonid's introduction. She paled at the thought that he was writing to tell her he'd signed the five-year stipulation. How could he have chosen this way to announce a decision about something so important? Why hadn't he telephoned her?

"You know what?" Anna announced, suddenly uneasy. "Let's do it the way Papa says." She opened the curtain. "I'll go into the kitchen and read the letter by myself, and after that we'll read it again together."

"But I want to read it now! I want to read it now!" Petya couldn't manage to disentangle himself from the blanket in time, and Anna was able to jump out of the bed. Ignoring her father's alert gaze, she hurried past him. "Is the gas on, at least?" she asked, drawing the kitchen curtain between herself and the others.

"We made tea."

Anna heard the quick, small steps as Petya ran across the living room, heard them stop suddenly as her father caught his grandson and tried with soothing words to prevent him from following her.

"But it's from Papa!" This protest was followed by a skirmish that ended only when Viktor Ipalyevich proposed an extraordinary, pre-dinner game of chess. Anna bent over the letter.

". . . I've never found anything so difficult," she read again, in her husband's forceful handwriting. "Let me simply describe what happened, and then you'll understand."

As Anna read on, she pulled up the chair and even had the presence of mind to light the gas with a match. She decided not to put the teakettle on to boil. When she was finished with each page, she laid it atop a neat stack, stopped once to decipher the word *inexplicable*, read the last lines and the greetings to Petya, and pushed the stack away. She leaned back and looked at her actual surroundings—the spice rack, the coating of grease on the heating pipe, the flecks of tomato sauce here and there. Looking out the window, she saw the swaying branches below her, the green that signaled the return of warm weather—in contrast to her cold apartment.

With one spring she was in front of the curtain; with two more steps, she reached her shoes and slipped into them. "I have to go back down . . . I forgot . . ." Without ending the sentence, she stepped out the door. On the second floor, she remembered that she'd left the gas burner on; her father would notice it before long, she thought. Bounding as though for joy, she dashed across the entrance hall and out into the street.

Spring had taken hold of the city and was tightening its grip a little more every day, making evenings like this one bright and warm. Despite the lateness of the hour, the sun was still sending out a few rays, the sky remained deep blue; it was the time of year everyone had been waiting five months for. Anna removed her felt jacket and slung it over her shoulder; in her flat shoes, she could walk fast. She crossed the Chaussée against the red light, got honked at, and a minute later reached the park. Even though the big trees hadn't yet leafed out fully, green had already won the ground battle, the forsythias were blooming, and there were primroses on the park lawns. Anna couldn't stand still; if she wanted to let the news she'd just read sink in all the way, remaining in constant motion was her only option. Leonid had gone on at great length and filled many pages to avoid the truth, but in the end he'd come out with it. The effect was powerful and simple at once. An emergency solution meant to take him away from Moscow temporarily had turned into Leonid's new future, a situation he desired, a complete change of direction. Oddly enough, Anna's first concern was the application for the apartment in Nostikhyeva, which she would now have to withdraw, because apartments of that size weren't granted to single mothers. At the end of his letter, Leonid, too, had mentioned a practical consideration: how to arrange for a seven-year-old to make the journey to Siberia alone. Leonid ruled out the possibility of his getting leave to fetch Petya from Moscow every time. He'd formulated his idea—the boy would spend the warmer months in Yakutsk—as vividly as if there were no doubt about its realization. He'd remained vague on the matter of whether or not divorce should follow their de facto separation. How heavily all this must have been weighing on his mind, Anna thought, and what kind of woman could have motivated him to make such a momentous decision? While marching at double time through an alley of acacias, Anna tried to picture the woman she'd just learned about for the first time. How extraordinary this Galina must be, she thought, to put the sober Leonid in such an agitated state.

She looked up. The deep blue of the sky was tinting the treetops, and all at once evening flooded the park. In spring, of all seasons, she had to get dumped! The fearful certainty that the whole thing was her fault, that she bore all the guilt for it, suddenly gave way to self-pity: Was she jinxed, or what? Could anyone imagine worse confusion than what she was floundering in? Was there an unluckier person in the whole blessed city of Moscow?

"The wind's going to carry you away, girl!" she heard a powerful voice say.

The fact that someone had called her "girl" made Anna turn around. Not far away, she saw a couple, the weatherproof kind of people who come out when the seasons change. Snow still lay in spots shielded from the sun, some patches of ice were not yet completely thawed, but these two had already come out to the park and built a fire, and now they were roasting shashlik on spits and baking potatoes over the hot embers; a supply of dry branches lay nearby, fuel for the fire. The two were comfortably ensconced in a pair of lawn chairs.

"Come over here! Why are you running around like that?" the woman said. "Sooner or later, you have to come to a stop, so why not here?"

Before she knew it, Anna had taken the first steps toward the fire.

"That's better." Despite the man's furrowed face, there was no telling whether he was forty or sixty; his beard grew from his throat to his cheekbones. "We'll eat in a minute. How about a little drink first?"

They pointed to the bottles standing at the ready behind them. There was no reason to refuse, not today, and so Anna allowed a beer to be pressed into one hand and a generous glass of home-brewed liquor into the other.

"What could make a pretty comrade run around in circles instead of strolling calmly on this lovely spring evening?"

"My husband wants to leave me." The answer was out before she'd formed the thought.

"What a dumb guy he must be!" the woman answered impassively. "Doesn't he have eyes in his head?" She cast a meaningful glance at her own husband. "A few years ago, this comrade here thought about moving on to greener pastures, too." She pointed a shashlik spit at her husband.

"That's not true anymore, hasn't been true for a long time," the bearded man said soothingly.

"What did you do about it?" Anna asked the woman.

"I let him starve." The woman held the meat over the flames. "The pantry was off-limits to him. If he needed food, let him get his fill from the other woman! You can't imagine how fast he came back."

"Obviously, none of that is true." The man clinked glasses with Anna. "The only reason I'm keeping quiet is so I won't spoil my darling's lovely story. Do I look like a man who would cheat?"

"You all cheat when you get the chance." The woman coerced Anna into lifting her glass. "If a pretty little mouth attracts you, or a skirt is lifted a few inches, you all start running like donkeys chasing carrots."

"My case is more complicated." The warmth of the liquor spread through her like a shiver, and Anna squatted down on her haunches.

"No, it's not," her hostess contradicted her. "It all just seems complicated. Men's heads are constantly throbbing with the fear of missing something. The gentlemen get a nice hen to share their nest, but after a few years, they want to see whether they've still got some rooster credibility. They flap around and crow, their combs swell, and they're grateful if they can mount another hen."

"The way you talk, Galina, light of my life. Always full of surprises." The bearded man opened his next beer and drank from the bottle in gurgling swallows.

"Galina?" Anna looked up at the woman, who was looming over her, brandishing her skewers like a sword fighter.

"And you, sister, what's your name?"

Anna laughed. "Is your name really Galina?"

"What's funny about it?"

"Galina is also the name of the woman who turned my Leonid's head."

Now the woman with the skewers laughed, too. "It wasn't me, that's for sure! You see," she said, teasing her husband, "there are tramps named Galina, too. What a lucky man you are!"

"That must be about ready to eat," he said, changing the subject.

The woman sniffed the meat, then blew on it and tasted it. "Just another minute, no more. The marinade is a poem!"

"Garlic and wine?" Anna asked.

"And red peppercorns."

The man spread a cloth on the young grass and put out a couple of glass jars containing pickled vegetables, followed by a loaf of bread. With a narrow, oft-sharpened knife, he cut off large chunks of the bread and gave one to Anna. "It's lovely to have company today. Don't be gloomy, my girl. Things will get straightened out, one way or another."

"Straightened out," Anna murmured. She broke off a piece of the freshly baked bread and chewed it slowly.

TWENTY-EIGHT

In the following days, the duty to carry out her mission for Kamarovsky merged, for Anna, with her need to talk to someone she could feel understood by. She thought about the mad coincidence that had made her and Alexey fellows in misery. Here was the jilted house painter, whose captain preferred his Siberian love, and there was the Deputy Minister, living on his own now that the influential cultural secretary wanted nothing to do with him. Had the consequences of all this turmoil not been so unsettling, Anna could have laughed at it. But they were, and so, one morning, heedless of her usual caution, she dialed the number of the telephone in the Drezhnevskaya Street apartment. The receiver was picked up on the second ring, and a muffled voice said hello.

"Have I . . . Is this Alexey Maximovich's apartment?"

"Anna?" said the voice on the other end.

"Yes. I apologize for disturbing you at this . . . you sound strange."

"I'm brushing my teeth," he mumbled. Various sounds followed: the receiver being laid down, footsteps, running water. "All done," he said cheerfully.

"I apologize."

"No, I'm glad to hear your voice. If you only knew how glad,

Annushka." Before she could reply, he suggested a meeting. "When do you have time? This evening? Tomorrow? Don't say no. Should we meet here . . . no, that's not a good idea. Somewhere else, some magical place . . . Hello, Anna, are you still there?"

Now that the meeting she'd wanted to engineer was going to take place without any effort on her part, Anna became wary.

"Let me arrange something for tomorrow," he insisted. "Let me surprise you."

"That's not necessary."

"Of course it isn't necessary," he said with a laugh, "but it will make me happy. I'll send Anton to you. Shall we say around seven?"

Anna agreed, said good-bye, and hung up.

Bulyagkov buttoned his shirt, tied his tie in front of the mirror, and noted that his double chin was becoming more unsightly every day. He gazed nervously at the telephone; he was expecting a call and had purposefully kept the conversation with Anna short. His cheeks burned from the shaving; he went back into the bathroom and applied the French cream. As he was rubbing it in, the telephone rang again. Bulyagkov took a deep breath and answered the phone.

"Alexey Maximovich?" said an unpleasant voice on the other end of the line.

"Yes."

"Something's come up. How soon can you be in the Ministry building?"

He named a time and hung up. The caller's unwillingness to say anything more made Bulyagkov confident that the something that had come up was what he'd hoped it would be. He left his apartment, watched the black ZIL pull up at the curb, and climbed in. Anton drove out of the narrow street and onto the Chaussée.

At the Ministry, Bulyagkov was welcomed by a hastily formed committee and informed that the Minister had fallen ill overnight with a severe case of intestinal flu. His physician had made an initial diagnosis of food poisoning, but the Minister couldn't remember eating anything he shouldn't have. The exact cause of his condition was still to be determined, but in any case, he was confined to his bed and, according to the doctor's report, in no condition to travel to Stockholm.

"Cancel" was the Deputy Minister's response. Without the top man, he said, the excursion made no sense; an international research exchange without the Minister for Research was an absurdity.

The committee granted Bulyagkov's point but objected that preparations for the trip had already consumed a considerable amount of funding, and that moreover the members of the scientific delegation had all arrived in Moscow already; how great their disappointment would be if they were now sent back to their research stations. Finally, they weren't going to Sweden merely to present their own science; in return, they expected to receive interesting information about various Western technologies.

Bulyagkov remained adamant. He'd only seen to the organization of the visit to Sweden, he said; he was unprepared in the science of the various fields and considered himself incapable of giving a proper speech of greeting.

The committee resorted to flattery. It declared emphatically that the Deputy Minister, with his background in the natural sciences, was the only person versed in all the department's interests. And even should he be compelled to improvise, he knew a lot more about chemistry, mathematics, or nuclear physics than any other official in the Ministry. Without naming the Minister, Bulyagkov's colleagues evoked his relative competence and made clear their belief that, when it came to science, the chief couldn't hold a candle to his deputy. Their adulation reached such a level that Bulyagkov stood up, walked pensively around the conference room, and stopped at the big window. He looked down to the street, his view of it already blocked here and there by a canopy of leaves. Alexey knew what his colleagues feared above all: They feared that his refusal could result in their being deprived of the amenities offered by a trip to the West. They weren't interested in science; they kept their eyes fixed on their privileges as Soviet representatives.

"What about the speech to the Swedish Academy?" he asked, acting hesitant again.

"Why not give the speech that was written for the Minister?"

"I can do that only if I do it in his name."

"Of course! Good idea! Respectful gesture!" some of the officials cried. They saw a ray of hope, but Bulyagkov announced that he would accept the mission only on condition of a unanimous resolution of the Chamber. This proviso was met with agitated objections: The scheduled departure was only forty-eight hours away, and it would be impossible to convene the entire Chamber in such a short time. The Deputy Minister appreciated that, but he insisted that there be a memorandum recording the proceedings in detail and ratified in writing by the members of the Politburo. His colleagues, feeling that success was near, promised to provide him with such a document, and then someone remembered that two of the high-ranking comrades had profited from the spring weather and taken a jaunt to the Black Sea.

While the committee was discussing how the required memorandum could be ratified "telegraphically," Bulyagkov was overcome by a serenity that he'd long had to do without. He'd assessed the men around him correctly and laid so many obstacles in their way that his departure would arouse no suspicion. These Russians, with their panicked need to shed the most flattering light on their performances in the little positions they'd striven so doggedly to occupy, would do everything to persuade him to agree to something that had been his plan from the very beginning. In these minutes, he saw the future in a larger dimension, and despite pangs of anxiety before the unknown, he felt that he was simultaneously at the end and at the beginning of something. He thought warmly about Anna's call, shook off a brief moment of suspicion about her motives, and considered the possibilities for the following evening. He wanted their date to be splendid and affectionate, impressive and intimate. When he thought of the right place, he cracked a narrow smile. He announced to his colleagues that he would await further developments in his office. By way of precaution, he would have the Minister's twenty-six-page speech of greeting sent to him, but he especially wanted to contact the Minister by telephone and offer him his sympathy and best wishes for a speedy recovery. The comrades in the conference room hailed this gesture.

TWENTY-NINE

The narrow street behind the Mozhaisk Chaussée was now so brightly lit at night that getting into the car under cover of darkness was no longer a possibility. While Anna watched the ZIL approaching, it occurred to her that in spite of all the changes, this one thing had remained constant; she might have broken up with Alexey, but Anton was still picking her up and bringing her to her unflappable lover.

"As punctual as clockwork," Anton said in his melodious voice.

"I've never said this to you, but you would have made a first-rate singer." She had her heart on her sleeve.

"To be honest, Comrade, I've done that." He turned around and drove onto the crepuscular boulevard.

"You're a singer, Anton? Really?" She laid her arm along the top of the seat, almost touching his shoulder.

"Once upon a time."

"In a chorus?"

"It was a provincial troupe. We brought a quite respectable performance of *Boris Godunov* to the stage. I was Boris."

"Anton, I'm amazed!" She tried to picture the inconspicuous, always clean-shaven man costumed as the imposing, bearded Godunov. "Why did you give it up?"

"There were several reasons . . ." He looked at her in the rearview mirror. "And I'd rather not talk about any of them."

Anna took the lipstick out of her purse, re-reddened her lips with the help of her reflection in the window, and pushed her hair behind her ears. There she was, being driven to her Arctic wolf, as happy and excited as if she hadn't told him, not a very long time ago, that it was all over. "Where are we going?" Anna asked, closing her purse.

"I was sworn to silence on that subject." Anton drove a short distance along the Smolensk Quay, avoided Kalinin Prospekt, and took the Garden Ring to Mayakovsky Square; on the left and on the right, Gorky Street glittered. He stopped in front of a building that Anna knew only by name and accompanied her inside. They crossed an elegant beige foyer. The staff of the Peking Hotel nodded to Anton as he accompanied Anna to the elevator, pressed the button for the top floor, and stepped back. The doors closed on his friendly face and moments later opened on an elegantly furnished vestibule. In the reflection of a gold-framed mirror, Anna saw Bulyagkov coming toward her. He was wearing a three-piece suit of dark wool that made him look thinner. Before either spoke the first word, Alexey embraced the painter, and they stood for a while in the little foyer with their arms around each other.

"Where are we?" She wiped lipstick from the corner of his mouth.

"Through a piece of especially good luck, I got the tower."

"The tower?" She let him lead her inside and stood before the most beautiful view she'd ever seen. Not far away, she recognized the tall buildings of MSU, the Moscow State University; Gorky Street was like a long wedge of light. Anna could see the Kremlin, with its glowing red star, and behind it the narrow streets where old wooden buildings pressed close to one another.

"Usually, this is a privilege granted only to the inner circle," Alexey said. "Or to foreign guests of the State."

"How wonderful," Anna said, embracing him a second time.

"People will think we're still a couple. The food in the Peking is supposed to be very respectable indeed." He tried to draw her into the dining niche, where a light meal awaited them.

"I don't want to eat now," she said, standing her ground. "I'd like to enjoy the moment."

"And might your enjoyment be enhanced by a little something to drink?" He pointed to a battery of bottles. "Even I don't know what some of this stuff is," he said, picking up a bottle at random. "You sounded so urgent on the telephone." He turned around. "Why?"

"Leonid left me."

It was so easy to say that, without tears, without loading the sentence with unhappiness. Alexey, however, seemed much shaken and inattentively set down the unopened bottle, which fell over onto the plush carpet but did not break. "But how can he . . . it's impossible," was all he managed to say.

"A whole year of separation is a long time." She found it amusing that *she* had to break the news gently to *him*. "There are beautiful women in Siberia, too."

"Siberia? I thought it was Sakhalin."

She told him about Leonid's furlough and his cowardly refusal to tell her the truth to her face.

"Wasn't he supposed to be granted his right of abode in Moscow this year?"

"Apparently, there are charms that can compete with that." Anna was pleased to think that she appeared strong and relaxed, while the news was having an amazingly strong effect on Alexey.

"I can only tell you how sorry I am," he said. He picked up the fallen bottle.

"Why? What does that change for you . . . or for us?"

"A great deal," he answered warmly. "I would have liked to know that everything was sorted out for you." He fell silent, uncorked the dark beverage, and sniffed it. "Old port wine, I believe. Give Leonid time."

He took two inverted glasses from a shelf. "In a few months, everything could be back the way it was."

"A few months." It sounded worse when he said it. "So now we're fellows in misery," she observed, shifting without a preamble to the other subject she wanted to talk about.

"What do you mean?" He poured some wine and tasted it.

She waited until he'd swallowed. "Why are you getting a divorce, Alexey?"

He stared pensively at the bottle, as if it were an object of great interest. "Kamarovsky?" he asked in an undertone. Anna nodded. All at once, the Deputy Minister's features relaxed. "Well, of course—the brotherhood must find that just fascinating."

"You never spoke a word to me about it. Why the sudden separation?"

"Nothing lasts forever." He could tell from her look that this trite observation wasn't going to satisfy her. Bulyagkov realized how close he'd let Anna get to the truth. If she wanted to, she'd be capable of correctly identifying the connections linking various events. He could act like a lumbering old bear, but now there were some holes in his coat, and Anna could already see through them. The splendors and delights of the Peking Hotel hadn't blurred her sight. Nor was her own pain leading her to talk only about herself; no, Anna looked more alert than ever. Bulyagkov considered this without fear and without any weakening of his feelings for her; but for the first time, he saw that the house painter represented a risk. "Medea and I will go our own ways from now on. There's absolutely no drama, you understand?" He went up two steps into the alcove and sat on a long couch with curved armrests. "Remember, I told you I was going on a trip?"

"Yes?" She followed him to the couch.

"I leave tomorrow. I'm leading the delegation to Stockholm." A mischievous look flitted over his face. "Why not come with me to the city where it's never hot, not even in summer?"

Her voice became unusually clear. "You're leading the delegation? I thought the Minister himself . . ."

Bulyagkov moved away from her. There was a short, aggressive silence.

"The Minister has fallen ill. An unforeseeable indisposition. Therefore I have to take his place."

"What's wrong with him?"

"He's got some stomach or intestinal problem. That is to say, he's puking his guts out. Maybe he ate something he shouldn't have."

"It's remarkable that he's come down with whatever he's got barely two days before such an important mission." He turned his head, and she stopped talking.

"You think he's not really sick?"

"Don't you know?" While Anna drank the heavy port, while he bent her back a little and kissed her temples, while she scrutinized the first-class wallpaper, whose seams were as good as invisible, she was tormented by the question of how Alexey could already have known a week ago that he was going to go on the trip if the Minister had fallen unforeseeably ill only yesterday.

"So you're off to Stockholm." As Anna cast about for a solution, she was slowly absorbed by the thought that Medea's fate and hers were beginning to resemble each other. She noticed that Alexey wasn't stopping at a little friendly snuggling and in fact had skillfully opened the hooks and pulled down the zipper on her skirt. Anna tried to hold on to her thoughts and resisted giving in to his caresses. Before her mind's eye, she passed in review the persons who were keeping the wheels of this whole business spinning. The Minister and his Deputy, Medea, and Lyushin, too, belonged among them, and of course Rosa and the Colonel, but as hard as Anna tried to give to each of them a shape in keeping with his or her function, they soon merged with the amorous play that Alexey was drawing her into. For the first time, he exposed himself to her, removing his jacket and vest and undoing his trousers. With his tie hanging over his shoulder, he surged over her, bracing his elbows against the couch's dainty backrest and keeping one foot on the floor. Surprised and excited, she accommodated him. Actually, she had come looking for consolation from her paternal friend, and now the old fellow, her wolf, was on top of her, penetrating her with his piercing eyes, kissing her earnestly, offering her his heavy body. The wallpaper had a pattern of crowns, which Anna found peculiar—obviously a failure of oversight when the choice was made. The crowns—dark blue against a pale red background—looked a little like flowers, too. Maybe, she thought, the paperhanger had hung the wallpaper wrong, and blossoms had become crowns. She whispered Alexey's name, and since the armrest was bruising her spine, she let herself slip to the floor. He lay on his back and, unembarrassed and playful, allowed Anna to caress him, raising his head to watch what she was doing; the lights of the capital shimmered behind her.

The tower, Bulyagkov thought; the pleasure of being with her here, with time and place joined in the best possible relationship. Coordination had ever been his greatest talent. He was humbly grateful to Anna, and he loved her for the year and nine months she'd given him.

THIRTY

At the same time, and yet eight hours later, Leonid detached himself from Galina after a long embrace. He couldn't use the dawn as an indication of how early or late it was; at that time of year in the North, dawn lasted half a day. She'd been sad the previous night; with greater detail than usual, she'd described her efforts to save an old man's life. He was a nomad by birth and a day laborer out of necessity, he had no place to stay, and the approach of the warmer season was his only prospect. But the nine months of winter had so consumed his strength that when the police picked him up in a tractor hangar, he'd collapsed and lost consciousness. When they brought him to the hospital, the police lieutenant had snidely remarked that it didn't look as though there was much to be done for him. Galina had given him a cardiotonic injection, put him in a clean hospital bed, and hooked him up to an intravenous drip. He was given chicken broth and bread. During the night, however, he'd undergone a remarkable transformation. Instead of drawing new courage to face life from the care and security he was receiving, the man had relaxed his grip on the last bands that held his existence together and, in the truest sense, surrendered. Combed and fed, and closely observed by the nurses, he'd appeared like a man resolved on his own death. His heartbeat and breathing slowing down, the man had lain there with a queer smile on his face and looked first at the worried night nurse and then at Galina. She'd cried out to him, begging him to stop acting like that and go on living. When his breathing stopped, Galina had considered a tracheotomy, but a comment made by the most senior station nurse had tipped the scales in favor of letting him go. *He knows his time has come*, the nurse had said. He'd died around eleven o'clock in the evening; his death was registered, and barely an hour later, his body had been transferred to the crematorium.

Leonid quietly rolled out of bed. It must be around five in the morning, he thought; he was supposed to muster the men for roll call at six. That didn't leave him much time, because the road to the base wasn't snow-free yet.

While he dressed, his eye fell on a cartoon in a magazine: A man, hanging over a pit where predatory teeth snap up at him, feels the branch he's clinging to breaking and remarks, "Good thing everything in life is temporary." As he left the house, Leonid wondered whether that wasn't exactly the situation he was in: unstable and temporary. Everything could change completely again at any time. Or could he start to look upon his hours with Galina, their nights in Yakutsk, as the beginning of a new future?

Anna's silence regarding his letter relieved him. At the same time, he found it unfathomable that she hadn't called or sent him a telegram or written. It wasn't in her nature to let things slide.

While Leonid waited in front of the house for the transport vehicle to pick him up, he was annoyed at both the women to whom he'd given control of his fate. Hadn't it been because of pressure from Anna that he'd moved away from Moscow, where he could have had a good life in an agreeable division? Didn't she bear the chief responsibility for the confusion that everybody—including, unfortunately, Petya—now had to deal with? And what about Galina's obstinacy in wanting to live here, of all places, here where her roots were and nowhere else? A good surgeon could find a position anywhere, including Moscow. Leonid had shaped a future for himself, but in reality, didn't it look as though he was letting the women make the decisions he should have been dictating to them? Was he a weak man, "henpecked," as in the old Yakutian fairy tale?

The captain stood still. The sense of being trapped and the shock of realizing how deep his doubts ran had made him shiver. He'd read and reread a great many fairy tales of late; of the three books in Galina's library, two were medical books, and the third was a collection of Siberian legends and fairy tales. In "The Tale of the Henpecked King," the king of the birds—the eagle—obeys his domineering wife's command to build her a special nest for her brooding time. He summons the birds of every kind, has a hole drilled in the beak of each one, and binds them together, so that Madam Eagle can brood comfortably on their plumage. When he counts the bound birds, he ascertains that one, the owl, is missing; he sends out messengers and has the owl brought before him. The owl excuses his absence by explaining that his eyes aren't fit for flying in daylight, and that night travel takes a great deal of time. However, he declares, on his way, he's had a chance to look around and see what's going on in the world. This makes the eagle curious; he wants to know whether the dead outnumber the living on the earth.

"If you count those who are asleep as dead," the owl replies, "the dead are in the majority."

"Is it more often day than night?" the eagle asks, and the owl replies, "If you count the dark Siberian days as nights, it's more often night than day."

"And now, tell me," the eagle continues. "Are there more men or more women on our earth?"

The owl thinks for a moment and answers, "If you count the henpecked men as women, there are more women on the earth."

The king of the birds starts, realizing that in order to be of service to his wife, he has tortured his fellows. Without hesitation, he sets all the birds free; in all their variety, they soar heavenward. And so it is that the owl, alone among birds, has no holes in its beak.

Leonid stamped his booted feet. Where was the damned car? It was almost time to sound the assembly, and here he was, walking up and down on the outskirts of this faceless city. I must take things into my own hands, he thought; I must find a way to stand my ground. Either I travel to Moscow and try to bring about a reconciliation with Anna, or I inform Galina that she can't count on me unless we relocate to the capital. Did I break my back trying to get a right of abode in Moscow for nothing? Did I make sacrifices for Anna so I could rot out here? A captain in exile isn't any better off than an ordinary soldier.

Leonid turned around. He'd walked some distance, and now an army vehicle was parked in front of building number 119 with the motor running. The driver wasn't looking out past the hood of his engine; instead, he was taking advantage of the officer's absence to have a smoke.

"Hey, soldier!" Leonid shouted, so loudly that an echo ran up and down the street. The driver clenched the cigarette between his lips and drove toward the captain.

Maybe, if we both make an effort, going on with Anna isn't hopeless, Leonid thought, but at the same time, he felt the impossibility of doing without Galina's warmth, her humor, her lustiness. He remembered the tension and gloom that had characterized the days he'd spent on leave in Moscow. Things can't remain as they are, he thought. He climbed into the vehicle and looked disapprovingly at the driver. I can't go back, and I don't know where I'm going if I go on.

"Go on," he growled to the corporal.

The latter kept his eyes ahead of him and steered around a wall of ice that the snow plow had shoved to one side of the road.

THIRTY-ONE

It was only as a private citizen that A. I. Kamarovsky found himself inside the Lenin Library. He'd changed from his winter-weight dark green suit to a dark green suit made of lighter material, but with spring windstorms in mind, he was also wearing his long scarf. A few yards away from him sat a young woman who had, he kept telling himself, *his* eyes. In addition, she wore steel-rimmed eyeglasses, just as he did. To avoid the fuss of borrowing a book from the reference shelves, Kamarovsky had brought one with him. He sat at one of the long tables. Rows of fluorescent tubes bathed the reading room in a sallow light that made him tired and offered no possibility of hiding in shadow should the student happen to turn her head in his direction.

The book was an advance copy of a volume of poetry, sent to Kamarovsky at his request. It was a slim volume, and the cover showed a flock of red birds flying out of a black sun. Why hadn't they put a hard cover on the first edition? Kamarovsky wondered; this floppy little book couldn't be displayed upright. Even though it was outside his authority, he resolved to make a telephone call to the state printing office. Why use half measures when it was a matter of lifting a writer out of obscurity?

Before opening the book, Kamarovsky cast a fleeting glance three tables ahead. How pretty she is, he thought, and he was unable to suppress the joy he felt at the idea that he deserved a lot of credit for that, too. If I were a young man, I'd find it a pleasing prospect to woo this attractive young woman. Even though he regretted that his only possibility of seeing her was to spy on her, there was something thrilling about it. The student had three giant tomes open on the table in front of her. Her pencil flew over her notepad; as she wrote, her glasses would slip down her nose, and with a swift gesture she'd push them back up. She's inherited my narrow nose, Kamarovsky thought, and so her glasses won't stay in place. When his daughter grew immersed in a passage in one of her texts, he opened his volume of poetry.

> *Viktor Ipalyevich Tsazukhin's legacy comprises thirty years of Soviet lyric poetry and is the expression of an epoch rich in hard-won victories as well as painful losses. Tsazukhin is a man produced by the Revolution . . .*

The Colonel snorted impatiently and flipped the pages to the end of the foreword.

"Where Does Russia Begin?" was the title of the first poem. Kamarovsky was immediately taken with the bright tone, with its direct, emotional appeal. Even though his assessment of the poem was rather blurred, he flattered himself that such verse had been published through his intervention.

What was she working on? He would have been all too happy to take a look at her books. Her decision to major in architecture filled the Colonel with pride. She's inherited more from me than she's willing to admit, he thought. *My child.* My child is growing up. Maybe she'll marry that fellow from Okhotsk she's been living with for a year. And even if she doesn't go back with him to his hometown, her profession will take her away from Moscow. They need good architects out in the provinces. If she's smart—and it goes without saying that she is—she'll go to one of the newly founded cities in the Tuvan SSR or Kazakhstan. The Colonel's eyes skimmed Viktor Ipalyevich's poem without apprehending its content. So far, there's nothing out there but a main road, electricity, gas, and water connections, and the CC's official mandate to build a city. What that city will look like will be up to the architect—namely my daughter. Now, that's going to require her to be away from Moscow for years, maybe decades. It could even mean that I'll never see her again in this life. Calm down, he said to himself, shaking his head, she's barely begun her studies, and you're already sending her out to raise up cities from the earth. In spite of this insight, he felt a sudden urge to stand up and walk over to her and present himself, a sick, gaunt person, a wearer of eyeglasses, the owner of some not very good teeth, a nervous man in the sixth decade of his life. If nothing in his appearance betrayed the office he discharged, how could she reject him? Didn't everyone want to have a father? How lovely it would be to discuss architectural topics with her. He was interested to know how she conceived of the building art, what architect or school of architecture most impressed her. Without a doubt, it's Le Corbusier; she must find his long, generous line simply compelling. The Colonel smiled, realizing that even in his thoughts, he tended to impose things on his daughter. Force of habit, Kamarovsky said to himself, habit of force.

He lowered his head with the idea of plunging into the world of Tsazukhin's poetry, but a brief, colorful vision made him look up again. It was a patterned blue dress, nothing unusual, but the Colonel thought that shade of blue was familiar. The pattern showed interlocking squares on a dark blue background. A light dress, worn with boots. Apparently, Rosa Khleb had been working in the reading room and was now leaving. She walked without haste, a notepad under her arm, her purse hanging from her shoulder. As far as the Colonel was concerned, her presence in the library aroused no suspicious speculations; the *Moscow Times* didn't have an archive of its own. He wanted to read another poem; at the same time, he wanted to observe his daughter; and he did neither. To someone who'd spent his whole life gathering and processing information, an inadvertent stakeout like this presented an opportunity it was impossible to pass up. Kamarovsky watched himself as he closed the book and slipped it into his pocket in a single movement, noiselessly rose to his feet, turned his head so that his daughter wouldn't recognize him, and stepped out. Rosa chose the way to the main exit, which in that massive building entailed a considerable walk. Kamarovsky stayed close to the wall, pausing in doorways, happy to find that he was still good at the old surveillance game, even though he'd long since delegated such tasks to others. He became so inconspicuous that nobody coming his way so much as looked at him; he was something on the fringes, someone who could observe undisturbed. Rosa entered a wide corridor that was in semidarkness because the electric lights had been switched off at the beginning of spring, and the daylight had yet to reach its full strength. There were many people in the corridor—small groups of students with serious faces, jovial professors, and someone who, in Kamarovsky's judgment, didn't belong there. The man wasn't in the habit of visiting a library; he had no book bag, no writing equipment; he was simply coming that way. Even if his aimlessness hadn't struck Kamarovsky, there were two other reasons for the Colonel to consider him attentively. For one thing, it looked as though he and Rosa were moving toward each other, and for another, Kamarovsky knew the man. He, too, was practiced in wearing a mask of inconspicuousness; his gait and body language were those of someone who understood how to remain in the shadows. Kamarovsky had a dossier on this man. Many years before, he'd embarked on a career as an opera singer, worn himself out in the provinces, taken to drink, been found guilty of assault in some jealous altercation, and done time for his offense. After his release, he'd been unable to find a job until, surprisingly enough, the Deputy Minister for Research Planning had taken him on as his driver. When Kamarovsky investigated this matter at the time, he'd found that Bulyagkov's chauffeur was a native Ukrainian distantly related to his employer. Since there was nothing unusual about giving support to a fellow countryman,

Bulyagkov had been allowed to have his way and Anton to remain in his service.

Now Anton was nearing Rosa, taking smaller, slower steps as he approached. While maintaining her loping gait, Khleb took the bag from her shoulder, opened it, pulled out something that looked like a brown envelope, and held it at her side. Now she was even with Anton, and now already past him. She hadn't altered the rhythm of her steps for a second. Rosa walked on; her light dress swayed around her legs. But it hadn't escaped Kamarovsky that the brown envelope had changed hands. For a fleeting second, the Colonel had seen the object in Anton's hand, and then the thing had disappeared into his jacket pocket.

Despite the long decades during which A. I. Kamarovsky had had to do with many different forms of treachery, what he'd just seen briefly took his breath away. In security work, nothing was feared more than the double agent, the person whom you allow to look into your arrangements and who then misuses the knowledge thus gained. Persons of this sort were superior to the average spy and at the same time the most morally reprehensible members of society. Kamarovsky turned his head away as Anton went by but immediately fastened his eyes on him again. Bulyagkov's driver consulted the signs posted at the next intersection of corridors, but where the man wanted to go was unimportant; in any case, he wanted to go where Bulyagkov was. Kamarovsky was equally uninterested in Rosa's destination; she'd already done the decisive deed. Oddly, the Colonel didn't immediately start to ponder his next moves. Instead he mused about his daughter. Incongruous as their worlds might have been, there was at least one good thing about his: He could be close to her from time to time. And this time, Kamarovsky's unconsummated striving for contact with his daughter had led him to make an interesting discovery, a revelation that threw new light on the Minister for Research Planning's unexplained illness. The news that Bulyagkov was going to fill in for his boss on the Stockholm trip had set off nothing more than a faint signal, but now all the Colonel's sirens were wailing. At this moment, Alexey Bulyagkov was probably on his way to the airport with the freshly stamped divorce certificate in his pocket. Somewhere along the way, there would be a meeting with Anton, who would turn over the brown envelope. Shortly thereafter, the Deputy Minister would climb into the airplane and fly out of Moscow, heading northwest.

While Kamarovsky was making deductions, while his every conclusion was laying open the next question, he reached the exit and went down the grandiose outer staircase. Whether it was because he'd been walking so fast, or because inexplicable little wheels that had hitherto spun independently in his mind had suddenly meshed and made sense and he'd become overexcited—for whatever reason, as he went down the stairs of the Lenin Library, Kamarovsky's head suddenly sank, his jaw dropped, his muscles failed at their tasks. He still had the presence of mind to reach into the pocket where he'd put the tablets, but at that same moment, he felt his hand go limp and knew it would remain powerless, stuck inside his jacket pocket. In a last effort to retain his composure, the Colonel turned in the direction of his office, which was only a few streets away. If he could only reach that address, the people there would know what to do. A grand mal seizure had surprised him at work more than once. His colleagues would carry him into the quiet room normally used as an intimidation cell. He'd lie there, mute and motionless; often he'd start to regain consciousness after a few minutes, but there had also been a few times when he hadn't come to for as long as ten hours. Waking up in that oppressively small room had always reassured him; in the small space contained within its four walls, the panic of losing himself and the shock of feeling strength and control suddenly flow out of him became bearable and, before long, subsided. In such cases, he'd swallow a tablet while still on his back, wait a little while for it to take effect, and then go back to work.

In the moments when the weakness was spreading through all his limbs, while his convulsing muscles were still trying to jolt themselves into action, Kamarovsky felt something strike against his hip: Viktor

Ipalyevich's book of poems. Even though his reason was already fleeing away and his thoughts becoming silhouettes, the Colonel retained the idea that the operation he most urgently needed to undertake would necessarily involve the Tsazukhin family. His knees buckled, and since he was incapable of extracting his hand, which was like a wedge inside his pocket, he couldn't break his fall and landed directly on his shoulder. He was aware of a hollow thud, and his head snapped backward. Good thing I have my hat on, the Colonel thought from out of nowhere, and then he saw himself rolling down several steps; what a joke, what a joke, ah, what a joke.

People didn't notice the accident until the older man was fully horizontal, his fall having come to a stop in the middle of the stairs. He lay with one arm flung out and the other hand in his pocket; his hat had slipped down and was hiding his face. Someone observing him from above might have thought he was in the classic orator's pose, except that he was delivering the oration while lying down. The circle of people around him grew tighter. A policeman reached the spot and waved to colleagues in an official car. Behind the policemen, an attractive woman in a blue dress appeared. Her face showed concern and skepticism and the pang of thoughts in turmoil. She didn't participate in the discussion about the cause of the accident or wait for medical help to arrive; she took the measure of the man in the dark green suit one last time, as though she were charged with ordering his coffin, and then she quickly left the square in front of the Lenin Library.

THIRTY-TWO

Anna had told Petya that on a day like this, you had to go to a park, and she'd chosen the Arkhangelskoye Estate. It was no surprise to discover that thousands of other people had conceived the same idea. As she and her boy turned off the street and walked down to the lower-lying gardens, they discovered a sea of colors—bright hats, vivid shirts, checkered blankets, and baby carriages. People hungry for sunshine had flocked to the park; they were lying about on its lawns or strolling along its paths or laughing, eating, and sleeping in boats afloat on the lake. It was only when Anna, on her way to the children's play area, reached the triple-spiral staircase with the café that she grasped the real reason why she was there. She'd returned to the place where she'd received the first, decisive information about how everything fit together.

In spite of the enchanted evening in the Peking Hotel, Anna had returned home uneasy, even ill-humored. True, she'd bidden Alexey a tender farewell and enjoyed their last embrace at his door, and yet during those very minutes, it was as if she'd looked into a mirror that had become immediately transparent, exposing many rooms on the other side. Later, in bed, Anna had reproached herself for the long time she'd spent seeing only the obvious in that mirror, namely herself, the Deputy Minister, and the pleasant world he'd opened up for her. Even when she'd become aware that Bulyagkov and Kamarovsky were working her like a puppet, Anna had considered it as part of the male power game. She hadn't yet been ready to see the secret that lay behind all that. The night had passed in restless dreams, and the morning had brought a stupid quarrel with Viktor Ipalyevich; in the end, she'd collected Petya and fled the closeness of the apartment for the park.

He dashed over the grass and along the water and came back with a hundred things to tell his mother about. A family of peacocks near the café drew Petya's attention; Anna allowed him to go closer to them, but cautiously.

Naturally, all the tables were occupied, but there, *there* of all places, at the table where Anna and Kamarovsky had sat, a couple stood up, left a tip, and walked off into the park. A woman with a camera hung around her neck hurried over, but Anna beat her to the table and ordered cakes and lemonade for two.

How long had it been since that August day when Kamarovsky had made her his peremptory offer? *Alexey Maximovich is in the public eye,* he'd explained, after shedding the mask of the innocent park visitor. *Special security precautions are taken for him.* But the decisive sentence, which Anna had—until today—overlooked because it was a matter of course, had been this: *Alexey Maximovich Bulyagkov is a bearer of the Soviet Union's state secrets. Therefore, it matters with whom he speaks, whom he meets, with whom he sleeps.* At the time, she'd assumed Kamarovsky was talking about her; the guilt she felt at having walked into the KGB's clutches as an adulteress had prevented her from drawing any further conclusions. Her face turned toward the sun, it occurred to Anna that Kamarovsky might not have correctly evaluated what he'd learned from his range of contact persons. He'd guessed many things and foreseen others, but he'd disregarded the essential. His biggest mistake was that he misconstrued Alexey's driving force. To Kamarovsky's way of thinking, and possibly to that of everyone in the state apparatus, all ambition was necessarily directed toward the next rung on the ladder of rank, the better position, the higher office: in Bulyagkov's case, therefore, the office of Minister of Research Planning. The competent organs had interpreted Alexey's dissatisfaction with his work as frustration at being the number two man. His infelicity, however, ran deeper than that. When he was a young man, the political apparatus of the time had forced him to give up studying for a degree in science, to leave his Ukrainian homeland, and to go into hiding. After his family's rehabilitation, it had been impossible for Alexey to take up his studies again, either because it was too late or for some other reason. In Moscow he'd met Medea, and through her and her family's influence, a door into the stronghold of power had opened for him. Once in the Ministry, however, he'd soon learned that all scientific research was subordinate to the apparatus and not the other way around. He hated serving only the regime; his passion was for science itself. *Had my life run in a different course, nothing could have prevented me from becoming a scientist*, he'd confessed to Anna. He'd revealed everything to her, piece by piece, hadn't he? But she hadn't been able to put them together.

She saw Petya throw some handfuls of grass at the peacocks, who were not impressed, and shifted to a thought that should have entered her mind a long time ago: Under cover of his official position, Alexey Bulyagkov was about to depart on a journey from which he would never return. What else could be the reason for Medea's sudden separation from her husband, if not her own protection? What about the physicist Lyushin and his double game, letting a scientific success be reframed as a failure, with Alexey's encouragement? Why was Alexey traveling to a scientific meeting in the West? In the West, Anna repeated inwardly, he's going over to the West! Was this intention belated revenge for the humiliation of his family? Was the Ukrainian paying the Russians back for having killed his father? At the same time, Anna found it incomprehensible that Bulyagkov, the weary wolf, a man she thought she knew, would be about to turn defector. He must have been planning it for months; therefore, he must have been lying to her for months, too. It seemed even more mind-boggling to think that Alexey must have devised and executed his plans under Kamarovsky's nose, and that he'd taken advantage of her only because he wanted her to report the obvious—but not the truth—to the Colonel. When she called up her mental image of her lover, his spongy face, his unkempt hair, it was hard for her to believe him capable of such calculation, of the circumspection and patience to carry out such a long-range plan. The very length of the plan, the preparation such a thing would entail, made Anna doubt her conclusions. Even if he felt so jaded, so frustrated by his lack of prospects and the treadmill of the governmental apparatus that he indulged in fantasies of departure, surely his sense of justice, his loyalty, and his patriotic feeling for the fatherland would regain the upper hand after a while.

But not if his fatherland isn't Russia, Anna thought. Not if the Central Committee doesn't represent the instrument of his political convictions and the Ministry of Research fails to come up to his standards of scientific advancement. Maybe enticements reached him from *over there*, offers that have given him hope of resurrecting, at this late date, his buried life's dream. Anna was certain that the people *over there* welcomed only those who brought something with them. Even though Anna had only an inexact notion of how Lyushin's work fit into the overall structure, she nevertheless understood that her own trip to Dubna had been part of the plan. She was supposed to deceive Kamarovsky about Lyushin's results.

She used one hand to fan her burning face, her eyes were red, and on this spring day she was feeling unseasonably hot. Only now did she discover that two plates of cakes and two glasses of lemonade were standing in front of her; she drank half the contents of one of them. Loud shrieking made her look up; the biggest of the peacocks clapped his tail together and made a run at Petya. Still clutching a handful of grass, the boy turned away and took off for the terrace. Close to his goal, he tripped on a sill and fell to the ground, fully expecting the bird to attack him from behind. But the peacock remained at a safe distance from the humans, ascertained that his mission was accomplished, and sauntered back to his peahens. Anna made her way between tables and reached Petya, who was so frightened he didn't even cry.

"That's what you get," she scolded him. "Come on, now, nothing happened. We've got cakes waiting for us. Want some?"

He let her lead him to the table, where the waiter stood ready with the check fluttering in his hand. Anna paid the check, sat down, and watched Petya as he ate.

Whom should she inform? Who was capable of soberly assessing her suspicions—for despite her certainty, that was all they were—and taking steps? Certainly not Kamarovsky; confiding in the Colonel was tantamount to throwing Alexey defenseless to the lions. It was too late for her to speak to Alexey himself; he and the delegation were meeting the press at that moment, and after the meeting, they'd go straight to the airport. Petya sat beside Anna, eating happily, his soul at peace. What was she supposed to do with him? She needed freedom of action.

"I have to make a phone call. Take the last piece with you."

"More juice," Petya mumbled, his mouth full.

"Later. You'll get some juice at home." Anna took his hand and drew him away from the café terrace. She spotted a pay phone on the other side of the ornamental stream and hastened toward it without paying much attention to whether Petya could keep up with her or not.

"What's the matter?" he whined.

"This won't take long." Anna kept her eyes straight ahead, ran over the little bridge, dodged two bicyclists, saw someone a little distance away also heading for the telephone booth, snatched Petya off his feet, and ran. Panting, she burst into the booth with Petya in her arms, closed the door, turned her back to the oncoming person, and put the first coin in the slot. She dialed Rosa Khleb's number. While Anna listened to the ring tone repeat itself unanswered, she admitted to herself that out of all the possibilities, she'd chosen the one that would thwart Alexey's intentions. If her suspicion were confirmed, he was planning to do something wrong, and it was Anna's duty to avert damage. Outside, the man who also wanted to use the telephone was only a few steps away. She was about to step out of the booth when she recognized Anton. Petya started to push the door open, but she took him by the hand. Anton looked at them through the glass panes.

"I have to talk to you," he said. "Not here. Let's go to the car." He pointed at the spiral staircase that led up to the street. Anna stepped out with Petya.

The boy dragged his feet, unwilling to go farther. "We'll be home soon," she said to encourage him. When they reached the street, Anna looked around for the black ZIL.

Anton indicated the automobile in front of them. "We're taking this one." He opened the passenger door of a Zhiguli and pulled the seat forward.

Stressed as she was, and unable to understand the situation, Anna laid her head back and laughed. The sun shone on her face. "What is this?" she cried, as if it weren't obvious that Anton was driving his own vehicle instead of the official limousine.

"It's as good as new. One point two liters, sixty horsepower, with a radio and genuine synthetic fur." He reached in and stroked the back of the seat.

Anna shoved Petya into the back and climbed into the passenger's seat next to Anton; they were sitting side by side for the first time.

"Would you like this?" He handed Petya an opened package of chocolates.

After a questioning look at his mother and a shy one at the stranger, Petya accepted the gift.

"How long did you save up for this car?" Anna asked.

"Six years."

"How did you track me down?"

"I went to your home, Comrade. Your father told me where I could find you."

"I'm surprised. He doesn't know you."

As though declaring that there was no time for such chitter-chatter, Anton leaned toward her. "But you and I, we've known each other for a good while, Anna Viktorovna. We've driven down many roads together. Something's happened."

"To Alexey? What? What is it?"

"He'll be taking off soon."

"So?"

"I *did* something for the Deputy Minister. Apparently, I was observed when I did it."

"Did what?"

"I took delivery of certain documents for Alexey Maximovich." Anton ran his hand over his forehead and through his oiled hair. "Someone saw me do that."

"Who?"

"Star-Eyes."

At first, the name and the man who'd spoken it didn't fit together. So Anton was in on it, too? Was everyone she knew involved in this affair? "What does that mean?" she asked in a whisper.

"The Colonel probably had a suspicion he couldn't substantiate—until today." Anton cleared his throat. "Now things look different."

Anna saw her line of thought confirmed in Anton's words. "Alexey wants to defect," she said grimly. "He wants to betray his country."

"He only wants to start a new life."

"But that's not possible. You have only *one* life, and you have to face up to it. You can't change it like a coat."

Petya stared in amazement at his impassioned mother. She rubbed his head and tried out a reassuring smile. "We're talking, we're just talking," she said.

"There's still time," said Anton, coming to his real point. "Alexey Maximovich must be warned."

"Why? Isn't he about to take off for his new country? He'll be in Stockholm in a few hours."

"You're mistaken. The delegation has a twenty-four-hour layover in Riga. It has something to do with an old invitation from the Latvian Central Committee. Bulyagkov's supposed to give a presentation there."

"So why are you coming to me with all this?"

"I thought . . ." He lowered his voice. "It seemed to me that the right person to warn the Deputy Minister would be someone he'd listen to, not just someone he trusts, but someone he has feelings for," Anton said, in a serious, businesslike tone.

"And that's supposed to be me? Why?"

"Because I don't know anyone else Alexey Maximovich really loves."

For a moment, there was silence in the little car.

"Who's Alexey Maximovich?" Petya asked.

"An old friend."

"If he's a friend of yours, why don't I know him?"

"He's . . . he's not here anymore." Anna looked out the window.

Anton opened the door. With a glance at the child, he signaled her to step outside.

"We're already outside," she said, getting out of the car.

They talked over the Zhiguli's roof. "We can be in Riga in thirteen hours," Anton said, as matter-of-factly as if he were proposing an outing to the Kremlin.

"We?" Anna made an effort to grasp the lunacy of the proposal. "And what do we do there?"

"You talk to him."

"If Kamarovsky knows what's going on, he sent his people there a long time ago."

"He hasn't done that, Comrade."

"Why not?"

"The current state of his health doesn't allow it."

"Have you done something to him?"

Anton smiled at her dramatic imagination. "The Colonel is an epileptic." He saw surprise, almost shock, on her face. "You didn't know?"

"How could I? Our meetings . . ." She fell silent.

"We have to make use of this grace period."

"It's not just Kamarovsky. He's certainly smuggled a couple of his people into the delegation, and they can draw similar conclusions."

"I don't think so. There's a particular, crucial point that the Committee for State Security has remained unaware of until today." Anton gave the boy in the car a friendly look.

"Please explain what you mean."

"I'd be glad to, Comrade. But we don't have time. You must decide right away. Otherwise, I'm going on my own."

"In this car?" she asked, almost amused.

"Don't underestimate my faithful Zhiguli. The gas tank's already full."

"Why not just call Alexey on the telephone?"

"In a hotel in Riga?" He tilted his head to one side. "You know why that's a bad idea."

Anna noticed that Petya was making signals to her through the window. She put her hand on the glass and answered his finger language. "I can't, Anton."

"In all this time, Alexey Maximovich has never asked anything of you. He isn't asking anything now, either. I'm asking you. I'm begging you to save Alexey Maximovich Bulyagkov's life."

Anna looked up at the tree in whose shadow the automobile was parked and saw that they were under a venerable Russian silverberry. Then her eyes slid down to her own fingers, which seemed to be holding Petya's hand through the glass. She asked Anton why he was so sure of reaching his goal; after all, there was a border in the way.

"I'm a driver," he said with a smile. "I've been a driver for so long I can hardly remember the time before I started. If there's anything I understand, it's driving."

Anna didn't want to be taken in again. She was tormented by the feeling that this affair would never end and that as long as she had anything to do with Alexey, her life would be turbulent and hopeless. Even now, when she was supposed to be free of him, he was dragging her back, pulling her behind him, entangling her in his guilt, giving her qualms, and she wanted out, she wanted to strip all that off like a soiled dress. But it was only an affair, she thought, kept up against my will—an affair that had already damaged various aspects of her life. What would have to happen before she could say the thing was finished, over, done with, one way or another? And so she was standing there, looking back and forth from the silverberry tree to her son in the backseat.

She cast about for a gentle way to tell Anton that his proposal was ludicrous and she wasn't available. Anton's hair was stiff with brilliantine, but as she turned her gaze to his questioning face, the wind tousled him and blew a lock onto his forehead. This little change had an effect: Anna looked at him no longer as Alexey's appendage but as an independent person.

"I'm going to take Petya home now," she said. "Wait for me in the little street." She bent down, opened the back door, slid the passenger's seat forward, and helped her son out of the car. "Are you hungry?" she asked. Petya shook his head. "Do you want to go home?"

They walked off together, hand in hand.

THIRTY-THREE

Nagged by the impression that she'd missed something crucial, Rosa Khleb stood by the unconscious patient's bedside. The KGB's elephant, the man who'd taught them all, lay before them in a pale blue hospital gown, felled by the illness people had whispered about for decades. Rosa and two colleagues found themselves in Doctor Shchedrin's clinic, in the section reserved for special cases. The room's furnishings were dignified and the prevailing silence extraordinary for a place in the heart of the city center. Outside, a young birch tree gave a touch of faux rurality to the scene.

Rosa's cogitations had yielded no conclusions. Almost mechanically, she'd checked the validity of her visa, which she'd been granted because of her work as a foreign correspondent. One of the two possible escape routes went through Prague, the other through Dresden; there was no getting around a stop in one of the Soviet Union's satellite countries. Rosa had the flight times for Dresden in her head. Her passport, the visa, and her press credentials as a reporter for the *Moscow Times* lay ready in her apartment. No request for foreign travel had been made for her, but that fact alone wouldn't be enough to arouse suspicion right away. The Khleb had taken many a spontaneous trip, on assignment for the newspaper or in the service of the Colonel.

It was said that Rosa was so beautiful as a girl that people in her vicinity would start to laugh or cry, because they couldn't stand it. She'd been called to Moscow to work as a "greeting girl"; when flowers and kisses were to be presented to friendly statesmen, Rosa had been the presenter of choice. She was the blond girl standing behind Kosygin when he addressed the Pioneers, and once, when the selection of "attentive listeners" at an appearance by Brezhnev in a synthetics factory hadn't seemed sufficiently telegenic, Rosa had been outfitted in work togs and placed in the front row. And thus, at the age of fifteen, she'd shaken the General Secretary's hand.

Rosa's beauty increased with each passing year; she became breathtaking and desirable, but her state propaganda assignments occupied her so extensively that she hardly had time for private offers. These were too numerous to count, some of them pushy, some polished, but no one could boast of any success. The blond, all-Russian girl was still a virgin when Kamarovsky received permission to train her for work in his department. He didn't go about it the way he usually did with future adepts—promises, intimidation of the parents, or blackmail because of past misdeeds. A. I. Kamarovsky counted on the seventeen-year-old's intelligence and vanity. When she appeared as a pretty ornament for the clown in the Russian National Circus, Kamarovsky waited for her behind the big tent in an official government car and took her to the Turkmenyev, a nightspot whose doors remained closed to ordinary comrades. Kamarovsky gave himself out as a big wheel with some numinous foreign committee and offered Rosa the possibility of accompanying him on a tour as a "friendship ambassadress." In spite of her popularity, Rosa Khleb had so far been a decorative face known only within the Soviet Union; when Kamarovsky offered her a broader opportunity, she showed even more enthusiasm than he'd hoped. He was amazed at how hard-nosed the young woman was when she spoke about putting herself on display, how accurately, even back then, she assessed herself and her value for the apparat. It had been child's play for him to transform his project into reality; a "finder's fee" forestalled Rosa's parents from worrying about her.

And so she had come into Kamarovsky's service and was at his side on the tour, which took them exclusively to Western countries. He was cautious enough not to burn Rosa out with normal missions; she didn't infiltrate anything, and she didn't have to sleep with Western politicians to pick their brains; the Colonel put his money, as it were, on her virginity. With her, he had something *inviolate* on his team, and therefore her assignments were of a particular nature. During a security crisis, negotiations led to an exchange of undercover agents. Fourteen men were set free on the far side of a bridge in the dark of night; when they reached their native soil, a blond angel was there to welcome them. Kamarovsky liked toying with such romanticism and used the beautiful young woman as a figurehead. Victory, freedom, revolution—hadn't such concepts always been symbolized by women, with scabbards slung from their waists and swords in their hands? Kamarovsky didn't flinch from dressing Rosa in attire appropriate to those iconic images. The uniform of an officer in the Red Army was tailored to her measurements, as was some traditional Cossack garb.

At some point, however, there came the day when Rosa's youthful magic had completed its service; she herself noticed this later than the Colonel did. Even the prettiest outfits could no longer hide the fact that she wasn't a girl anymore. When Rosa, too, became aware of this, Kamarovsky unscrupulously exploited her disorientation. The KGB was all she knew; a return to normal life would have necessitated the kind of trivial activities for which she'd long since been spoiled. The Colonel had Rosa go to journalism school, and while she was still taking courses, he employed her in assignments related to the news services. He lifted his prohibition on her having her first boyfriend, who was himself a journalist and, naturally, Kamarovsky's man. As expected, a normal sex life did away with her aura of inviolability; from that point on, she was only one of the attractive women on external duty. She slept with a Western diplomat, compromised him as directed, and produced the desired results. However, Rosa Khleb's youthful fame precluded planting her as a decoy in some Western embassy, and therefore she was given short, concise assignments, among them the recruiting of the house painter Anna Nechayevna. It had taken Rosa only two meetings to gain Anna's trust and deliver her to the Colonel.

What neither he nor anyone else in Moscow knew was that Rosa's abilities had also attracted notice outside her own sphere. During one of her trips as a foreign correspondent, she allowed some harmless banter with a Swedish Ministry official to turn into something more. The Swede turned out to be in the service of the French, who subtly conveyed to Rosa that it made no sense for a stream of interesting information to flow in only one direction; the heavier the traffic, the greater the likelihood that both parties could profit from it. Of course, money played a role in Rosa's decision, but even more important was her desire for revenge on Kamarovsky, who'd pushed her into an irreversible career. Maybe it was also that she'd been to Paris, Stockholm, and Vienna a few times too often to be able to forget the delights of private property. From that point on, the Khleb played a childish game with herself: Since she confided secret details about her department to her Swedish lover and only to him, she could maintain the illusion that she was simply chatting with a friend and not committing treason. In return for her information, she received payment from the French, which the Swede concealed by means of discreet transfers to a Stockholm account. One day, in the course of a meeting in Switzerland, he informed her that a man at the second level of the Soviet hierarchy wanted to change sides. She'd been assigned to establish contact with this man, to learn his intentions, and to find out *what he intended to bring with him*. A complicated ritual had been required to make Alexey Bulyagkov pay attention to her and then to convince him that she, Rosa, Kamarovsky's devoted follower, was the person charged with responding to his signal. After long negotiations,

Rosa's suggestion was accepted and Stockholm agreed upon as the best place for Bulyagkov's defection.

Outside the birch leaves were quivering; Rosa's colleagues had opened the window and were having a smoke. The reason why Rosa felt she might have missed something had to do with the location where Kamarovsky's seizure had laid him low. When he'd described the symptoms of his disease to her for the first time, Rosa had been fascinated by the idea of a "grand mal," a sudden illness that fell upon its victim like a punishment from heaven and paralyzed his entire organism. Why had he collapsed right in front of the library? What was he doing there, and why had he chosen this day, of all days? Rosa's experience with the KGB had taught her that when it came to making any sort of transfer, subway stations, major intersections, museums, and libraries were the best venues; she'd been certain she'd chosen the right spot for her convergence with Anton. Should she have left the country right away, as soon as she saw Kamarovsky sprawled on the steps? Was it still possible for her to leave now? But wouldn't that be acting too rashly if the Colonel had been at the library only by chance, if he hadn't even seen her? As a member of the inner circle of Kamarovsky's collaborators, she'd simply had to show up at the hospital, Doctor Shchedrin's medical paradise. The Colonel's peaceful sleep made Rosa think her speculations were improbable; nevertheless, she'd informed Anton of her suspicion. In case of necessity, he was to prevent Bulyagkov from walking into a trap.

The spring, Rosa thought, the spring lures you in and clasps you tight, its breezes blow away clear thoughts until you're dizzy. If she had to stand around in Shchedrin's clinic and discuss the consequences of the department leader's temporary absence, the spring didn't care. It made the birch wave to her through the window, made the birds chirp and the clouds, no longer low and heavy, sail gaily through the upper sky. Rosa went over to the window where the others were gathered, turned down the offered cigarette, and listened to what her colleagues had to say.

THIRTY-FOUR

How green, how splendid, how light, Anna thought, conscious of every breath she drew into her lungs. Why would she be happy at a time like this? Did it take so little to transform her feelings? Or was everything else simply too much, and too awful? She felt like a child who runs and plays and works herself up to such a pitch that she can't stop laughing. "Where are we?" she asked, turning to Anton.

"We haven't gone very far yet, Comrade. We're not even to Volokolamsk."

"So why is everything so beautiful here?"

"I take it you don't leave Moscow very often."

"You're right. Not since before this past winter. And a terrible winter it was." She clenched her fists in her lap.

"This is fertile country, with gentle hills and woods full of oaks and willows. Willows grow here, Comrade, because there's so much groundwater. And the sky is always in motion."

The road was patched in many places, and if Anton failed to dodge a pothole, his little car snapped and crackled. "We're on the old Volokolamskoye Chaussée," he informed her, answering her earlier question. "You might think the M9 would be faster, and you'd be right, except traffic's always bottled up around Krasnogorsk at this time of day, so we avoided that. Once we're past Volokolamsk, I'll swing onto the main highway."

Anna listened to him with only half an ear; she was almost wholly captivated by what she was seeing. They went through a village where only the utility poles revealed what century they were in; the wooden houses with their colorfully painted window frames, the meadow edges, the piles of firewood, birch and pine, depleted by the long winter—all these indicated a time that had passed and yet was obstinately holding on in this inconspicuous spot.

"It really blows hard out here," she murmured, observing a tree bent diagonally by the west wind. Something was being hawked on the side of the road, but Anton was driving too fast for Anna to be able to make out what the offered wares were.

"The train would have been another possibility," Anton said, resuming the small talk. "The Baltic Railroad, Moscow to Riga in one day."

"Why didn't we just take the train, then?"

"We still can if something goes wrong with the car. I've learned one thing from Alexey Maximovich: 'In love and on the run, you must always have two ways out, Antosha.'" In sudden high spirits, Anton leaned on the horn. "Words to live by," he said.

"He chose a single way this time," Anna pointed out. "With no turning back."

"I don't know. You may well be right, Comrade."

"Please call me Anna, like everyone else."

"I can try." He smiled. "But habit, Comrade, habit's a big, strong horse that pulls in only one direction."

Now that she was talking to him at some length for the first time, Anna realized that Anton was no urbanite; he was a country boy, and his years in Moscow hadn't succeeded in driving that out of him.

They reached Volokolamsk and shortly thereafter left it behind. Anna saw the golden towers of a cathedral shining between houses, and then a swanky house, once a noble's residence, that had been turned into a club building for the agricultural combine. Beyond the town limits, Anna admired the private vegetable gardens, where bean plants and lettuces were sending their first shoots up into the light. Anton took the feeder road to the big highway, and their pace increased substantially.

"Do you know what's special about Volokolamsk? When the Nazi troops were advancing on Moscow, this was the farthest they got."

"Here? I thought that was Yakhroma. On the trip to Dubna, we were told—"

"Yakhroma? Nonsense!" he said vehemently. "It was Volokolamsk, I can assure you. I know the history. Twenty-eight soldiers under General Panfilov managed to destroy dozens of Nazi tanks before they themselves were killed. There's a monument to the twenty-eight heroes in Volokolamsk." He gave Anna a penetrating look. "*Here* is where the Wehrmacht was brought to a standstill, not Yakhroma!"

They left the Moscow administrative division, crossed into the Tver oblast, and an hour later were nearing the town of Rzhev. Anna grew tired and even briefly fell asleep. A noise as loud as an ongoing explosion made her start awake in terror. "What is it?"

"Sukhoi Su-9," he said, smiling at her and pointing skyward.

The sound faded away and came back. Another black fighter plane swept across the clear sky, leaving its noise far behind.

"Where are we?"

"There's an air force base a few miles from here," Anton said, shouting over the roar of the jet engines. "That one was a Tupolev." He leaned forward and struck the dashboard. The temperature gauge needle bounced. "I think it could use a little drink," Anton said. He patted the steering wheel. "It won't be long, my thirsty friend."

The town lay a little distance off the M9. Anton stopped in front of a simple house on the outskirts. A woman was outside, weeding her vegetable garden. "It's better if you ask her for some water," Anton said, handing Anna a jerrican.

She got out, stretched, and walked toward the fence. "Excuse me, Comrade . . ."

The woman, bending to her work, hadn't heard Anna coming and jerked herself upright. As a sign of her innocuous wish, Anna held up the container. "Could you give us some water?"

"Water? How about a glass of lemonade?" She stuck her little knife into her pocket and opened the garden gate for Anna.

After a brief glance at Anton, Anna followed the woman into the house and entered a living room where her eye was struck by something she would never have expected to find in such a place: silver-gray wallpaper with a white pattern, perfectly hung and cleanly finished at the top, a hand's width below the ceiling. Light, freshly washed curtains were suspended from gleaming, gold-colored rods, meticulously aligned with the top line of the wallpaper, and alongside them hung drapes with a dark brown pattern. Anna noticed a television set, a house plant, and even central heating.

"You've got a lovely place here," Anna said. "How did you get ahold of this first-class wallpaper?"

"My brother's the local priest," the woman explained. "I'm his housekeeper."

Behind her, Anna spotted a cross and some pictures of martyrs. "Your brother?"

"Our members spend generously," she said, plucking at the lace tablecloth until it lay smooth. "Are you hungry, my girl? I've stuffed some hardboiled eggs."

"Thanks, but we're in a hurry." Anna turned toward the kitchen.

"The wallpaper was a gift from God's children in our kolkhoz," she said. Then she laid her hand on the samovar. "But surely you'll drink some tea, won't you?"

"Many thanks, but no. Maybe on the way back." Anna pointed to the jerrican.

"We could have filled that in the garden," the woman said, clearly irritated by the rejection of her hospitality. She gruffly ran her hand over the cherrywood sideboard, as if she'd discovered a speck of dust on it. Then she accompanied Anna outside again, turned on the water faucet at one corner of the house, and, while the container was filling up, peered at Anton. "Yours?" she said, meaning the man.

"His," Anna answered, pointing at the automobile. Just then, Anton lifted the hood.

"Where are you headed?" The woman tried to decipher the license number.

"To visit some friends."

When Anna brought the water, Anton thanked the woman with a nod. Apparently forgetting her garden work, she went back inside the house.

"What took you so long?" Anton asked, closing the hood.

"She has beautiful wallpaper on her walls."

By the time they passed Rzhev, the day was drawing to its close. Anna tried to sleep, but the road had become worse, and she was constantly shaken awake. Anton looked at his watch. "We won't reach the border before midnight," he said.

The landscape turned monotonous; Anna's happy feeling had vanished. She thought about the hours that lay before her; she'd see Alexey again, but she wasn't expected this time, and the circumstances were thoroughly transformed.

"Didn't you say you'd taken delivery of some documents for Alexey?" Anton nodded. "And so you turned those documents over to him?"

"When I drove him to the airport."

"But then . . ." She sat upright as though jolted. "Then you had time to warn him in Moscow!"

"No," he said softly.

"I don't understand." A pothole made Anna's chin bounce off her chest.

"You knew Kamarovsky saw you. Why didn't you tell Alexey before he got on the plane?"

"Unfortunately, I didn't know that." He clicked his tongue. "She didn't call me until later, when Alexey Maximovich was gone. She told me about Kamarovsky."

"Who?"

And so Anna learned that the agent for internal security, Rosa Khleb, whom Anna liked to think of as a modern witch, was capable of even more artfulness than she'd imagined. Anna listened in amazement as she learned that the Khleb and Bulyagkov had been in contact for at least a year, and that it was she who had worked out his escape plan via Stockholm. Anton was even able to report that an untimely overlap had taken place the last time Anna visited the Deputy Minister in the Drezhnevskaya apartment: The mysterious visitor was Rosa; she was the one who'd brought Bulyagkov the little parcel, and it was her footsteps that Anna had heard sounding in the stairwell.

They passed villages and little towns; the sun shone red in their faces and finally disappeared; Anton began to smoke, which was the only hint he gave that he might be getting tired; and while all this was going on, Anna was arriving at the realization that she, who had considered herself so clever and calculating, who had even reproached herself for her great cunning, was nothing but a beginner. The game had gone on without any participation from her. She hadn't even known the rules—she was just a piece that had fit in. She'd done exactly what she'd been expected to do. And at this moment, Anna saw that as her greatest defeat.

THIRTY-FIVE

The Kremlin stands above the city; above the Kremlin stands only God. The fortress was rebuilt eighteen times; why eighteen, the man in the pale blue hospital gown wondered. The first stone wall was erected in 1366; Ivan III's architects put up twenty towers, a palace, their city's first fortification. Kamarovsky was gratified to ascertain that his eyeglasses had been taken away from him; the unreliable things only stopped him from seeing connections properly. They were Italians, he thought; in those days, the Italians were the best builders. They put twenty streets and ten squares inside the Kremlin walls—a tour de force of fortification architecture. Why did Napoleon have all that burned down? Out of vexation, Kamarovsky thought, nodding. Who wouldn't be vexed, after dismantling the biggest country on earth, to wait in vain for someone to come and submit to him? One of the people in the room giggled, and Kamarovsky looked around; that was no giggling matter. Napoleon must have felt like a spurned lover, sitting there in the Kremlin, with not a single Russian showing up for a rendezvous. While he let his *capitaines* plunder the city, he overlooked the fact that it was already the middle of September: time to start getting ready for winter. The fire he lit in Moscow wasn't hot enough to warm his army. He who burns something down makes a site for reconstruction, Kamarovsky thought.

Thicker walls this time, and then, later, they set shining, red-ruby-colored stars on the tops of the towers. "Ruby stars"—the words resounded in him. The sound evoked something like beauty, still incomprehensible, but it announced its presence. The beautiful, the great—it flowed into him like a stream, penetrating him. He took several deep breaths.

"In the past we had no fatherland, nor could we have one," Kamarovsky said. "But now that power is in our hands, in the hands of the workers, we have a fatherland, and we will defend its independence." The Colonel made a great effort to recall who'd said those words. Not Vladimir Ilyich, the patient was sure of that, but of course it had to do with him, as did everything else. Kamarovsky nodded: Everything else. No, those words came from the great speech given in the Grand Kremlin Palace to the graduates of the Red Army Academy on May 4, 1935. I was there, the patient thought. By that time, Vladimir Ilyich was long dead. I heard the speech, and I understood. Why was it so important to remember the Kremlin and the beautiful stars shining on its towers? Red stars, ruby stars, the Colonel thought; in the past, he'd sometimes called her *Rosa, my ruby star*. Whoever saw her today would hardly have been able to envision how bright this Russian soul, how beautiful this most beautiful of Soviet girls, had been.

He struggled to keep his thoughts from falling into confusion again; he dared not go back there, where they all became one. Kamarovsky propped himself on his elbows. The cathedral, he thought, built in 1457 under the direction of the Italians—here stood Ivan's throne under the carved pavilion roof. The bell, the Tsar Bell! Remembering the bell was important. It was supposed to sound out from the Tsar's Tower, but that never happened.

"It never happened!" he shouted into the room, trying to avert another collapse. "Right from the start, the master founders struggled with difficulties in the casting. Who would build such a monstrosity? Over twenty feet in diameter, just imagine, to this day the biggest bell in the world!"

The bell meant—he sank back down onto the pillows—the bell

meant a certain place. Not the Kremlin, not the pit where it was cast, not the pedestal where it still stood. The bell meant . . . the library! Of course, the library. Kamarovsky had been there and observed a young woman who knew all about the Kremlin Bell, who'd studied it closely.

Now the Colonel was waking up and calming down. The multiple ideas in his head fell together and made room for the one idea that he could grasp. He let the calm sink into him more and more deeply, and behind it he could feel himself reviving. A. I. Kamarovsky looked around. His vision was still blurred, obviously, because he didn't have his glasses. It wasn't about the bell, he realized, nor was it about the young woman in the library that bore Vladimir Ilyich's name. But in its halls, yes, Kamarovsky had seen someone. His memory came back slowly, gradually, and in the end he knew that the person he'd seen had been Rosa, his *ruby star*. After he was sure he'd identified all the connections properly, he rang for the nurse and had her call Doctor Shchedrin.

"I want my car," he told his old friend.

"Some other time, my dear Antip Iosifovich," the doctor said. "You can go for a drive some other time. Not today."

"On the contrary," the Colonel said with a smile. "Some other time, you'll keep me here, maybe forever, if it comes to that, because I surely can't take many more attacks like this last one. But today, my friend, even with the best will in the world, I can't stay."

"And where do you want to go, Antip?" the doctor asked, looking at him earnestly.

"What's today?" Kamarovsky thrust his hands behind his back, trying to reach the strings of his hospital gown.

"Wait, I'll help you. Today's Tuesday."

"If today's Tuesday . . ." Unceremoniously, the Colonel allowed his friend to undress him and watched as the nurse, at Shchedrin's behest, fetched the green suit from the closet. "If it's Tuesday, I don't need a car, I need a helicopter. I have to get to Riga as quickly as possible."

"Ah, Antip Iosifovich, that's not good for you." The doctor put together the necessary medications for his friend and in the end gave him back his spectacles.

As they approached Novosokolniki, the darkness became definitive. Anna couldn't have said whether the incessant rolling and thumping and rumbling was caused by the road or by the throbbing pressure in her head. The distance they'd come seemed immeasurable, the distance yet to go endless. She stopped looking at the odometer; it was too disappointing to see how slowly they were approaching their goal. Stupid fantasies fluttered through her brain, probably because of an offhand remark Anton had made. As they were leaving the metropolis behind, he'd called the provinces west of Moscow "the Land of the Old Believers" and told her that the people here made no distinction between life and death and would secretly keep their dead loved ones in their homes.

In the smoke from his cigarettes, with visibility limited to the small stretch of road directly in front of the headlights, Anna passed into a kind of comatose state, swinging between waking, dozing, sleeping, and reviving. A long, interminable sleep was something devoutly to be wished, a sleep between this world and the next, and so it didn't seem particularly surprising when she recognized Alexey in the darkness, lying there in state. The wolf's eyes were closed, but his ears were pricked up, as if he could hear, even in death, what was going on around him. A veiled woman, the widow, stepped to the bier; Anna pictured Medea, stony-faced, under the veil. At the head of the casket stood Colonel Kamarovsky, not in a dark green suit, but in the sumptuous regalia of a metropolitan, black and gold, with which his steel-rimmed spectacles seemed out of place. In the next moment, the nameless place turned into Anna's own sleeping alcove, but bigger, as though it were a deep, deep cave in which the wolf, an old hero in fabulous leather clothing, lay dead. It was obvious to her that traitors had assassinated him, but that he could still escape his end if only someone would bring him the water of life. In these familiar surroundings, Anna looked for herself in vain, but there was the television set, and here was Viktor Ipalyevich, bent over his notebooks. The metropolitan said a prayer and recalled the hero's accomplishments in the service of science. When Anna tried to take a better look, she realized that it wasn't Medea who was wearing the veil, it was she. How amazing, to be the old wolf's widow, and yet it was only logical, because only a young person with a fighting spirit could give him the water of life. Anna was alert, excited, and happy until she suddenly noticed that Anton, without warning, was turning off the M9.

"Where are you going?" she asked from under the veil.

"Those two are a little too *inconspicuous* for my taste," he said, leaning into the steering wheel and holding on. The turnoff road was haphazardly paved, and the Zhiguli skidded uncomfortably.

"Who?" Anna asked, wide awake.

"Two Volgas, for the last six miles." He looked in the rearview mirror and nodded. "Just as I thought."

Anna, too, could see two pairs of headlights follow them onto the side road. "Now what do we do? Should we talk to them?"

"That would take time." He stepped on the gas. For the time being, the headlights disappeared behind a curve in the road. "We can talk later."

"If they're already following us here, then they're surely waiting for us at the border!" Anna said, her voice growing hysterical and her breath short.

Without answering, Anton drove still faster, jerking the car from one side of the road to the other and avoiding the worst holes.

"You'll never shake them off!"

"In love and on the run, you need two ways out," Anton said. There was no trace of nervousness in his deep bass. He forced the car along so fast that Anna could do little but hold on tight. The Zhiguli bounded over bumps, slid sideways, and lurched dangerously, but it always righted itself and found the middle of the road again. The trees became shapes flashing past them. Anton maintained one hand on the gearshift, kept the engine turning at its top rotation speed, and reacted to curves and rising ground before Anna became aware of them.

"There." He took one hand off the steering wheel and pointed at the forest. "We're driving parallel to the railroad. A few minutes through the woods, and you'll reach the tracks."

She was listening to him breathlessly. "Walk along the tracks, and after a few miles, you should see the town of Maevo. Do you have money?"

She reached into her bag. "And where are we going to meet?"

"We won't meet again." Anton drove around a pothole. "The train will be safer and more comfortable."

He braked hard, and the car came to a lunging stop close to the edge of the forest. "We're about an hour ahead of the night train."

While he looked in the rearview mirror, Anna opened the door. "Just a moment, Comrade," Anton said. "How do you expect to find Alexey Maximovich?"

The pursuing headlights flashed above the top of the hill behind them. In the seconds that remained, Anton gave Anna the name of a hotel. Then he closed the passenger's door and drove off, without a word of encouragement or farewell.

Anna stood at the side of the road, facing the woods. Then, not looking back, she began to put one foot in front of the other, stepped among the trees, and fell, somehow ducking as she did so. Before long, the lights were there, the noise of the engine even with her, then already past. She raised her head, turned, and saw the brake lights flicker, go out, and flash again before disappearing into the terrain. Almost as if lost in thought, she faced forward again. The forest looked so thick that there seemed to be no way through it.

THIRTY-SIX

Rosa's apartment wasn't very nicely furnished. She could have afforded good furniture, and she even knew the channels through which it could be procured, but she had no appreciation for it. A room and a half in the Arbat district, overpriced, viewless, and ugly to boot—that was Rosa's residence. The bedclothes were seldom changed and the table was wobbly, with its veneer lifting up around the edges. She had no carpet—the floor covering was made of some synthetic fiber—and a single picture hung on the wall. The sofa served as a clothes closet. Thick dust covered the stove; Rosa didn't like to cook and had never learned. A jar of prunes was in the sink, but she couldn't remember why she'd bought it. On a shelf stood a few books, including a much-talked-about novel that she'd placed there, ready to be read, but it remained unopened. She came home only to watch television and sleep; if she had to attend to something important, she did so from her office at the newspaper, and she never had guests. When colleagues expressed interest in Rosa's private life, she fobbed off their questions with insinuations. She was indifferent to people. Women didn't interest her, because most of them thought of nothing but getting married and starting a family, and they asked no more of life than to wallow at home. Rosa hated men; she found it absurdly easy to see through the swaggering way they marked their territory. Russian men were ugly and inclined to corpulence, with fat thighs and unclean skin. They smelled so bad it could make you sick. There was a time when Rosa thought she'd like slender men with dark hair; a week in Rome had cured her of such romanticism. The men there, more agile than Russians, behaved like street mongrels, panted and howled after Rosa, made lewd movements, and didn't give up even after being whacked on the nose. She despised good-looking men still more than those whose crudity and tactlessness made them loathsome right from the start. Men had always been blinded by Rosa's beauty; when she was younger, the degrees of male primitiveness had amused her; these days, she considered her condescension justified. A dark line under the eyes, and already men's heads turned in her direction; some shadow on the lids, a red mouth, and entire packs would change direction, cross the street, and follow her like children behind an organ-grinder. If in addition her dress was stretched tight over her bottom, if high heels presented her bosom and backside in their best light, men could no longer be differentiated from beasts. In her early twenties, Rosa had thought she could grow accustomed to being touched by animals. Her work and her curiosity about life had led her to disrobe in front of them and spend naked hours with them. As the years passed, however, her revulsion hadn't diminished; on the contrary, it had grown with every guy.

Simultaneously with this growing awareness, the most abstract thing in the world had become, for the Khleb, the most important: She loved money, in whatever form it appeared. She liked banknotes in packets and preferred newly printed bills to used ones, and there were evenings when she would sit happily for hours in her ugly apartment and count her assets. Since the possibility of a sudden trip abroad could not be disregarded, Rosa had converted her "savings" partly into various foreign currencies but mostly into gold leaf. She arranged it in clear plastic folders, touched it for its color, and even laid the cool metal on her skin. Rosa undressed for gold and covered herself with thin sheets of it.

Not only for lascivious reasons, but also for practical ones; should the day come when she would have to take flight, gold leaf could be hidden everywhere on her body, and who, Rosa asked herself, would dare approach so close as to discover her riches?

Tonight the desire had come over her, and she'd taken out all her treasure. The artistically printed paper money lay on the table. She'd set aside the rubles; only foreign currency counted. She placed pound notes next to Swedish kronor because of their similar dimensions. Rosa found German money cool, even repellent in its presentation; she didn't like those cold-eyed faces. Dollars were ugly money, as lacking in interest and culture as the people that issued them. One good thing about dollars, however, was their uniform color. Rosa played with the green notes, smiled at the stupid heads printed on them, switched to the pounds, and ran her fingers over the British queen's crown. She went to the sofa, stretched out on it, and opened a folder. She'd turned the heat up high, so even though she was completely naked, the temperature was comfortable. Delaying gratification, she thrust her hand into the folder and fingered her gold until she could stand it no longer, removed the first leaflet, and wrapped it around one calf. At first, she savored the coolness of the little sheets, but then she began to apply them more quickly. She wanted to transform herself into a golden mummy and rejoiced in the reflection of the gold every time her breast heaved.

As she stroked her throat with a golden leaf and laid it across her Adam's apple, somebody rang her doorbell. She could feel the big vein pulsing—this was no ordinary visit. Since she lived on the fifth floor, she should have been able to hear footsteps on the stairs long before the doorbell rang, but whoever was outside had come silently. Because of her training and her familiarity with the way those people worked, Rosa knew what was happening. There must have been some twist she'd overlooked. She should have followed her first impulse, collected her gold and her money, and left the country. The decisive time had come, and she'd missed it. A long time before, she'd seen this moment in a dream: She was standing on a scaffold, and Kamarovsky looked up at her and told her he always won the game. Then he gave the signal, the trapdoor opened, and Rosa plunged through it and fell until the rope stiffened and her neck broke with a snap. Swaying in the wind, she watched the Colonel leave the place she recognized as the rear courtyard of the Lubyanka, where obstinate remnants of snow remained, even in spring. Sometimes, even as a dreadful accident is happening, one thinks it unreal or believes it can still be averted, and so Rosa remained on the sofa, completely covered with gold. The interval between the first and second ringing of the doorbell was incredibly long. Rosa was familiar with this technique, too: They didn't want to strike terror into the delinquent's heart prematurely; he should open the door without suspicion. She let the second ring fade away and forbade herself to hope that the visitors outside would simply leave.

Rosa raised her head. After all, everything was done; she'd known more of life than most people do. She'd been honored, feted, admired, she'd seen the world outside socialism, felt the frisson of evil, performed the reprehensible with a cool hand. She no longer expected anything new; from now on, life would repeat itself. Rosa stood up. Sweat and surface tension kept most of the leaves clinging to her; she stepped to the window and stood there like a golden statue. From outside the door, she heard the inconspicuous rustling with which her colleagues were searching for the right tool. They had to hurry. Soundlessly, Rosa opened one side of the casement window and, as she did so, saw her arm. Did she want to land on the street like a gold angel or strip off the gold leaf first? Why should she allow her stupid colleagues to enrich themselves with her savings? It would be better to let the people down on the ground find her as she was; they'd struggle with their scruples at first, but in the end they'd help themselves from her bloody corpse. She smiled, grabbed the window frame, heaved herself up with one foot on the radiator, and watched as several golden leaves fluttered away into the night.

With a sudden jolt, the apartment door gave way. Three men in uninspired raincoats entered the room and looked around. The sight of the money on the table held their eyes for an instant, but not long enough for Rosa to clear the windowsill. The first man caught her by the leg, the second sprang to his aid, and together they dragged her, naked, back into the room. While the men gazed at her in amazement, while the abhorrence she felt for them set in like a reflex, her reason told her that a period of unspeakable suffering lay before her.

She pointed to the money. "And what if I propose that you help yourselves?" she asked, making a pathetic effort.

"We'll do that one way or another, Comrade." The man grinned and opened his raincoat.

THIRTY-SEVEN

Thicket and underbrush, pitch-black night. Had Anna considered that she was not only subjecting herself to incredible unpleasantness but at the same time taking part in something that would be classed as subversion, her impulse to turn around and go back to Moscow as quickly as possible would have looked like the only rational response. But in that night-shrouded no-man's-land, whipped by tree branches, frightened by animal sounds, with no guide to orientation other than Anton's injunction to find the tracks of the Baltic Railroad, Anna stumbled onward, come what might. A peculiar magnetic force had taken possession of her, pulling her along, compelling her to keep advancing on the impassable path whose goal was named Alexey. The stronger the doubts that plagued her and the greater her fear not only of doing the wrong thing but also, and more simply, of heading in the wrong direction, the more resolutely Anna struggled on. In all the months they'd been together, she'd gone to Alexey dozens of times, but never with such commitment, never with the feeling that she was going not the right but the only way. In many spots, the ground, thawed by the spring sun, had turned into a swamp; she sank in it up to her calves and consequently did her best to give the lowest terrain a wide berth. The time her walk was taking seemed interminable. Mustn't the train have passed already?

But Anna hiked on and on, until at last she tripped over an obstacle and fell flat. It was the aforesaid tracks, and the tree above her was no tree, but a power pole. Worn out and bloody-palmed, she started walking west on the cross ties.

Sooner than expected, lights came into sight, silhouettes darker than the sky appeared, sounds reached her ears, and more incredulous than relieved, she reached the little town of Maevo. She was able to purchase a train ticket without standing in the usual line, and the cashier had kindly informed her that the train would arrive on time, that is, with the usual delay. While she was asking for information about the formalities at the Latvian border, she heard the locomotive pulling into the station, and she was directed to join the little group of night travelers and board the train. There were amazingly few passengers in the carriage; Anna heard someone remark that trains headed in the opposite direction were always full. She fell exhausted into a seat, listened for a while to her breathing as it slowed down, and soon dozed off. Her nap seemed to have lasted only a few minutes, because when she started awake, they were arriving in Isakovo, an hour and a half from the border.

A large family of Latvians, returning home from visiting relatives and laden with leftovers, boarded the train. They spread themselves out near Anna and reveled in their memories of the festive hours they'd spent. Anna thought about why her family had always been so small. The war had carried off her paternal grandparents. Her mother's parents had moved away from Moscow, and by the time Anna was born, both of them were dead. Viktor Ipalyevich had no siblings, and Dora, too, had been an only child. Petya, Father, and I, that's the yield of the Tsazukhin family, Anna thought. And then there was Leonid. She wondered why she'd never wanted a second child. A job like hers was sought after because it paid well, and until such time as Leonid would attain a higher rank and more pay, income had taken precedence over her desire for more children. So now he was a captain—and he lived in Yakutsk. She realized that of all the questions currently pressing in upon her, the one about whether or not to have another child was probably in last place. And yet, the unity displayed by the Latvian family over there awakened a longing in her. How confident those people were, how protected they felt in the cozy bosom of their family.

Anna tried to snatch an hour's sleep before reaching the border; according to the schedule, the train was due to roll into Riga around dawn. She took off her shoes and made herself comfortable, taking up two seats, but she couldn't manage anything deeper than a light doze. She saw the signs for Dmitrovo glide past—at this time of night, there were no passengers either boarding or leaving the train. The conductor came through the car for the second time. Although he'd already taken Anna's ticket, he stopped in the aisle and stared down at her as she lay curled up on the seats. She pretended to be asleep.

At Zaistino, border officials got on the train, two in police uniforms and one in civilian clothes. Anna sat up properly, rubbed her bleary eyes, and got her identity papers ready. She observed the plainclothes official; the man was obviously drunk. He was doing a good job of holding himself steady, but his skin and eyes betrayed him.

The large Latvian family was subjected to exhaustive scrutiny. The patriarch of the clan gave good-natured replies, while the women, intimidated, remained silent. It struck Anna that the Russian border cops were treating the Latvians as though they'd been granted the privilege of traveling in Russia, but now that period of grace was over, and they must scurry home to their "sister state" as quickly as possible. The officials' condescension and rudeness irritated Anna. They gave the members of the family their documents back, approached Anna's seat, looked at her—and continued on without a word. She expected the men to check her on their way back through the car, but soon they opened a door while the train was still moving and stepped off. They were in the no-man's-land between the two border stations; a little farther on, Latvian officials saluted and took over the train on their native soil. While Anna was watching the exchange and trying to find an explanation for such lax bureaucracy, an automobile stopped on a gravel road near the railroad line. Everyone except the driver got out and boarded the train.

There was no reason for her to feel proud or elated, and yet, at that moment, Anna thought her adventure remarkable. Increasingly confident of actually arriving in Riga before too long, she even grew convinced that Anton had been nimble enough to shake off his pursuers. In her inexplicable cheerfulness, Anna saw herself as a genuine traveler, riding the night train on a flying visit to Latvia. While she was imagining her meeting with Alexey, the door opened behind her. She assumed that the Latvian officials were now doing their duty, and so she collected her identity papers, turned around, and looked into A. I. Kamarovsky's eyes. In spite of the mild temperature, he was wearing a winter coat. He looked hollow-cheeked, even deathly; his innocuous smile didn't suit his wasted face.

"Your blushing cheek shows me that you find it exhilarating, just as I do, to run into old friends while traveling." He threw off his coat, spread it on the seat, and sat down next to Anna.

A great heat rose in her, as if she'd taken some fast-acting poison. Words fled from her mind; there was nothing to say.

"You probably find it impossible to sleep in trains, too," he said with a benign smile. "So we may as well talk. We still have a while to go before we reach Riga. What would you like to talk about?"

She refused to put up with his taunting. If talk was what he wanted, it had to be the real thing. "I didn't know anything about all this," Anna said.

"Of course you didn't. If you had, your behavior would be completely incomprehensible." He raised his hands, indicating their unreal situation: Anna and the Colonel, their faces illuminated by the cold nighttime lighting, and behind them the big Latvian family, sound asleep. Kamarovsky pulled the skirts of his coat over his lap. "At the next stop, we should get ourselves something to drink. Have you ever been to Latvia before?"

She shook her head.

"I know practically nothing about it myself. That's about to change." The Colonel raised his eyeglasses and rubbed the bridge of his nose. "However the two of us work out what's going to happen," he said softly, "it won't be easy, and I won't hide from you the possibility of an unpleasant outcome."

"Have you got Anton?"

"Anton's insignificant. A loyal liegeman of his false lord." Kamarovsky stiffened. "In a nutshell: Bulyagkov must not leave Riga. He must be stopped, one way or another."

"One way or another." She repeated the Colonel's words and understood that he was speaking of life and death.

"The last thing we want is an arrest outside Russia. It mustn't look as though we're recapturing an escaped bird. But at the same time, the bird must be prevented from singing. Do you understand, Anna?"

Even though the possible consequences for Alexey terrified her, she was relieved that the Colonel was eschewing all bombast and rhetoric in discussing the matter. It wasn't a question of hunting anybody down, but of correcting an erroneous development and preventing it from doing damage.

"I've never needed you so much as I do now," Kamarovsky said soberly.

"What can I do to change anything?"

"Unfortunately, we won't be able to know the answer to that question until after the fact. The important thing is for you to see the background issues in their proper proportions."

From the day when Alexey had told her his story—the biography of a student who'd been brought to Russia clandestinely and forced into an uncongenial career there—from that moment on, Anna should have faced up to those background issues. She'd neglected to do so and instead acted as a mother, as a wife whose marriage was slipping from her grasp, as a daughter who wanted her father's happiness. Whenever a change had occurred, she'd adapted to it and hoped that time was on her side. Alexey, on the other hand, had looked far into the future and known their time was limited. He'd treated Anna like a lover, but also as an instrument of his purpose, and he'd never taken his eyes off his goal. And now, Kamarovsky was demanding that Anna confront this man, and that she do so in full awareness of the "proper proportions." In the woods and on the train, her spirits had risen at the prospect of seeing Alexey again, of being, in a way, his savior; but the idea of contacting him as Kamarovsky's advance guard literally revolted her. At the same time, she had to smile at the Colonel, because his faith in her capabilities seemed unbroken.

"Please inform me, Comrade," said Anna.

He nodded. Before he began, his eyes wandered to the window. "I can't believe it's already getting light outside. We're farther north than Moscow, but it's unusual to see a dawn like this back home." And with that, he turned to her again.

THIRTY-EIGHT

Bulyagkov was sitting in the bar at the Hotel Riga, surrounded by professors. The establishment had closed long since; only the visitors from Moscow were still being served. The Deputy Minister understood the unconstrained exuberance displayed by the scientists, eight men and three women; they were about to put on the biggest public performance of their scientific careers. Again and again, he toasted with them, but he himself drank moderately, even though his desire for stupefaction was great. The day had included much unpredictability; for example, to Bulyagkov's surprise, his baggage had been inspected. He'd opened his suitcase and the briefcase inside it and then looked on wordlessly as the uniformed official took out Nikolai Lyushin's dossier. This folder contained many scientific documents, however, and the official had failed to notice the only one that was explosive. He'd leafed through the pages covered with Lyushin's microscopic handwriting and then thrust the folder back into the briefcase. Bulyagkov had stood and watched the operation calmly, but when the Kyrgyz mathematician, waiting her turn, cast a curious glance at the document, Bulyagkov, as if inadvertently, had blocked her view with one shoulder.

After a short flight and a warm welcome by the Presidium of the Latvian SSR, the schedule had called for a bus tour of the city, which meant that Bulyagkov and the delegation were driven past the Old Town on the way to the Palace of Science. There was insufficient time for extensive sightseeing; therefore, the Deputy Minister had merely unveiled a memorial tablet to the founder of the astrophysics observatory. The Russian delegation had shaken hands with a delegation of Latvian scientists; in the brief speech of greeting, the hosts' sorrow that not a single one of their number would represent the Soviet Union in Stockholm had been impossible to ignore. After that, the leader of the Riga City Soviet had taken charge of the group and led them on a brief walking tour, beginning at the square dedicated to the Latvian Red Riflemen. Finally, the delegation had been brought to the Riga, a bulky hotel on the Muscovite model, and Bulyagkov had taken a room on the fourth floor. After a short rest break, the delegation had been driven to an unusual building on Komjaunatnes Street that looked like a Florentine palazzo but proved instead to be the headquarters of the Supreme Soviet of the Latvian SSR, where the banquet in honor of the Russian guests had taken place.

In his speech, after first expressing regret for the Minister's illness and apologizing for his absence, Bulyagkov had delivered a spirited paean to Latvia's industrial achievements that had been received by the hosts with applause and brotherly kisses. Relieved at having discharged his duty, the Deputy Minister had sat still for the Party secretary's answering address as well as four additional speeches before the meal was served.

After dinner, Bulyagkov had received his second surprise in the person of the Latvian professor Otomar Sudmalis, who'd expressed his joy at meeting the Deputy Minister, a man he knew to be in close working contact with Nikolai Lyushin, with whom the professor maintained a regular correspondence. Sudmalis, it had turned out, was well informed, dangerously well informed, about Lyushin's work; the professor was acquainted with certain results of Lyushin's researches about which the Ministry, thanks to Bulyagkov, had remained ignorant. He'd answered the Latvian's questions in general terms, built a hedge of verbiage around prickly details, and pretended to be drunker than he was. In the end, although he couldn't feel he'd satisfied the other's curiosity, Bulyagkov believed he'd at least given him the possibility of presenting himself as an authority.

Under normal circumstances, the Deputy Minister would have stayed late on such an evening, as the secretary of the Latvian Central Committee was a man without affectations and, for a leader of the apparat, amazingly communicative. But shortly after midnight, Bulyagkov, thinking about what was to come on the morrow, had caused the delegation to leave the banquet and return to the hotel.

The next unforeseen event had occurred around one in the morning. Back in his room, Bulyagkov had already removed his tie and loosened his belt when there was a knock on his door and a visitor announced herself: Professor Tanova, the mathematician from Kyrgyzstan. When he'd opened the door, the entire delegation was there. Someone had pointed out, to general amusement, how easy it was for a woman to get into the Deputy Minister's room. Bulyagkov had joined in the laughter and accepted the invitation to go downstairs for a nightcap.

The wallpaper in the bar was the color of ox's blood. The Russians were still sitting there, drinking Latvian vodka and eating smoked fish, when dawn began to light the sky outside. In a few hours, they were scheduled to have breakfast with some deputation—Bulyagkov had forgotten its mission—before boarding the plane for their 12:05 flight to Stockholm. Having been born on the twelfth day of the fifth month, Alexey Maximovich took the departure time as a good omen. He knew himself well enough to be certain that he'd get no sleep this night; the liquor was good, and the Kyrgyz woman had a smile that would be able to sustain him through a few more drunken hours.

As his glass was being refilled, he forbade himself speculation about what lay ahead. He was afraid of coming to the conclusion that the weights on the scales were unbalanced, and not in his favor. Medea's face came into his mind. At first, she'd overtly threatened to denounce him, and she would have done so, too, had she not been the one who'd lured him into his current life and watched him go to ruin in it. As lovers, they hadn't been suited to each other, but as a soul mate, no one would ever be closer to him. It must have been an enormous sacrifice for her to have agreed to his plan, he thought, and she'd probably already begun to regret it. She might even—as soon as he reached safety—admit what she knew. Medea had never been able to live a lie. Lost in thought, Bulyagkov struggled to follow the Kyrgyz mathematician as she told a long-winded story; he didn't fail to notice that she'd moved her hand on the couch closer to his thigh, and he hoped day would come soon.

He considered how it was possible to love a woman for nearly two years and, at the same time, callously make use of her. It wasn't his character that he was calling into question, it was the phenomenon of deception itself. Right at the beginning, he'd told Anna that she would never have anything to fear from him, and yet he'd lied to her every time he'd seen her. His behavior seemed to him so duplicitous that he couldn't help seeing in Anna, too, in Anna who had defied him, a woman with two faces. One was gentle, candid, the face of a woman nearing the end of her twenties who wanted more from life than climbing on scaffolding day after day. The other was the artful Anna, who, aware of her own immorality, had spied on him. In a woman like Rosa Khleb, those opposites wouldn't have been at all incompatible: She deceived some people and played them off against other people, because the center of her interest was always and only Rosa Khleb. Bulyagkov had never known a woman so immoral. She hadn't betrayed him and his purposes to the KGB for one reason and one reason alone: He paid her better. The cunning idea of poisoning the Research Minister two days before his scheduled departure had been Rosa Khleb's.

Alexey shifted himself away from the Kyrgyz woman. He didn't want to compare Anna with the Khleb, and he couldn't equate what he was doing with Anna's weakness. He'd probably never see her again. He peered gloomily into his glass.

You're a monster, he thought. How often have you had slogans promoting the worldwide equality of all mankind on your lips? You used them in speeches and conversations while you were building your private, individual dream. He loosened his tie. No, that wasn't right; he *had* believed, he still believed, that the world needed to be remade, and even that the Soviet empire was the right power to precipitate the revolution. But he couldn't make out the people capable of such a feat. The petrifaction had progressed too far; the system now defined itself only by its immutability. Was it worth it to be loyal to such a power, to make sacrifices to it with an eye to future generations? He'd often discussed that with Medea, who would challenge him to think in larger historical dimensions. It would take more than a few years to transform the world, she'd say; it would take time for the good and noble forces to gather together and overcome the alliance of the exploiters. On such evenings, inspired by his wife, Bulyagkov had felt his faith restored. But the next morning, in the Ministry, the truth appeared once again before his eyes.

The big things are simple, he thought. Never in history has the development of a plan for life brought any sort of advancement to mankind. But what was Alexey Maximovich's idea of "simple"? If I were fifteen years younger, he said to himself, it could have been a life with Anna. She was the simple solution to all the intricacies that entangled his existence. She was the warmth he longed for, the light he would have gladly followed, the love his heart so badly needed. Although fully aware of his own sentimentality, Bulyagkov called Anna's image to his mind—her thick hair, her kind eyes, her seductive mouth. He saw her like that, standing before him, and standing at the entrance to the hotel bar.

Bulyagkov thought he'd been carried away by his fantasies, thought he was mistaken, thought his drunken eyes would soon see that the woman entering the bar was actually the waitress. It wasn't possible that Anna was in Riga, and out of the question that she'd come into this oxblood-red room and, stepping deliberately, approach the still-boisterous group of eleven scientists, who only now noticed her. When the head mathematician from Novosibirsk shouted a loud greeting and indulged himself in the commonplace about the latest hours that bring the prettiest guests, Bulyagkov realized that Anna Nechayevna, in the flesh, was there in front of him. Wherever she might have come from, and for whatever reasons, she'd made her way to where he was. He loved her for that, right then. But in the next moment, anxiety seized him. He raised his head to see if others had come in behind her, but she was alone. Her demeanor indicated that she was glad to have finally reached her goal.

"Where did you come from?"

The group fell silent, emanating curiosity.

"This is Comrade Tsazukhina," he said awkwardly. "She's brought me some papers I forgot, documents I need for the presentation in Stockholm." He straightened his tie. "Thanks for taking the trouble to come so far."

Anna stood there and waited for him to invent an excuse for the two of them to leave the bar.

"Well, then, we should go over them right away," Bulyagkov said, rising to his feet. "So you can finally go to bed, Comrade."

Accompanied by the scientists' farewells, in which there was no lack of double entendres, and followed by the Kyrgyz woman's disillusioned gaze, he took his leave and, with a gesture, showed Anna the way to the elevators. After a few steps, they were alone.

"You're crazy," he whispered, grabbing her hand.

"No, the crazy one's you."

He saw the seriousness in her eyes. "You know?" Then, after a breathless pause, he asked, "Who else knows?"

She pushed the button. "Come on." The elevator doors slid open.

They kissed on the way up, not out of passion, but in order to exclude the possibility of speech from the little space they were riding in. He pressed her against him; she clung to his shoulder. They stood there like that, in the deepest despair.

While they walked through the fourth-floor corridors, he kept his eyes fastened on her. Anna didn't return his gaze. Bulyagkov opened the door of his room, and together they walked over to the window to watch Riga wake up. The hotel stood opposite the National Opera House, and behind that was the park with the Lenin monument.

"If you'd told me yesterday I'd be seeing all this today, I would have laughed at you."

"It's a lovely city," he said. "I've always liked it."

He fell suddenly silent, whereupon she said, "Anton begged me to do this. He wants to warn you."

"Why didn't Anton come himself?"

"He tried to. He . . ."

After the hours she'd spent conjecturing how this meeting would go, Anna suddenly knew nothing more. The wolf was in the trap, the trappers were getting ready to come for him, and he was too tired and too old to slip away from them this time. She looked at his eyes and the purple rings around them, the sullen mouth, the bowed shoulders. She tried to look beyond all that and see the Ukrainian boy who loved mathematics beginning his university studies in science. It was of course necessary to stop Alexey from going through with his plan, but was it also right? Anna was indifferent to Kamarovsky's interests, but she wondered whether she herself was ready to play Judas. Her breath streamed in and out; she saw the morning light reflecting off the glass table and the reflection trembling on the wall. Medea let him go, Anna thought, and she knows him better than anyone. Who am I to play the part of fate? With a sigh, she realized it was no longer a question of that. She was only the messenger who was supposed to make it easier for him to lay down his arms.

"Are they already in the hotel?" He looked at his watch.

"I don't know." The light hurt her eyes, and she drew the curtain partly closed. "They've got Rosa."

His weary face twisted into a sad smile. "I see." Bulyagkov slowly ran his fingers through his hair. "I'm not going to get to Stockholm. Is that right?"

Anna saw no possibility of crossing the ten feet that separated them, taking his hand, and giving him an answer that would make his situation look good. On the morning of the execution, it was hard to say anything encouraging to the condemned. Alexey had put himself on a cliff from which there was no climbing down, only plummeting.

"What do you want to know?" Asking this question, Bulyagkov seemed suddenly distant, as though he didn't wish to be disturbed while deciding on his next move.

"I want to know why you waited until you were practically about to leave before you started your divorce proceedings."

"Are you asking me that as a woman or as an agent for internal security?"

"As an agent, I'm supposed to ask you for the briefcase," Anna replied. "They want you to turn it over to me."

"And what am I offered in return?"

"Safe conduct home."

He folded his arms in disdain. "Either you or they are unclear about the use of pressure. Where's the advantage for me?"

"There isn't any."

"So why should I consider accepting?"

"Because you're not a traitor."

There was silence for a second. "But they'll treat me like one." He vented his frustration with a sharp gesture. "My case is so hopeless that it'll be hard to find a lawyer to represent me."

Anna touched the curtain: cheap material. "The people you'll be dealing with are human," she said, her face turned away from him.

He laughed. "That's the negotiation strategy they told you to use? Humanity?"

"You're a Russian," she countered.

"You know I'm not."

"You belong to this country and this society. You're one of us. You don't belong in Stockholm, where they'll pay you and stick you in some hiding place. You think the dreams of your youth will come true there?

It doesn't happen like that! Whether as a traitor or a minor criminal, you won't be young again. But you're still the Deputy Minister for Soviet Research Planning. That's your fate, and no one can save you from it."

"Apparently, someone will, and pretty soon." He put a hand over his eyes, as though suddenly exhausted.

"That's the consequence of what you've done, but it's not the end."

He looked at her furiously. "What do you know about the end, you with your twenty-nine years?" He went into the bathroom without waiting for an answer. She could hear running water.

"Do you want to drag Medea into all this? And Lyushin?"

He dried his hands. "You're concerned about Lyushin, a man who's never out for anyone but himself? The die is cast." His expression changed into a sad smile. "In love and on the run, there are always two possibilities."

"Do you think so?"

"Do you remember the little package that was delivered to me that afternoon?"

"You mean the one Rosa brought you?"

"They've instructed you well." He nodded. "The package contains a gift."

"For whom?"

"For the captain of the transport ship that's sailing from Riga today. Stockholm can be reached by sea, too."

"What would that change?"

"I'm still interested in living, you see." He went to the window again. "Going back means death."

"How do you know that?" Impulsively, she stepped in front of him.

"Well, what does Kamarovsky have in view, then? Privileged treatment in a labor camp?"

"Why do you keep asking what others will do for you? What have you done for us?"

"Oh, Anna." As though to distinguish her, he laid his hand on her shoulder. "You're the best thing that could have happened to Kamarovsky. You're someone who's calculating and idealistic at the same time. It's quite a stunning combination."

"I'm someone who loves you." She didn't budge.

"I love you, too." He compelled himself to be sober. "But did you really come here with the intention of talking me into giving myself up?"

Some seconds passed. "We've told a lot of lies in all these months. And nevertheless, we've stayed together. We've done each other good. I came here today to make an end of lying."

"And after that?"

She took his strong hand and laid it on her cheek. "I don't know. But I know it's already better, now that we're being honest with each other for the first time."

"It's too late for that." He detached himself from her. "I have to get on that ship."

She thought his brusqueness was an act. "You think you're not free in Russia? You think going somewhere else can change anything? Have you considered the fact that you'll be taking *yourself* around with you, wherever you go?"

"Stop it. Those are just words, and I've heard enough of them."

"Today . . . no, yesterday, I saw a lot of our country," she said. "I had no idea of the expanse of it, the light, so many impressions—"

"Save your breath," he said dismissively. "You're not getting me back with litanies to Holy Mother Russia."

"Then forgive me for . . ." She took a step back. "For being pushy." She waited to see whether he'd do anything to prevent her going.

The corpulent man stood at the window in his shirtsleeves. Some strands of hair hung down over his forehead, and his left hand was clenched in a fist. Anna went to the door. The sun must have risen behind the hotel, because when she looked at him for the last time, the city was colored a gleaming pink. The man's dark silhouette was outlined against it. He turned his back to her and thrust his hands into his pockets.

THIRTY-NINE

How hot it was. In heat like this, Anna felt sorry for the fat woman rolling the hot blacktop smooth. Wearing black overalls, the worker sat in her steamroller and drove back and forth over the closed-off stretch of Bolshaya Sadovaya Street, always close behind the tank car, which poured out its contents in a stinking rivulet. The expression on the steamroller driver's face wasn't peevish, only concentrated; Anna spotted a pretty wedding ring on her dirty hand.

It was really too hot. Minutes earlier, when they'd come walking along the river, they'd seen thousands of half-naked people lying on the ground, even though the sun was hidden behind veils of haze. It was getting close to seven-thirty, but people didn't want to go home yet. The day had been enchantingly beautiful, the sun-drenched city gleaming in the hot air. Women wore their lightest clothes; older ladies kept handkerchiefs in their sleeves, ready to dry off forehead and neck from time to time. Ice-cream stands and eau de cologne vendors were doing a booming business, and laughter was everywhere in the streets.

"It's getting close to seven-thirty," Viktor Ipalyevich said, putting his hand inside his open shirt, where gray fuzz grew high on his chest.

"We have enough time." Anna liked the breeze her skirt stirred up when she swung her legs. Given the occasion, she had hesitated no longer to buy the desert-colored dress with the strawberry print; the price was, of course, an impertinence; on the other hand, nobody else had a dress like that. At the next corner, a little girl was running around without paying attention to the traffic. She wore a white kerchief, and she was pursuing a paper airplane that someone had thrown. Instinctively, Anna held Petya's hand more tightly. Wearing his only suit, the boy trotted along beside his mother and grandfather.

"We should have taken the subway." Tsazukhin wiped droplets of perspiration from his beard. "When I get there, I'm going to be covered in sweat."

"On a day like this, nobody goes underground voluntarily." Anna checked the armpits of his light-colored suit jacket for stains. "A festive day, a day in your honor," she said, teasing the poet. "And all Moscow is invited."

"All right, all right, that's enough."

They reached the boulevard and strolled toward the Conservatory building. Suddenly, Viktor Ipalyevich slowed down. "Hasn't anyone come at all?" he asked anxiously. "What did I tell you? Nobody wants to sit inside and listen to contemporary poetry on a fine June day."

Secretly, Anna feared he might be right. When snow was piled a yard high and only narrow paths were shoveled clear, when light had been absent from the city for months—that was the best time to enter interior worlds, to be edified by literature, music, or theater. Who would go to the Conservatory to hear poems in June?

"They're probably all inside already," Anna said, encouraging her father.

"Nonsense. On a day like this, they'd stay out in the evening air until the very last bell."

A pale-faced Doctor Glem leaped out at Tsazukhin. "My dear Viktor Ipalyevich," he cried, his voice implying trouble. The chairman of the artistic board was wearing a light-colored suit identical with the poet's, but enlivened by a red breast-pocket handkerchief.

"What is it, Doctor Glem? What's wrong?" Viktor Ipalyevich tried to adopt a patronizing tone. "There's no audience, is that it? I told you to reserve one of the smaller halls. Who needs a big stage for a book of poems and—"

"You're here at last!" Glem cried, interrupting him. "We called you and called you, and then we even sent someone in a car to fetch you. Where have you been?"

"We went for a walk in the delightful summer air," the poet said in self-defense.

"You went for a walk on the evening of your great occasion? A thousand and more are waiting for Tsazukhin, and he's taking a leisurely stroll!"

"A thousand and more? How can that be, a thousand and more?" He stared at Glem in confusion. "We're not supposed to start until eight o'—"

"Seven-thirty, Viktor Ipalyevich, seven-thirty!" cried the chairman of the artistic board, relieved to see the muddle cleared up so easily. "Didn't you read the invitation to your own reading?"

"Seven-thirty?" He turned around. "Anna, did you know . . . seven-thirty? We were just loitering around, and I thought it was almost seven-thirty, but . . ." He jerked his head up and looked at the clock on the building: 7:37. "My dear Glem, I'm so terribly sorry, naturally I'll have to make an apology." He stamped his foot. "I hate unpunctuality!"

"Go on in, Papa, it's all right." Anna took him by the shoulders and pushed him toward Doctor Glem, who joined in the effort to soothe the poet.

"Everyone's having a good time, they're all patient, they're glad to wait for you. Come on, now."

"I'm melting in my own sweat!" Tsazukhin said feverishly. "I would have liked to freshen up, maybe take off my shoes for a few minutes."

"How about some cologne water? That will make you feel better." Glem looked gratefully at Anna, who continued to push her father forward. "Things are going to turn out fine, after all."

As he'd done the last time they were in that building, Glem's assistant welcomed the poet's party and escorted mother and son into the auditorium while Tsazukhin was being brought onstage. And as she'd done the last time, Anna shuddered as she stepped into the artists' box: Down in the orchestra seats, in the tiers, and all the way up in the galleries, Moscow society had assembled. In the front rows, she recognized some prominent and important people, along with her father's colleagues and assorted wives, grandfathers, and aspirants. As she'd done before, she pushed down the folding seat and occupied it. The only difference this time was that little Petya was sitting next to her, not Leonid. The parapet was too high for the boy to see over, so he folded his seat back up and sat on the edge. "All these people came to see Dyedushka?" he whispered.

"A thousand and more." The flapping and fluttering in the theater made Anna smile. People cooled off by fanning themselves with their programs; others even used, for the same purpose, their newly purchased volume of the poet's verse. Anna's eyes shifted over to the side stalls, which were reserved for the nomenklatura. Comrades in dark suits were sitting there, some of them without ties, their shirt collars turned out over their jacket lapels. She recognized one unprepossessing face from newspaper photographs: The Minister for Research Planning entered, took a seat, and gestured to his wife to do the same. The places around the Minister filled up quickly; the Deputy Minister was not among those present.

At that moment, the house lights went out, and a spotlight shined a circle of light on the red curtain, which immediately swooshed upward to reveal a simple lectern, surrounded by a colorful stage set that belonged to a student production at the Conservatory. Doctor Glem stepped to the lectern first, was welcomed by friendly applause, and launched into his introductory address: "Viktor Ipalyevich Tsazukhin's legacy comprises thirty years of Soviet lyric poetry and is the expression of an epoch rich in hard-won victories as well as painful losses."

Anna's attention was suddenly distracted by a late guest, whose arrival went unnoticed by the audience. An invisible hand had opened the door for him; without a sound, he'd gone down the aisle to the side stalls and taken a seat among the influential personages. He wore a dark green suit and had apparently been in such a hurry that he was still holding his hat in his hand. For a moment, he listened to Glem's speech, and then, all at once, he turned his head to the left. In spite of the darkness, his eyeglasses reflected some stray spotlight beams; A. I. Kamarovsky looked up at Anna, as if he knew that she and no one else was sitting in the artists' box. It seemed to her like a greeting.

Doctor Glem reached the end of his introduction, announced the guest of honor, and considered it necessary to call for applause. The thousand drowned him out and welcomed Viktor Ipalyevich. Kamarovsky, too, clapped and looked on benevolently as the poet, whose career would have turned out differently had it not been for the Colonel, walked to the lectern.

It had been impressive—beautiful and rich in ethical content. It had been worth the trouble. Kamarovsky slipped off his street shoes and removed his jacket. On that particular evening, it might have been desirable to sit out on the balcony in his underpants, but A. I. Kamarovsky didn't do anything in his underpants. So he merely opened the balcony door and looked out into the mellow night. Even though it virtually never got dark at that time of year, the Kalininsky Bridge was a band of shimmering light, and the river reflected the opposite bank; it was as if the buildings were dissolving in the black water. In the distance were the lights of the Ostankino television and radio tower—1,660 feet high, Kamarovsky recalled. Satisfied, he closed the door. It was a special night. New things were coming; the Soviet poet Tsazukhin's triumph belonged among them. As for old things, tonight they would be disposed of. Kamarovsky had played a decisive role in both processes. He went over to his desk. Without turning on a light—the reflection from the street lights was enough—he opened a folder. It contained handwritten notes, most of them in cipher. Kamarovsky let the pages slip slowly through his fingers; he understood not a sentence. His accomplishment lay in the recovery of the material. Nikolai Lyushin's trial had commenced, in camera, closed to the public. It was essential to give him a strong warning, but without dampening his scientific zeal. He must learn that the agencies overseeing his work were its protectors, not its censors, and that he would do well to trust them. His assertions that he hadn't knowingly done anything illegal were noted in the transcript.

Kamarovsky closed the folder, withdrew to the dark part of the room, and, with a sigh, sank down onto the sofa. The night was progressing; at this rate, it wouldn't last much longer. He'd seen Rosa one last time, but she hadn't noticed him. Her beauty had seemed to him like a mask on her devastated face. He hadn't succeeded in making her believe she'd gotten off so lightly; Rosa knew what path she was on. In the foregoing weeks, she'd given up everything that was of any interest. She'd done it almost unbidden; corporal punishment hadn't been necessary. For one whole day, she'd allowed herself to be encouraged by a hint that now, turned in a double sense, she could be sent out into the field again. The following night must have made it clear to her that she was of no use to the KGB anymore. From that point on, Rosa's spirit was broken. She knows what's coming, the Colonel thought, she just doesn't know when. The reason for his decision lay in the plain fact that in this case, deterrence was inevitable. Kamarovsky took off his glasses in the darkness and put them on the armrest, ready to be snatched up again. In the shadowy space in front of him, he saw Rosa as she was being taken out of her cell. He saw his protégée, the most beautiful Russian girl he ever met, walking down the corridor. The ceiling lights made her shadow appear now in front of her and now behind her.

Kamarovsky had charged "Bull-Neck" with handling the matter. No, you couldn't say he'd actually *charged* him; a hint had sufficed. Bull-Neck looked upon it as a distinction and was glad to oblige. As usual, the prisoner would have an escort: one man in front of Rosa, and Bull-Neck behind her. He'd prepare himself soundlessly, and at the moment when the man in front disappeared behind a turning in the corridor, the execution would be carried out.

In other words, the condemned would neither hear the sound nor feel the entrance of the projectile. It was like sitting on a seesaw and then being catapulted up to where everything lost itself in white. Looking at it that way, he could say that Rosa knew what was happening to her but would not herself experience it. I'm the only one, Antip Iosipovich thought, who will comprehend Rosa's death. He picked up his glasses and rose to his feet. At the age of only fifteen, Rosa Khleb had handed our General Secretary a bouquet of flowers; she had kissed him and been embraced by him. How many Soviet girls receive such an honor? He turned on the television set.

FORTY

Captain Nechayev had been instructed to detach teams from each company and deploy them to assist in earthmoving. There was a shortage of heavy equipment, and the men complained about the back-breaking labor. After the hard winter, maintenance work on the regional railway line could no longer be postponed. When Leonid inspected the tracks, it looked to him as though drunken giants had been at play with the railroad. Along a five-mile stretch, the formerly straight and level track embankment was warped into a line that undulated up and down like a wave; the steel rails, as thick as a man's arm, had bent as though they were made of wax. Damage from freezing had been followed by the thawing of the ground, which then turned into mud. There was nothing here that could be repaired; everything had to be ripped out and built anew.

The first lieutenant in the corps of engineers told him, "We've used this method before in regions where the ground thaws ten feet deep in summer and the whole countryside is transformed into a morass."

It was decided to move the line over several miles and with the help of mining machinery build a new embankment six feet high, using for ballast a mixture of rubble and crushed macadam. If you let the material subside for a year, the engineer said, it will form a layer practically as hard as concrete, and then new cross-ties can be laid on that. The dismantling of the ruined track and the construction of a provisional road had already been coordinated between the railroad administration and the army. The new track bed had to be completed in no more than three months, before winter brought everything to a standstill again.

"A year of track replacement traffic," Leonid said. He feared a high cost in material as well as elevated administrative expenses. The engineer announced that he would place cranes on both sides of the worksite to assist in loading and unloading freight. The provisional road was to be built of wood, because a wooden road could be built more cheaply and also in the shortest time, and the used-up planks could ultimately provide fuel for winter heating. Leonid admired how confidently the engineers went about their job—making calculations in terms of tons and cubic feet and battalion-strength work crews—and how little they cared about obtaining proper authorization for what they did.

From earliest youth, Leonid had felt a romanticized interest in woodworking. He liked it when the screaming saw cut the first wedge out of a tree trunk and the tree shivered from root to crown. He'd been amazed to discover that the lumberjacks always knew what direction the tree would fall in, and he would look on in excitement as a toppling giant ripped through the undergrowth and crashed to the ground, where saws immediately sprang upon the fallen victim. The result of these memories from Leonid's time as a Young Pioneer was that he'd made arrangements to participate in the construction of the wooden road himself. The people performing the work were carpenters and joiners; Leonid and his soldiers were there to assist them.

On that morning, the force at the worksite was visibly reduced. Leonid checked the list and saw that many soldiers had reported sick, and there was a general shortage of helping hands. When a carpenter operating a circular saw needed an assistant, Leonid took off his uniform jacket, set his cap aside, and pitched in. The machine was an elderly table saw, on which rough blocks were being cut at a 45-degree angle, a task that required a steady hand. The carpenter worked at a leisurely pace. After an hour, Leonid's hair, shirt, and pants were sprinkled with chips. He felt free and happy, and from time to time he squinted into the sun, which shone in a cloudless sky. He lifted the next block onto the metal table; the carpenter held the wood in position and pushed it steadily onto the spinning blade. Suddenly, the block jerked to one side, Leonid reached for it, the carpenter screamed something—they both saw, too late, the branch hidden in the face wood. Leonid couldn't get free in time and was literally sucked in by the saw blade; he watched his hand disappear into the machine. He felt an itching sensation that made him think it couldn't be so bad, but then a gush of blood poured out. The carpenter pressed the emergency button, and the rotor came to a stop. Leonid staggered backward; when he looked at his hand, it seemed to be part of someone else's body. He turned his head away and collapsed. The carpenter tore his shirt into strips and pressed them on the wound to stop the bleeding. Someone else informed the medical service.

When the doctor arrived, he determined that the injury should not be treated in the small military clinic and contacted the local hospital. The surgical department was told to prepare for an emergency case, and the morning shift got one of the three operating rooms ready. The worst thing for Leonid during the twelve-mile drive to the hospital was the howling of the siren. The military physician had given him a shot, and the infusion bag was swaying over the captain's head. At brief intervals, the doctor measured his blood pressure, which was falling dangerously. "Hang on there, buddy," the doctor said, chewing the ends of his mustache.

Leonid knew the door his stretcher was carried through; he'd often picked up Galina there. The corridor, the pastel green tiles—everything was familiar to him. The next time he raised his head, he was looking into Galina's gray eyes. Behind her, the military doctor was leaving the operating room.

"It's your thumb," she said.

"Like before, remember?" Leonid saw her furrowing brow and explained that right before their first real date, Galina had performed a thumb amputation.

"Well, you've taken care of the amputation yourself." She gave a sign to her assistant, who pulled off Leonid's boots. "A clean slice," Galina said. "Unfortunately, nobody thought to bring your thumb along."

"It's lying out there in the sun." Inexplicably cheerful, he tried to sit up. "What are you doing with my foot?"

"I have to tell you, your chances are fifty-fifty." Galina bent over him so that he couldn't see what was happening at his other end.

"What chances?" Her blue, bonnetlike scrub cap made her face look slightly absurd.

"I did an operation like this once before." She laid her hand on his forehead. "For the amputation, you'll receive a local anesthetic. Later, for the operation, you'll be out cold."

"I thought I'd already done the amputation myself." He would have loved to touch her neck, but he felt too weak.

"I'm going to take the second toe from your left foot." She checked to see how far away her colleagues were. "And then I'll give it back to you as a thumb."

It took a while for what she'd said to get through to him. "Is that possible?"

"I've told you and told you, this is a particularly good hospital. When will you finally believe me?" She raised the surgical mask to her face. Immediately afterward, he felt an unpleasant sting that hurt worse than everything that had come before. Galina stuck him twice more, gave the needle to the nurse, and straightened up. "One minute, and then you won't feel anything." She came back to the head of the operating table. "We're equipped for microsurgery." She put a finger on his carotid artery. "The operating needles are so thin you can't see them with the naked eye."

He was enjoying her touch. "But . . . how will you do it, then?"

"I'll operate under a microscope. First I'll connect the bones with a steel pin, and then I'll sew everything together: nerves, tendons, arteries, skin. The thinnest capillaries must remain open so that blood can flow through them. Precision work, my dear."

He looked at her with astonished eyes.

"And the worst part of it is . . ." She turned around. The assisting nurse indicated that the local anesthetic had taken effect. "The worst part is that the operation can't be interrupted. That means I won't be able to go to the toilet for six to ten hours." Her voice took on a tender tone. "What a girl won't do for such a stupid captain."

He wanted very much to kiss her, imagined how it would be, and watched as Galina stationed herself next to his foot and pulled the instrument table closer. "So," she said. "We'll talk again in a few hours." She put on a pair of spectacles that resembled binoculars, nodded to her colleagues, and began.

As he laid his head back down, Leonid tried to pick up a signal from his left foot, but he could feel nothing. Then a peculiar thought filled his mind. He was probably the only person in the world whose lover—his life's partner, his woman—was cutting the second toe off his left foot and then sewing it onto his right hand as a thumb. And for that reason, even though he wasn't yet conscious of doing so, he decided, in the minutes before he was put to sleep, to stay where he was. He decided on Galina, on life in the coldest inhabited place on earth, and decided to sign, with or without a new thumb, the five-year clause for Yakutsk. He was relieved at having finally taken that step, even if only in his mind, and he concentrated on the soft, focused sounds coming from the surgeon at the foot end of his table.

FORTY-ONE

The officials of the Moscow City Soviet had sent their apologies, and only the Party secretary for Karacharovo had come to the ceremony. Complex two-one-five was finished; in the bright, sunny weather, the pale gray of the facade made a friendly, even elegant impression; on winter days, it would look different. Anna's combine was lauded for having not only accomplished its own mission but also taken up the slack for other crews. The very next day, the families would show up with their household goods, and that evening, the first lights would appear in the windows. If there were still some splashes of the facade paint on the windowpanes, that was because the dismantling of the scaffolding had been scheduled before the arrival of the window washers. The condition of the front yards and inner courtyards, which were full of construction waste, had to do with the protest of the landscapers: They were there, they said, to plant trees and grass, not to get rid of crap left behind by others.

"New living space for eight thousand comrades," cried the Party secretary. For the sake of projecting the proper image, the women were in their work togs, but on this day, none of them was going to come anywhere near a trowel. They were holding plastic cups; beer had been served, and sausage rounds lay ready on wooden platters. Anna was feeling melancholy; she would have liked to confide in her colleagues, to tell them that this morning had deeper significance for her than the dedication of two-one-five.

Her farewell to the combine had required only a formality, a five-line document, a stamp, a handshake from the official in charge—and with that, Anna was free of her employment. But her colleagues must not know about any of it; the reason for the change in Anna's life had to remain a secret. She touched glasses with the secretary and her comrades, laughed about the unsatisfactory tap of the plastic cups, and accompanied the others to the second floor, where a tour of the model apartment was programmed to take place. Unimpressed, Anna trotted with the rest from room to room, mistrusting the superlatives the Party secretary strove to produce.

With the handing over of the keys to the first renter, the little celebration came to an end. As she had done for years, Anna got on the workers' bus, kept quiet during the drive, and, when they reached Durova Street, said good-bye to her colleagues in the usual way. As the bus pulled off, she felt heavyhearted.

Everything had begun with Leonid's call. The captain had telephoned at sunset; she didn't know what time it was in Yakutia. He'd sounded warmhearted, resolute, and gentle. Tactfully and fondly, he'd informed her that after a brief hospital stay, he'd finally gotten around to doing the paperwork, and announced that he was going to remain in Siberia for another five years. Several responses lay on the tip of her tongue, but she made none of them and simply wished him well. They'd spoken softly and laughed about this and that; on the miracle of the thumb graft, Leonid had remained silent. At last, they'd come to speak of the factor that made their plans so fragile.

"What are you thinking about doing with Petya?" she'd asked.

"I wanted to hear your opinion first."

"Do you want to see him?"

"Of course I do. But I thought—look, any objection you make is justified—you see, summer here is incredibly short. Basically, preparations for winter have already begun again." Leonid was babbling a little because he didn't have the heart to express his true desire.

"Do you want him to visit you?"

In the ensuing silence, she'd felt he was trying to keep his composure. "I'll take care of everything. Everything," he'd said. "We Siberian officers have special privileges."

"You Siberian officers," Anna had repeated sadly.

"Our service flights offer a lot of convenient transportation possibilities. Petyushka will be amazed!" They'd talked about the timing of the boy's visit, and Anna had agreed to an early departure. After that, she'd let him in on her own plans.

He'd reacted with a question: "What about your job?"

"The combine can't keep the position open for me. I'm just on the list."

"What does that mean for our right of abode in Moscow?"

"*Our* right of abode?" For the first time, she'd realized that the categories "we" and "us" had changed their meaning. Shortly thereafter, they'd ended their conversation, alleging, mutually and unconvincingly, the high cost of long-distance telephoning.

Many things had to be made ready. Anna had stood in line for hours in various offices, because Petya needed his own passport. She also had to complete the real preparation, the mental one. Anna looked at her plan as a sort of experiment, which could be studied in depth and broken off at any time.

The great moment lay ahead of them. The six-year-old was going to be allowed to fly before his mother had ever seen the inside of an airplane. Petya was so excited that he'd thrown up at breakfast. He spent his days babbling practically nonstop and would not leave his grandfather in peace. The old man let his grandson feel his love in the form of patience. All the time, Viktor Ipalyevich was equally stirred up, but as long as Petya was home, he kept it to himself. In the morning, he dedicated himself to his work; later, he went for his walk, had a drink at the place on the corner, and met Petya at his school. After the boy had lunch, they would play chess. But it wasn't the same as before; both of them felt that each game just meant that there was one fewer to go before the last one.

Anna hadn't known that Sheremetyevo Airport contained a military section, where the army used a civilian runway. The aircraft Petya was supposed to fly in was an old Tupolev; a few days earlier, Petya and his grandfather had looked at some pictures of the plane.

Noon was approaching: time to leave. Viktor Ipalyevich heaved several sighs, unable to hide how stricken he was. Since the Nechayev family moved into his apartment, no day had passed when grandfather and grandson weren't together. In spite of all his eager anticipation, Petya cried, embraced the old man, and wouldn't break off until Viktor Ipalyevich finally placed the boy's trembling hand in his mother's, and Anna tugged Petya out of the apartment. The stairwell echoed with Petya's cries of "Dyedushka!" Once on the street, he calmed down, and Anna explained to him that they'd see each other again in the fall. Meanwhile, on the fourth floor, the poet was weeping snot and water.

To get to Sheremetyevo, they had to transfer twice, but at last the bus stopped in front of the departure terminal. After a bit of wandering around, Anna was informed that she should have gone in by another entrance. A calm telephone call was made and Petya's name and passport number conveyed to the person on the other end of the line. Anna was beginning to fear that her son might miss his flight when a young female officer came up to her and introduced herself as Petya's traveling companion. Her uniform looked smart, and she wore her cap at a jaunty angle.

"I'm afraid I can't take you through the security gate," she said, pointing to the restricted military area. "Would you like to tell Mama goodbye here, Petyushka?"

The little boy was too confused and excited to start crying again.

Wide-eyed, he hugged his mother, barely listened to her exhortations, felt that she was squeezing him harder than usual, and turned around several times to look at her before disappearing down the corridor, hand in hand with his companion. Long after he was well and truly out of sight, Anna continued staring in his direction, and then she burst into tears. She hurried up to the visitors' terrace and persuaded herself that she had picked out, among all the planes preparing for takeoff, the one that would carry her youngster to Siberia.

She'd arranged everything so that she would spend the next three days alone with her father. This was a mistake. Had the mutual suffering caused by the pain of parting been limited to one day, it would have been easier for both of the afflicted parties. As it was, they put on a show of grotesque normalcy and thus subjected their emotions to undue stress. During the course of those few days, Viktor Ipalyevich Tsazukhin came to the realization that he would probably spend the last quarter of his life alone. Suddenly, his one-and-a-half-room flat looked incredibly big. How could an unspectacular existence require so much space?

"Now you'll finally be able to sleep in your own bed again," said Anna, encouraging him.

"The devil I will. I'm used to the sofa, I'll stay on the sofa."

"You can have guests. You can invite whomever you want."

"Who'd want to pay a call on me, except maybe death?"

He meant it as a joke, but it was a heavy moment for both. They went to the table to eat the meal Anna had prepared, but neither of them liked it much.

"You've got it good, escaping the muggy metropolis in summer," he said, teasing her.

"I have no idea what the weather's like there."

All the windows were open. The apartment smelled of benzine.

Anna left the following day. She'd taken the big suitcase down first, but then, considering the few things she really needed, she'd decided on the smaller one. As though to reassure herself that it wasn't going to be forever, she hadn't packed any winter clothes. Viktor Ipalyevich insisted on accompanying her to the train. When they reached the platform, sweat was running down from under his cap. Anna had the good luck of finding an open seat and heaved her suitcase up into the overhead rack. She couldn't open the window, so she went back to the door of the car. "Take care of Mama's grave," she said, the only thing that occurred to her. "It gets overgrown so fast."

Viktor Ipalyevich promised and then asked, "Has the entire world gone mad?"

She embraced him, climbed into the train, and didn't watch him as he walked with drooping shoulders to the exit.

The car doors closed automatically, and the train left the Kiev Station exactly on schedule. It was terrible to be unable to ventilate the compartment. Unrestrained by their parents, three children performed gymnastics. The grown-ups were eating kohlrabi from a plastic container on the seat between them. "You have to put lemon on it to keep it fresh," the woman said, offering Anna a piece.

An hour passed. She didn't stare out into the landscape rushing past or take part in the conversation around her. The trip would be long, but she wasn't going too far away. No one had urged Anna to do what she was doing; no one would have even thought of making such a request.

"It can't have been just a question of patriotism," Kamarovsky had said.

Anna had gone up to the apartment on the eighth floor one last time. She'd looked out over the river; even with the balcony doors open, the apartment had been stiflingly hot.

"Bulyagkov could have escaped. If he'd really wanted to on that morning, he could have got away with it. When you're in a seaport city, you can always find a way out."

Feeling peculiarly at ease, Anna had sat beside the Colonel on the sofa. His reflecting eyeglasses lost their effect if you got close to him.

"He handed over the briefcase without stipulating any conditions or getting anything in return. Why, Anna?"

"I don't know, Comrade Colonel."

"Then all I can do is to thank you." He laid his hand on hers. "I know that I owe you a particular debt of gratitude."

"Why? What have I done?"

"You saved a life. In every conceivable sense. You did it for love, and apparently . . ." A rare smile crossed the haggard face. "Apparently, love was also the driving force for Alexey Maximovich." He cleared his throat. "As an officer, I'm satisfied. As a man, I'm impressed."

Anna had asked what would happen to Alexey and learned that he'd been placed under house arrest since turning in his written resignation. She'd imagined him sitting in the Drezhnevskaya Street apartment, the place they had used like a dream of exile. The doubting wolf who'd turned out to be a patriot would no longer get his meals from the fancy food shop; he'd receive them from the hands of his guards. Maybe they'd taken away his belt and shoelaces and forbidden him to lock himself in the bathroom.

"Alexey Maximovich must be purged of his doubt and punished for his attempted treason," Kamarovsky had said, stepping behind his desk. "It has been announced that the sentence to be meted out to the patriot Bulyagkov will take the form of banishment." As though troubled by some irregularity, he picked up a sheet of paper.

"May I see it?"

That was not allowed, and neither was a telephone call. Kamarovsky had made no objections to a written communication.

"The best thing to do would be to leave the envelope unsealed," he'd said as she was leaving. "I shall read your correspondence with great interest."

For a day and a night, Anna could find no words, but on the following day, she'd written the letter all in one burst. She'd dropped it, unsealed, in the appropriate place. Twelve hours later, the reply was lying in one of the scarred mailboxes on the ground floor, where Avdotya was always busy.

With the closed envelope in her hand, Anna had run outside. She'd restrained herself from taking out Alexey's letter until she reached the park. Then, leaning on the trunk of an elm tree, she'd begun to read.

Now, with the letter in her lap, Anna was sitting in the boisterous train compartment. Making sure her traveling companions couldn't see, she carefully unfolded the pages for the umpteenth time. What tiny writing for someone who wrote with such a strong hand, she thought. His *m*'s were hard to distinguish from his *i*'s, and in general, as far as form was concerned, the Deputy Minister hadn't made much of an effort. *The Deputy Minister?* Anna stared at the pages. She still thought of him in his official capacity, even though everything had changed for him. They hadn't seen each other since their dawn meeting in Riga.

Anna yanked the door open and barged into the corridor. People were standing, sitting, and passing the time here, too. She made her way to the end of the car and stood alone on the little platform. What was she about to do? Moments from the past crossed her mind: When Viktor Ipalyevich, sitting down to work, took off his woolen jacket, and you knew that spring had come. Petya's thrashing in his sleep, which infallibly meant that he'd tell her about a fantastic dream the next day. The joy she'd felt when the mortar on her trowel had the right consistency and went on smoothly. A life in Moscow would have lain ahead of her! She thought about the streets of the Arbat quarter in the snow, the feeling inspired by passing the illuminated Kremlin late at night.

Even as Anna was evoking pleasant memories of what she'd left behind, one thing was clear to her: She had to face the unromanticized truth. She looked more closely at the point her life had reached. Her marriage hadn't blown up, it had simply come apart. The housing situation—the cohabitation with her father, the bed sharing with Petya—how much longer could that have lasted? Anna was anxious about how her son would react to the new woman at Leonid's side, and she recognized the difficulties the boy would have as the child of a broken home, but all the same, the breakup had been inevitable. She smiled at herself when the thought crossed her mind that she was following her heart, just as Alexey had done when, with full awareness of all the consequences of his actions, he'd gone back to Russia.

Anna became conscious of the fields that went on forever in the gently rolling countryside. What crops were being cultivated there she couldn't say. When she went back to her compartment and had to ask one of the children to get out of her seat, something remarkable occurred to her. Since she'd finished her job training and married the non-Muscovite Leonid, she'd had only one goal: to obtain the right of abode in Moscow for her family. She'd filled out innumerable forms, she'd had her name and Leonid's added to lists, she'd been friendly with office supervisors; in long conversations with her husband, she'd considered whether she'd left anything undone; the goal had justified any means. And now, when the Nechayev family's assignment to their new apartment was only a formality, Moscow was going to have to get along without them. Leonid had settled into his new Siberian nest; Anna was about to turn her back on Russia. Only Viktor Ipalyevich remained the die-hard big-city dweller he'd always been. From now on, he'd be able to distill Four-Star Tsazukhin in his kitchen undisturbed.

Anna felt so blithe and gay that she began a conversation with the people in her compartment. They came from a small town in southern Russia and spoke contemptuously of Ukrainians, although they admitted they'd been "down there" only once.

How strange, Anna thought. We're supposed to live in equality, but the desire to be different remains obstinately strong.

The closer they got to the border, the emptier the train became, until at last Anna was alone in the compartment. She dozed off and started awake to see a uniformed man holding out his hand to her. She performed a hectic search for her papers and experienced a few bad moments while the border policeman paged through the document and finally handed it back. The landscape was in no way different from that on the Russian side, and yet Anna caught herself thinking that now she was in a foreign country. Half an hour later, the train reached the station that was the goal of her journey, a small town near Kharkov. She carried her suitcase along the only platform, crossed the waiting room, and emerged into the open.

She'd traveled practically a whole day to wind up now, at twilight, in such surroundings! Gray-brown buildings with missing plaster, a collapsing barbed-wire fence, a street full of potholes, the rusting skeleton of a cannibalized tractor at the side of the road. Across the street, a storefront whose sign was missing so many letters that the word *bakery* could barely be deciphered. Anna's heart sank; in the middle of the street, she turned round in a circle. Silence reigned, but somewhere far off, a generator was running. The air smelled like fire.

Alexey had written about a house in the country, a house formerly used by the district surveyor, namely his disgraced father. As she read those lines in the letter, she'd imagined the living room with its tiled, turquoise-blue woodstove, the old-style wide floorboards, and the kitchen built out of silver fir. The water in the pipes froze regularly, he'd written, and you had to put scuttles filled with smoldering coals against the walls so the pipes would thaw and water could flow again. The toilets were outside; you had to go downstairs to the first floor and then out to the privy; on winter nights, you could find yourself walking through snow in your nightshirt. So as not to exaggerate the romantic appeal of the place, he'd said, he had to report that there was electricity and that telephone service was due to arrive at some point. Full of expectation, Anna had read that the roof ridge had borne the snows of two hundred winters without yielding and was still dead straight. Alexey had also written about the small piece of land he wanted to farm; he was thinking about cultivating maize and beets, along with salad herbs. When she pictured the convicted former ministerial official bending over his beets, Anna had smiled, and yet everything was coming together into one image.

Now, however, Anna was surrounded by ugliness, provincialism, and decay, and all her old doubts fell back into place. How was she going to tell Petya about the new man in her life, a man only fifteen years younger than the boy's grandfather? What was she supposed to live on? Would she try to find a house-painting job in Kharkov, say, and hire herself out for Ukrainian—i.e., starvation—wages?

In the radiant certainty of having made the wrong decision, under the sudden impulse to undo a terrible mistake, Anna turned around and started to run back to the train station . . . until a spot of color brought her to a halt. It wasn't an unusual color for a car, but somehow that particular greenish-gray vehicle seemed familiar. In some confusion, Anna put down her suitcase, raised her other hand, and took a step toward the Zhiguli, whose driver was just getting out. She could see a second man in the passenger's seat, a heavy, gray-haired fellow who in spite of the heat was wearing a woolen jacket. Anna avoided a puddle, pushed her hair behind her ears, and walked faster. Whether she wanted it to or not, her heart was laughing.

A NOTE ABOUT THE AUTHOR

MICHAEL WALLNER is the author of the international sensation *April in Paris*. He lives in Germany, where he is an actor and screenwriter, and divides his time between Berlin and the Black Forest.

A NOTE ABOUT THE TYPE

This book was set in Adobe Garamond. Designed for the Adobe Corporation by Robert Slimbach, the fonts are based on types first cut by Claude Garamond (c. 1480–1561).